Wrangler *in* Petticoats

**Center Point
Large Print**

Also by Mary Connealy
and available from Center Point Large Print:

Sophie's Daughters Series
Doctor in Petticoats

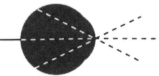

**This Large Print Book carries the
Seal of Approval of N.A.V.H.**

SOPHIE'S DAUGHTERS

Wrangler *in* Petticoats

MARY CONNEALY

CENTER POINT PUBLISHING
THORNDIKE, MAINE

This Center Point Large Print edition
is published in the year 2011 by arrangement with
Barbour Publishing, Inc.

The text of this Large Print edition is unabridged.
In other aspects, this book may vary
from the original edition.
Printed in the United States of America
on permanent paper.
Set in 16-point Times New Roman type.

ISBN: 978-1-60285-949-4

Library of Congress Cataloging-in-Publication Data

Connealy, Mary.
Wrangler in petticoats / Mary Connealy. — Center Point large print ed.
p. cm.
ISBN 978-1-60285-949-4 (library binding : alk. paper)
1. Women painters—Fiction. 2. Cowgirls—Fiction. 3. Cowboys—Fiction.
   4. Montana—Fiction. 5. Large type books. I. Title.
PS3603.O544W73 2011
813'.6—dc22

2010040910

Dedication/Acknowledgment

He hath made every thing beautiful in his time.
ECCLESIASTES 3:11

I got the idea for this book about a Western artist from a very good friend, Karen Cooper (www.karencooperpaintings.com).

Karen lived next door to me years ago. She was raising a houseful of little ones about a quarter of a mile away from me and my houseful of little ones. Neither one of us had given much thought to writing or art. Though Karen was always an artist. I can see that now. She has a wonderful gift of color and making her home beautiful. The closest I came to being a writer was scribbling all over my children's baby books. Still, I did a *lot* of scribbling.

When I talk to Karen now, she uses interesting "inside" language about art that I find fascinating; and I tried to catch that attitude, that way of looking at the world, in Logan McKenzie.

On the wall right in front of my computer is an original Cooper. Every time I need inspiration in my writing I look up at that beautiful bouquet of bright red flowers Karen painted and remember who I was and who I am, how far I've come, and how wonderful the journey has been along the way.

And I want to dedicate *Wrangler in Petticoats* to Bob and Gloria Breckenridge for all the interesting information they shared with me through a very special book about the famous Western artist Charlie Russell. I learned a lot about historical painting techniques, tools, and attitudes. Thanks Bob and Gloria.

One

Sally McClellen fought to control her temper and her horse.

But her horse wasn't the problem. It was her temper upsetting the horse. He wouldn't have been acting fidgety if it weren't for her testy grip on the reins. So any trouble Sally had was all her own doing.

"None of this gets me one step closer to Mandy. She needs me." Sally was so anxious to get on down the trail she thought she might explode.

They rode around the curve of a steep mountain trail and in the distance caught their first glimpse of a river lined with high banks of stunning red rock.

"Sure it's a pretty sight, but—"

"It's more than pretty. It's *beautiful*." Paula McGarritt, Sally's traveling companion, looked at her and smiled. "Admit it. It was worth riding out here."

Mrs. McGarritt knew full well how impatient Sally was, but Mrs. McGarritt, sweet and friendly as she was, didn't let anyone push her around. The colonel's wife sat her horse sidesaddle in a proper riding dress. She had made her opinion known early and often about Sally's manly riding clothes and her habit of riding astride.

"It *is* beautiful." Sally stifled an irritated sigh. They were here now, staring at the rocks. As if none of this group had ever seen a rock before. They all lived in west Texas or New Mexico. Their whole world was pretty much made of rocks.

Sally relaxed her grip on the reins to spare her restless horse. They'd be at Mandy's in a few days. Less because they'd abandoned the trail and gone cross country. But Colonel McGarritt had agreed to the shortcut because he had a hankering to get out of the train and see some wild country. When Pa had asked if they'd see Sally safely to Mandy's house, the colonel had studied the area and decided he'd like to see several places along the trail—this canyon among them.

He'd have just stayed on the train, though, if it wasn't for Mandy living in the middle of nowhere with her no-account husband. So, Sally took the detours that interested the colonel and his wife in the best spirit she could manage. Griping didn't help and it made everyone else miserable.

Which wasn't to say she hadn't done plenty of it. But still—the group had voted. She'd lost. This was America. "Thank you for insisting we ride out here."

8

"You're welcome." Mrs. McGarritt grinned at Sally, not one bit fooled by her forced politeness. The older lady reached out her hand and Sally clasped it.

"Spectacular," Colonel McGarritt said. "Absolutely stunning."

Sally tore her eyes from the view to intercept Mrs. McGarritt's smug look. Paula was too polite to say, "I told you so." But Sally caught the superior look and didn't even mind.

Much.

The crimson bluffs were magnificent. But was it worth the time they'd wasted abandoning the most direct path? When Mandy might be in trouble? She was at least suffering from terrible homesickness. Her last letter had been a poorly concealed cry of loneliness. But with a third baby on the way and no womenfolk within fifty miles, she really needed the help as soon as possible.

No, this wasn't even close to worth it.

Only by sheer force of will did Sally keep her hands loose on her reins and a smile on her face. They had plenty of time to get to Mandy's before the baby came. And Sally knew, from the map Mandy had sent, that the site of her new home was going to take this party a long way out of their way, and the group had all gone along with it; and they'd been a sight more mannerly about it than she was being.

Mandy would soon have her third baby in three years of marriage. She needed help. A woman's help. Luther and Buff did what they could, but they had no place at the birth of Mandy's baby. Sally offered to go.

Ma and Pa had a dim view of Mandy's husband and they'd relented, though they'd made a fuss over losing another daughter to Montana. But Sally had promised not to let Montana keep her. She'd promised it wouldn't be forever. A year at most. Sally would help with the babies. Probably end up spending the winter with Mandy and no-account Sidney, then head home.

And now, instead of making the best time possible, here she sat staring at the admittedly beautiful canyon and river God painted with a blazing crimson brush.

She and Paula McGarritt rode with six men. All but Sally were making their way to Seattle. The group had been forming before Sally had gotten the idea to travel to see Mandy.

Pa would have never allowed Sally to travel so far alone. But once Pa had heard of this group of sturdy men, and the stalwart Mrs. McGarritt who would act as chaperone, he'd relented. Now the travelers were slowing Sally down.

She was well aware she should be ashamed of herself. Then she noticed she'd tightened her hands on the reins again and her horse was tossing its head. Sally relaxed and sat with the most patience possible beside Paula, who wore a prim riding skirt, her gray hair neatly hidden beneath her bonnet, her spine ramrod straight.

Sally knew about tough and considered herself as tough as they came. But she had to admit, the nearly sixty-year-old Paula McGarritt could keep up with her. Maybe not in a footrace, but the woman was frontier born and bred, and she was at home in rugged conditions. And these were rugged indeed.

Though Mrs. McGarritt had clung to her proper clothing to take this ride, Sally had slipped away once they'd left the train and changed into her wrangler clothes. Mrs. McGarritt had scolded, but Sally, already chafing under the delay, refused to change back, so Mrs. McGarritt had relented and allowed Sally to wear chaps and ride astride with a rifle strapped on her back.

Sally had won that small battle but lost on the sightseeing trip. Now here they were looking at pretty rocks when they should be making tracks for Mandy's house.

Mrs. McGarritt said, "Let's ride down closer. I want a better look."

Sally didn't like it, but she said nothing, resigned to the delay. Now she rode along to take a closer look than their bird's-eye view from a mountain crest. They funneled down the narrow trail.

The trail made its serpentine way down the

11

mountain. Sally admitted it felt good to be on horseback again after the long train ride. They wove around a curve.

Sally looked at the sheer drop to her left and swallowed hard. They were as far out in the wilderness as a body could get. And this side trip down to those red rocks served no purpose. Food to hunt, cattle to round up, fine. But to stare at rocks, no matter how pretty? Sally shook her head but remained silent.

The land dropped off for a hundred feet on her left. The horses' hooves scratched along on the loose dirt and round pebbles. The trail was a steep slope downward, which meant slick even on this bone-dry day in June.

As the trail twisted, Sally saw the end of this dangerous stretch only a few yards ahead and breathed a sigh of relief to pass this particularly treacherous section of the trail. Now with only a few more tortuous yards to cover, Sally relaxed. "Mrs. McGarritt," she called out, wanting to tease the dear lady again about dragging Sally along on her joyride.

Paula, below Sally on the trail, gained nearly level ground. The cliff no longer yawned at her side. She turned in her saddle, smiling. "You can thank me later, girl. When you're dressed like a proper young lady again."

Thank her? Not likely and well Mrs. McGarritt knew it. The two of them exchanged a warm smile. Mrs. McGarritt really was a sweetheart, for a tough old bird.

Once she looked away, Sally gently brushed her fingertips over the front of her broadcloth shirt and felt the ribbon beneath the rough fabric. No one knew of Sally's fondness for ribbons and a bit of lace. She went to great lengths to keep her little bows and frills hidden, pinning them on her chemise when no one was around, removing them before laundry day so even Ma wouldn't see.

Admiring pretty things felt dangerous to Sally, so she didn't speak of it. Pa loved having her at his side on roundups and working the herd. For some reason, Sally felt certain that if she went girly on her pa, he might not love her as much. Oh, he'd always love her. She trusted in her pa's love. But he might not love her in the same way. With Beth and Mandy gone, Laurie owned Pa's heart as the princess. Sally's place was beside him riding the range.

Trusting her horse to manage the steep trail, Sally pondered this spark of womanly weakness that drew her to lace and frills and such nonsense. Her foolish daydreams ended with the sharp crack of gunfire.

Paula McGarritt slammed backward off her horse.

Sally's world slowed down and focused sharply as it always did in times of danger. Her hand went to her rifle before she spun to face the shooting.

Another bullet sounded, from above. Someone shooting from cover.

Smelling the burning gunpowder, hearing the direction of the bullets, Sally's gun was firing without her making a decision to aim or pull the trigger.

Mrs. McGarritt landed with a dull thud, flat on her back, behind her horse's heels, a bloom of red spreading in the center of her chest. She bounced once, kicking up a puff of dust, then lay still, her open eyes staring sightlessly at the sun.

Sally raged at the fine lady's death and focused on an outcropping of rocks hiding one of the outlaws. Her rifle fired almost as if it had a will of its own. The rock hiding the assailants was in front of other, larger rocks, and Sally consciously aimed for a ricochet shot, hoping to get around the stone.

A barrage of gunfire kept coming at her.

She dragged bullets from her gun belt as she emptied her weapon then reloaded as bullets whizzed by her head close enough she felt the heat of them.

They came from a different spot. She aimed in the direction of the shot and pulled the trigger as a second member of the colonel's party was shot off his horse, then a third.

Her horse staggered toward the cliff side, hit.

Sally dived to the ground, throwing herself to the cliff side of the narrow trail, with only inches to spare between her and the edge. Her horse went down under the withering fire and fell toward her, screaming in pain.

Gunfire poured down like deadly rain.

Sally was now sure there were three of them. They'd lain in wait like rattlesnakes, attacked from the front, rear, and directly overhead, and were picking them off with vicious precision. Cold-blooded murderers.

Rolling even closer to the cliff, Sally avoided the collapsing horse. Raging at the senseless killing, she used her mount's thrashing body for meager shelter.

Fighting her terrified, dying horse, Sally rolled to her left just enough to twirl her rifle in her right hand, cock it, aim, and fire. She'd yet to see any of the coyotes who were attacking them, but aim was instinctive and she trusted it.

The men around her, the ones who hadn't died in the first hail of bullets, battled with her against the dry-gulchers shooting from cover. Sally saw Colonel McGarritt take one agonized look at his wife lying dead and turn back to the assault from overhead. He had a rifle in his right hand and a Colt six-shooter in the left. A constant roll of fire came from him as if his rage and grief were blazing lead.

A quick look told Sally only four men had

survived the first shots. The cover was bad. Another man jerked backward, struck the ground hard, and collapsed on his back.

A cry from overhead told Sally somebody's bullet had found its mark. There were three shooters. With the cry, one of them quit firing.

Another of her companions collapsed to the ground. There just was no shelter. The horses weren't enough. Sally's horse neighed in pain and made a valiant lurching effort to regain its feet. The movement sent the horse—and Sally— dangerously close to the cliff. Bullets whizzed like furious bees from two directions. Sally aimed at the source of that vicious raining lead and fired as fast as she could jack another bullet into her Winchester.

Another yell from overhead and another of the three rifles fell silent. One was still in full action and she aimed in that direction.

A shout from behind told her Colonel McGarritt was hit, but his gun kept firing.

A bullet hit the trail inches from her head and kicked dirt into her eyes, blinding her. It didn't even slow her down because she was aiming as much with her ears and gut as with her vision. The remaining shooter switched between Sally and Colonel McGarritt with a steady roll of gunfire.

Sally clawed at her eyes to clear her vision in time to see Colonel McGarritt drop his gun and fall limp on his back. She was the last one of their party firing. Everyone was either dead or out of action.

God, have mercy on all of us. Have mercy on me. God, have mercy. God, have mercy.

Her trigger clicked on an empty chamber and she shifted to reload her Winchester. A bullet struck hard low on her belly. Her arms kept working so she refused to think of what a gut shot meant.

Praying steadily for mercy, for safety, for strength to survive the horrible wound, she squinted through her pained eyes to see her horse, riddled with bullets, kick its legs and make a hopeless effort to rise. Furious at the death and destruction around her, Sally was too disoriented to know left from right.

The dying horse staggered up then fell toward her. Sally rolled aside but not far enough. The horse slammed her backward. Clawing at the rock-strewn trail, she felt the ground go out from under her.

She pitched over the edge of the cliff and screamed as she plunged into nothingness.

"We got 'em," Fergus Reynolds yelled and laughed when the last one went down. He pushed back his coonskin cap and scratched his hair, enjoying the triumph. "We earned our pay today. Let's go collect."

He rose from the rocks he'd chosen for their vantage point on the trail and headed for his horse. Swinging up, he thrust his rifle in his scabbard and kicked his chestnut gelding into motion.

That's when he saw his brother. Dead. Curly Ike, with that same weird streak of white in his hair that Fergus and Pa both had. He lay sprawled in the dirt, his chest soaked in blood.

Fergus tasted rage. No one killed one of the Reynolds clan without punishment.

He, Tulsa, and Curly had a habit of keeping their ears open in town. This bunch had gotten off the train and talked of the trail they'd take, straight out in the wilderness. There was some sight out the way these folks were riding that drew a small but steady stream of sightseers, so Fergus knew right where to lie in wait.

Fergus and his gang had gotten to their vantage point and been ready. Only after they opened up on them did Fergus realize that they'd taken on a salty bunch. Most of the folks that rode this trail were easy pickings. But not this crowd. They'd fought back hard, thrown themselves off their horses and scrambled for shelter, their guns in action almost instantly.

"That cowpoke who went over the cliff shot me!" Tulsa came down the trail toward the horses, raging. "Creased my shootin' arm."

Fergus looked at his saddle partner and

wondered bitterly why Tulsa was alive while his brother was dead. Fergus remembered from his youth that his family had been one for feuding and fighting for family. It burned him now that his brother was dead. But those who had killed him were beyond paying for that. The family sticks together.

Fergus even thought of his name. His real name. One he'd left behind long ago. "Curly's dead."

Tulsa fumbled at his blood-soaked arm, trying to stop the bleeding. He barely spared a glance at Curly, and that made Fergus killing mad. "I put a bullet in the gut of the one who went over the side. He was still aiming and shooting when he was gut shot. He was dead while he was still fightin'. He was just too stupid to know it."

Fergus could taste the rage and the need for revenge. But how did a man avenge himself against someone who was dead?

"He got off a lucky shot." Tulsa flexed his hand as he rolled up his shirtsleeve.

No luck, nohow. Skill. Cold-blooded warriors. Fergus and his saddle partners had never had much trouble finding a few travelers who could be separated from their money. They'd loiter around town, watch for people heading out into the back country, then ride ahead and lie in wait. They picked folks who were passing through so no one noticed when they didn't come back to

19

town, and wherever they were going, if people there missed them, they didn't know where to start hunting.

But today they'd bought into the wrong fight and it had cost his brother's life.

Tulsa's arm worked, and no bones looked broken. But a shot like that would keep Tulsa laid up for a few days. He wouldn't be any good for shooting for a while. And Tulsa was a crack shot. With Curly dead, they were out of action for a while.

"The one you're talking about, that went over the cliff, had himself a mighty nice Winchester," Tulsa muttered. "We won't get to strip nothin' offa him."

"He screamed like a girl when he fell." It fed a hungry place in Fergus's gut to listen to a grown man scream.

"I don't like him getting away with his gun, even if he did die for his trouble." Tulsa pulled out a handkerchief and tried to tie it around his bleeding arm, his eyes blazed with hate.

Fergus thought of his brother. They'd been riding the outlaw trail together for near twenty years. "I want to go down there and make sure he's got nothing left. Not a dime in his pocket and not a bullet in his belt." Fergus ran his hand over the bandolier belts he strapped across his chest and kept filled with bullets. There were empty spaces now, but Fergus would refill them

20

soon. He liked having a lot of firepower close to hand.

Fergus turned from the people they'd killed, sprawled on the ground, including a woman, and looked at the cliff. They haunted this area and they'd turned the bottom of that cliff into a graveyard. If they wanted that sharpshooting cowpoke's rifle and money, they'd have to climb down to get it. A chill rushed up Fergus's back when he thought of going down there. Death wasn't something Fergus worried about much. Not his and not anyone else's. But he didn't want to wade into a graveyard where nobody'd bothered to dig holes.

A graveyard he'd created. They'd been throwing their victims over that cliff for three years.

The sick fear made Fergus feel like a yellow belly, and that didn't sit well. So maybe he ought to go down and see his handiwork. "We'll have to go a roundabout way to get down there then hope we find the cowpoke's body. Some of that drop is sheer, but there are enough trees his body could have snagged anywhere."

They made their way down to where their day's work lay bleeding into the dirt. The three of them had made a good living on the fools who passed this way. Now there were only two of them.

There was talk about sending armed men into Yellowstone to protect the visitors, and that would settle the whole area. But nothing had come of it so far. And while they dithered, Fergus lived mighty high on the hog.

But he'd just paid one ugly price for his easy living. His brother was dead.

TWO

Sally slapped into a branch. It scraped her belly and she clawed, but the branch snapped.

On. Falling.

Down. Slowed by the tree but not stopped, just beaten and dropped. Slapped and let go. Battered and bleeding and falling, hurdling, plunging.

That cliff had been sky high. Now she'd return to earth. Trees grew parallel to the cliff. She skidded between tree and stone, slashing through the skinny top branches, slamming into thicker ones, only to hit the top of the next trees and their frail upper reaches.

Twigs stabbed at her face and neck. She clawed at the trees, trying to find a way to stop, save herself. The branches she managed to grab broke, not even slowing her down as she plummeted toward the rocky ground far below. Another hard blow, this time to her back, as she tumbled. Then another and another.

She rolled and slammed her stomach into a thicker branch. For a second she stopped. A pine tree—tougher than the aspens—snagged on a buckle. She fought for a hold. The branch tilted. The needles tore at her flesh. The sheer cliff was within her grasp, but too smooth to find a handhold.

Sliding toward the rock wall, for a second she was pinned. Solid, sheer rock on one side, bristling pine bowed but unbroken.

Her head swung down as she hung from her belly. Her hands scrambled for a solid hold on the tree or the granite. Fingernails ripped at unforgiving rock. Her flesh shredded on prickly pine.

As she dangled, her eyes blinked open and she looked straight into the startled face of a man. A man perched in a nearby tree like a two-hundred-pound squirrel.

The horror on his face told her, even in an instant, that he'd seen her fall. He knew he was watching someone die. He shouted and reached for her. But he might as well have been a mile away. There was too much distance between them.

Sally had one heartbeat to know he wasn't part of the shooting from overhead. Her second heartbeat held pity for him. He was watching something ugly. Something no rational human being would want any part of.

She knew she didn't want any part of it.

"God, have mercy," she cried out to the Lord and also to this man. It was almost as if their souls touched in that single look.

In those fleeting seconds she let herself be completely alive. Looking into the man's eyes, probably the last human being she'd ever see, was as powerful as any moment of her life.

Even as she clawed at the branch, it slipped through her buckle. She knew unless she got ahold of something solid, she was going to be with God this very day in heaven, because she still had a long way to fall and a hard meeting with the ground.

With her eyes, she told that man good-bye, told the whole world good-bye. She regretted knowing how her family would grieve. Pa would blame himself. Ma would hurt nearly to death. Mandy would have no one to take care of her. Beth would relive this and want so desperately to help. Laurie would cry. Her little brothers would want to.

Her weight tore her loose from the ponderosa pine and she plunged. She hit sturdier branches with a sickening thud, face down. The air slammed out of her lungs. The tree gave again and she fell, hit and fell, hit and fell. The rock on her right grated her skin. The tree on her left seemed to take pleasure in its slapping leaves, occasional sharp needles, and harsh, scraping bark. The world set out to do every bit of harm it knew.

She had no idea how far she fell, if it was for a long time or if the world had just slowed down as she plunged to her death. And then the ground, rushing toward her. Nowhere left to fall.

A sudden blow wiped it all away.

Logan McKenzie slapped one hand to his Colt six-shooter when he heard the gunfire.

Of course it was gone. Left on his horse rather than climb a tree with it. Nothing much to shoot in a tree.

He looked up, not sure what he'd do with the gun from here anyway.

The shooting went on and on. He was no hand at such things, but he knew there were a lot of guns. Something terrible was happening up there.

A sudden, terrible crack of branches drew his eyes still above him but lower. Something coming straight for him.

He caught the branch of his tree and swung himself aside only seconds before a huge form hit right where he'd been sitting.

As it plunged past, he recognized it. A horse.

Dear Lord God, what is happening?

More shattering branches. More gunfire.

This time, whatever fell wasn't so close. He turned to face whatever was next.

Another horse. It whinnied, terrified. Horrified.

The sight of that huge brown body plunging past him was sickening, shocking. A sight burned in his brain he would be forced to live with for the rest of his life.

Logan's prayers grew and spread.

The gunfire went on.

No way to go up without going down first. Logan dropped his sketchbook and pencil and rushed, hand over hand, to the ground far, far below. He'd descended no more than a dozen feet when he heard something else falling toward him and turned to see, to dodge.

A woman slammed into a branch of a tree next to him. Only a few yards away. Her belt snagged on something and she hung, stopped in her fall for a precarious second. The space between them wasn't far . . . just too far. There was no way to reach her.

Logan cried out in anguish, and she looked right into his eyes.

A terrified, beautiful woman. Long blond hair trailed and tangled with the branches. All of her terror passed between them.

The world stopped spinning. She let him into her soul through her eyes. Shared her pain, terror, regret.

The connection was unlike anything Logan had known. She handed her life to him in that frozen moment. Endowed him with her beating heart and her gasping lungs. Left them to him like an inheritance as if she knew, seconds from now, she'd no longer need them.

She even somehow let him know she was sorry. Sorry to be dying and sorry he'd been forced to witness it.

He moved to get to her, save her—though the space between the trees made it impossible. He knew it. She knew it.

Farther down maybe. If she hung for a few more minutes he could get across.

The limb that held her snapped and she fell.

"No!" Dropping hand over hand, he raced down the tree. It cut at his hands and tore at his clothes as if the tree itself was trying to stop him. He tried to follow the woman with his eyes.

She'd vanished after the horses.

The tree clawed his hands. Like all of nature, it could punish someone who wasn't careful, and he wasn't at all. The urgency was too huge.

His prayers weren't words anymore, just groans too deep for words. Screams of regret that he didn't utter aloud. Desperate longing that he could get to her. Save her. But it was too late, far too late.

He tore a layer of skin off his right forearm as he went down and down and down. The branches got wider and sturdier. He noticed but ignored the fire in his hands from the scraping bark.

When he hit the ground, he skidded along the steep ground, mostly on his backside, descending, slamming into the tall, slender aspens that covered this mountainside. Looking everywhere for the woman.

Because he skidded right past it, he grabbed at

the sketchbook he'd dropped, barely aware that his hand had closed over it.

There she was! Covered in blood. Lying motionless—certainly dead—against a pile of talus rock gathered by avalanches over centuries.

Swallowing hard, shocked by an urge to cry, mourn her, Logan kept moving, the sight of her terrified eyes burning in his head like a red-hot iron. He felt bound to her, even in her death. Their eyes meeting was the most intimate thing Logan had ever shared with another human being. He'd be haunted by that unspoken scream for help—help he hadn't given—for the rest of his life.

He needed to see to her burial. As he slid and ran toward her, he planned to see if she carried anything with a name on it. He could tell her people what had become of her. Try to explain what had happened to her, though he had no idea.

He ran, slipped on some loose rock, and ended up sliding, head first, belly down, right up to her side. He rolled sideways so he wouldn't skate into her, careened into a pile of rocks, and came to a sudden, stunning halt. He scrambled on his hands and knees to her side.

Her face was covered in blood. She had on chaps and a leather jacket. Men's clothing. Shredded and tattered but protected by the rugged clothing far more than she'd have been in gingham and petticoats.

God, the poor soul, bless her. Take her into Your arms.

He reached a shaking hand to press against the blood-soaked front of her shirt, to feel for a heartbeat. Before he even touched her, her chest rose and he snatched his hand back. She was alive.

Logan looked up—forever—to where she'd fallen. The top of this cliff wasn't visible with the many trees in the way. Logan remembered the gunfire. It was well no one could see down here.

He turned back to her. She lay flat on her back, arms outstretched. Her hair spread wild and white-blond in all directions. Her face was covered in blood. He thought of Wise Sister, his housekeeper. She knew healing, but he was miles and miles from his home and Wise Sister's help.

Stopping her bleeding was within his skill. Logan stripped off his buckskin jacket and cast it aside, glad for the warm day. Then he tore his shirt off so fast he popped a few buttons. He tried to rip it in half, but the sturdy fabric wouldn't give.

He snatched the knife out of his boot. As he did, Logan noticed a fetid smell. For some reason the smell poked at him like a warning of danger, as if he wasn't already enough on edge.

He shook off the strange tension caused by that scent and cut through his shirt's tough bottom hem, then ripped it in two up to the back of the neck. He needed the knife again to get through that. Then he formed a pad of cloth. Because the woman was so still, he spoke, if only to keep himself company. "I'm going to just press on the fastest bleeding wound on your forehead."

Pausing, he knew he was wasting time speaking to her. But it pushed down his fear of harming her. "I won't move you at all. Just let me staunch the blood. We don't want you losing any more, now do we? I'd say you've got the amount you need in your veins and we shouldn't waste a drop of it."

A second rivulet appeared out of a spot farther back on her head. He used a corner of the cloth pad to stop that.

The woman was wearing an outlandish getup—men's clothing from top to bottom—but Logan thanked God for whatever had prompted her to dress this way. The top button of her broadcloth shirt was torn away, and he caught a glimpse of pink ribbon right at the hollow of neck. Somehow that pleased him, though he had no idea why it should.

A closer look and he saw a little scar, tiny but nasty looking, right at her throat, as if someone had stabbed her in the neck. What in the world had caused that? And how had she managed to survive it?

As he knelt there, pressing gently but firmly on the worst of her cuts, he had time to study her and saw a rifle on her back. He noticed the strap holding it there and that the buckle, right at gut level on her left, was smashed. A flattened bullet protruded from the metal. A bullet that would have killed her if the strap hadn't stopped it.

A small breeze kicked up, swirled around him, and stirred up that smell again. He looked around while he pressed on the woman's wounds. There were dense woods all around the pile of avalanched rocks. The smell seemed to come from everywhere and nowhere.

Death.

Old death.

How old was this avalanche? There were slides like this all over in the mountains, and it was a normal thing to come upon shale slides blocking a trail. Logan had done enough reading about land formations in the Rockies that he knew it was called talus. Most likely this slide of broken rock fragments was recent and it had killed an animal as it swept down.

He did his best to ignore the stench and fussed with the wounds until he'd stopped all the bleeding he found. He'd been forced to work at his father's side as a child and knew a bit about doctoring. She should have stitches on these largest cuts, and a quick check showed him no broken bones that he could find. As for her insides, her spine, her neck, who could say what damage had been done?

"I'd say you're all fixed up now, except you're

still out cold." Kneeling by her side, he watched her breath, and then he watched some more.

"I don't think I dare to move you. But then I don't really dare leave you lying here, either." He glanced up that cliff. No more gunfire. His fingers itched for his Colt and he took an oath then and there to never walk away and leave it in his saddlebag again. But he had her rifle if there was trouble.

"My horse is just down the hill a ways, picketed on grass. This hill turns much flatter about a hundred yards down past these trees. I could take you home." Her chest rose and fell a bit more deeply. He pressed a hand against her wrist and found a steady pulse. He'd been trained to the extent his father could jam knowledge into his stubborn head. But for the most part back then, he'd daydreamed about the great outdoors and wondered about the next picture he'd paint. And now, when doctoring skills might save a young woman's life, he was stuck here with a sketchbook and little else.

"If you've got parts inside broken up, you'd be getting weaker, and you don't seem to be." He didn't know what he was talking about. Still, it stood to reason. "You seem to be all in one piece. No unnatural twists in your arms and legs." Of course her arms and legs were completely covered. "I'll bet you'd be fine if I hauled you on a long horseback ride."

Her response was as expected. Total silence.

Logan stared at her, willing her to come back to him, answer him. Praying she would. He really wasn't much good for anything but drawing pictures. And, though he definitely excelled at that, it was a foolish mission in life, or so his father said. And in many ways Logan agreed. The only real reason he didn't stop was because he couldn't.

"I think, from the look of you, you'd consider my drawing as foolishness, too. Although I suppose your clothing is a bit foolish for a woman, so maybe you understand someone who's a little different. Of course you've chosen clothing that is, above all else, practical. So I suspect you're dead set on being practical." Logan sighed. She'd be as annoyed with his painting as Father.

He could do nothing other than stay, keep a vigil over her. She'd wake up or she'd die. The thought hurt deep in his chest, and Logan prayed silently for a long while, hoping up here in the mountains they were just a bit closer to God in heaven. That was foolishness, too, because God was right inside Logan's heart no matter the altitude.

"What happened up there, anyway?" Logan looked up, up, up. There'd been no shout from above. No one climbed down to search for this young woman. Of course, who could scale that slope to come down and check?

And if someone did come, well, would that be good or bad? There'd been a lot of gunfire up there. "Which usually means good guys and bad guys. No way of saying whether someone coming down here had it in mind to make sure you're dead or to save you if you're alive."

Although if someone was worried about her being alive, there should have been a shout or two. Calling her name. It didn't bode well for whoever had been with her. He looked down at her.

Her eyes flickered open.

He scrambled on hands and knees and bent over her.

"All dead."

He read her lips more than heard her. He leaned down to within an inch of her, hoping to catch any other words she uttered.

"Shot. Dry-gulchers. God, have mercy." The young woman reached to her side with a trembling hand and fumbled for the muzzle of her rifle. The muzzle barely showed by her right hip. The butt was visible above her left shoulder. She'd fallen all that way, was only semiconscious, yet her first act was to reach for her weapon.

"I'll protect you." He said it and knew it was an oath before God. "I'll take care of you and see you get home."

Logan was no gunman, no cowboy, no

mountain man. He hunted elk . . . to draw them. He would rather sketch a grizzly bear than shoot it for its hide. The wild things seemed to know that and leave him alone. But he'd been living in a hard land for three years and he'd learned a few things. Wise Sister and her husband, Pierre Babineau, had seen to it.

Wise Sister, the wizened Shoshone woman who tended to his home, was in charge of putting meat on the table, and she did her job well. Logan didn't concern himself with how.

"Can you move?"

The young woman blinked at him, and her beautiful blue eyes focused a bit as if she were trying to force herself to understand.

Logan pointed upward. "You fell from way up there. I can't get you back up there, not without about a full day of winding around. If I did get you up there, we wouldn't want to see what happened. And there might be danger if we rode that way." Logan would have faced it if he'd been alone. But with this young woman, so injured, there was no possible way.

The woman stared at his lips as if focusing every ounce of her efforts on comprehension.

It made Logan overly aware of his lips for some odd reason. "I'm going to take you to my cabin. It's a long ride. We'll be pressed to get there before dark. But it's the opposite way from whatever trouble happened up on that mountaintop. I've got a woman at home who is a Shoshone healer. She'll help take care of you."

"Help?" The woman lifted the hand that had reached for her gun and rested it on his upper arm.

Logan smiled at the life that seemed to burn like blue fire out of her eyes. She was a tough one, all right. Maybe she had been up there alone. Maybe that's why no one had come. Dry-gulchers, she'd said. All dead. Maybe she'd been referring to her horse. Horses, there'd been two. But maybe one was a pack animal. He glanced around and didn't see either of them. Either they'd fallen farther down the mountain or gotten stuck higher up.

Such violence, such a waste of life. He knew that nature was full of violence. Bears ate fish. Mountain lions ate deer. Wolves ate rabbits and a pack could pull down an elk. Yes, there was violence out here and he respected that as the way of nature. But only man killed senselessly.

"I'm going to carry you to my horse now, miss." He looked down at her and wondered if she could think clearly enough to tell him her name. "I'm Logan. Logan McKenzie."

"Logan?" Her eyes blinked slowly and she stared at him as if her vision was blurred and nothing she saw made sense.

"What's your name?"

She might have been carrying papers in one of

her manly pockets. Those would tell her name. But Logan hadn't gotten around to searching her before she awoke, and now that she was conscious, he certainly wasn't going to be frisking her. She just might be able to get to that gun. He didn't underestimate her.

"S–Sally."

She definitely sounded like the West. Her few words carried a drawl that was in stark contrast to the clipped tones and upper crust accent and snooty vocabulary he'd been raised with in New York City. His voice set him apart and he'd been trying to learn Western lingo. Learning the culture fed his art.

"I'm Sally Mc—"

A low growl cut off her words and pulled Logan's gaze up.

Wolves. Three of them, crouched low, barely visible in a clump of quaking aspen trees just across the talus slide.

Ah yes, violence in nature indeed. They smelled the blood. Or they smelled whatever scent of death lingered at this place.

"Rifle. Get my . . . my Winchester."

Logan was more inclined to get his sketchbook. They were beautiful creatures. But one of the wolves inched forward, ears lying back, looking ready to attack.

Logan slid his hand behind her neck and lifted her carefully to ease Sally's rifle off her back.

37

She reached for it but he stood, the heavy iron steady and familiar in his hands. He realized just how much he'd learned in his years in the wild and how little he fit with the people back East, where he spent his winters.

"Are there more of you?" He raised his voice, hoping the wolves would back off. Wondering if there might be more than these three. Hiking and studying nature had taught him that a pack was usually larger. Although in the summer they weren't as likely to gather in large groups.

The wolf wasn't impressed with his shouting and inched closer.

He cocked the rifle, a Winchester '73 like Babineau favored, aimed at the nearest really fat tree, and pulled the trigger.

The animals vanished as swiftly and silently as wraiths.

Wise Sister had scolded him when he'd admitted he often left his Colt in his saddlebag. This proved her right. He should keep it close to hand. Of course, he usually didn't hang around in the forest soaked in blood.

"You missed." The woman, Sally Mac, tried to sit up, levering herself forward with one elbow as if to wrest her rifle from his hands.

"No reason to kill them." He admired tenacity, and Sally had a bundle of it.

"They're wolves, what . . . other . . . reason d'you . . . n–need?"

Logan smiled. "You seem to be recovering." He remembered how she'd carried the weapon. He'd do the same. He slung it over his own shoulders, adjusted it like she'd had it, then crouched and eased his arms under her.

He hiked long miles and was prone to climbing trees and rocks and wading in fast-moving streams to experiment with angles on a painting, so he was fit enough. And she didn't weigh much anyway. He carefully lifted.

She gasped in pain.

"I'm sorry." He looked down at her and she quickly suppressed the sound, closing her eyes as if she'd shamed herself with that sound of pain. He began walking, careful to jostle her the least possible amount.

He skirted the avalanche, taking a longer but more easily hiked path to the lower grassland where he'd picketed his horse. As he reached the end of the talus, he passed through a thick stand of trees and kept his ears and eyes open for any sign of the wolves. None jumped him. And then he stopped, the shock so sudden he jerked poor Sally Mac and squeezed another gasp out of her.

Her eyes flew open. "What?" Then she looked in the direction he was staring, shouted, and struggled against his grip.

"No, stay still. There's nothing we can do for him." If it was a him. A . . . skull. A human skull, someone obviously long dead. Logan thought of the wolves and looked more closely at the skull. It was possible it hadn't been so very long.

"That one?" Sally pointed away from the skull Logan stared at.

Logan gave her a startled glance then followed the direction of her eyes and saw another skull. As his vision widened, he saw a bone . . . likely a human arm but possibly not. Logan didn't want to believe he stood in the middle of a ghastly burial ground.

Then he looked back, all the way up to where he'd heard the gunfire.

Three

I'm not riding down there." Tulsa rubbed his arm. The man was always moving, nervous, with weasel eyes. Fergus got tired of it, but Tulsa didn't miss much and that was a worthy skill. But without Curly around, Fergus found Tulsa wearing on his nerves worse than usual.

Fergus had torn strips of cloth off the dead woman's skirts and saw just how deep that gouge was that cut Tulsa's forearm. No doctor around to make pretty stitches so Tulsa was going to have an ugly scar to remember taking his first bullet, and that was if the wound didn't turn septic and kill him.

"I am. That cowpoke killed my brother. I'm hunting up what's left of him and taking it for myself." Fergus was so sick of Tulsa's whining he had a very pleasant daydream about putting a bullet in the man. He restrained himself. He didn't want to ride these hills alone. Three had been the perfect number for waylaying those who came riding through.

"Long trip down for a rifle." Tulsa turned back to stripping their victims of valuables. Tulsa was skin and bones, except for a potbelly. His legs were so bowed no one had to say out loud he'd been next thing to born on horseback and wasn't a man to walk when he could ride. He was a hard man for all his whining, and a dead shot. He'd never been so much as scratched before. That creasing bullet had cut into his pride as much as his arm.

Fergus could use that. "If you ain't in, I reckon I'll meet up with you in town later. It don't sit right to not take somethin' back after that no-account killed Curly Ike and shot you. He might have a few dollars in his pocket."

"Lookee here." Tulsa pulled a fat envelope out of a saddlebag. Money, paper money, spilled out and Tulsa hurried to grab it. Then he looked up at Fergus. "Two horses went over with that cowpoke."

The horses that had lived had run off. Fergus saw one far down the trail that had stopped to graze. Those saddlebags looked fat, too.

"It's a rich group." Fergus's eyes narrowed as

he added up the wealth he'd have if every saddlebag had this kind of money. "By the time we round up that horse down there, we'll be halfway to the bottom of this cliff anyway. I say we go down there and have a look around."

Tulsa frowned, greed warring with his desire to do as little work as possible. Then a gunshot rang out from far below.

They both rushed to the edge of the cliff but could see nothing.

"Whoever you shot must have survived the bullet and the fall." Tulsa scowled. "We've never had anyone live to go to the sheriff before."

Fergus looked at the dead horse beside him. "We can't hoist this horse over the ledge, so someone's gonna see we've left trouble on this trail."

"We have us a stake, 'specially if we find good money in the other saddlebags." Tulsa's eyes slid back and forth like a sneaky ferret. "We might want to move out for a while. Take it easy. We might have enough to have an easy-livin' winter in San Francisco."

"And we'll let this trail cool down for a while." The bitter loss of his brother was almost forgotten as Fergus counted the money he might well find in the saddlebags at the bottom of this cliff. "When our cash runs out, we'll come on back. Plenty of curious folks comin' into the area. Most head for those geysers in Yellowstone, but there are always a few fools that come up here."

The two men exchanged a harsh, greedy laugh.

Tulsa shoved the last sightseer toward the edge of that cliff. Then they both set out to take a much longer but less deadly way down.

Logan heard something coming. Falling.

It stopped overhead and there was no more sound. But he suspected it was another member of this woman's party being tossed over the edge. Only the fact that she'd fallen had saved her life. If she'd been up on that trail, wounded, they'd have finished her off and cast her over. "Were there many with you up there?"

"Yes. All dead. All but me." Her head sagged against him, her cheek resting on his chest, as if the last of her strength was spent.

Logan needed to stay and bury the dead. A white bleached bone was only a few feet away from him on this crude burial ground. The men who had attacked Sally were savages worse than the most vicious wolves.

Logan knew he had no choice about walking away. He had to see to the living. Between the wolves and the wounded woman, Logan could do nothing but go on. He knew now why the wolves stalked this area in a pack. There was an unnatural supply of food.

Sickened, Logan began walking with his

delicate cargo. He'd come back. Identify these bodies if possible and inform their families. Then report this to the authorities.

What authorities? There was no law out here. The place was almost completely empty, though travelers to Yellowstone had increased the chance of a few wanderers coming down these mountain trails. A fact evil men had no doubt discovered.

Logan suspected these men loitered around town and followed sojourners into the wilderness. That would explain how they knew where to position themselves to waylay people.

A perfect place for lawlessness of the worst sort.

He picked up his speed, heading for his picketed horse. Hoping he wasn't hurting Sally. But considering the wolves, both animal and human, which would have definitely been on her had she been alone, getting out of here was about the only real choice he had.

Settling in to take the long strides he'd learned while hiking miles and miles in these rugged, beautiful, wooded mountains, he glanced down and saw that her eyes had closed. Passed out again.

Regret hit him hard. He'd hurt her. Holding her closer was his only way to apologize. He walked along with painful care and prayed over her, and for the others who had died here.

They were beyond help. She had a chance.

A wild cry overhead pulled his eyes upward and diverted him from the brutal ugliness he'd just encountered. He stopped to drink in the eagle soaring, playing on the wind, lifting and falling, wheeling and diving. Majestic and free and glorious.

Dear Lord God, bless the souls of those who died here. Help me protect this young woman from the dangers in this beautiful creation of Yours.

His throat ached with the beauty of it. With the beauty of this entire, spectacular corner of the earth. He could stay here and draw forever. And he just might.

Looking back down at the battered woman, he saw past the blood to how perfect her face was. Bone structure that sang to his artist's heart as surely as the victorious eagle above. Blond hair that had fallen out of a braid. That little pink bow peeking out. The cruel scar at her throat.

Why was she dressed like a man? He wondered about it, but he didn't object to it in the least. He believed in letting people live their own lives, in their own way. It's what he'd wanted desperately from his father.

He reached the clearing and breathed a sigh of relief to see his horse, a sturdy brown gelding, still there, cropping grass. A vision of peacefulness in this valley of the shadow of death. Beyond the horse he saw the white-capped mountains.

A flicker in his artist's heart made him wonder if he should paint the ugliness of nature, too. There was no power in art if it wasn't honest. Logan wanted to do work that mattered, that lasted. But the ugliness of what he'd seen back there in that talus slide was a depth of ugliness Logan didn't believe would fit in the artistic world. He'd consider it. Wolves, death, murder. It would be drawing tragedy and sin and hate. Did God give him this gift and hope he'd use it in such a way? Logan couldn't decide.

His father's oft-repeated opinion that Logan was wasting his life echoed and taunted. His father saw death, fought for life, and even if he lost, went on to fight again.

Was Logan less courageous than his father? Was choosing to draw his pictures a way to run from the ugly side of life? Logan had always believed he was showing courage to follow this leading from God, but maybe he was, in fact, a coward. All of this doubt assaulted him as he approached his horse in this wild setting.

Logan looked back at the perfect beauty of his sleeping patient. How his father would tease him about trying to doctor someone after Logan had turned his back on the profession. Now Logan wished he'd at least listened more. Then he'd know better what to do. Instead, he'd spent his childhood with his head in the clouds. Drawing and dreaming. And now, when a bit of medical knowledge would possibly save a life, he had none.

He let her beauty pull him away from the ugliness he'd seen. He wanted to paint her. Use his precious oils to catch the color of her white-yellow hair and sapphire eyes and the depth of the soul he'd seen as she hung in a tree just past his reach.

Later. But it would happen.

He would paint her face. He rarely did portraits, but this one he must do.

He laid her down on the ground carefully, saddled his gelding, and mounted with Sally cradled in his arms. He gave the animal a gentle kick.

The horse knew the way home, even though it was hours and hours away. The old boy was fat with grass, but he knew there'd be a bait of oats waiting so he moved along with little guidance.

Which left Logan free to give all his attention to the beautiful Buckskin Angel that had fallen from above to land in need of his care.

The Rocky Mountains truly were a land of contrasts.

Near miraculous beauty . . . and murder.

Four

Where's Sally?" Mandy's heart sank as she saw Sidney alone in the buggy.

She'd expected Luther and Buff back days ago with her little sister. Sidney tended to make his trips to town stretch to a week. Luther and Buff could make it in two brutally hard days. Now, after days of tension that had stretched her temper tight as a fiddle string, Sidney had returned with no Sally and no Luther and Buff.

Mandy looked at the two men who rode behind Sidney. His bodyguards. Bodyguards were as ridiculous as the house Sidney was building.

She ignored the hammering going on behind her. Men were hard at work building Sidney's ridiculous mansion, thanks to all that ridiculous gold.

"Sally wasn't there, but there was a message from her." Sidney, who'd gained weight steadily since he'd found his gold, lumbered down from his ornate buggy, its sides gray instead of proper black. Just as Sidney's suit was gray and Mandy's dress. The gray was custom-made and far more expensive than a black buggy. It was like the man was *looking* for someone to overcharge him. "Luther and Buff left town ahead of me to meet her. There was a note saying they'd left the train and would be coming from a different direction. I expected to find them all here."

Mandy had to fight back a cry of disappointment. "It's not like Sally to let anything delay her."

"There was a letter from Texas. From your ma and pa." Sidney smiled his superior smirk that told her how little he cared for her parents. Then he reached his plump, dimpled hand into the inner pocket of his suit with deliberately taunting slowness and produced a tattered envelope. Opened.

It was all Mandy could do not to go after him with the butt of her Winchester. Just like every day.

She controlled the urge with little effort. With practice, a woman could learn to do almost anything. "Does the letter say she'll be late?"

The letter Sidney carried had been written to her and her alone. Her parents always wrote the letters with only Mandy's name on the outside. Their way of being stubborn about the fact she'd married a man who already had a wife . . . almost.

Not that Mandy had known that at the time.

And the wife had, after all, been dead.

Not that Sidney had known *that* at the time.

Still, even without his name on the letter, Sidney always opened it and read it on his way home from town.

Mandy had her teeth clenched behind her smile.

"The letter is old, sent before Sally started out. We have worthless mail delivery out here." Sidney shook his head and sniffed in a way that made people dislike him. People including her.

How could Sidney think they'd have mail delivery when he picked a house site at the top of a mountain slope? He didn't expect it, not really. He just liked sneering.

Sidney tossed the reins of his team of grays to the taller of his two bodyguards. Bodyguards, what nonsense. A man guarded his own body out West.

These two were tough men, Mandy had no doubt, but they rarely spoke, and she didn't like what she saw in their eyes, cruelty and arrogance and sometimes, when they fastened on her, something ugly. Something that made her keep her rifle close to hand day and night.

"They'll be here soon. It'll be nice to have some company." He might even mean it. Sidney rarely covered his feelings. A fact Mandy deeply regretted.

A stiff upper lip sounded like heaven. Rather than jump up and down and start screaming and fretting over the delay or worrying over her missing little sister, Mandy just kept smiling. Sidney didn't like her all worked up. Pleasant, calm, polite, restrained. Above all restrained.

She'd become a master at restraint almost equal to her sharpshooting.

And at night, if she had the occasional dream about her hands wrapped around Sidney's flabby neck, well, she never actually touched the man, so no harm was done. In fact, it was possible that's why God had created dreams.

"Pa's home!" Little Angela came charging out of the cabin. Just past two, she was a fireball. Lively and bright and full of sass. And dressed in gray.

She reminded Mandy of her sister Laurie so much it was like a constant ache in her throat. Mandy had a big hand in raising Laurie, so turning all her love to this little tyke was a simple task indeed.

Angela ran straight past Mandy to her pa.

Sidney caught Angela up in his arms with a grunt of effort. "Hello, sweetie. I've got a surprise for you from town." Being wealthy had agreed with Sidney to a certain extent. Being a king—at least in his own mind—suited him right down to the ground.

A loud cry from their cabin turned Mandy's attention. She looked over her shoulder at the small but adequate cabin Sidney had paid someone else to build before he figured out just how much money he really had.

Little Catherine was awake. Hungry no doubt. Mandy needed to get her weaned before the next one came. But with both of their milk cows dried up, waiting to calf, milk was scarce up here in the high-up hills where Sidney seemed determined to live.

Luther and Buff would have brought supplies from town, but they'd been focused on picking up Sally. Then, since she hadn't arrived, it appeared that they'd turned their attention to figuring out why.

Which would leave the supplies to Sidney. Who came home empty-handed.

He stood Angela back on her two wobbly feet, handed her a licorice stick, and shooed her away like an unwelcome fly. But he had hugged her nicely first.

"Can I read the letter, Sidney? While I see to Catherine?" Mandy used exactly the correct tone. Not over eager. Pleasant, restrained, restrained, restrained.

Mandy adjusted the rifle strapped on her back. She'd begun to leave it off occasionally after their first year out here. Hung it over the door in the tidy little cabin. Then Sidney had struck it rich and hired his bodyguards with their watchful, hungry eyes, and she'd clung to it, either within grabbing distance inside or strapped on her back outside. She even slept with it beside her bed.

The taller of the two men gave her a long look behind Sidney's back, and Mandy was grateful that she was in an advanced state of pregnancy. Sidney had kept her in that state ever since they'd gotten married.

But Mandy didn't mind. Her daughters were the best part of her marriage. No contest.

God protect me. And protect Sidney from me.

She shouldn't ask. It wasn't properly restrained. But she couldn't stop herself. "Sidney, did you remember to bring supplies from the general store?"

Why they needed supplies when they were surrounded by mountains teeming with food was beyond Mandy, but she knew with Luther and Buff riding out to meet Sally and bringing her the rest of the way, there was only the food that she fetched with the business end of her rifle, or what Sidney brought from town. And going hunting when she was eight months into her confinement, with two toddlers in tow, was a bit much. Not that she hadn't done it. The hunting was hard enough, but bleeding and gutting a deer, then hauling her catch home and butchering it taxed her right to the limit.

Luther and Buff had left plenty of food. But that was before any of them knew about the men coming to build the new house even farther up the hill.

Sidney, not a practical man at the best of times, had neglected to mention the work crews, who had arrived shortly after he left. All Sidney knew was there was always food on the table somehow and he ate his share and more with great enthusiasm. He had no personal curiosity about how it got there.

"No, I didn't have time for that, Mandy. I had business to see to. Important business." Sidney came into possession of his kingly voice with little provocation. Mandy would have liked to shove that attitude of his right down his throat.

"As if eating isn't important?" Uh-oh. That was definitely not properly restrained.

The baby cried again, louder. Mandy needed that letter before she settled in to feeding Catherine.

Sidney's eyes flashed in his puffy, pallid face—temper, always sullen, pouty. One more word from her, and he'd probably not speak to her for days. Oh, she was tempted. She was more than tempted.

"Sidney, how am I supposed to feed five workmen, your bodyguards, plus our two children and you without food?"

Sidney crushed her letter in his hand. Mandy felt as if he'd physically crushed her heart. What if he destroyed it? What if there was news? Beth was expecting a baby and Mandy knew it might have come by now.

She thought about her rifle on her back in such a sinful way she was horrified. Restraint.

God protect me from my temper. And mostly, protect Sidney from it.

"I do everything around here." Sidney lifted his fist, holding the letter in a tight ball, but Mandy could smooth it out easily. "I provide you with luxuries your *father* never dreamed of."

Sidney pulled a match out of his pocket. The man had taken to smoking expensive cigars since the gold mine had come in. So a match didn't necessarily mean disaster. He could be planning to smoke.

"I will not put up with your constant nagging." Sidney struck the match and held it to the paper.

"I'm sorry, Sidney. So sorry. I will never speak like that to you again." She held her breath. Prayed. Her fingers had an actual itch on the tips and it would scratch them very nicely to grab her rifle. She wouldn't shoot him of course. But just one well-placed butt stroke to the head—

"See that you don't, woman. And get in the house. It's not proper for you to flaunt yourself in front of the workmen. Will you never learn decent manners?" He very deliberately dropped the letter to the ground and stomped on it as he walked past her without looking at her.

"Yes, Sidney, I'll be right in." She rushed for the letter and snatched it up. She looked up to see the bodyguards smirking at her.

One, Cordell Cooter, who held the horses, was tall and thin and young. The other, Nils Platte, was stocky and older and hard. Both treated her with disdain to match Sidney's. Although

Cooter's disdain was different. Mandy saw contempt in the eyes of both men, but Cooter's contempt had more to it. Mandy couldn't define it, but she knew it wasn't decent and she knew she'd never want to be at Cooter's mercy. Of course, she'd prefer not to be at Sidney's mercy either, and here she was. It crossed Mandy's mind that the two might one day be forced to protect Sidney from her.

Angela grabbed onto her leg, and Mandy tried her best not to look devastated by Sidney's humiliating treatment. But one look at little Angela's expression told Mandy she'd failed. Her precious daughter had tears brimming in her eyes. She looked to her mama for comfort, and Mandy could barely find the strength to hold a frown off her face. She picked up her daughter and hugged her tight, smelling the fresh scent of her recently washed blond curls.

Restraint. She had to learn restraint. Sidney knew too many ways to make her regret it if she didn't.

"Protect me, Lord," Mandy whispered against her baby's smooth, pretty pink cheeks. "Protect us both."

Catherine wailed inside. The baby kicked in Mandy's belly. Angela's tears spilled over. And Mandy restrained her temper, shoved the letter deep in the pocket of her gingham dress, and tried to figure out how to feed eleven people with bare cupboards.

She was a good shot. And she had a vigorous garden. She'd manage.

Being rich had turned out to be terribly hard work. Being married to a man who thought he was the King on the Mountain had turned out to be a nuisance.

"We shoulda met 'em by now." Luther looked sideways at Buff. Worry was riding them both hard. So hard Luther had spoken aloud what they both knew without words.

"Just keep headin' to meet 'em. All we can do." Buff pulled the crude map the colonel had sent along with the train, along with a note from Sally saying they'd cut days off the trip by heading cross country rather than riding all the way to Helena.

"Could we have missed 'em turning off the trail somewhere?" Luther reached for the map and studied it. "Or missed the place where their trail intersected with the trail from Helena to Mandy's cabin?" Luther wasn't much of a one for talking, but this needed to be hashed out before they rode another step—maybe in the wrong direction. They were already inching along, studying sign. Sally should have been here by now.

"Reckon they ran into trouble." Buff stared down through the rugged country the colonel had said they were riding through to get a look at some of the scenery along the trail Lewis and Clark had ridden so long ago.

"Only reason for 'em to be this late." Luther folded the map and kicked his horse forward, his stomach stomping on his guts as he thought of all that could go wrong in country this wild.

Five

Logan barely paid attention to where they rode. The horse knew the way after all. Instead he focused on the woman in his arms.

They'd been riding for hours when they finally reached the carefully concealed trail that led home. He still had a long stretch to go, but now they were on the final leg, climbing to the heavens. Logan's heart beat harder as he thought of what was waiting up there—the glory of God's creation.

He looked down and saw Sally's eyes flicker open. Blue eyes. Magnificent. Like God had mixed the colors Himself and taken long hours to get a once-in-a-lifetime shade of pure, vivid blue.

Her eyes narrowed. "Who are you?"

"My name is Logan."

"Logan?" Confusion dimmed her expression for a moment.

"Logan." He smiled. "Logan McKenzie. Don't you remember from earlier?" Logan tried to think how to ease her worry. "You fell. I found you unconscious, but you woke up for a while. Long enough to tell me your name is Sally. I'm taking you to Wise Sister, the Shoshone woman who cooks for me and looks after my house. She knows medicine. We weren't safe back there."

"You're the mighty wolf shooter." She frowned and her eyes slid to his shoulder where she could no doubt see the butt of her rifle. He wore it just as she had, strapped across his back.

Since he'd deliberately missed the wolf, Logan didn't take offense. "Yes, I scared off a pack of wolves. Can you tell me if anything hurts particularly? I'm no doctor." Something he'd never regretted until now. "I couldn't leave you there, so I'm taking you to Wise Sister." He spoke slowly, clearly, hoping she could remember this time.

Sally pushed at his shoulders and tried to sit up. She cried out in pain. Her well-tanned skin turned an alarming shade of gray.

"What?"

"Something's wrong. My—my—" Her left arm was tucked between their bodies, but her right arm was free, and she clutched her chest with a gasp of pain.

"You fell a long way. I couldn't see any obviously broken bones, but I wouldn't be surprised."

"And my leg. My right leg."

"I'm sure being moved is agony, but I couldn't

leave you and you needed care. Lie still." He lowered his forehead so it rested on hers, trying to soothe her. "We'll get there."

He didn't say it would be a long time yet. He'd set out yesterday and intended to stay out overnight tonight and maybe longer. He wanted to do a thorough sketch study of the crimson rocks he'd found in that area. He'd planned to sleep out. He'd never expected to turn around and ride all the way back home only an hour after he'd perched in his tree. "Can you go back to sleep? That would make the trip pass more quickly for you."

"I—I don't think so. My leg is on fire. God, have mercy."

Logan pulled away from her to look at her leg, completely covered by her buckskin pants and, below that, the heavy Western boots she wore. He carefully reached down and lifted a bit of her pants leg. The pants weren't overly tight, and he could see that her boot was firmly in place. He inched the pants leg up with one hand until he found the top of the boot and his stomach twisted.

Her leg, right below the knee, was swollen until her skin sagged over the top of the boot. It had looked fine during his early inspection for wounds, but now it was an awful sight. There was no sign of bleeding or a protruding bone, but the boot had to be cutting off her circulation.

He prayed silently as he lowered the buckskin. *God, give me guidance. Speak to my heart, put wisdom in my head.*

Overhead the scream of an eagle drew his attention. Logan looked up, not to watch the magnificent bird, its white head gleaming against the blue sky, but to reach out for God and acknowledge man's lowly place and God's ruling hand.

He looked at her and saw she had a knife in a sheath at her waist. A knife to slit the boot? Though he felt pressed to get to Wise Sister as soon as possible, he had to do something about that constricting boot.

Urging his horse forward, he sought a likely place to dismount. When he found it, he stepped off onto a stirrup-high, flat stone and lowered Sally to the rock.

She gasped as he eased his arms from around her.

"I'm sorry."

"My chest feels like it's being chawed on by that pack of wolves you missed."

Logan controlled a smile. Which wasn't hard. All he had to do was think of her leg.

"I'm going to cut your boot."

"No, don't touch me, please." Sally made a single forward motion then gasped in pain and subsided.

"I'm sorry. I've got to loosen it. Your leg is so

swollen I'm afraid the circulation is cut off. You could lose your leg."

The pretty jawline firmed. Her teeth clenched so hard, Logan was afraid she'd grind them down flat. She kept her eyes wide open, looked straight up at the sky, and gave a single nod of her head. "Do it."

"I'll be as gentle as possible." He raised her pants leg just past the top of her boot and pulled his knife out of his boot. He kept it razor sharp at all times, but boot leather was tough.

"Is it broken?" Sally stared at his face but stayed flat, making no attempt to see her leg.

Logan thought that was more because it hurt to move than a sign she had any faith in him. "It must be, Sally. I'm sorry to say that, but it, well, it's bad, broken or sprained, either one." Logan couldn't imagine a sprain swelling like this. "I'm going to have to"—Logan swallowed hard—"get my finger between your leg and the boot."

"Quit talking and get on with it," Sally said between her teeth.

Sliding his finger in was a terrible business. He had to do it or he'd cut her. He got the slightest fraction of an inch pulled away and touched the boot with his knife. The tough leather cut, but not easily. He fought it, inch by inch, doing his best not to move her leg. Sally wore a heavy, manly sock under her boots and that gave her a bit of protection against a slip of the blade.

The swelling didn't let up; in fact, as they got to what Logan hoped would be a slender ankle, the boot only seemed tighter. Sally cried out when he touched her ankle and then went limp. He looked at her quickly. She appeared to have fainted, which was a mercy for her. Hadn't she asked for God to have mercy?

Still careful, even with her unconscious, Logan cut all the way to a thick seam near the boot heel. It wasn't so tight there, and with a sigh of relief, he decided it was enough. It gave him a partial view of her stocking-clad leg, which showed no signs of bleeding; and it didn't look like the bone was displaced. What was left of her boot made a good support for her ankle, so he didn't remove it.

His stomach twisted as he took one careful look at her gray complexion. He'd hurt her terribly. Unable to resist, he ran a finger down the soft curve of her cheek, drawn to the delicate beauty in the buckskin outfit. The combination spoke to his artist's heart. How he'd hated hurting her.

Sheathing his knife, moving as cautiously as possibly, he gathered her back in his arms, climbed on his horse, and rode on. After three years out here, he'd learned to be savvy about a trail, leave no tracks. He'd never felt threatened—until today—but Pierre and Wise Sister were knowing people and he took their advice to heart, if for no other reason than because a man being out here in the wild might scare off wildlife and he didn't want that.

Now he approached the well-hidden trail to his cabin on rocky ground where no hoof prints would show. His sure-footed horse had taken this same path many times, and he did most of the work, picking his way up the steep, rocky path.

When Logan finally crested the top of the mountain, he breathed a sigh of relief to see Wise Sister walking up to her cabin from the west, her bow slung over her shoulder, a quiver of arrows on her back. She spent time hunting many days, and he'd feared he might wait hours for her to come home and help.

It wasn't the first time that she'd been exactly where he needed her at a crucial time. He'd never really figured out how she did that.

Wise Sister wasn't one to let someone ride up on her by surprise. From the moment he saw her, she was watching. He couldn't even see her expression from this distance, but she must have taken everything in, his unexpected return and the woman in his arms, because she rushed to her cabin. By the time he rode the rest of the way home, smoke was streaming out of her chimney and he could smell something herbal in the air.

Then Wise Sister came out of the cabin, her long hair, more white than gray, in two braids that hung down her back. She came to him and reached up her arms. Logan knew she was uncommonly strong for a round, old woman.

"She fell. Mind her leg. I think it's broken. Her ribs, too."

"Hush." Wise Sister gave him a look that would have shut him up without the single word.

Wise Sister spoke broken English and Logan knew a lot of Shoshone words. They managed somehow. When Wise Sister's husband, a French fur trader, Pierre Babineau, had been alive, he'd interpreted for them. Babineau had also, working with Wise Sister, built a cabin just for Logan and hunted food. Logan paid them generously, one of the perks of having a good market back East for his paintings. They all got along well.

But this year, when Logan had come back in the spring, as he'd done each year while he worked on sketching the scenery in the area, Wise Sister had been alone and there'd been a grave dug beneath a towering pine tree marked with a rustic cross. Since then she'd quietly and competently seen to Logan's needs alone.

The honest truth was, though he trusted her with his life, Logan considered her a formidable woman and a little scary. So he handed Sally over without protest.

She took Sally into her arms and, in her quiet way, took complete charge. She hurried into the cabin, leaving Logan to tend to the horse.

Six

Logan turned his gelding loose in the rough corral Pierre had built. The horses Logan used to pack in all his painting supplies in the spring looked up and snorted at their friend as it trotted into the pasture.

He hung up the saddle and bridle in a little shed with quick, practiced motions, his mind on Sally. He'd grown up with horses. Saddling a Western animal was a bit different, but it came easy.

Rushing in the gathering dusk, he headed straight for the small cabin behind his, but he realized with a pang that it bothered him that Wise Sister had taken Sally into her cabin rather than his. Of course she had. It made sense. It would be improper to care for a woman in his house, since Sally might well be laid up for a long time. But Wise Sister's cabin was half the size of his. The women should live in his cabin and he should take the small one. And besides, knowing it was ridiculous, Logan couldn't help but feel like Sally was his.

As he reached Wise Sister's door, he paused, not wanting to burst in and catch a glimpse of an exposed limb. Swallowing hard as the exposed limb notion flickered through his head, he admitted that he hadn't thought much about women since he'd started working on painting the scenery in the Rockies. He picked the wilderness and there weren't any women here, so he didn't bother thinking about them.

But right now, there was no denying he had himself some thoughts. A woman, whose limbs might be exposed, had been dropped from the heavens into his arms. That made her a gift from God straight to him, and he was strongly inclined to accept that gift. With a grin, he decided he probably needed to consult Sally on that. Then he knocked and waited a moment.

"Come." Wise Sister wasn't for saying a sentence when a word would do.

Logan entered the cabin, always amazed at the lifetime of beautiful things Wise Sister had gathered. She was above all a practical woman, but her home wasn't practical. It was beautiful . . . and rich in sentiment.

The artist in him loved the beaded dresses, furred window covers, woven baskets, and dyed and knotted wall hangings. The one-room cabin sang to Logan's heart. He always wished for time in here to touch the textures, study the vivid colors, learn this different kind of art than what he was used to.

All of it soothed his soul, but none of it pleased him as much as the picture Wise Sister hung in a place of honor. He took one second to look at the portrait he'd painted of Wise Sister and Babineau. He'd done well with that one, capturing Wise Sister's calm and her deep, dark, patient eyes. And he'd found the wild man in Pierre Babineau and put him on the canvas. He was a perfect match for Wise Sister's quiet strength. The contrast between the two shone out of his picture, and Wise Sister had honored him indeed to hang it among her lifetime gathering of precious, beautiful things.

Logan moved to the foot of the bed where Sally lay flat on the large bedstead in Wise Sister's cabin, wearing a nightgown he recognized as his housekeeper's. It covered Sally from neck to toe. No limbs exposed anywhere.

Sally's gaze rose to his as Wise Sister stood beside her, tearing a sheet into strips. "I reckon I've got you to thank—" She stopped, obviously not remembering his name. He'd told her twice already, but she'd had a bad day.

"Logan."

"Thank you for seein' to me, Logan." She spoke as if moving her jaw was painful. Logan suspected there was nowhere on her that didn't hurt. "Wise Sister says I have a broken leg and some badly cracked—if not broken—ribs."

"Wrap leg now." Wise Sister lifted the cloths she was tearing.

"Let me help." Logan stepped forward, closer to pretty Sally.

Wise Sister pointed to a thin, flat board, about four inches wide and ten inches long, lying on the floor by her feet. "Cut in half." Wise Sister reached for the board, lifted it, and drew a finger across the board.

If Logan cut it correctly, it would be two boards, each five inches long. He took the wood outside to the chopping block and whacked it in half with a single, well-placed blow.

When he got back, Wise Sister shoved two socks at him. "Wood in socks."

He understood her order. It made no sense, but he understood.

As he covered the boards with the socks, Wise Sister set aside her pile of cloth strips and turned her attention to Sally's leg. Sally lay with her eyes closed.

Logan noticed two boots on the cabin floor, one cut nearly in half. On a chair next to the boots he saw Sally's clothing. Chaps—of all things for a woman to wear. A fringed leather coat. Broadcloth pants and a shirt with an ugly splatter of blood across it. There was also her chemise, bloodstained and ruined. It lay in a heap on the floor and looked as if Wise Sister had cut it off. He noticed a feminine pink bow on the front of that chemise. It looked almost silly lying amidst the mannish clothes. There was no blood on the ribbon. He didn't know that much about women, but his mother had liked frills and ribbons. He was glad this bit of frippery had survived for Sally.

Wise Sister gently eased a long sock onto Sally's badly swollen foot.

Logan turned to watch Sally's expression. His teeth gritted in sympathy for her pain.

Sally's neck arched back, pressing her head against the pillow. She never made a sound, but the color leeched out of her face. Her eyes closed and cords stood up in her throat. Her clenched jaw told Logan she was in agony.

"I'm going to pray while we work, Sally." Logan lifted her hand and saw white knuckles and an iron-hard fist.

Sally nodded almost imperceptibly. "God, have mercy."

He was surprised she could get words through her tight jaw. Logan spoke aloud to God, asking for the pain to end. Asking for healing and safety from those men, whoever had attacked her. He felt God come very near, as so often happened out here.

Once he ended the prayer, he began to talk, hoping the sound of his voice would be a comfort or at least a distraction. "I feel as if the mountaintops put me close to God. This corner of creation is God at His most miraculous. I think of this place, especially Yellowstone—I go in there for a few weeks every year—as being a gift from an artist God."

"I need your hands, Logan." Wise Sister gently positioned the sock-covered slats on the sides of Sally's terribly swollen ankle. "Hold."

Letting go of Sally wasn't easy, but Logan slipped his hand free and helped Wise Sister.

Sally swallowed hard and her jaw relaxed just a bit.

Hoping it distracted her, Logan went on while Wise Sister began her wrapping. "At the creation, the heavenly Father used these mountains as His canvas," Logan continued, trying to express in words what he couldn't get so many people to understand. Why he spent his life out here painting. "When I ride into Yellowstone, I paint the waterfalls and rugged canyons, the blasting geysers and primordial woodlands, the boiling mud pots and steaming hot springs. To me, all of that is an expression of God's love for the world He created."

Her tight jaw relaxed just enough for a smile to creep onto her face.

"There are pools of water in Yellowstone that are unlike anything I've ever seen before. It's so colorful, like a rainbow in the water and sometimes in the air above the water, too." Logan was doing his best to help Wise Sister and pay attention to Sally's expression at the same time, to call a halt if she appeared to hurt past what she was able to bear. She seemed to be listening, so he went on. "The geysers are so strange and beautiful. It's hard to believe they even exist. I've never seen anything like them before. Water, just spouting right up out of the ground. And there are a whole bunch of them. Some of them just come and go whenever they want. One they call Old Faithful."

Sally's mouth barely moved as she responded. "I've heard of it."

Logan saw Wise Sister wrapping around and around. Sally's ankle was now so thick with the white cloth that it should hold the bone steady enough to heal.

"Keep talking." Sally's request was more of an order.

"It fires off a spray about once an hour. And it's so hot you have to stay well back."

Sally's eyes were open a slit, boring into Logan as if she were trying to climb out of her body and into his. Which Logan couldn't blame her for. She couldn't have been real thrilled with her current condition.

"I stay there a few weeks and paint. Then I come back here. Wise Sister and her husband Pierre have lived here for years. I met Pierre when I first came into the area, and Pierre acted as my guide. He told me he lived in a spectacular place. We came up here, where he'd lived with Wise Sister for years. I asked if they'd stay on, work for me, help me find my way in these mountains."

Logan glanced at Wise Sister, who caught the look and shooed his hands away from Sally's ankle, then nodded encouragement for him to keep talking. Holding the limb motionless seemed to be helping because a bit of color returned to Sally's cheeks.

"For three years I've been coming back here." Logan went back to holding Sally's hand. "Pierre and Wise Sister built my cabin for me, with huge windows to let in the light and the view. And as I got to know them, Pierre the rover, Wise Sister the homemaker, I came to love it here. I hope to come back every summer for the rest of my life. Or at least until I've painted it all. Which should take the rest of my life, so that's the same thing."

Sally caught hold of his hand so tightly Logan wondered if he'd be able to paint when this was done. He found he didn't really care enough to let go.

"I've had the notion that maybe this is where God had the Garden of Eden."

A soft sniff of humorous disdain sounded from Sally, and she wrinkled her nose and spoke through gritted teeth. "Too hard of a land for the Garden of Eden."

If she could laugh at him, it was a good sign she was listening . . . and maybe not hurting so badly.

"It is that. True enough. And it sounds to me like the Garden of Eden was an easy life. But the beauty makes up for it. It's staggering. The sun rises from the east in a splash of glory. It's often blazing red in the west at night. There are majestic elk, powerful buffalo, towering lodgepole pines, and soaring eagles. God has created many beautiful things, including—" Logan checked himself before he mentioned Sally. She was so lovely. "Surely God never has created anything more beautiful."

Wise Sister worked quickly, gently binding Sally's leg.

Sally swallowed convulsively but never once cried out. Logan was impressed beyond words.

When the leg was tightly bound, Wise Sister brushed Sally's hair back from her face. "Ribs next."

Sally gulped audibly.

"You." Wise Sister looked at him and he straightened, ready to do whatever would help most. "Go." Wise Sister jerked her hand toward the door.

"But I—"

A threatening grunt erupted from his housekeeper's throat. "Woman. Only women."

Logan knew wrapping ribs was the usual treatment. And that no doubt needed doing without the nightgown in the way. He wanted to stay and help. But as usual Wise Sister was terrifying, also undoubtedly right. He left, but he didn't like it.

He paced, went into his cabin, twiddled his thumbs, and went half mad with worry and impatience before he remembered he knew how to draw. "I can sketch her face." He slapped his shirt pocket. No pencil. He'd lost it when he'd dropped his sketchbook. He was always scrupulously careful with his equipment because of the work it took to haul it in here. But a woman had been plunging past him after all.

It didn't matter, he had another pencil. Rushing to the trunk he hauled in here every year, he threw open the lid. "Got to get her face down on paper." It burned in him. To think he'd forgotten.

He pulled out a fresh sketchbook. "Can I do it? Can I capture her beauty and courage?" He only knew he'd never be satisfied until he'd given it every ounce of his talent and effort.

Each spring, he also brought canvas and as many pots of oil paint as he could carry. Then he steeped himself in this magnificent place and immersed himself in art all summer.

The winter began threatening in September. Leaving would have torn Logan's heart out except it was about the same time he ran out of canvas and oil paint and sketchbooks. So, he hauled it all home, sold what he could bear to part with, and spent the winter in his parents' house in New York City painting, using his sketches and memory to supply the colors.

He took his first stroke of pencil on paper and felt all his nervous tension melt away as it always did when he let himself get lost in his art.

What would his family think of Sally's

portrait? His doctor father and four doctor brothers loved him and admired his work, all while telling him good-naturedly that he was out of his mind to spend his life drawing pictures.

They'd calmed their teasing some since he'd started making a solid income with his painting, squeaked his way into a few museums, and appeared in the pages of *Harper's Weekly*. They were almost used to his scenery. But they'd never seen a drawing of a woman he'd done. Even the one portrait he'd done of Wise Sister he'd left behind for her.

Sally's face appeared on the paper as if it flowed out of his fingertips. He didn't hesitate for a second. The ability to draw and paint was something he'd been born with, and even he didn't understand it. But with or without understanding, he was completely confident when he was creating.

He filled the first sheet with a profile, another one of her sleeping, another one of her in his arms. As he drew that, it struck Logan that he'd never attempted to draw a picture of himself before. He just let the image come, but wondered if that was what he really looked like. Could a person have an honest image of himself?

Next he caught her terror during the fall and lived that horrifying second again, when she'd caught on that branch and their eyes had met and he'd reached out but not far enough. The picture was awful. Drawing her fear was like living it through her. It was an honest picture, but painful to see and too personal. Logan tucked it into his trunk, not eager to see it again.

He drew her from the back, with that rifle in place. He drew her in chaps and wrote the words "Buckskin Angel" across the top. Then he thought of that tiny ribbon and used his imagination to put her in a dress.

Wise Sister pushed the door open, looked around the cabin, and made an unbelievably rude noise. "Done. Go."

She waved a shooing hand at him, then hustled to his fireplace and began building a fire. Only then did Logan realize night had fallen. A lantern was lit. He supposed he'd done that at some point.

Shaking his head, he made a pile of his drawings, amazed at the number he'd done, and put them off to the side. He saw the fire catch, then Wise Sister—as she always did—stopped to stare at Logan's favorite painting—*Blazing Land*.

He'd done it the first thing when he'd come back this spring, of the view outside his window. A brutally beautiful sunrise, the snowcapped peaks in the background and churning water in the foreground. This was a picture of the spectacular place he'd chosen to build his cabin, at the most glorious moment he'd ever seen.

The color of the sun that morning had turned everything outside his window into dancing fire. Logan hadn't done a bit of sketching. He'd just stretched his canvas and started painting. He hadn't been able to confine *Blazing Land* to a smaller canvas.

It was a foolish picture, Logan knew. First of all, huge. What had possessed him to use so much of his precious canvas on one painting? And the style, not his usual.

He'd had it churning to try his hand at a new style they were calling Impressionism. He'd studied it during the winter, and that perfect sunrise had demanded to be done in that style. He wanted the strong, undiluted colors. He wanted to paint in the outdoors and try to capture a moment and a feeling and a flash of sunlight, rather than go out to sketch and come back inside to create.

He'd done lots of sketching outdoors in his earlier years, especially tramping around Yellowstone. Who could stay inside in this stunning wilderness? But now he was doing the actual *painting* outside. He loved the slash of the paint knife and the thick colors until the painting was almost three dimensional. But such a huge picture . . . it reached the ceiling of his cabin, and the walls were eight feet high.

But he hadn't worked outside with *Blazing Land*. If he'd painted it outside, he couldn't have gotten it in the door to his cabin. Now he couldn't get it out. If he did get it out, he couldn't pack it on horseback to the nearest town. If he could figure a way to pack it to town, it wouldn't fit on the train.

If he somehow found a train car that could handle it, he couldn't find a home or museum anywhere that could get it inside *its* door.

Add to that, the Impressionist style was still controversial and often rejected by museums outright. No museum would want it.

It had been pure indulgence. A foolish picture indeed. And yet he couldn't stop himself from doing it just the way he had.

Logan seriously suspected that Wise Sister thought he was an idiot. But as Wise Sister studied that painting, the feeling bloomed like the most glorious flower that she understood, at least a little, that art could have value.

Her scowling, taciturn expression softened, and Logan knew that, as much as Wise Sister scolded, she approved of him in a way that defied her own common sense. He was surprised to realize it meant more to him than the highest compliments of the art critics back in New York.

He smiled as he hurried out to visit his Buckskin Angel.

Seven

Sally hurt like she'd been thrown off the back of a bucking bronco, then stomped on by a longhorn bull, then chawed on by a lobo wolf.

Worse yet, God, have mercy, she was feeling a lot better.

It had been a *pack* of wolves chawing while Wise Sister had splinted her leg and wrapped her ribs. Besides the breaks and bruises, she'd taken several blows to the noggin, and her vision was blurred. She'd sworn Wise Sister was three people at one time. But maybe that's just because the quiet old woman hurt her as bad as three people. Three people with wolf teeth.

She'd finally—almost fully—remembered what had happened, and her heart was hurting as bad as her body. Mrs. McGarritt—dead. The sight of Paula McGarritt, lying dead, on her back on that trail—Sally'd had one brief heartbeat to see her and the sight haunted her now every time she closed her eyes.

Colonel and Mrs. McGarritt had been close family friends. They were honorary grandparents to Beth and Alex's baby. The others riding with Sally were solid, knowing hands. Soldiers almost to a man. Tough, competent, trail savvy, and they'd been mowed down by yellow-bellied cowards.

Sally had done her best to put a bullet or two into them. The others with her had done their share, but Sally had heard the wrong guns still firing as she fell. The dry-gulchers had won. Sally had to figure everyone with her was dead. The members of her company would've come if they were alive.

As vague memories returned, she knew there'd been no sounds from above, except what she knew were bodies being thrown off the trail. From the bones she'd seen, Sally knew for a fact those coyotes had done this before. They were making a living at it.

But they'd made a mistake this time. The colonel was an important man with important friends. He came from a well-respected family that owned a big chunk of land in New Mexico. The colonel wasn't going to be shot to doll rags, tossed over a cliff, and forgotten. Folks would come hunting and they'd stay on the hunt until they had answers.

Someone would come for her, too. Sally had sent that letter on to Luther and Buff, who were to meet her train and guide her out to Mandy's. She'd be discovered missing within days.

Luther was smarter in the woods than Pa, even Ma. Maybe not Beth, but no one was better than Beth. Luther would be back-trailing her as soon as she didn't make the place where this shortcut crossed the trail to Mandy's.

If the man—Logan—who'd found her hadn't hauled her a day's ride away from that hill, Luther might be there to find her already. But Wise Sister was certain Sally had needed doctoring, so it was as well Logan had done what he'd done.

Didn't matter nohow. Luther'd still come, just take him longer. Luther and Buff could read sign like the written word. They'd come and find her, and she'd be on her way to Mandy's.

Urgency pressed on Sally when she thought of Mandy with a baby on the way. The last letter they'd gotten from her was as polite and perky as all Mandy's letters, but Sally had heard a thread of desperate loneliness in Mandy. Ma and Pa must have, too, because they agreed to let Sally come north and stay.

Suddenly Sally wanted to see her pa so bad it was the worst pain of all. She'd tried so hard all her life to be special to him. And she knew he loved her dearly, especially if she rode at his side and worked the ranch hard. Why had she ever left home? To her horror, she burst into tears.

The door swung open and her rescuer walked in. He saw her tears, and Sally waited for him to run.

Fine with her. She couldn't seem to stop crying and she didn't need to shame herself in front of a strange man.

"Sally." He said her name like a prayer and

closed the door—with him on the inside. He hadn't run? What kind of strange behavior was that for a man?

Instead, he hurried to her side, just like she wasn't bawling like a motherless calf. Pulling up a chair with a scratching noise that made her head ache, he sat beside her and lifted her hand with such gentleness she only cried harder.

She swiped at the tears streaming down her face with her free hand but decided it would hurt too badly to pull free of his grasp. Besides, it felt nice.

"What can I do to help you?" Logan leaned close and whispered. "I'm sorry I left. Wise Sister threw me out. I wanted to stay and help but"—he smiled sheepishly—"I'm kind of afraid of her."

A ripple of laughter broke through Sally's shameful tears. "Nothin' you can do. I reckon I'm just beat up is all."

"Beat up." Logan produced a snow white handkerchief and handed it to her. "Broken leg, knocked cold, fell off a cliff, shot. Yeah, I think *beat up* about covers it."

"I'm seeing two of you." She mopped at her eyes but kept a hold on his hand. It made the world spin just a little less.

"A concussion."

"What?"

"Doctor talk." Logan smiled.

Sally felt an ache in her chest that wasn't the same as her battered ribs at all. Still, what else could it be? His eyes, a warm brown that matched his unruly hair, seemed so full of sympathy Sally clutched his hand even tighter.

"My father's a doctor." Logan rubbed his thumb over her palm, like a caress, and it distracted her from her tears. "It's what they call a hard whack on the head that knocks you unconscious and makes you see double."

"Or triple."

"Ouch." Logan winced. "It'll clear up in a day or so."

"My sister's a doctor, too."

"Really?" Logan sat up straight, eyes wide with surprise. "A woman doctor? I've heard of a few of those, but not many."

"Well, to hear Beth tell it, they weren't real nice about it. But she managed to find a doctor who'd let her study with him. And now, in Mosqueros—in Texas where I'm from—we only have her and her husband to do all the doctorin', so folks let her help them—some—as long as Alex is there, too. Makes her cranky, but she puts up with it."

"It made me cranky when my father tried to *force* me to be a doctor."

"Instead you live in the middle of nowhere on a mountaintop?" Sally narrowed her eyes as she tried to remember and that made her headache

84

worse. "We did ride to a mountaintop, didn't we?"

"Well, I suppose, though there are higher mountains around it, so maybe not the very top." There was a look in his eyes that drew her—warmth, depth, kindness. He was different than any man she'd ever met.

"No one for you to doctor around here."

"Except for the occasional woman who falls out of the heavens." Sally was surprised she had the strength to make even that weak joke.

He flashed a smile full of even white teeth, a generous and easy smile that made her want to see it again. She tried to think of something else funny to say, but that also made her headache worse. In honesty, breathing made her headache worse.

"First time I've ever wished I'd paid closer attention when Father was trying to wring a little help out of me." His nice smile faded, replaced with regret. "I know I hurt you bringing you up here, but we couldn't go up the way you came down. Those men, whoever shot you, were still up there, or they could have been. I felt like you had to have care. Wise Sister knows everything."

"Everything?" It made Sally think of her ma, and she almost started crying again.

"Well, maybe not *everything*." Logan studied her and his thumb rubbed her palm again as if he could see her struggle. "So far she hasn't taken

85

up painting and bested me there." Logan looked at a woven mat hanging on the wall. "Although she made that, and to me that makes her an artist, even though it doesn't require paint."

Sally hadn't paid much attention to her surroundings, but she'd noticed this mat of knots and dyed string, beads and bits of feather and fur. As she studied the wall, she saw more. She saw carved leather and a soft, beaded dress that made her heart ache a little. There was a painting, too. And Logan had said Wise Sister didn't paint. That must mean that he did it. And thinking about a man paying attention to the beauty of a woven mat made her headache much worse. And had he said Wise Sister hadn't bested him at painting?

"But she's better at everything else." Logan diverted her with his story and his strong, callused hand. "As soon as you're healed, I'll take you back to town." Logan frowned. "The trail isn't safe, though, I guess. Judging from the other bodies we found." Logan looked warily at her. "Do you remember that?"

Sally nodded. "Awful. Those men have killed before. That's not a heavily traveled trail, but it gets a few people passing through. Pretty clear those back shooters watch the trail for riders."

"I know the dangers of the wild, steep trails and grizzlies and landslides, but for some reason I thought I was safe out here from man." Logan gave a brief, humorless laugh. "I found out today that's not true."

His eyes widened. "You know, I ride in on that trail when I come in the spring. I'm lucky they haven't shot me."

"Come? In the spring? Why?"

Logan leaned closer and Sally saw a light in his eyes that was almost frightening. She hadn't considered him anything but sweet. Until now. Maybe a mite stupid to have hauled her so far from where Luther'd come huntin'. A knowing man might reason out that if someone came trailing her, he oughta make it easy for them to find her. But besides that, he'd been sweet. Now he looked, well, just a bit shy of loco.

"I'm painting the Rockies."

All Sally could think of was the whitewash Pa had brought home to use on the cabin back home. "Painting the Rockies?"

"Yes. I'm an artist. Oil paints, pencil sketches. I'm going to start sculpting, too. I've been studying up. I think I've got it figured out."

"An artist?" Sally wondered why he didn't just say, "I'm a no-account bum." How could drawing a picture put meat on the table?

"I've discovered this miraculous land, and I'm going to spend every summer here until I've explored it all."

Exploring made some sense. After all, pioneers were explorers in a way, and Sally's ma had been a pioneer in west Texas. So, if he was looking for new trails for cattle drives to the west, or rich hunting and trapping grounds, or crop land, or a grassy valley to run a herd on, or even a place to dig for gold, she could understand it.

"Yes, I'm finding every beautiful site in the area. I go out to places like that canyon where you were, and I do a study of it."

"You study?" Like a school boy?

"A study." Logan nodded cheerfully as if he hadn't just admitted he was a bum. "I do a fast draw—"

"I'm a pretty fast draw myself." He'd finally said something that made sense.

"You can draw?" Logan perked up.

Truth be told, so did Sally. If the man was good with a gun, he couldn't be completely worthless.

"Yep, I can get my rifle into action faster than almost anyone, except my sister Mandy. She's the fastest draw in our family. Maybe in the whole West."

"Oh no. I mean I do a fast drawing of an area. A drawing, like with a charcoal pencil on paper? That kind of drawing."

Sally's headache was getting worse every second he talked.

"I've found my calling. Some of my work is—" He shrugged as if regretting he'd started that last sentence.

"Is what?" Sally tried to remember the last

88

time she'd drawn a picture. There'd been a few stick figures sketched into the dirt . . . when she was five.

Of course, the colonel had drawn a map to send on to Luther.

"Well." He shrugged again, almost as if he were embarrassed. Which Sally could well understand. "I've been hung in museums."

"Hung? Like you stole a horse and a posse caught up with you and—"

"No." Logan smiled and it had the odd effect of easing some of the headache his nonsense had caused. Didn't do a thing for her broken leg, though.

"Hung like they bought a painting from me and hung it on their wall." He actually blushed just a bit.

"Oh." Now Sally could understand the blush. It was embarrassing to admit to spending his life painting. Such enthusiasm to waste over something so useless. Although the barn had looked mighty nice after it'd been whitewashed.

"How do you have time?" Sally shook her head and instantly regretted moving. "On my family's ranch, it takes all of us working hard to keep the ranch going and hunt game, tend the garden and haul water. You don't have a herd, I s'pose." She felt some pity for him but tried to conceal that.

"Wise Sister does all that. Well, not ride herd, since I don't have one." Logan smiled.

Sally frowned. "She can't do it alone."

"Sure she can. She always has."

"Always?"

"This is my third summer out here." Suddenly Logan looked over his shoulder, as if he could see through the door to Wise Sister. "Her husband was alive until this spring, though." Logan looked back at Sally. "Is it a lot of work to keep a cabin going? She's never complained."

Sally remembered a few words of complaint just in the time Wise Sister had been tending her. Of course, Logan might be too busy drawing his pretty pictures to hear the fussing. And Sally had to admit, Wise Sister was quiet in her complaints.

In fact, she'd said little or nothing, but Sally, knowing the way of the West, had apologized for making so much work for Wise Sister and putting her behind. Sally knew Wise Sister was now going to have to work twice as hard and three times as fast to get a meal on for supper. Especially since Logan had left yesterday with no plans to return for a while.

"Yes, it's a lot of work." Sally narrowed her eyes. "You really don't know what all needs to be done every day to run your property? You really don't help at all? You don't do the huntin' at least?"

"I don't hunt much. It would scare the animals away from the cabin. I don't want that."

Sally's mouth gaped open but no words emerged.

"Maybe you'd better tell me what all there is to do." Logan planted his elbows on his knees.

He sounded like he cared. Just because he was ignorant didn't mean he was stupid. Sally knew the difference. He'd asked; she'd tell him.

"She has to hunt for your food. Hunting takes a long time. Maybe she sets snares. Do you have chickens?"

"No."

Sally sighed. "Do you eat a lot of rabbit and—" Hesitating, Sally said, "I don't rightly know what wild chickens you've got around here. Back home we've got pheasants and grouse and some wild turkeys. But mostly we eat chickens, raise 'em right in the yard. Saves a lot of time."

"Well, there are beautiful birds and animals in the mountains. Geese and ducks in many different species. Ptarmigans, pheasants, grouse, and wild turkeys. The bald eagles and golden eagles are the best."

"Best tasting?"

Logan jerked and sat up straight, glaring. "No, not best *tasting*. The best to *draw*. They're beautiful, and the way they soar on the wind and play—"

Sally snorted. "You don't have a lick of sense, do you?"

"I've heard that before, believe it or not." Logan tilted his head at her.

Sally would have rolled her eyes heavenward, but she was pretty sure it'd hurt. "No surprise there."

"I want to paint you." Logan leaned closer, and he quit looking her in the eye. Instead he focused intently on her.

She felt as if he'd forgotten about her and only saw the pieces. It was an unpleasant feeling, and she resisted—only due to the pain she was sure would follow—shoving him back. "Paint me." She knew he wasn't talking about whitewash now. He'd better not be.

"Yes, I've already started. I made sketches, but I'll want you to pose, too, and—"

"I'm leaving as soon as I'm seeing only one of you, so don't bother getting out your paintbrush."

The door swung open and a gust of wind came in with Wise Sister, her hands full. "Storm." She wrestled the door closed without Logan offering to give her a hand.

Sally scowled, and that hurt, too.

A rumble of thunder accompanied Wise Sister's word. Distant, but Sally realized it had gotten dark, fully dark. She'd thought it was sunset. She'd lost all track of time, but now it appeared clouds were the culprit, or part of it. "There goes any trail we left." Sally looked at Wise Sister.

"Someone will come?" Wise Sister carried a pot with her, steaming and savory.

Sally wasn't sure she could keep anything down. Her headache made her stomach swoop around. But she hadn't eaten since breakfast, and she knew bones and bruises knit best on good food. "Yes, I have friends who'll be searching. How far is this from that trail?" Sally looked at Wise Sister, figuring her for the person in possession of good sense in this room.

Logan answered. "We rode nearly all day. Not fast, though. It's a long, treacherous climb down to that canyon."

Sally did her best not to groan. She reckoned her best wasn't that good.

"Bad trail." Wise Sister set a plate on the table as the sky opened up. "And now the rain washes it clean."

Sally accepted that. She also knew Luther and Buff. They'd read what happened on that trail. They'd look for her body. When they didn't find it, they'd search. Her heart warmed to think of the strong men who loved her. Which made her think of Logan—the fastest draw in the . . . museum.

"I have to go back." She glanced at him but mostly just focused on Wise Sister.

Logan jumped as if she'd poked him with a branding iron. "Not until I've painted you."

"Not until your head clears and your leg is fit to ride." Wise Sister looked at the leg, which lay propped up on a rolled-up blanket. "Two weeks.

Much hurt. Much harm to you if you go sooner. Four weeks better."

A month? "No, I can't do that." Sally looked at Wise Sister. She just couldn't add another job to the older woman's day, so she turned to Logan. "You're going to have to go get them."

"Get who?"

"Luther, a friend. Luther and Buff will come hunting."

"Buff?" Wise Sister seemed distracted for a moment but didn't speak.

"Yes, they're friends of mine who were meeting me in Helena. I sent a note that we'd left the train and I'd most likely beat 'em to Mandy's house. They'll ride to the spot we were supposed to cross the trail, and when we aren't there, they'll start heading out to meet me. They'll find the spot where the ambush happened and start hunting me. You're going to have to go out and find them and bring them back here. I can't leave them riding all over this wilderness for a month."

"The trail isn't passable in this weather." Logan looked at the window, peppered with hard, driving rain.

"Smoke signals," Wise Sister said.

Sally nodded. "Yes, good. How deep in the woods are we here?"

"The trees get deep behind the cabin," Logan said. "But in front it's clear. It's a spectacular view."

Sally couldn't imagine what that had to do with anything. "Okay. Luther might be here already. If not, he'll be on my trail within days. We can start a signal fire and—"

"What if those men see the signals?" Logan asked, shaking his head. "Smoke will signal anyone, good and bad."

Sally felt a flare of irritation that Logan didn't deserve. He was right. And she didn't want to hear about it.

Wise Sister scooped some stew onto a tin plate and tapped her metal spoon with a harsh click. "Time now for food and rest. Tomorrow we plan."

Sally fell silent. Wise Sister brought her the plate, pulled a fork out of the pocket of her beaded buckskin dress, and handed it to Sally.

"I'm—I'm not sure—" Sally gulped. "I might not be able to—to keep it down. I'm feeling sorta sick." She looked up at Wise Sister.

"One bite." Wise Sister urged the plate on Sally, and the rich smell of stew teased her and settled her twisting stomach a bit. "Then rest. Then one more bite." The woman's face was lined with deep wrinkles. Her dark skin fell in somber lines, but there was understanding and kindness in her black eyes.

"Thank you." Sally's eyes filled with tears again. What was wrong with her?

"Good girl. One bite. Then you rest." Wise

Sister brushed Sally's hair back. Wise Sister was a short, round woman, her long, dark braids shot with gray. Though there was no physical resemblance, her strong, competent hands reminded Sally of her ma. Which made her think of Beth and what a skilled doctor she was. Which made her think of Mandy and how much she longed to see her big sister, meet her babies, help her when the new one came.

Logan leaned in and drew Sally's attention. "I'll ride out to meet your friends, Sally. I'll give them another day to get to the area, if you think your friend Luther is that close. The rain will let up and the trail will dry and I'll go."

"Helpless as a pup." Wise Sister frowned at Logan.

A flare of lightning flashed in the window, followed by a clap of thunder. Sally's stomach clenched from the thunder and worry about Logan out there with those back-shooting yellow coyotes. And her headache pounded like a drumbeat. "You can't go out there with those men." Something turned over deep in Sally's heart to think of Logan riding that dangerous trail. She remembered little of it, but she'd gotten an impression of it, and Wise Sister's furrowed brow told her everything else.

"I ride that trail out of here all the time. I may not go all the way to town, but I've never had trouble wandering this land." Logan's expression went grim. "Your friends are in danger if they're coming for you."

Sally wanted to deny it. "Buff and Luther are tough, knowing men. They'll ride careful." But the colonel was a tough man, too. Luther would ride wary. Still, the thought of him and Buff dying on that trail, cut down like the colonel and his wife, made her eyes burn again with those shameful tears.

"Eat now." Logan didn't run from her tears, again. Sally was amazed and, though it shamed her to admit it, a bit pleased. Never once crying—well, almost never—for her whole life had proved to be a burden.

"I can't go in the rain so we have time to think of something." He gently gripped her hand, and their eyes met and held for long seconds.

Sally had already decided he was a useless, no-account kind of a man. But something in those warm brown eyes seemed to give her strength. And how was it that a no-account man had strength to share?

But he did. And right now, Sally needed every bit of it.

With hands she couldn't quite control, she took the plate and fork from Wise Sister and ate a shaky bite of the stew. For a second she didn't think she'd be able to swallow it. The meat—she recognized venison—was tender, and there were carrots, potatoes, and onions in the thick gravy.

But even with everything cooked to melting tenderness, it worsened her headache when she chewed.

Logan rested a hand on her shoulder as if he knew, and Sally remembered the many times her parents had seemed to almost read each other's minds. She looked up at the concern in his eyes. That hand and the worry steadied her and she found she could swallow.

Wise Sister came on her other side and took the plate, as if she knew the weight of that small, tin dish with its bit of food was more than Sally could handle.

Coddled and surrounded by their concern, Sally, who took great pride in her toughness, let the bite of food settle, and she found it did awaken her appetite and make her feel stronger. Her vision even cleared until she was only seeing one of each of her new friends. She ate steadily. "This is delicious, Wise Sister." She managed a smile and shared one with Logan, too. "Thank you both for all you've done for me."

They both smiled and murmured kind words.

Sally had nearly finished the plate when a wave of exhaustion swept over her. "I think I need to sleep now." Sally's eyes drooped.

They flickered open when Wise Sister took her fork out of her hand. She saw Logan pull the blanket up to her chin.

"Thank you." Her eyes fell closed again.

Tearing through treetops. Certain death, pain, terror, falling, falling, falling.

A tight scream from her own throat jerked her awake just as she'd have hit the rocks at the base of the cliff.

Logan was there on one side, Wise Sister on the other. Neither had moved. Both were staring at her, worry cutting lines into their faces.

She hadn't even gotten fully to sleep and now she was afraid to close her eyes again. Would she face this same nightmare every time she slept? Maybe for the rest of her life?

Fergus heard the first wolf and whirled around, expecting to see the brute charging him out of the scrub. That's how near it sounded.

The howl was answered by a pack . . . close at hand. All around them.

Fergus clawed at his Colt and brought the gun up, but with nothing to aim at. The howling went on, echoing, eerie, so wild it sent chills up Fergus's backbone. The howling bounced off the mountains, surrounding them until it sounded like a hundred wolves.

His gun still drawn, Fergus noticed his hand shaking, and he would have ridden away if it hadn't been pitch dark. And if he hadn't needed to pretend like he wasn't a skeered rabbit.

It had taken the rest of the day to find their way across broken ground to the bottom of the cliff the cowpoke had fallen over. First they'd chased down the horses and stripped them of cash. That had taken awhile. Then they'd found it hard going to recognize the bottom of that cliff. Things had looked different down here.

What had finally told them they'd found the right place was the smell of death. Dead men, dead horses. And not just those who died today. Older. Rotting. And those demonic howling wolves had eaten the flesh of men before. That's why they hunted in this area most likely. And they might want more. They might have learned boldness.

Even that smell hadn't driven him and Tulsa away, because they'd found a lot of money in the saddlebags. And two horses had gone over the cliff. And that cowpoke had killed his brother. Fergus ran one unsteady hand deep into his hair, over the white streak that he'd always had in his black hair. Right at his temple. He'd heard that gunshot from down here. That cowpoke must have lived. If he had, where was he? Somewhere out there, armed and more dangerous than the wolves?

Besides killing his brother, the cowpoke was a witness. He'd seen nothing, hadn't he? How could he have? Fergus had never broken cover. But had Curly or Tulsa? They all three had that matching streak of white. Fergus might be picked out by that single feature.

"We ought to pack it in." Tulsa had whipsawed back and forth between wanting the money and wanting a soft bed. Now he sat by the fire, foot tapping, fingers running round and round on his Winchester while they listened to those ghostly howls. "What's say we head for town in the morning?"

"Go if you want. That cowpoke killed my brother. And if we find enough money in those saddlebags, we'll be walking in high cotton for a long time." Fergus knew the money was a bigger draw than avenging his brother.

Tulsa was a cousin, not a brother, so he didn't care much what happened to Curly. Now Tulsa reached under his coonskin cap and rubbed that funny strip of pure white hair. Same spot as Fergus's.

He didn't think worse of Tulsa because of his caring about the money and not Curly. That was normal, and Tulsa'd throw in because of it.

Tulsa grunted his agreement, and Fergus knew the money was a stronger pull than the bullet hole in his saddle partner's arm. They weren't quittin'.

Fergus lay awake, his Colt six-shooter clutched in his hand, his bandolier refilled and within reach, listening to those haunting sounds as the wolves talked to the moon. He thought of that single gunshot they'd heard. Someone was definitely alive down here, but it couldn't be that puny cowpoke. Fergus had seen his bullet strike. But if it *wasn't* him, then who?

Whatever happened down here, Fergus had to track it down and make sure it wasn't going to cause him trouble down the line. Fergus prided himself on being a thorough, careful man.

The next morning, it didn't take ten minutes to find trouble. Fergus crouched by one of a thousand paw prints. "Those wolves weren't here just by chance. This place is thick with wolf sign."

A curl ran up his spine. The wolves were used to feeding on human flesh. They lived right down here. Waiting, probably, for food to come falling from the sky. Fergus had been feeding a wolf pack. Now they were prowling close by and not of a mind to be kind to the man who fed 'em.

"Look at that slope." Fergus was daunted by what they were up against. He pointed up at the trees that seemed to grow straight out of the side of the mountain, point upward, and grow hugged up close to the rock face. "I don't see the cowpoke or any sign of the horses. They could be snagged on that slope anywhere. We'd have to be mountain goats to find 'em. And that's if the wolves didn't drag them off."

Tulsa snarled, as likeable as the wolf pack, and started scouting.

They found bodies all right, some they'd tossed down yesterday, some a lot older. Fergus kept looking up at those trees. The bodies were up there. Between the heavy woods and the wolves, it was looking like a long, hard job.

All day they worked, scaling the cliff a long way up.

"There's nothin' here, Fergus."

Then Fergus spotted a horse. With a shout, he scrambled toward the dead critter and found a rich stash in the saddlebags. Waving the money over his head, he yelled, "This is enough to keep me on the hunt."

They spent all day finding both horses and the rest of yesterday's victims, but there was no sign of the cowpoke nor his rifle.

As sun began to set, Tulsa and Fergus set up camp again.

"Could he have survived, Fergus?"

"I gut shot him. He's dead. Even if he survived the fall, the bullet I put in him would have finished him. Wolves must've drug him off."

"Then who fired that gun?"

"Maybe he lived through the fall and got a shot off. A signal for help or something. But he can't have lived. It's still the wolves."

Tulsa grunted and twitched. "Reckon. We'll hunt farther down the cliff tomorrow. No wolf is going to drag a body far."

Fergus tried to settle in to sleep, but the quiet started him into twitching as bad as Tulsa. Yes, they'd found enough money to make their day's work worthwhile. But searching the ugly burial ground gnawed at his gut. He felt his sins crowding in on him as he saw the death he'd visited on people. Hunting for a dead man spooked him. A dead man who'd vanished.

"Let's get out of this boot hill to sleep. Those wolves think they own that stretch of hill." Truth was, Fergus wasn't afraid of a few wolves. It was the ghosts that seemed to haunt this land. Not that he believed in ghosts, but if there was such a thing, then this would be the place for them.

Tulsa nodded and they rode off from the unholy graveyard.

They slept and went back to their search the next day. It was almost sunset when they finally found something that made no sense.

"What's a pencil doin' out here?" Fergus held it up. A pencil sharpened and showing no sign of being weathered.

"It just fell out of the pocket of one of 'em we shot, Fergus." Tulsa kept working around the ground, moving farther and farther downhill.

"None of 'em fell here. Not all the way down this far."

Tulsa looked at the cliff then at the pencil. "A wolf carried it away?"

"No teeth marks I can see. And no wolf tracks here. If a wolf dropped it here, it could have only been a day or two ago. There was a storm before that, and there'd be tracks if it was after the rain."

A pencil? A strange pencil with thick lead. Fergus studied it then started looking for sign that someone else had been here.

"Down here, on the flat," Fergus called over his shoulder.

Tulsa headed down. "A horse was picketed."

Someone had ridden away from here.

Crouching to the ground, Tulsa pointed to a single set of footprints. "How could our cowpoke have ridden away? And how could he have a horse handy?"

"Looks like whoever it was carried a heavy load." Fergus looked up that long, tree-covered mountainside.

"No one could survive that." Tulsa stared and scrubbed his hand over his bristly face and felt his stomach growl.

"Nope. I know where my bullet hit. But maybe whoever was down here took the man off to bury him."

"Why not just bury him here?"

Fergus shrugged. "He was carrying something heavy and the tracks are right to've been made the day we hit those sightseers. Even if it don't make no sense, he must've taken that cowpoke off to bury him. And if he did, he stripped the gun and any money from the guy. That means he took what's ours." Fergus liked the idea of someone to hunt, someone to hate. He liked the wild places. And now, with someone to hunt, he felt like a wolf again . . . instead of a haunted man.

"Whoever took that cowpoke has his gun. He owes me." Tulsa looked at his bandaged arm. "That means I've still got a chance at some payback. The tracks go off to the west in a straight line."

"Two days' head start."

Fergus didn't care, they could catch up.

A smile cracked on Tulsa's face. "A slow-moving horse carrying a heavy load."

A sudden rustling in the woods drew Fergus's attention to the gleam of a pair of yellow eyes.

Wolves. Looking at him. Wondering if he'd make a good meal.

Fergus pulled his six-shooter. The wolf must have seen one before, because it darted from sight before Fergus could take aim. He shot in the direction of the wolf anyway but didn't hear a yelp.

Too bad. It would have felt good to kill something.

Then, knowing just how the wolf felt when it locked eyes on prey, Fergus turned to Tulsa. "Let's track that rider down."

They mounted up and headed west, setting a fast pace.

Eight

Mandy shouldn't have asked Sally to come. What had she been thinking? Mandy had to accept her life, and wanting her sister—any of her sisters—around was pure selfishness.

When she'd gotten the letter saying Sally was coming, she'd been so thrilled she'd had her hands full keeping her usual restraint in place. And the letter had come too late to stop Sally, which Sidney would certainly have done. But by the time word arrived, Sally was already on her way with the colonel and his party as escorts and the directions to Mandy's mountaintop home in hand.

Mandy thought of Sidney's bodyguards, Cooter and Platte. Sally might not even be safe. Although with Luther and Buff close to hand, no one would hurt Sally or Mandy. But her old friends weren't here now. Mandy had always disliked and distrusted the men Sidney hired, but she'd never really feared them because Luther was always nearby.

Mandy suspected being far gone with child kept the guards away, and though she didn't like all the workmen, they'd shown no signs of ugly intentions toward her. But she was coming close to the time of birthing her baby.

Her condition kept Sidney away, too, for which

she was profoundly grateful. He still wanted her right beside him in the night. Said it was her place, and she reckoned it was. But mercifully, her rounded body didn't inspire his husbandly attentions.

She could barely stand to be close to him. She'd gotten to spending most of the night drowsing in her rocking chair. The children often woke up, which irritated Sidney something fierce if they disturbed him. This way she could see to them better, and the distance from Sidney was better for her chances to sleep anyway. Nightly, Mandy waited until Sidney fell asleep and began his raucous snoring then slipped out of bed.

Now, she settled in her rocking chair, made as comfortable as possible with blankets and a stump pulled in for a footstool, and regretted writing and inviting any of her family to come. She'd even managed to sneak the letter out to the mail, which had been no small trick because Sidney always read any letters she wrote.

But Luther had taken this one to town and mailed it for her, and now Sally was coming. And Mandy had put her little sister in danger, both on the long trail and here once she arrived—if she arrived.

Mandy looked down at the rifle that lay on the floor beside her chair and knew neither she nor Sally would be easy women to hurt, but where was Sally?

She was in danger certainly. Although perhaps Luther had found her already and was heading here. There was no way to send word, living up at the top of this treacherous mountain, a long, long ride out from Helena.

The new house was going to be nothing short of a mansion. Mandy marveled at it as she watched it being built. They'd used dynamite, the explosions terrifying, to clear a road to pull in timbers and stone. Gray stone. Sidney had been so excited when he'd told her it would be gray. Like his name.

He'd even named it. Gray Towers. Mandy had heard of such things, and a person often named their ranch, but a house? It just seemed plain boastful, and she knew Sidney meant it just that way.

The trail as it was now was steep, with high sides cut away by the blasting. Those trails were impassable last winter when they'd stayed here in the cabin, and before the blasting, they'd only come in and out on horseback. Now they were wider, but not much.

Sidney had his shiny buggy. Maybe, if she got lucky, the house would be finished and Sidney, with his bodyguards, and all the workmen would ride to town just before a big snowfall and end up locked away from her for the winter.

Mandy smiled at the very thought. And he couldn't even blame her. She'd warned him of the certain winter blockage. And they'd lived it last winter. But instead of moving them down closer to Helena, he'd widened the trail leaving it even deeper and more prone to being cut off. Even widened, it was a dangerous trip down to the perfectly nice cabin they lived in before the gold strike. Worse yet, they were moving farther uphill even from the cabin they were in now. It was another mile up a path that would give a mountain goat the vapors, on a trail skirting sheer cliffs, to reach the new house site.

Mandy went out and looked at the slowly rising house every day, stunned by the sight of it. They'd rattle around inside that monstrosity. How would they keep it warm? Did Sidney expect Luther and Buff to cut enough wood to fill that whopper of a house with heat?

A cry pulled her out of her dark thoughts and she rose quickly. Catherine was awake. She should want the little girl to sleep through the night, but Mandy always felt relief when Catherine cried. Now if Sidney came out and checked, it would be obvious that Mandy had been forced from their bed.

He liked her right there beside him. Like the idiot didn't leave her alone for days at a time when he went to town.

Mandy hurried into the girls' room and scooped her pretty baby out of the cradle Luther had built. She quickly carried Catherine back to the rocker Buff had built and settled in by the potbellied stove Luther had hauled from town. Then she settled in to sing quietly and nurse her baby. The little one barely fit around Mandy's expanded stomach, but they'd learned to manage.

Mandy hoped the cow calved before the baby came. It should. Otherwise she'd be nursing both children because there was no milk. As it was, Angela was doing without. Not a good situation for a two-year-old. Not a good situation for an expectant mother. For a rich person, Mandy had quite a time feeding her family. Sidney might manage to get fat, but Mandy and the children were lean and now, with Luther and Buff away, downright hungry.

Mandy turned her thoughts away from her worries and brushed her hand over the bit of dandelion fluff that was Catherine's hair. Catherine was soon done eating and fast asleep in Mandy's arms. She just held the baby and rocked her for the pleasure of it now. The baby's hair was white and fine, very much like Angela's had been. She wondered if this time she'd have a son. Resting her hand on her middle, she pictured a rambunctious little boy around the house and almost wept for how much she missed her little brothers.

Sidney didn't comment much on the children, but he seemed to think it was fitting that Mandy remain constantly in a family way. Except for the unpleasantness involved with becoming so, Mandy didn't mind the babies either. Her life made sense when she held her girls in her arms.

A sharp squeak came from the porch that ran along the front of the little cabin, right near the window that was beside the door.

Mandy's blood ran cold. She moved without even thinking. She had the rifle in one hand and the baby in the other. She rushed, silently, into the girls' room and laid sleeping Catherine down, praying silently that the little one would stay asleep.

Then she stepped back into the main room, her nerves cool, her ears focused on the outside. She swung the door open to her own bedroom. "Sidney," she said, keeping her voice low so whoever was out there wouldn't hear. She heard her husband mutter and snort. She hissed, "Sidney, get up."

It didn't sit right to go on into the room. She wanted her own body between whoever was out there and her children. But Sidney wasn't going to respond without some encouragement. She walked to his side and shook his pudgy shoulder. "Wake up!"

"What? What's going—"

Mandy slapped her hand over his mouth, and even in her desperate hurry to get back to investigate that sound, she might have slapped a bit too hard and enjoyed it a bit too much. It almost pushed back the cold because of the heat of that bit of violence. "Shhhh. Quiet." Her eyes had adjusted to the dark enough that she could see him looking at her. "There's someone outside our door."

His eyes narrowed and he jerked his chin to show he understood her.

She removed her hand, resisted the urge to wipe his touch off her palm, jacked a shell into the chamber of her Winchester, and left him. He needed to know, but she honestly doubted he'd be any help.

She went out into the room she'd left only moments before and moved quickly across the split log floor. Pressing her back against the wall, she positioned herself with the front door on her left and the window where she'd heard that footstep on her right. Their table stood in front of the window. She held her rifle in two hands, against her chest just above her round belly, barrel pointed up, her finger on the trigger.

The curtain was pulled shut. She was always careful about that because of the workmen and the two bodyguards who stayed in the bunkhouse. She hated the idea of their walking past the house and looking in the window at her.

Her senses were alert. Her nerves like steel. Steady as a rock. And cold as death.

She looked to her right, at the window, but she listened the way she and her sister Beth had learned to listen, with total attention, eyes and ears and nose focused. Her hand was steady on the trigger, trusting her instincts. Instincts could be a simple whisper of warning from God. Mandy was always open to that.

Who was out there at this time of night? The workmen and Sidney's guards slept in the bunkhouse closer to the new house.

Sidney came to their bedroom door and she was surprised to see a six-gun in his hand. And he looked comfortable holding it. "Where?" He moved his lips but Mandy understood.

She jerked her head at the window.

Sidney came across the room to the other side of the window, the table between them, and pressed his back to the wall just as Mandy had. His belly stuck out almost as far as Mandy's did, too. To Mandy's surprise, he was taking her very seriously. Mandy had never seen him like this. Sidney was a pouter, a city boy. He hired people to defend him—bodyguards.

Mandy supposed, in their way, Luther and Buff were her bodyguards, though no one had ever called them such. She knew Sidney tolerated them simply because he couldn't get rid of them. Luther had made it clear from the beginning that he wasn't leaving and that was the end of it. And Sidney didn't fuss much. After all, Luther and

Buff did almost all the work a man should do to run a home—hunting, skinning and tanning hides, cutting firewood, making shoes, doing the heavy work in the garden, and caring for the livestock.

Mandy wished so much that it was them making that noise. That in a few moments a knock would come at her door and Sally would call out, with Luther right behind her, both of them grinning, safe and happy to see her.

No knock sounded. No shout of hello.

She should have felt fear. In a detached way, Mandy knew that. But instead all she felt was calm, nearly irrational calm. Her eyes met Sidney's. A lot passed between them with a look. Who was out there? They'd never had trouble with thieves.

Sidney was very crafty about his money. Mandy had often thought that her husband had wiles unbecoming an honest man. There was no stockpile of gold here at their home. He kept the bulk of his money in a bank in Denver—a bank chosen specifically for its tight security. When Sidney needed more, he traveled to Denver, made his purchases, and returned, with a bit of cash but no gold, ever. Mandy had never seen it and she'd never been to Sidney's mine.

The noise didn't repeat itself. When minutes ticked by and there was nothing else, Mandy finally felt her instincts relax, and as before, she trusted them. She straightened away from the window.

"Whoever was out there is gone."

"You're sure you heard a man, not a deer or the wind rattling branches?" Sidney had that look on his face. Sneering. As if the sight of her with the rifle was a disgrace.

The insult was too much with the tension of the moment. Another time she'd ignore it, but right now she wasn't able to let her husband get away with. "I know the difference." The venom in her voice surprised even her. Maybe she wasn't as calm as she'd thought. Her tight grip on her rifle scared her a little. "We'll talk about this tomorrow. Go back to bed." She spoke like a general ordering a private around. She never, ever took that tone with Sidney.

He looked from the rifle to her eyes and back. Mandy wasn't sure what he saw, but for once he didn't make a snide remark. Instead, he swallowed hard, then went to his room and quietly closed the door.

She settled into her rocking chair with her Winchester on her lap. After a few minutes, she calmed enough to let go of the icy chill that had helped her be the fastest shot most anyone had ever seen. She began rocking.

Mandy could have gone back to bed, she knew, but instead she stayed in her chair and had a fierce little talk with Sidney inside her head. She decided that this was the last time she was going to keep the words to herself. Restraint wasn't getting her anything.

Tomorrow morning, she'd see if Sidney could handle the unrestrained version of the woman he'd married.

"We're not gonna find those tracks now, Tulsa." Fergus settled into the hideout they'd skedaddled to when the clouds started to build up. The trail had been simple to follow for a long time, but now they had no direction.

"I've been thinkin'." Tulsa tore a chaw of tobacco off with his teeth.

Fergus resisted the urge to ram his fist into Tulsa's face. They were cold and wet and a long way from easy food and the comfort the money bulging their pockets could provide. "'Bout what?" Fergus didn't let any of his mad sound in his voice.

"We both know that rider was hauling too big a load."

Fergus couldn't help but listen. Tulsa had a lot of bad qualities, but he was a crack shot and he was a hand at reading sign. Fergus knew better than to talk when Tulsa was thinking about a trail.

"I think whoever you shot off that trail lived."

Fergus shook his head. "He was gut shot. I saw the bullet hit."

"I know you hit what you aim at, but it's not the first time a bullet ricocheted off a belt buckle. That rider is carryin' a double load. We saw those horse's tracks coming into that clearing, and where he'd been picketed was clear. Then on the way out, the hooves dug deeper."

The rain peppered outside this overhang they'd found along the base of a cliff. The two of them knew a few bolt holes in this country. This was a good 'un, the kind of place a posse would ride right by, but it wasn't so good for getting out of the rain. The rain wasn't falling smack on their heads, but every gust of wind blew a face full of water in. They sat and listened to the pouring rain and the occasional crack of thunder and considered what it all meant.

"Even if he lived, he never saw us," Fergus said. "He's no danger to us."

"Sure he is. We've had a nice quiet little business riding some of the back trails in here. There's no law, and as long as we kept moving around, no one even seemed to notice. A few greenhorns turn up missing, no one thinks much of it. They was ridin' into a rugged country to see the sights, hoping for a closer look at some mountains. Bad things happen in rough country so who's going to care? But we've never had no one live."

"Nope." Fergus stared into the black night. A blaze of lightning lit up the sky and Fergus thought it was the most desolate sight he'd ever seen. This was a strange land and it had more than its share of things to draw the eye. He understood why people might want to hunt around out here just for a look-see. Even if he thought 'em fools for doing it. But right now, to Fergus, it was the most godforsaken place on earth.

"No sheriff out here in the wilderness so we've been left to ourselves. But if someone went in and told that he'd been attacked and his party went missing, a U.S. marshal might get sent in here. We haven't been that careful in the towns around here. It wouldn't take much of a marshal to figure out we've been spending money with no sign how we earned it. We've even sold a few stolen horses too close to town. If that man you shot lived, we either need to shut him up or quit the country." Tulsa turned to stare at Fergus, and a slash of lightning lit up their damp little corner of the cliff.

Fergus stared at Tulsa then turned back to the storm. "It's the best I've ever had it. Easy money. Plenty of it. No lawmen to be seen anywhere. I'm not ready to quit."

They sat quietly as the storm raged on. Fergus knew without asking that they'd made a decision. He figured Tulsa read things exactly right. Hard as it was to believe, that skinny wrangler had lived and found someone to care for him.

Pure blind bad luck for Fergus. "You've read it right, I reckon. We got nothin' else to do. We might as well see if we can pick up his trail. The way he went don't lead to any town. He's going up into the highlands. That cuts down on the land we have to cover. A mountain man must have come down out of the high-up hills and been passing through. If he found the wrangler I shot and took him in, then we'll have to kill the mountain man, too."

"A man who survives that fall after he's been shot is a tough man." Tulsa spoke quietly, but Fergus heard the hunger in his voice. Tulsa was a man who liked to kill. "And a mountain man ain't one who's easy to sneak up on, neither."

"So we ride careful." Fergus rested his head against hard, damp rock and longed for a dry bed and a hot meal, but he didn't say the words that might persuade Tulsa to quit the search. Right now, wet, cold, miserable wasn't so good, but this was the easy life, and he wasn't giving it up. "A little rain won't stop us from finding them."

Nine

It took Sally three days to snap.

"I've got to get out there." Sally threw her blanket off. "Luther and Buff will be hunting. They're in danger. All I've got to do is get down to the lower valley and they'll find me."

She was swathed in a thick nightgown from neck to ankle. She had one of her thick socks on her healthy foot and a huge bandage on her broken one. But still, she should have remained demurely covered.

Wise Sister gave her a quiet look that almost made Sally settle down.

Of course Logan didn't use *looks*. He'd rather talk a thing to death. "You stay in that bed." Logan hurried to cover her again.

"I can't lie here like this. I can't stand it. I'm losing my mind." Her behavior was outrageous. Even with Wise Sister here it was improper to push back her blankets in front of Logan. She knew it but she couldn't control the burn that she had to *do* something. And her clothes had vanished so it was the nightgown or nothing. Honestly, she felt like a fox with its foot caught in a trap, and she was ready to start gnawing. Her foot even hurt enough to make that seem real.

She wrestled with Logan over possession of the coverlet and managed to get her feet swung over the edge of the bed. She only did it because Logan was afraid to stop her. He worried about her pain all the time so she knew he was fully aware that she hurt in every inch of her body, and he was too careful with her to grab her anywhere.

She sat up. Her broken leg bent at the knee and her foot dropped to the floor. Pain shot like burning arrows up her body and met up with her

121

battered ribs, and the two joined forces and attacked her fragile skull.

"You can't go anywhere." Logan glowered.

"Too soon." Wise Sister came up beside Logan.

"You've been saying that for three days."

"And we've been right for three days. And we're *still* right." Logan spread his arms wide as if he was going to herd her back into bed.

How often had she used the same approach with a stubborn cow? And she didn't appreciate that the comparison had occurred to her.

"I have *got* to get out of here." She scooted forward, hoping to stand on her good leg and— what? Hop down the mountain? Even scooting was too much. She couldn't bite back a gasp of pain when she put the least bit of pressure on her foot.

The fact that it was all impossible didn't deter her. "Now what have you done with my clothes?"

"It's still raining, Sally." Logan stepped back, tidy in his black pants and vest. The sleeves of his white shirt were rolled up to just below his elbows. The man never worked harder than lifting a pencil. Or leastways, she'd never seen him.

Wise Sister had some traps and they'd had muskrat stew for the noon meal. Logan, well, she'd never seen him do a thing but draw pictures.

Wise Sister turned and picked up what looked like folded, tanned leather. "You go soon. Not today. Not in the rain."

Jerking her head around to glare at the window, Sally saw the dreary rain that had fallen off and on for days. There'd even been snow one night. Sally had awakened in the dim light of morning to see the window coated with it.

"Luther is out there by now. He'll be so worried." Desperation reared up until she felt like she was trying to stay on the back of a wild stallion. She couldn't let her old friend wander those hills searching. She felt the guns of those outlaws drawing beads on Luther's back. She could close her eyes and imagine Buff shot, bleeding, dying . . . like Paula McGarritt.

Every time Sally closed her eyes, Sally saw Mrs. McGarritt being slammed out of her saddle. She'd been awakened by nightmares every night. Wise Sister would be awake and soothe her and help her relax back into sleep.

And now, today, she was done letting Luther and Buff risk everything to find her. But there was no way to walk out of here and she didn't have a horse. Logan did, though, and she wasn't above stealing one. Sure that was a hanging offense as well as a sin, but it wasn't like she planned to *keep* it.

Wise Sister knelt on the floor in front of Sally and unfolded the leather.

"What's that?"

"Moccasin. Much tough buckskin. Protect leg on long ride."

Sally flinched, knowing it was going to hurt to put that on no matter how gentle Wise Sister was.

Wise Sister looked up from where she knelt, and Sally saw the sly expression. Sally got the message. There was no need to say it out loud.

"If it's too painful for you to let her pull on that moccasin," Logan went ahead and said it out loud, "then how do you expect to ride down the mountain, then travel for a long, rugged ride in a rain storm?"

Sally fought back the urge to slug him. It helped that just forming a fist hurt like the dickens. "Just fasten the moccasin. A body's gotta do what hurts sometime. Give me my rifle. I feel edgy if I can't grab it."

Sally looked from Logan to Wise Sister and back. She didn't like what she saw in either face. Not that they were going to stop her, but that they didn't believe they'd have to when it came right down to it. She was sorely afraid they were right. "I've got to try."

Wise Sister nodded.

Logan shook his head.

"I'll do it without you if I have to." Sally would dearly love some help. "Ouch!" Sally's leg caught fire, and though she'd like to blame that on Wise Sister, the elderly woman had been

124

terribly careful while she adjusted the soft boot.

Wise Sister finished lacing on the knee-high moccasin, then got the rifle and leaned it against the bed.

Sally felt some muscles unknot, knowing she could fight if she had to.

"If you're going to be stubborn, we can try." Logan came close on her left, slung the rifle over his shoulders. He did it smoothly, which didn't match with what she knew of him, that he was a citified sort of man, not given to the outdoors or manly ways.

Sally would have preferred the gun in her own grasp, but it would have hurt her chest too much.

Wise Sister stood on her left. They gently took her arms. Lifted. Wise Sister looked grim. Logan grimaced as if he felt Sally's pain himself. In fact, the way he watched her face, she suspected he was just mimicking the expression on her own face, though she fought hard to keep her pain from showing.

Sally rose. Every inch she gained burned like fire, on her leg, through her chest, in her head. She had bumps and bruises all over her body, including an ugly, blackened bruise low on her belly where that bullet had struck her belt. It hadn't penetrated her skin, but it had slammed into her hard. Her arms were bruised but her shirt had spared her cuts and scrapes. Her hands were awful to look at, her nails broken, her palms raw from where she'd tried to catch hold of tree limbs and the rock wall she'd fallen past. She'd been spared a mirror, but she could feel the scratches and bruises on her face.

And Logan still wanted to paint her. Ridiculous.

A lot of her wounds hurt bad enough to put her in bed, but it was hard to even notice them with her leg screaming at her to lie back down and her chest punishing her for every breath. She didn't let a single squeak of pain loose. "Let's go." Sally spoke through clenched teeth. "I've got to find Luther. I can't just lay here in bed while he's out there searching, putting himself in danger."

A look passed between Wise Sister and Logan that clearly said they thought she was an idiot. Well, she wasn't. She was desperate.

They made it to the door before Sally's vision started to tunnel and go black.

When she woke up she was back in bed. She didn't know how much time had passed.

Wise Sister said, "I'll go."

"No, I'll go," Logan cut in. "You've got to stay here and see to Sally."

"I leave sign for a knowing man. Buff. I know this man. I know how to tell him of you."

"You know Buff?" Sally asked.

Rather than answer, Wise Sister said, "I know wild places." Wise Sister looked with some compassion at Logan. "Better than you."

126

"Yes, you are better than me, but the ride down this mountain is too dangerous." Logan crossed his arms. "I won't let you ride out of here, and I can't stay alone with this young woman. She would be ruined. We'd have to marry."

That gave Sally a jolt that had nothing to do with a broken leg.

"I'll be gone only one day. Back by nightfall. No harm to Sally. No need to marry."

That sounded like Wise Sister thought Sally needed saving from such a fate. Well, it was a fact that marrying the strange painting man wasn't the way she saw her life going.

"I go afoot."

"In the cold and mud?" Logan's jaw got hard.

"So, I get cold. I get muddy. What is that to me?" Wise Sister looked at the window, sheeted with rain.

Sally's guilt was flooding worse than the weather.

"No." Logan slashed his hand to make it final. "I'm going."

"You can't move quiet." Wise Sister snorted at him. "Bad men find you. Hurt you. Force you to lead them to Sally then kill you, then come for her."

"I ride out of here all the time."

"Not in this weather." Wise Sister sounded wise, stubborn but wise. "Not with bad men around."

"Those killers have been around a long time. We saw evidence of that at the base of that cliff." Logan looked at Sally, and she saw how sickened he was by the proof of her attackers' ruthlessness. She wanted to think of him as weak for it, but truth be told, it was sickening to her, too.

"Better then that I go." Wise Sister's round face lined in downward curves as she frowned.

Sally looked back and forth between them until her neck protested and her head started to ache. She was still the best one for the job.

True, she had broken ribs. And an aching head. And a leg that wouldn't hold her up. And she'd fainted the first time she'd stood upright.

But except for that, she was the best one for the job.

"I won't let you risk it." Logan crossed his arms.

"And I won't let you be hurt." Wise Sister jammed her fists on her rounded waist. "You paint good. Important for you to be safe. I go."

The last drew Sally up short as she tried to keep up with the argument. Wise Sister worried about Logan's painting? Wise Sister seemed so sensible. Although, as Sally looked at the cabin, a lifetime of pretty things filled every inch of the wall, every corner. Everywhere Sally looked the cabin was touched by beauty. She thought of the pretty ribbon she'd had on her chemise and knew beauty could live alongside common sense.

"And I won't stay here"—Logan jabbed a

finger toward the floor—"warm and dry and safe while you risk—"

"Stop!" Sally yelled—which hurt her face.

The two nursemaids turned from bickering with each other to face her.

"Neither one of you is going. I am."

Matching stubborn scowls appeared on their faces. Sally was annoyed to realize that, whatever their squabbling, they did agree on something. Keeping her corralled. Great.

"But not today."

Logan's shoulders relaxed.

"Best to wait." Compassion appeared on Wise Sister's face. "Your friends will ride careful."

They both seemed to get over their earlier upset instantly. Sally got the sneaking suspicion that making her feel guilty was the whole point.

It didn't matter. They were right. No one, least of all her, was going anywhere today.

"I get food as soon as you're comfortable." Wise Sister straightened Sally's blankets with quick, gentle movements.

While Wise Sister fussed over her, Sally looked at Logan. "Your painting is important? Wise Sister thinks so." Sally could not imagine how a sensible woman like Wise Sister could be so foolish.

Sally did her very best to keep her expression bland so as not to let Logan see that she thought he was an idiot.

· · ·

It was obvious Sally thought his painting was a waste of his life.

"It's the highest compliment anyone has ever given me. Wise Sister not just *liking* my paintings, but believing there's value in them." Logan nodded to Wise Sister. "She has an artist's soul. The dye she's used to color her weaving, the porcupine quills to create pictures in a basket, the softness of the furs and the supple leather she works with, all of it is art. It's not practical, but she can't deny her love for making things beautiful."

Wise Sister sniffed.

Logan studied Sally for a few seconds. "I want you to see some of what I've done. You thought you were up to a long ride in the cold rain. How about a fifty-foot walk across to my cabin?" And if it hurt her, it might calm her desire to go anywhere for a while.

"Okay, I reckon I'd like to see what whiles away your time, leaving all the work for Wise Sister."

It pinched, but Logan was able to smile at her. He'd had plenty of practice at smiling through insults. "Can we take her over to the other cabin?" He glanced at Wise Sister.

She was silent for a moment—but then, Wise Sister was silent for most moments. "We try." Wise Sister picked up a slicker, one left from

Babineau, and slipped it over Sally's head. With the slicker in place, Wise Sister pulled Sally's blankets back.

The slicker was large enough to cover Sally from her neck to her moccasined foot. Sally began to inch off the bed.

"Don't move." Wise Sister jabbed a finger at her.

"Now do you get why I think she's scary?" Logan whispered, not even pretending to be quiet enough to keep Wise Sister from hearing him.

Wise Sister rolled her eyes.

Sally smiled.

Logan's fingers itched for his pencil to capture the gentle curve of Sally's lips.

"Tell me to stop if it hurts." Logan eased one arm behind Sally's slender waist and another under her knees, cautious about every move. He kept his eyes on her face, knowing her well enough already to understand that she wouldn't admit to pain. She'd fainted from it without a word of protest only moments ago. Gently, he lifted her in his arms. She didn't cry out, didn't even flinch, but he saw lines deepen around her mouth. "Are you sure you want to go?"

Her jaw was clenched so tight, Logan didn't think she was up to speaking. But she nodded, the faintest of motions. Then, an inch at a time, she slid one arm up and wrapped it around his neck. For a second their faces were close . . . very close.

"Are you sure?" He hadn't meant to whisper. But on the other hand, no sense yelling when someone was only inches away.

"Sure about what?"

Their eyes held and Logan found something for the first time in years that seemed more important than painting. Sally's arm around his neck moved restlessly and Logan felt himself pulled closer.

His gaze flickered to her lips and back to her sky blue eyes. "You're so beautiful."

A tiny smile perked the corners of her lips. "I am?" The words were little more than a sigh.

"More beautiful than the mountains and waterfalls and soaring eagles."

The moment eased a bit when Sally's smile stretched wide. "I'm prettier than jagged high-up hills; running water; and a hook-nosed, bald bird?" The smile turned to a laugh. "I reckon you think that's flattery, don't you?"

Somehow, put like that, it did seem less than a compliment. But her laugh took the sting out of his usual incompetent ways with people, women especially. Despite his upbringing, Logan knew he had an uncivilized streak, especially when good manners came between him and his art. He belonged out in these mountains alone. "Wait'll you see more of the Rockies. I'd love to take you and show you Yellowstone. You'll know I've just given you the highest praise."

"I've seen enough. Rich hunting land and good grazing, but too rocky to grow a crop. I reckon a body would find a spot for a garden here and there."

Wise Sister draped Logan's coat over his shoulders and dropped his Stetson on his head. He'd have walked outside without either if the elderly woman hadn't thought of it.

He moved slowly in the rain, leaning forward so the broad brim of his hat sheltered Sally. Maybe he should just give it to her and let the cold water soak in and cool his overly warm thoughts about this pretty woman.

Wise Sister went ahead. The two of them lagged behind, protected and dry in the soaking rain until Logan felt like they were in a cocoon, wrapping them away from the rest of the world.

He had to round the cabin to go in the front door, and he stopped under the wide eaves of the house. "I like that you've come out to my land, Sally." Logan's whisper wasn't necessary now. But his voice wasn't working just right and that was all he could manage.

"I was passing through, heading to see my sister is all." Her arm flexed on his neck and seemed to pull him closer.

"I'm so sorry you were hurt. It's nothing short of a miracle that your buckle stopped that bullet and you fell all that way and survived." Logan's throat swelled as he thought of what a close thing it had been.

"And that you were there to find me and care for me." Her fingers shifted and slid up his neck, touching his hair.

He'd let it get ridiculously long since he'd come out here. "It wasn't your time. God wasn't ready to take you home yet."

Sally nodded, almost imperceptibly, but Logan saw it and liked that she had a solid acceptance of life and death.

It would be so easy to lean just a bit closer. To see if Sally's smile tasted as pretty as it looked. Logan closed an inch and then another. Sally did some closing of her own.

A sudden gust of wind blew water straight into Logan's face, and it worked as well as if Sally had slapped him. He straightened. "What am I doing?" He shook his head as if he were a wet dog. "I can't get involved with a woman out here."

Stiffening in his arms, Sally said, "Involved? You think I want to get involved with a man who paints pictures instead of doing proper work?"

"Just because he saved your life?" Logan relaxed and smiled. He actually liked her in a safer kind of way—when she insulted him. He understood insults. They were so common. It was Wise Sister's approval that confused him. Sally's pretty smile confused him more.

"Well, yes." She sounded less belligerent. "You did do that, didn't you?"

"Yes, I did." An impulse made him do the very thing he'd already decided not to do, thanks to that God-given splash of cold water in the face. He leaned down and kissed Sally right on the lips.

He lifted his head. Their eyes met and held.

"You are way, way prettier than a hook-nosed, bald bird."

"Thank you." Sally smiled and the intimate moment passed.

Gone but not forgotten, Buckskin Angel.

Logan moved on toward the cabin.

Wise Sister had already thrown a chunk of wood on the burning embers. She moved to grab a pot, fill it with water, and set it on to cook. Wise Sister never seemed to move quickly, but she got everything done with almost frightening efficiency. She looked up from the fire and smiled.

It took Logan aback some. Wise Sister didn't show much of what she was feeling. As far as he could tell, she'd never pined for her husband. If she missed Babineau, Logan didn't know. She'd never once complained. Of course the man came and went some, prone to heading for the hills a few times every summer. Maybe she was used to his absence.

For the first time, Logan felt bad about the way

he'd treated Wise Sister. He considered her far more than a cook and housekeeper. He thought of her as a fellow artist and his friend. But he hadn't been a very good friend. He was just so used to her not talking much. It had never occurred to him to try and draw her out.

"She needs rest." Wise Sister went to the dry sink and began skinning potatoes. Wise Sister was a genius at drawing food out of this rugged land.

There were papers and pencils, paints and paintbrushes all over. Noticing how cluttered it was, Logan felt embarrassed at his housekeeping, but he wasn't negligent of the things that mattered. All the brushes were carefully cleaned, all the pots of paint meticulously sealed. He knew he'd need every drop of the paints and each bristle in his brushes. They could be ruined so easily.

Logan settled Sally on the chair next to his kitchen table. He took a moment to be glad that he had a separate room for his bedroom because it would feel awkward to bring Sally into the place he slept.

Logan cautiously slid his arms away from her, watching for any sign she might not be able to sit alone. He hurried to get his other chair and carefully propped her foot on it. "Are you all right?" He put a folded blanket on the chair to cushion it.

"I'm fine, but why did you—" Her eyes went past him and landed on *Blazing Land*.

The shutters were closed on the oversized windows that covered most of the front of the cabin, one on either side of the cabin door. There was no glass in them. Glass would have been hard to get in here without it breaking.

Besides, Logan wanted lots of natural light and he wanted to hear and smell the outdoors, as well as see it. When the shutters were open, it was almost like the whole front wall was missing. Babineau had thought he was foolish to ask for those huge openings, but the man had grudgingly followed Logan's instructions. Now, as Logan always did when the windows were closed, he'd moved *Blazing Land* to lean in front of the window on the left side of his door. It brought the outside in for him.

Other, smaller paintings leaned against the wall, surrounding the room. Logan had worked feverishly since he'd arrived in early May. The desire to capture the unspoiled beauty here drove him like nothing ever had.

He thought of the murder he'd happened upon and the evidence that it had happened before. Logan had ridden that same trail to come into the area in the spring. Yet he'd had no idea of the danger.

Babineau had often preached to him about it being a lawless place. And Logan had learned to be mindful of the world around him. But he'd never caught a hint of danger beyond what was normal—grizzlies, mountain lions, rattlesnakes, and steep trails. Logan trod the trails carefully and wisely, and because of that, he'd believed he had no cause to fear this land. It saddened him to know those days were over.

Sally studied the painting, and Logan waited, hardly aware that he'd quit breathing. For some reason, having Sally believe in him meant everything.

"That's it? That's what you've spent your time doing when you should have been helping hunt for food?"

Maybe it meant a bit too much. "Well, I *have* done other—"

"Quiet," Wise Sister cut Logan off. She said to Sally, "Look again. Give it time."

Sally glanced at Wise Sister and something passed between them that Logan couldn't interpret. He was never much of a hand with women. In fact, he'd never been much aware of anyone around him. His head was in the clouds, always searching for beauty so he could express it through his paintbrush.

Sally turned back to the painting with a shrug. Logan decided maybe she needed a *lot* of time. Hours. Maybe days.

Remembering how Sally had chastised him about his treatment of Wise Sister, he left Sally and went to Wise Sister's side. "Can I help you?"

She dropped a whole potato in the pot and splashed hot water on the front of Logan's shirt.

He stepped back, waving a hand at his shirt, pulling it out from his stomach.

"Sorry." Wise Sister studied him a few seconds then must have decided he'd live. "Help?"

"Yes, help you make supper. I never help around here, and I'm sorry for that. I didn't realize quite what a huge job I'd given you, without Pierre around. That was unkind of me."

"Can you cut up a parsnip?"

"I don't even know what a parsnip is."

Wise Sister jerked her head in the direction of several whitish vegetables lying on the table.

"I—uh—suppose I could learn."

"Thank you." Wise Sister gave him a smile that was a bit sad around the edges. "Some days, yes, help. Not today. Easy meal today."

Logan stared at her and she looked back, solemn but kind and serene. Finally he shrugged. "Okay, but I'm serious. I'm going to start helping more."

"Rain has slowed. Open that window." Wise Sister pointed at the shutter on the right side of the door, the side that didn't have Logan's painting leaning on it. Logan thought that might qualify as helping. He didn't remember Wise Sister giving him very many orders before. Well, occasionally she ordered him to get out of the cabin. But this was different.

He obeyed her quickly, going outside to work under the broad eaves. The shutters hung from leather straps and they were heavy to swing open. Wrestling with them, Logan got one side open and looked in to see Sally still looking at *Blazing Land*.

He finished quickly then came back inside. Even with the day overcast and rain dripping heavily, the gloomy cabin was considerably brighter when the shutters were open.

Maybe Sally would like the painting better in good light. Logan couldn't stand the suspense, which was really stupid of him. Why be in a hurry to have this pretty woman cut his heart out?

He pulled up the one other chair in the room and sat beside her. She cast him a look out of the corner of her eye then went back to *Blazing Land*. He couldn't decide if that was because the picture drew her back or because she was obedient to Wise Sister. He was sadly afraid it was the latter.

"Ever since I was old enough to pick up a pencil, pictures have come out of me." Logan felt compelled to try to make Sally understand. "My mother says I was drawing dogs and kittens when I was three years old."

When would he learn it was useless to try to

explain? But, like a fool, he kept trying. "I don't know why. I only know it's a gift God gave me. Not just the talent for it, but a love for it, too. I feel more alive when I'm painting than any other time. I can't claim any credit for it because it was simply mine from birth. Colors and shapes almost shout out to me, asking me to capture them on canvas. I see a color I love, and I start mentally mixing the paints, trying to figure out how to get that exact shade."

Logan rarely tried to make anyone understand. His family on occasion. They loved him and worried about him. Wise Sister seemed content to go about her life, doing her job, caring for Logan and his home, without making much effort to understand him. But he wished wildly that Sally would. "Painting isn't something I *do*."

Sally turned from the painting, and Logan regretted he'd distracted her. "What's that mean?" Her brow furrowed. At least she was listening.

"It's something I *am*. It's how God created me. He gave me a love for art and a longing to draw and paint that is almost like—like thirst. Not many people understand. They think I should do something more . . . useful. The simple truth is I can't stop any more than I could stop drinking water. I know it's not a practical way to spend my life. If I could stop, I would. It would be

141

much more comfortable to live on a doctor's income, in a modern house back East, with easy access to water and food. I've got four brothers and they all followed my father into the medical profession. They all live in warm homes in New York City. I miss them."

"Lots of hills and trees to paint back East, aren't there? Why here?"

"A good question." Logan smiled. "I read about it. The geyser in Yellowstone, Old Faithful, is what drew me to begin with. They mostly write about that in newspapers back East, but there were several articles that talked about the unusual sights. I just had to see them. Then I got here and, yes, it was spectacular but there was more. I wanted to get into the mountains. I met Pierre, and he brought me to this place where he'd lived with Wise Sister for years, said it was the most beautiful place he'd ever seen. That's what you were doing out here, wasn't it? Looking at the scenery?"

"The group I was with was excited about the scenery. I only wanted to take the shortest route to my sister's house. One of the men in our party used to scout in this area and he knew about those red canyon walls, and the colonel and his wife wanted to see them. I didn't want to veer right nor left on my way to Mandy's house." Sally's expression closed and Logan thought of the people who had died with her. "I thought it was foolishness. I need to get to my sister. She's gonna have a baby anytime. My folks said I could go and stay with her awhile. My ma thinks she's married to a no-account man."

"No-account because he doesn't work the land, hunt for food . . . because he doesn't provide well?" Logan had just described himself. Sally's parents wouldn't approve of him either.

Not that it mattered. Despite that kiss under the eaves, that moment of closeness that was more than he'd ever shared with another human being, this wasn't a life any woman wanted to share with a man. He accepted that.

"Sidney's rich, for a fact. But there's lotsa ways to be no-account that don't have a thing to do with money. And by all reports, Sidney is all of 'em."

For some reason, that came as a relief to Logan. It sounded like Sally had a good grip of what really made a man "no-account." If only he didn't rank as one . . .

Sally's eyes wandered to *Blazing Land*.

"I know this isn't a . . . a . . . normal painting." Logan looked back at his much-loved creation. "I've got lots that are more traditional. But this is a new technique. I studied it over the winter. Some people are calling it Impressionism. It uses the sunlight, how it shadows things at the exact moment you're painting. Instead of mixing colors to make a shade, you put the colors side by side. It's bolder. The paint is thick in places, translucent in others. I use a knife for most of it instead of a paintbrush. I'm trying to catch more than a view. I'm trying to put—right on that canvas—how I *felt* as I watched that sunrise."

"But it's not the way it really looks," Sally protested. "A painting oughta show the way things really look, seems to me."

Logan nodded. "Many would agree with you. But it's an interesting way to look at the world. I enjoyed doing it." Logan turned from his painting and smiled at Sally. "I appreciate that you took the time to really look." Then, with only the smallest hesitation, he reached up and rested one finger on Sally's chest. "Art is in here."

Sally frowned. "What's that mean?"

"It means if *you* like it, then it's good—for you. If you don't like it, then it's not good—for you." Logan tapped on her chest gently. "You get to decide. No one tells you if you're right or wrong."

"Well, it's a strange painting, but I won't say flat out I don't like it. I suppose it's just too *different* for me to know what to think, leastways right now. But it does give me a feeling of what it must have been like to see all those colors splashed across the sky."

Logan lowered his hand, satisfied. His eyes slid from the painting, which he loved, to the vicw through the open shutter, which he loved more. His breath caught.

At his gasp, Sally turned and looked. "Elk."

"Elk." Logan saw that their antlers were sprouting fast. He wanted to draw them in all stages of growth.

"Beautiful." Logan reached for his pencil.

"Supper." Sally reached for her rifle.

Logan almost lost the gun slung across his back because he hadn't been ready, but he managed to keep her from disarming him. "Hey, we can't shoot them."

Sally tore her eyes away from the elk, almost as if it were painful. "Sure we can." She tugged on the rifle and groaned in pain.

Wise Sister moved fast, for a slow-moving woman, and put herself in front of the window. "Can't shoot from cabin."

"Why not?" Sally looked at her rifle again and glared at Logan.

"His rule." Wise Sister jabbed a finger at Logan.

Sally shifted her glare from Wise Sister to Logan. "Why would you let food wander right up to your back door and then not shoot it?"

"Because they won't come back."

"What?"

Wise Sister sighed. "True. Gun scare elk away."

"We can eat for maybe a month on one. Who cares if they run off after we shoot one?"

"He cares." Wise Sister jerked her thumb at Logan.

"I want them to feel safe here." Logan smiled. "They won't if we shoot one. That is so obvious."

"That is so stupid."

"But, if they find out this is a dangerous area, then I can't draw them from the cabin." Logan looked out and saw that they'd come within one hundred yards of the cabin. He wished they'd feel safe enough to let him touch them. He also wished Sally's mouth wasn't gaped open with no words coming out.

"Give up," Wise Sister muttered and exchanged a look with Sally.

Sally closed her eyes and sagged back in her chair.

"Supper soon." Wise Sister looked at Logan. "Plates. You put plates on table. And get my chair. In my cabin."

That perked Logan up considerably. Wise Sister was going to let him help. He adjusted Sally's gun across his back.

"Hey, leave that here." Sally sat up straighter but it hurt.

Logan saw that clearly in her face, though of course she made not the slightest noise at the pain.

"I think I'll take it with me. Just in case."

"In case what?" The fire flashing out of the pretty little woman's eyes nearly burned a hole in his shirt.

"In case you get hungry in the one minute I'll be gone." Logan left the cabin. It hurt for her not to understand him. Of course he expected it, but he'd hoped. Still, seeing her frustration, her annoyance, laced humor in with his disappointment. She really did think her way was best. Strange place this West. Too many guns, not enough respect for nature.

Of course, he'd scoot his chair up to an elk steak as quick as anyone. Wise Sister had brought down at least one elk since he'd arrived in the spring with her trusty bow.

She didn't like guns, he'd learned. She could do whatever needed doing with her swift, silent arrows. How far had Wise Sister hiked to get that elk? How far had she hauled it? How had she lifted the carcass to cut it, bleed it, and butcher it? He'd never asked. He'd just picked up his fork and enjoyed.

He went into Wise Sister's cabin and picked up a chair. Wise Sister had one, Logan had three, all four built by Babineau.

Everything was built by Babineau or Wise Sister. Everything in this cabin, keepsakes and bits of beauty, had been collected or created over a lifetime in these mountains. Logan saw his picture amidst Wise Sister's things. As always, he was deeply honored he'd rated a few square feet of her precious space.

She did like him and she even respected him.

But he wasn't taking on his fair share of the weight of living in the West. He'd definitely change that and start doing what he could to ease Wise Sister's workload.

As he exited the cabin, he paused to study that small herd of elk. It might be conceit but he thought he recognized them. Of course the bull—there was only one of them—but even the two dozen or so cows and their spring babies each had a personality. The yearlings were sprouting modest racks of antlers. One adult bull, still a youngster, snorted at that old king on occasion, but he always backed down.

Logan loved trying to sketch that tension and the power in their little skirmishes. Logan was sure it was the same herd as last year.

Reasonably sure.

He'd already sketched the bull elk that stood so proudly on an overlook—on guard, remote, proud. The big animal was well gone on this year's magnificent rack of antlers. By autumn they'd be spectacular. He'd stand up there with his chest thrust out, his head held high, protecting his family.

Logan thought of wounded Sally and could understand just how the bull felt. But he couldn't imagine shooting at them. In Sally's mind that probably made him a no-account weakling.

He thought of that kiss they'd shared and wanted another. But it wasn't a wise thing to do, kissing a woman who called him stupid with nearly every breath. Even if she didn't say it out loud.

Logan wasn't incompetent. And he could shoot an elk if he had to. He wouldn't starve for his art. He'd gotten used to the wild country. And he wasn't as good slipping around as Wise Sister, but he'd learned to move quietly, without drawing attention to himself, so he could ease up on some shy critter. He didn't mind hiking, and he was comfortable sleeping on the ground in a bedroll. He'd taken to the Western land well, learned his way with a gun and a campfire and a rugged trail. He wasn't afraid to sleep outside.

He and Babineau had spent most of the first summer camping in Yellowstone. When he'd returned in the spring, he'd met Babineau and gone into Yellowstone again, but only for a few weeks. Then they'd come here for the rest of the season. And Logan had found he had his own elk herd and persuaded Wise Sister not to use it as a food supply.

Logan grinned when he thought of that confrontation, translated by Babineau. Wise Sister had chalked him up as a complete fool. Logan tried to explain that a man couldn't always find an elk to draw when he wanted one. It made no sense to scare off a handy herd.

Even then, when she'd thought he had no common sense, she'd liked his paintings. He'd painted the portrait of her and Pierre, and she'd given it a place of honor. And best of all, she'd agreed, grudgingly, to hike away from the cabin to hunt for food.

Logan needed to keep Sally disarmed until she saw the light. Logan looked at the elk and the elk seemed to look back and even, maybe, be thankful that Logan was willing to annoy the woman he found so fascinating.

"You're welcome." Logan gave his four-legged friend a nod of understanding and thought the elk got it, however fanciful that notion. "You should be flattered, old boy."

The elk lowered his head as if to threaten Logan and ask why.

"Because she's really cute."

Ten

Luther jerked back on his reins so hard his mount reared and snorted. "That's Sally's horse."

Kicking his chestnut gelding forward, he galloped toward the carcass of a dead horse. He swung down, crouched low to see the McClellen brand. Even with the rain, Luther could see what else had happened here.

Death.

Luther looked at the steep rock wall that lined the trail and saw, in a few spots sheltered from the rain. "Blood. Lots of it."

150

His eyes met Buff's and they both knew without speaking. Too much of it.

Luther's jaw got so tight he couldn't force words through. He and Buff went over the trail carefully until it had given up all its secrets. They found spent shells where someone had shot from cover and left one of their own behind, not even bothering to bury him. Then they looked over the cliff.

"If she went over this she's dead," Luther said, not because it helped to talk but because saying it out loud was almost necessary, to force the possibility into his brain that he could have lost one of his precious girls.

"Let's go." Buff swung up on his horse and headed down with no further words.

It was a long, long way down the trail. Then they had to wind through a land so rugged it was almost impossible to get to the bottom of that cliff.

It was a day's work studying the carnage at the bottom of the trail. They didn't know how many people had traveled with Sally, but they found enough death down there to account for a good-sized group. The one thing they didn't find was any trace of Sally.

Luther knew it wasn't reasonable to hope Sally had lived through that turkey shoot up on the trail, or lived through falling over a cliff. But she wasn't here and that meant she was somewhere else. He couldn't stop himself from hoping.

About nightfall, they found where a horse had been tethered; and in a spot sheltered from the rain, they studied the sign.

"Two riders. Same tracks of the coyotes who mowed down the colonel and his party. Leading extra horses. Horses they stole from Colonel McGarritt." Luther's gut burned hot. "Dry-gulchers." Sally's party had been hit hard. Luther had seen what had happened on that trail above. Sally, his little cowgirl, had to've been right in the middle of it.

They hadn't found her body. Nothing could tie these tracks to Sally, not well enough for a judge to find them guilty. But Luther knew what he knew. He could find the men who'd done her harm. Right now there were no tracks to follow, but Luther could make out which direction they headed, and the lay of the land made only one direction possible. Luther would find them. And when he did, he and Buff would get answers. "The colonel had friends. Won't be just us who comes a-runnin'."

"Clay might head up, too. Not one to leave his little girl's safety to someone else." Buff grunted and chewed on a chunk of beef jerky as they mounted up.

That sounded like hope to Luther. A little girl's safety meant a little girl who was in danger, which meant a little girl who was still alive.

"We're heading into a mighty wild land." Luther kicked his horse and went forward on the wet ground. The men they were tailing were heading for high ground.

"Best get after Sally." Buff was obviously impatient with Luther for his chitchatting.

They rode on, through woodlands and shale slides, down ravines and along treacherous slopes. Spreading out, checking side trails, as the day wore down they finally picked up the hoof prints of the men who'd done the shooting. They followed as they lost the light and could see the men they were after meandering, like maybe they were searching for something.

Searching for Sally.

The tracks they followed turned and headed for a gap in the mountains. "Leave a marker for anyone coming after us." Luther jerked a thumb at a small sheltered spot in the treacherous trail, just a few yards from a meandering creek.

"Good spot to camp." Buff swung down and Luther did the same.

"I itch to keep going, but this land will break a horse's leg easy as not." Luther began gathering firewood as he wondered at the land around them.

"Mind that itch. Could be more than frettin' over our Sally." Buff laid out the pile of stones for Clay. "Had a hankerin' to see her again. Been too long."

"Didn't like leavin' Mandy with that no good husband of hers neither." Luther built a fire small enough to fit in the crown of his Stetson. No sense tellin' the outlaws where they were camping.

"Money didn't do that polecat no good." Buff stripped the leather off his horse.

Luther shook his head. "Had a chance I think, till he found that gold. Might've come around to being a decent man. Now he just needs someone lookin' out for him all the time." Luther stopped and turned to Buff. "I don't feel right about huntin' Sally and lettin' Mandy stay home alone."

"Woman oughta be safe in her own home. And Mandy is a pure pleasure to watch with that rifle. Never knew no one who could best her—man, woman, nor child." Buff smiled like a proud papa.

Luther knew how he felt. They'd had a hand in raisin' the McClellen girls and were happy with the way they'd shaped up. Women fit to tame a wild land.

"Mandy needs us, no use denying it. But she can watch her back for a few days, especially with Sidney back home. He's not gonna be able to beat anyone who braces him, face-to-face, but he's hired hisself a pack of coyotes. None of 'em'll come at Mandy directly, not while Sid's around. We just gotta get back before he takes off for another one of his weeklong trips to town."

154

Luther took the coffeepot off his pack horse and turned to dip it in the stream they'd chosen to camp beside. "Look at that, Buff."

A huge grizzly lumbered out of the woods on the far side of the fast-moving water. Luther heard Buff's gun cock a second after his own. The bear looked them over, woofed at them a few times, then kept coming over the broken land that sloped downward to the rushing creek. Two cubs frisked out of the forest behind her.

"She's never seen a man before, nor a gun." Luther glanced at Buff, who'd come up beside him. "Doesn't know to be afraid."

"How deep is that water?" Buff asked.

"Hard to say. I hope she stays on her side."

They watched the massive bear and her rollicking babies drink long and deep. The animal acted like exactly what she was—the biggest, meanest animal for a thousand miles. She wasn't afraid of anything. She'd never seen a man, never seen the damage a Winchester could do.

Luther had just a few minutes to feel bad about encroaching on her kingdom, knowing flying lead would knock her off her throne in a heartbeat.

She drank as the sun lowered, and finally, her thirst quenched, she turned and waddled back toward the thick growth of pine and aspen, her cubs wrestling and gamboling along behind her.

155

"We'll stay here and eat, but I think we'd better move away from the water to camp. If one mama grizzly drinks here, others, not quite so friendly, might." Buff turned back to his fire while Luther filled his coffeepot.

While they ate, a herd of elk came down to drink. A golden yellow cougar with four cubs came, too. And a couple of deer, a pair of wolves, and a lone moose, with a short growth of antlers. Other, smaller animals passed by, too, before Luther and Buff finished their quick meal and moved on to a better, less popular spot.

"If our girls had only those animals to face they'd be just fine." Luther spread out his bedroll and contemplated two-legged critters and how much more trouble they could be than the four-legged variety.

He was worried sick, but he ended the day a lot better than he'd begun it, with the discovery of Sally's dead horse.

This morning he'd known she was dead. Tonight he had hope.

If she'd somehow survived that fall, then she had a fighting chance of surviving until they could get to her. He'd helped raise those McClellen girls. He knew what they were made of. He figured they'd be fine if they were ready for trouble.

Except maybe Sally wasn't fine.

That made him sick, and as he lay down, he

wished a grizzly would charge him to give him something more pleasant to think about.

Mandy didn't normally speak to her husband if she could help it. That had been her policy for the last couple of years. But last night she'd finally figured out that it wasn't a good strategy for a marriage.

"There was someone outside last night." Mandy put her fork on the dinner plate with a sharp click of metal on glass.

With Sidney's suspicious nature, who knew? He might actually decide they shouldn't live all the way up on this stupid mountaintop. They were a long way from the law up here. A long, long, long way.

"So you say. I didn't hear anything." Sidney shoveled a massive amount of food into his mouth three meals a day. Mandy noticed the blotches of grease at the corners of his mouth and had to force herself not to grimace. Sidney set his fragile coffee cup down on its fussy little plate. Sidney had insisted on buying the glass dishes.

Mandy admitted they were pretty, but she missed the duller click of tin on wood. "Well, I did, and I trust my judgment a lot better than yours." Those were fighting words, Mandy knew it, but it was fine with her. She and her husband were about two years overdue for a good fight.

Sidney's eyes narrowed. Mandy pushed her plate back, crossed her arms on the table, and leaned forward. They were on opposite ends, much like where they'd stood last night. Armed, working together on something for once.

She did her best not to start yelling. That wasn't going to help. Although she held the idea in reserve in the event she needed it later.

"What exactly did you hear?"

Mandy prayed to God that, despite showing all sorts of signs of being a halfwit, Sidney would know enough to trust her on this. "Someone stepped up on the porch. Right by this window." The window the kitchen table sat in front of. "It was a man, I'm sure of it, not an animal or the house settling or the wind. Someone snooping around. I turned the lantern on when I got up with Catherine. I think, whoever it was might have been thinking of coming inside."

Mandy shivered, remembering how she'd felt—watched. The windows had curtains but the fabric was thin. A man could watch through the windows and see pretty well inside. At least make out her form in the rocker. And the glass and curtains certainly wouldn't stop a bullet.

Sidney seemed to take her very seriously. Mandy was grateful for that . . . for his sake.

His eyes shifted as he frowned. "I've regretted a few of the men I hired to build the house."

Mandy sighed with relief, though she didn't let

Sidney see that. She was no longer going to twist herself into a knot hoping for Sidney's respect. Starting today she was going to demand it.

"And what about the two men who ride with you? I don't trust them either." Mandy had never gotten Sidney to listen to a word against Cooter or Platte. Of course, Mandy rarely spoke to Sidney, so it's not like he'd had a lot of chances. And why wouldn't he be suspicious? So far the only people he hadn't suspected of wanting his gold were Catherine and Angela. And he'd probably get around to that when they were a few years older.

Sidney did what he did best: quietly blamed the whole world for trouble of his own making. "I hate to fire any of the men because the house is a big project and it needs a lot of workers. But I'll look into it, see if anyone admits to being out for a walk last night."

That wasn't good enough but probably all Sidney was capable of. She'd protect this family herself.

"Why did you build up here?" Mandy expected little but criticism from him. But Sidney was talking a bit, and she was genuinely interested. She hoped he could tell. "I would have thought you might want to go back East, to a more comfortable life. The living is hard out here."

Mandy didn't mention train travel and the fact that she could occasionally go visit her family if they lived nearer civilization. She could go maybe twice a year, for six months each time.

She remembered that, at the beginning, when Sidney was more vulnerable to her opinion, before gold had made him believe he was royalty, he'd admitted his mother had been disreputable. It was possible there was something back East that Sidney wanted to stay far away from.

Sidney, maybe distracted by his paranoia, didn't snap at Mandy. "There's just something about that spot, up on the mountaintop." He pushed back the curtain and looked out the window up at his monument to his own greatness. "When I first hired my assistants"— only through sheer willpower did Mandy keep from rolling her eyes at Sidney calling Cooter and Platte his "assistants"—"we scouted around looking for a building site. I loved the view from here, and this cabin seemed adequate to our needs. But now, with the children coming . . ." He gave Mandy's stomach a satisfied look that made her uncomfortable.

She had a feeling Sidney thought to keep her in the family way for most of her life. She loved her children, but she wasn't a bit fond of Sidney. And some . . . closeness to him was required for all those babies to come along.

"We need more space, and once I was up here, I looked around and realized the view was even better from up there."

Mandy had a sudden image of Sidney getting into that house and realizing there were even higher peaks around. It was high up, but it wasn't the very top of the world after all. They'd have to move again and again, higher and higher. Maybe he'd think the house had to be bigger every time, too. Pretty soon she'd be living in a castle atop a snowcap.

Since he was talking pleasantly for a change, she carefully kept from snorting in disgust.

"We'll be happy up there, Mandy. You wait and see."

The way he said it pinched Mandy's heart. She really was fed up with her husband and, because of that, didn't spend much time trying to understand him. She thought, in fact, that she *did* understand him. He was an idiot, she understood that completely. But he sounded sad when he said that. As if—"Aren't you happy now, Sidney?"

His head came up, his eyes wide, as if her questions startled him.

Knowing how moody he was, Mandy told herself she probably shouldn't pursue it, but it didn't hurt to try to have a good relationship with her husband. It was probably a waste of time, but it didn't hurt to try. "You're healthy. We're all healthy. We're rich. We have beautiful children. Why wouldn't you be happy right now?"

"I—I *am* happy, I suppose, but I could be

161

happier. I just need to get our lives in order and then we can finally settle down and live in contentment. I can have what I need to be happy and you—you can put down that rifle you always keep at hand and be a proper woman."

The part about her being proper wasn't new. She leaned forward, restraining her temper. "You don't know me at all, do you, Sidney?"

Scowling, Sidney said, "Of course I know you. Don't be ridiculous."

Praying for the right words, Mandy said, "You want to find happiness for yourself. You think you'll find it with the right house and the right view and the right amount of money, and I hope you do. I hope you find whatever it is you're searching for. But you owe me the same thing. I'm a woman born and raised on a Texas ranch. I lived with my ma and little sisters, a real hardscrabble life, for two years before she married my pa. I learned—"

"I know all that." His expression closed up.

Mandy kept trying. "The thing is, you want contentment and happiness, and I want them for you. But do you want *my* contentment? Do you even know me well enough to care if I'm happy?"

"What have you got to be unhappy about?" The growling was starting.

"I was the best sharpshooter on the McClellen ranch, Sidney. Do you realize that?"

"I've heard you say you're a good shot."

"Not a *good* shot, the *best*. One of the best in all of west Texas, my pa used to say. I use my rifle to feed *this family*, but it's more than that. It's a talent I have that I'm proud of." And a little scared of, but she didn't say that out loud. "It's not something I do for lack of womanly manners. It's a big part of who I am, the skill that came from needing to be accurate, from living a rugged life where we needed to put food on the table to survive, then later from competing with my sisters and Pa and Ma."

Sidney stared at her as if wishing she'd say something that made sense.

"Your contentment seems to require making me over into a wife you can be proud of, but you owe me the respect of being proud of me *right now*!" Mandy saw her fists clenched and forced them to open.

Lord, protect me.

Right now she needed the Lord to protect her from her own temper. She felt the cold that came over her when she was shooting. The icy cold that steadied her hands and calmed her nerves. Her eyesight seemed to sharpen. The world slowed down. It was always in the back of her mind that one of these times, when she held her gun, her blood flowing like sleet in her veins, she might not come back from the cold. This time she might stay frozen forever.

Above all, she knew that this fighting fury, calm and deadly, had no place in this talk with her husband. She tried to push the cold away.

"I hope and pray for your happiness and want you to be content, but you owe me that right back. Instead of *fixing* me, you need to take pride in having a wife that can out-shoot, out-rope, and out-ride almost every man in these mountains." Leaning forward, trying to pierce Sidney's cloddish opinions, she added, "When am I going to get that from you?"

"Get what?"

"Get *respect*." She slammed a fist on the table, and when she did Sidney's eyes focused on her.

Until this moment, he'd quit listening. Was she surprised?

Sighing, Mandy leaned back. "Get you to embrace what I *am* instead of trying to mold me into whatever twisted vision of perfect womanhood you have inside your head."

"I respect you, Mandy. I just wish you were more refined. You were brought up in a wild place."

Mandy's eyes went out the window to the back of beyond where they lived. There was no place wilder than this.

"I respect who you are, but that doesn't mean you can't learn more womanly ways, better manners."

Better manners? Maybe she'd say "please"

when she took the butt of her gun to his head. And "thank you" after he passed out on the floor. She fought down the cold. It seemed like when a woman tackled a big old fight with her husband, she ought to at least be fiery hot with rage.

"Look at how I've changed since I found gold." Sidney touched his chest with his widespread fingers, flashing his stupid ring at her, caressing his dark gray suit and white silk shirt with the foolish string tie that only had a use, as far as Mandy could see, if Sidney suddenly needed to brand a fractious calf. "I dress better, ride in a better carriage, conduct myself like a wealthy man ought. That's all part of finding contentment."

And what about finding your teeth when I knock them out, huh, Sid?

"Oh, before I go up to see how the work is progressing on the house, I forgot to mention that I bought a team of horses when I was in Helena."

Spending money like it was fresh milk he was afraid would go sour if he kept it around too long.

It was a shame there was so much of it, because if it ever ran out, Sidney might stop being such an arrogant halfwit.

"We could use a couple for the girls." Mandy allowed him that. Buying horses wasn't a pure waste. "They'll need gentle saddle ponies. Did you—"

"I didn't get *ponies* for the children to ride, for heaven's sake." He looked at her like she'd lost her mind.

Well, considering the man she'd married, he might have a point.

"It's not ladylike for a woman to ride a horse. I bought a new carriage and need a matched pair to pull it. I would have preferred grays of course. But these are the best so I bought them. I found a breeder over by Divide who, the word is, has the prettiest pair of black thoroughbreds anyone in these parts has ever seen. They're two-year-olds, out of a black stallion he owns that seems to be famous through the whole state. I bought them, and he's delivering them as soon as they're thoroughly trained to pull a buggy."

"Divide?" Mandy's stomach swooped. "A black stallion?" That could only be—

"Tom Linscott." Sidney pushed back from the table. "He was in Helena delivering his herd. I'd asked about horses and they pointed me in his direction. He seemed really interested in our new house and where we lived. He'd heard of me, in fact. I suppose I need to get used to being an important man."

He'd heard of Sidney all right. When he'd come to visit and Sidney wasn't home—the summer she and Sidney had gotten married. Tom had wanted to see the little foal Belle Harden's mare had delivered out of his stallion. And he'd stayed all day and done the work a husband should have done. By the end of that day, he'd known exactly who . . . and what . . . Sidney was, without Mandy saying a word.

"He'll be a month at least delivering them because I insisted he not try and unload inferior, badly trained animals on us."

"Did you say that to him?" Mandy swallowed hard, remembering Tom could get cranky, especially about his horses.

"I told him my expectations, of course."

And he let you live? Mandy didn't say that out loud, but she was impressed with Tom's restraint.

"I told him where we lived, and he said he'd come on up. Remember, we raised a foal out of his stallion that first year we lived out here?"

"I remember," Mandy said faintly. She also remembered that Tom Linscott had touched a very tender place in her heart at a time when she wasn't very happy with her husband. She'd been glad not to see Tom again.

And now she would. And she was even unhappier with her husband now than then.

At least she wasn't cold anymore.

She ran her hand over her stomach and was grateful Catherine cried from the bedroom. She didn't have good control of the expression on her face and wasn't sure what Sidney would see.

She rose from the table, but before she turned to fetch her little girl, the itching of guilt made

167

her more forgiving of her husband. "I want you to be contented and happy, Sidney."

She wanted it for herself too, badly, because right this moment she was as restless and discontented as any woman who ever lived. She thought of Eve in the Garden of Eden, reaching for that apple, and knew how a woman could be wildly tempted to do something she knew was wrong.

"It's something I pray for—your happiness." And she was going to start praying harder, for all of them. "But contentment isn't going to come from gold or a fine house or the best horses or a grand view from a mountaintop."

She thought her expression was one she dared to let Sidney see now. She hoped. Turning to him, she spoke kindly, with her whole heart. "Happiness is inside of you. It comes from being at peace—with yourself, and mostly with God. It usually grows best when you're *giving* rather than taking. We're so far out we can't attend a church service, but I worship with the children on Sunday mornings. You could join us. You could—"

"Mandy," Sidney cut her off in that arrogant voice that made her think of the weight of her gun on her back.

She realized that she'd just asked Sidney to accept her and respect her. Now here she stood trying to change him.

"Don't start that." Sidney waved his hand impatiently, dismissively.

Mandy noticed again that ring on his hand. It fit, which must mean it was new because his fingers had gotten fat along with the rest of him. It was a large, rather ugly ring that looked like he'd had a gold nugget made into a piece of jewelry. He might have been wearing it for quite a time. Mandy realized that she'd gotten into the habit of ignoring him whenever possible.

God, please protect my husband from that day when I really explode.

Mandy was genuinely afraid that day was coming soon. She'd seen and heard the explosions when they'd blasted a trail up to this pass. She sometimes imagined her own temper detonating.

Boom!

And from now on she was going to quit fearing that. She was no longer going to be the wife Sidney wanted her to be.

Sidney stood from the table and headed for the door. Going to check on his mountaintop castle.

Starting right now . . . in fact, she'd already started . . . she was going to be herself, no matter how much Sidney disliked that.

Another thought struck Mandy hard. It was so obvious she almost smiled. She had never succeeded in being *good* enough for Sidney. All her efforts and they'd been a waste of time. Oh, sometimes for a few hours she'd been able to please him, but she'd never been proper enough, restrained enough. And that wasn't for lack of trying.

It was just the cold, hard, dirty truth that Sidney's unhappiness was something that had nothing to do with her. Though he blamed her, it had everything to do with him.

So she couldn't even say she was failing. The truth was she was wasting her time trying to suit him, trying to be restrained enough for him to be happy with her. Mandy vowed to herself that she wasn't doing it anymore.

She watched Sidney leave, wondering what the future held for her and her unhappy husband.

Tom Linscott's face immediately came into focus, vivid and clear, every feature etched in her mind. Which was frightening because she'd only seen him once, and that had been over two years ago.

She turned her thoughts back to violence against her husband, which somehow seemed far less sinful. If she lost her temper—truly, horribly lost it—Sidney might be finished with her, and she might get herself sent down the road . . . all the way home to her parents in Texas.

Mandy tried very hard to convince herself that would be a very bad thing.

Eleven

Seven days since she'd fallen off a cliff. Sally hadn't gotten free yet, but this was it. Now it was time.

Sally watched Wise Sister clean up after breakfast, waiting impatiently for the sweet lady to go away.

"This is for you." Last night Wise Sister had sewed busily for the entire evening, and this morning she'd laid out a beautiful doeskin dress, tanned nearly white. Now she presented that dress to Sally.

"Really?" With a gasp of pleasure, Sally reached out and touched the beautifully tanned dress. Somehow that dress seemed to bring all the parts of Sally's nature together. It was practical and tough. But it was beautiful and so lovely to touch. Sally realized as she took the dress from Wise Sister that her heart had longed for the creation Wise Sister was working on.

"Your clothes are ruined. Ripped. You need something." The kind Shoshone woman slung her quiver on her back. "Get dressed."

The elderly woman headed out to hunt so Sally had only Logan to contend with.

Her leg was still as broken as it could be, no denying, though the swelling had gone down a bit, and Wise Sister had tightened the splints and the leather moccasin to fit. But her ribs were feeling a lot better. Now, every time she moved or breathed, it felt like being clubbed with a dull hammer rather than like wolves gobbling down her chest. A big improvement.

Her headache was gone. That gave her the most hope. She'd been practicing sitting up whenever she got left alone for a minute, and all day yesterday she'd managed it without the room spinning. She'd stood one-legged a few times, too, clinging to the bed carefully so she wouldn't fall and make her injuries worse.

And now she had clothes. That had been a big problem holding her back. Sally ran her hand over the fringe along the arms and skirt and a few rows of beads that Sally would have protested about if she'd realized who Wise Sister was making the dress for. It was a shame to waste such fussiness on Sally. Such pretty fussiness.

Her Winchester was there, too.

Sally chafed to think of her chaps and broadcloth pants, but she'd seen herself that they were destroyed. She thought of what Ma would say if she knew Sally had changed into her manly clothes after she'd left the train. Ma would be annoyed at her behavior, but those clothes, tough and protective, had helped save Sally's life. Ma would forgive all Sally's outrageous behavior and give thanks because of that.

A tiny twist of pleasure forced Sally to admit it

would feel good to wear the doeskin dress. And it would be much easier to put on, considering the sorry state of her ribs and leg. Eyeing the doeskin, Sally knew that this morning she was going to get dressed and get out.

So what if she was on top of a mountain? She'd scoot downhill on her backside if Logan wouldn't give her a horse. One way or another, she was going.

Sally figured to dress then go find herself a sturdy crutch. She knew she'd never get far without being caught, but if she could get up and prove to Logan and Wise Sister that she was capable, they'd lend her a horse and let her get on with it.

This was the West, and out here, just like in Texas, people forked their own broncs. This was Sally's problem, and she'd solve it.

She moved slowly, careful not to jar her aching leg. Standing, she had only two hops to reach the dress. She made that with only a token protest from her battered body. She sank into a chair and took it slow and easy pulling on Wise Sister's gift.

The tanning had taken a lot of time and was already done before Sally had come crashing into Wise Sister's life. Sally wondered what Wise Sister had been planning for the lovely piece of goods.

Studying the cabin, Sally knew Wise Sister

might have had grand plans to decorate the leather and use it in her home somehow.

Sally listened carefully as she pulled her dress into place. Once it was on, she also noticed the bit of ribbon that had been on her chemise. It had been lying on the table beneath the dress. The pin she used to keep it in place and remove it to be hidden at the end of the day was there, too. Not a speck of blood on her secret, womanly indulgence. She picked up the bit of foolishness and, with care, found a seam inside the soft dress and pinned the ribbon in place, out of sight.

She hurried to finish dressing, worried that Logan might come to the cabin. With her ears peeled, she prepared to yell out for him to wait until she was decent. When he saw her dressed, she fully expected him to start yelling right back.

She wasn't interrupted and was soon fully dressed, even getting her remaining boot on her good foot. That made her feel steadier. She sat, gathering her strength, wondering exactly where she'd have to go to get a crutch, when she heard a footstep at the door.

There was a knock, which there had never been before, but then Sally realized how rarely she'd been left alone. One of her two caretakers was always with her. Humbly, she had to admit that they'd taken good care of her.

"Come in." She squared her shoulders, bracing for the fight she intended to win.

The door swung open and Logan stepped in and smiled. "We knew you were ready to get dressed. I see you've finished."

It irritated Sally to find out her scheming and plotting had, instead, been predictable. "I'm dressed and ready to go." Sally crossed her arms, delighted at how little that hurt.

"Wise Sister has already gone to scout for your friends. Your breakfast is ready over in the other cabin. Shall I carry you over there or bring it here?"

"You made me breakfast?"

"No, of course not." Logan shuddered. "I want you to get better. What I'd cook might well set you back. Wise Sister made it before she rode out."

"She shouldn't go out there. It's dangerous."

"She's only going for a few hours. She said something about Buff, but I didn't understand it. Just that Buff would read her sign. Does your friend speak Shoshone?"

"Not that I know of."

Logan shrugged. "Wise Sister is sure she can leave a sign your friends can follow but stay clear of anyone else who might be prowling around. We talked about it, and she convinced me I'd only make things worse." Logan smiled.

He wasn't a very normal sort of man. Her pa wouldn't have been happy about a woman doing a job he saw as his. And most men wouldn't laugh at themselves. Sally found that the attitude was refreshing. But Logan was strange, with his odd painting. Maybe he'd learned to accept others in hopes they'd also accept him. She wondered if he liked her pretty new dress.

"Wise Sister left some heavy branches. She said she thought you'd be able to fashion yourself a good crutch with it." Logan came up beside her, swung *her* rifle over *his* shoulders and scooped Sally into his arms.

Whatever kind of bad job he was doing of caring for himself, Sally had to admit the man was strong.

He lifted her with ease and smiled down at her. "Let's go. You can eat, and I can paint you."

Sally felt a very strange twist in her gut that she didn't understand, and her arms seemed a bit too natural wrapped around Logan's neck.

Logan stopped. "Do you mind getting the door?"

Sally grinned. They got into his cabin the same way.

He settled her at the table with such gentleness Sally couldn't stop from whispering, "Thanks."

Logan paused as he slid his arms free of her back and knees, his face too close. His eyes were an odd shade of deep brown, and this close she could see they were shot through with an almost golden yellow stripe. Though he acted gentle, those eyes made her think of the eagles that soared overhead in this strange land. Predator eyes, strong, dangerous. There was a depth to them that made no sense. The man painted when he should be chopping wood and hunting for supper.

But, though she didn't understand the way he lived, she saw in him patience, confidence, an assurance that, though he knew he didn't exactly suit the world, he suited himself. It was amazingly attractive.

It reminded her for a fleeting second that she dressed like a man and worked a man's job. And yet she apologized to no one for her behavior. Could it possibly be that deep down, she and Logan were a lot alike?

Then his eyes changed. Where once there was kindness and concern, the depth now held warmth. More than warmth . . . heat.

He kissed her.

He certainly shouldn't be doing that. She pulled back to tell him to stop, but he followed along, and she forgot what she was going to say.

His hands touched her face, and he tilted her head gently and deepened the kiss.

Her hands came up to rest on his wrists. To hold on. Tight.

She wondered at his talented, strong hands and how gentle they were.

Something awoke in her that she hadn't known was sleeping. An affection for Logan bloomed that was a mismatch for her opinion that he was a no-account kind of man.

He raised his head so their lips separated, and Sally followed after him and brought him back to her, back to that kiss.

Logan straightened away, his eyes on her as if she were the most beautiful thing he'd ever seen, even better than a hook-nosed bald eagle. "Let me draw you, exactly like that."

Scooting her chair close to the table, he sat around the corner from her, only inches away. His sketchbook was laying right there, and he picked it up. It was never far from his hands. He began drawing while Sally wondered what he saw in her that he found so fascinating, that made him share a kiss then grab a pencil.

"You can move if you want." He looked up from his drawing but it was a studying kind of look.

"Really? I thought you'd want me to sit still." So that meant she was obeying him, even while she was still planning to tell him he had a lot of nerve to just announce he was going to draw her picture.

Not to mention kissing her.

And he *hadn't* mentioned it once he pulled back. She'd noticed that clear enough.

God, have mercy. I want him to kiss me again.

"No, moving is good for me. I can see different angles of your face, catch the way your bones and muscles work together. I can catch shadows from the light coming in through the window." He reached past her and pulled a red-and-white-checked towel off a plate on the table, revealing scrambled eggs, a slab of venison, and a square of cornbread covered with honey. "I'll pour you some coffee."

Logan set his sketchbook aside as if it hurt him to let it go, grabbed the coffeepot off the stove, poured a black tin cup full of the steaming liquid, then hurriedly returned the pot with a clank of metal on metal and rushed back to sit beside her and resume drawing.

"You hadn't oughta kissed me like that." Sally hated saying that. Hated knowing she could never let him do it again. He'd done it before, and she'd thought that was the end of it. Now he'd sneaked past her again. "It's not proper."

He looked up from his drawing, but his expression showed no agreement with her or regret that she'd just told him he couldn't kiss her again. Instead he just studied her for long quiet moments with those deep, probing eyes. It seemed like he was trying to see inside her head.

Which she sorely hoped he couldn't, because she didn't want him to know how much she'd thought of their first kiss. How often she'd imagined having another . . . which she just had . . . and how much she regretted that she had to call a halt to such nonsense.

Finally, he went back to drawing.

Sally decided not to mention the kiss again and invite another such long look.

She ate quietly, savoring the meat and eggs. She'd seen no chickens, but maybe there were ducks and pheasants around. Wise Sister would know how to rob their nests.

She stared out the windows, wondering about the kiss and Logan's single-minded painting and the work a lone woman would have to do to provide this meal, when she noticed how far and wide she could see. "You've got both your shutters off today." The south wall of his cabin was almost completely open.

She sought out the huge painting, now leaning on the east wall. "What made you paint it in such an odd fashion? It doesn't look real. I thought a painter's skill was judged by how much his pictures looked like what he was drawing."

Logan smiled, looked up from his sketchbook, opened his mouth, and then stopped. "I need you to take your hair down, catch the light on all that yellow gold."

Her hair was in one long braid that had swung over her shoulder and hung down nearly to her lap.

"I'll do it." He reached over, without asking so much as a by-your-leave, and tugged on the leather thong Wise Sister had given her to contain the braid.

"What are you—"

"Got it. Thanks." He tossed the strip of leather onto the table next to Sally, set the sketchbook beside the hair tie, and with quick movements undid her braid then pulled her hair into disorder.

"You—wait—I don't—" Sally sputtered, shoving at his hands, but it was too late to do a thing.

His hands lingered on her hair far longer than Sally thought was necessary. Their fingers were intertwined. She ought to stab him with her fork, but her breath caught as she saw his eyes slide from her hand, tangled in his fingers, to her eyes.

With a shake of his head, he let go of her and went right back to drawing. "*Blazing Land* is the name of the picture. It was"—he looked up from his drawing and smiled—"pure indulgence that I painted it. A waste of paint and canvas, a huge picture impossible to take home."

He looked at the wall-sized painting behind his back. A rueful smile bloomed. "But it was like I had that inside me. I couldn't do anything else until I—got it out—got it out of the way." He stared at the picture, then shrugged his shoulders and went back to drawing.

Then she looked a bit farther and saw a smaller painting. The big one demanded attention, but the smaller one . . . "Is that—me?" She sat on a horse, dressed in pants and her buckskin jacket, the horse in motion under her while she focused completely on something beyond the picture. She held the reins in one hand, a rope coiled over her head in the other, a lasso she was almost ready to throw.

Logan looked up, followed the line of her vision, and smiled. "Yes. Another thing I had to get out of my system." He looked back at her. "Except, I don't seem to have quite done that yet. I get up in the morning thinking to capture another sunrise, and all I can do is study sketches of you."

He made a move that looked like he was going to touch her hair again, then stopped and jabbed his pencil at her plate. "Eat. You need food to knit your bones. That's what Wise Sister said."

"You've never even seen me on horseback."

"Well, not while you were conscious."

That's right. He'd carried her home. Just swept her up and whisked her away, like one of his eagles carrying something back to its nest. Eagles did that with food.

She shook off that thought and studied the painting he'd done of her. The picture seemed to move. It was alive, dust kicking up, the horse wheeling, obeying the pressure of her knees. She could feel herself—in the painting—riding, concentrating, aiming that rope. She could smell the sweat a person worked up and the horse, the dust, the cattle she'd have been working. "That's—that's—you're really good."

Logan looked up and grinned. "Well—it's not humble to admit it, I suppose, but, yes, I am really good."

He reached for her again, this time not checking himself, and stroked one finger down the side of her face, around so he touched her chin, staring at her in that intense way. Frowning, he said, "It's not a normal pastime, painting. But since I can't seem to stop and can't focus on anything long enough to find a more useful career, I'm just giving it all I've got."

Logan quit touching her then looked over at the painting of her for a minute. He snapped his fingers and lunged out of his chair toward the other side of the room where a square of cloth covered something on a table. He pulled the cloth away, and Sally saw another picture of her, dressed in buckskin again. A twinge of embarrassment surprised her. He'd never seen her in women's clothes until today, and he'd yet to comment on Wise Sister's gift.

She thought of the way he'd kissed her. She'd never considered kissing much. When she was around men, it was either her father or brothers or men she was trying to outdo in some way. She wanted the cowhands on her family ranch to respect her. And there was no place for kissing in that. Nor had she ever wanted there to be.

It hit her suddenly that she spent most of her life proving herself to men and when, as she always did, she proved herself better, she looked on them with pity. So, if a tough Texas cowboy couldn't win enough respect to awaken some affection, how could a man who painted pictures?

Simple answer was he couldn't. And if she didn't respect him, then she shouldn't be kissing him. She thought of her big sister Mandy, married to a man her parents loathed . . . Luther hated. Sally suspected Mandy hated him, too, once she'd gotten over being addle-headed in love with him at first.

It could happen. A woman could fall for a no-account man. Or a man could appear to be of some account then prove himself later to be a scoundrel and a liar, as Sidney had.

Sally knew that lesson from hearing about her big sister, mainly through letters they received from Luther, but some of it had sneaked into Mandy's letters, too. Mostly she knew how Mandy felt just because of the complete lack of any affectionate mention of Sidney.

Mandy was the smartest, toughest big sister a girl could have, and she'd been tricked into marrying a man who was busy night and day wrecking her life. Now it looked like Sally might have that same inclination. In fact, as she thought about it, Sally remembered the stories she'd heard about her own pa, the first man Ma had been married to. Though Sally could barely remember him, her sisters claimed he was a hard man to have around. So even her ma had been lured into a bad marriage.

And Beth—well, Alex had turned out to be okay, a fine man in fact. But that was just pure good luck. When Beth married him, it didn't look like she'd done one bit of a good thing.

Sally stroked the tiny scar on her neck.

"What is that?"

Abandoning her dark thoughts of no-account men, Sally touched the bit of redness that was never going to fade. "My sister Beth's husband—"

"The doctor," Logan supplied, drawing away.

"Yes, he . . . well, he did a little bit of surgery on me."

"On your throat?" He looked up, horrified.

"Yes, it was the day he married my sister. They'd only met a few hours before. My throat swelled shut when I was stung by a swarm of bees, and he cut here." Sally drew one finger down that tiny scar and thought kind thoughts about Alex. Maybe Beth *had* known what she was doing.

"He made a hole into my—well—my lungs, I guess. I don't reckon I know exactly what he did. But he cut here, below where my throat was swelled shut, and blew through a tube to keep me alive until the swelling went down."

"I've never heard of that." Logan shook his

head as if denying it and studied her neck more closely. "I don't remember much about my father's doctoring advice, but I know a person can't be having his . . . or her . . . throat cut."

She saw a flash of anger on Logan's face, as if he were mad about Alex cutting into her. As if he'd like to protect her from any such violation. His concern and anger appealed to her in a way she couldn't describe, since she'd never felt such a thing for a man before. "Alex knew what he was doing, I'd say. Though I was unconscious, I suspect I was grateful enough for the air when it started flowing again."

Sally was warmed by Logan's protective anger, and she could see how a woman could be lured toward a man who wasn't what she wanted. It happened too much, too easy. And maybe especially her family seemed apt to make stupid choices in men.

Which explained why she was thinking about Logan's kiss. And even worse, wondering how she could get him to kiss her again. It was probably in her blood to do stupid things when it came to men.

It was almost a comfort to decide what she was feeling wasn't her fault. In fact, it cheered her right up to blame this on her mother.

Twelve

Logan slashed at the canvas with a kind of victorious violence.

He loved painting like this, with a knife instead of a brush. Thick paint, vivid colors. Sunlit scenes . . . and faces.

He'd brought a lot of supplies with him this year, thinking to ride into Yellowstone with Babineau as he had last year. The agreement he'd made with Babineau was the same as the year before. They'd meet at the train station. Logan would leave half the supplies stored at the train depot and Pierre would help him haul the rest into Yellowstone. Logan would paint there for three or four weeks then they'd take his finished work back to the train, ship it home, pack the stored canvas and paints, and ride to the cabins, where Wise Sister waited. She never followed after Babineau when he went wandering.

Except Logan had arrived and waited. Waited several days. Precious days of the short Rocky Mountain summer. But Logan finally had to admit that Babineau wasn't coming. He'd left word, bought some pack horses, loaded his supplies, and gone into Yellowstone himself. He'd survived somehow. In fact, he'd gotten lost in his work.

While he was in Yellowstone, he'd painted Old

Faithful and a dozen other geysers. He'd spent an entire week doing sketches of the waterfalls and the Yellowstone River. He'd also painted the new bridge spanning the river and the tent city that had grown up around Yellowstone like an ugly sore on the beautiful land. These he might be able to sell to newspapers or magazines. He might write about the people coming to Yellowstone, too, try his hand at a bit of storytelling to go with his art.

He'd done it all alone and found pride in knowing he could handle it. Then he'd packed the paintings back to the railroad station, crated them, and shipped them home. Then he'd picked up his stored supplies and set out for the cabin. He'd ridden there several times with Pierre and he'd known where he was going. He'd hoped.

He'd also hauled in the supplies he'd known were needed for the summer at the cabin. He'd found his way easily, wondering where Pierre had gotten to. He'd found Wise Sister alone, with a fresh grave that told its own story.

Wise Sister had gone on with her life and taken care of Logan's house, and Logan had let her. He'd never considered that he was asking too much of the woman.

He'd wanted to load six or even ten horses with canvas and paint. In fact, he'd planned to do just that next year if he sold enough of his paintings. But the grass was sparse up here, the corral small. Wise Sister took the horses daily to graze and drink water, and now Logan realized how much work that was. He couldn't add more horses to her daily chores.

But this style of painting was going through his supply of paints fast. Soon he'd have to be content with sketches. That chafed like wool on a sunburn. Maddening to know that, for lack of paint, he'd have to give up on this task that burned him alive with passion and pleasure. Next year he'd bring more. He had to, somehow.

As he painted, the sun lowered in the west. The mountain peaks would swallow it up long before true sunset. He felt exhilaration in the movement of his muscles and the emotion that flowed out from him onto the canvas. And as those emotions rose, another painting nudged him, haunted him until his mind wouldn't stay on this canvas.

Before he lost the light, he set his paints aside for a blank canvas and returned to his more traditional style of painting. Slowly Sally's face emerged. Her expression was perfect, the exact way she'd looked after he kissed her. It was the face of a woman in love. He doubted that she was, at least not in a deep and lasting way. But at that very moment, when she'd been in his arms, maybe there was a trace of truth in it. What would he give to have Sally look at him like this every day for the rest of his life?

The painting drew him just as powerfully as his

slashing knives and violent red sunsets. It awakened something in him that burned in a different way than the pleasure of painting. But burned just as hot. Nothing—no one—had come close before.

He looked away from his work to watch her fashioning a crutch out of the sturdy forked branch Wise Sister had left behind. Practical woman, handy with a knife. She'd been at it all day, whittling at the wood and stitching a leather pad for her arm. She was an artist in her own way, though she'd probably punch him for saying such a thing.

She glanced at him, as if she were aware of his every move, even with her attention firmly fixed on her carpentry work. Then her eyes went past him to the painting.

He watched the play of feelings cross her face and wanted to sketch every one of them. Annoyance, unwilling fascination, curiosity, he thought maybe he even saw just a flash of respect. He loved her expressiveness. She hid nothing of what she felt, a completely open and honest human being.

"That is a stupid painting."

Painfully honest.

"You made me look dumber than an empty-headed maverick calf."

He'd made her look like a woman who'd just been kissed and wanted to be kissed again. And maybe, from her point of view, that equaled dumb.

"I paint what I see, Sally. I saw that look in your eyes the moment after I kissed you."

She pointed the razor-sharp knife she'd brought over the cliff with her at his nose. He was glad he was a few steps away.

"We aren't going to talk about that. We agreed."

Smiling, Logan looked at what he'd created, what he'd found in her. His heart ached as if he'd taken that knife right between the ribs because he knew Sally would never stay here with him. She thought he was a fool.

Not only did she not want him, he didn't want her. Not really. He'd be a bad person to tie in with. He was obsessed with painting. Look at poor Wise Sister; she'd been working like two people and he'd never noticed. He got so caught up in his painting he was thoughtless of everyone else.

"I'm too selfish of a man to ever kiss a woman." Logan didn't look at her. He was afraid of what he'd see. Despite her anger, he knew she longed for there to be more between them. But despite that longing, she'd leave. It wouldn't take much for him to be on his knees begging her to stay. "I—I shouldn't have done that. It's dishonorable to give you hope there could be something between us."

"I have no such *hopes*."

The anger in her voice made him look.

"My *hope* is to get out of here." She glared, that wonderful expressiveness, those blazing eyes, that perfect, silken skin. He'd never seen anything more beautiful, and while he drank her in, he saw her hand tightened on the knife. "If you think I'm *hoping* you'll decide I'm *worthy* of the great artist—"

"I know you're leaving," he cut her off. Logan was tempted to smile, but mindful of the knife and her temper, he didn't. He loved her spirit, her strength, even her honest disparagement. At least he could trust her to say exactly what she thought. But he thought it was fair to at least fight for her good opinion of him. "That day you went over the cliff, you were dressed like a man."

She didn't stab him, so he continued. "That's what you like. That's how you're happy."

She arched her brows, as if surprised he knew that and accepted it.

"That's odd behavior for a woman, but I find I like it well enough. It makes sense to me that you'd dress in a way that's comfortable and, even more importantly, safe."

"My thinking exactly." Sally sniffed and turned her knife back to working on her crutch.

He knew it would soon be done. Then she'd either walk out of here or her family would show up and take her away. Whichever happened, the end was the same. The prettiest, most fascinating woman he'd ever known would be gone.

What's more, he didn't want her to stay. He knew himself well enough to know that she'd come to hate him. The sun would be coming up, or setting, and the land would be ablaze with violet light or a crimson glow, and he'd ignore her and race against the movement of the sun and the fading of the day to catch the color and depth of it.

She didn't have much respect for him, but she didn't hate him. If she stayed, if he begged her and cajoled her and made promises that might be beyond his ability to keep, she might be persuaded. A few more moments in his arms and all the pretty words a man could say, and he might catch himself a wife. But she'd end up hating him. The very thought broke his heart.

"So, why can *you* be different, live to suit yourself, turn up your pretty little nose at conventions and I can't?" Logan quit talking and waited.

She set her knife on the table. "It's different, what I do."

"How?" He set his own knife aside.

"What I do makes *sense*. I may be different but I'm practical. I dress like this to get my work done."

"So, I live out here and paint because that's *my*

193

work. I don't see how you can disdain what I do while you go around doing exactly as you wish, even though it's not a bit normal."

Glaring as if she could burn a hole straight through him, Sally sat, her jaw clenched into a tight, straight line. At last she leaned back in her chair and relaxed. "I suppose that's fair. Though I don't see how drawing your pictures puts food on the table. I help take care of my family. You do nothing but draw."

"You said you have a sister who's a doctor, right?"

A smile curved Sally's lips, and Logan could see how fond she was of her family. "Beth's a doctor, that's right."

"Well, how does doctoring put food on the table? Does she go hunting after her workday is done?"

"They buy food at the general store."

"I buy food with the money I earn painting."

"No, you don't. You make Wise Sister go hunt it for you."

"But I pay her to handle that. If she's working too hard, I didn't realize it, and she's never come out and said it's too much for her. I can fix that. I can help her more or hire someone else to help her. But hiring her is the same as your sister, Beth, and her husband going to the general store."

Sally stared at him. Then her eyes went to the

194

picture he was painting of her and slid on past it to *Blazing Land*. "You think you'll find someone to pay you money for that picture of me?"

Logan would never part with this one, not for any amount of money, but he decided not to tell Sally that. "I've found a good, steady market for Western art back East. I'll load my work onto my packhorses in the fall, before the winter closes down on me, take the train back to New York, spend the winter painting from my sketches and my memory, and sell the finished works. I'll make enough to come back next summer."

"And that's it? For your whole life? No family, no children?"

The thought of no family and children, while pretty Sally sat there, was an ache in his chest. "This is my calling. I feel it as if God had carved it into a stone tablet." He looked out the wide-open windows and saw the herd of elk, *his* herd of elk, wander out of a draw about a hundred yards away. "And I'm—I'm self-centered. You've convinced me of that. I'd make a bad husband, a worse father, because if the light was right, and the clouds were a perfect shade of red, I'd pick up my paints and work."

He thought of how he'd been able to ignore his father. Logan could never have been a doctor, he knew that, but that didn't mean he had to be disrespectful of his father's wishes and wisdom. "I'd pick my art over my family every time. God

195

may judge me for a sinner, but He also gave me this passion, this burning need to put the world on canvas."

"You could be less selfish. You could put the sin aside and live a better way and still paint."

"I can't." Logan studied the bull elk as if he held the meaning of life. "I've known myself long enough to know I can't."

The young upstart in the herd lowered his antlers and pawed the ground, and the bull turned to face the challenge yet again.

Seeing the elk pulled Logan's attention to the table in the corner. Yet another type of art he was attempting. He stepped toward the object covered with a wet towel.

"Can't or won't?"

Her voice stopped him and made him realize that once again his art had come before someone's needs. She sounded sad, which made him want to comfort her, and that reminded him of their kiss. She had a right to believe he wouldn't be kissing her if he couldn't have an honorable interest in her. And he'd just admitted he didn't.

"Can't or won't, in the end, the result is the same, Sally. A wife would end up being hurt. That's reason enough to never take one." To take his mind off the unruly image of Sally being his wife, he strode to the table and lifted the damp cloth to reveal an elk, fashioned out of clay. The animal stood proud, its chest out, its antlered head tilted nose up, mouth open, bugling to the sky.

Logan had found clay along a riverbed last year, so this winter he'd studied with a sculptor in New York and had come to love the touch of the clay on his hands. He studied the statue, nearly a foot tall, including the elaborate antlers, then went back to studying his living subject out the window. The bull and his young adversary circling each other. Sparring, charging, angry, violent. Logan wanted to capture it all.

A slow, quiet sigh pulled his attention away from the elk. And he lost all interest in the struggle of the two strong male creatures and turned to something a hundred times more interesting.

Sally.

Their eyes met and that kiss was between them like a living, breathing, burning thing.

"I reckon then," Sally said after far too long, her voice unsteady, "you'd better not kiss me again. You'd better stay away from me."

Logan nodded and moved closer to her. "You're right."

Their eyes held. The moment stretched.

Reminding himself that art was truth and he needed to be as honest in his life as in his art, Logan said, "I think I probably will kiss you again, Buckskin Angel."

His determination to stay away battled the force of his attraction and made him think of the mountains, made of stone, and the fact that they weren't all that solid. In fact, there were avalanches all the time. "I'm not sure if I *can* stay away from you."

Shaking her head, Sally turned her attention to the elk statue. "You made that, too?"

"Yes." Logan heaved a sigh of relief at the new subject. "I've been studying sculpture. I wanted to try and get all the sides of a subject instead of the flatness of painting."

"So it dries and you haul it back to New York, too? It's made of clay, isn't it? That isn't very strong, especially not the antlers. You'll never get it all that way on a train without breaking it."

Logan nodded. "Probably not, but I'm going to coat it in plaster to take it home. Then when I get there, I'll cut the plaster away from the clay and have a perfect mold of my statue. I'll cast that mold in bronze and have something that will last forever."

"Plaster? You have plaster here?" Sally sat up straighter.

"I brought some because I knew I wanted to attempt this."

"Where is it?"

Logan pointed to a chest near the back of the cabin.

"We can make a cast for my leg with that. My

sister did that when a patient had a broken bone. It'll be sturdier than this leather boot, and I can ride a horse more easily. With a plaster cast on my leg, I can get out of here."

She sounded so excited, Logan's heart sank. Of course she wanted out of here. She wanted to be on her way. She wanted to find her family and get on with her life.

He wanted that for her, too. But it made him sad that she sounded so excited. In fact, it made him more than sad. It made him a little angry. He was tempted to refuse her the use of the plaster. She only needed to stay a bit longer. Another week or two and her leg would probably be fully healed.

Besides, he wasn't done painting her yet. He wasn't done kissing her either.

Wise Sister picked that moment to come home.

Logan smiled to think that the old woman had just saved Sally from finding out all the things Logan wasn't done with.

Thirteen

Wise Sister came into sight through Logan's oversized windows and saved Sally from wiping that smug smile off Logan's face with her fist.

Wise Sister moved quietly, smoothly, with no apparent haste, but she was a woman who got things done. She'd left this morning, probably before dawn, and now here she was back with a haunch of venison over her shoulder.

Sally couldn't wait to hear what had happened. She stood, grabbing her crutch.

"Stay put. You'll fall." Logan stepped away from his sculpture toward his stupid painting that looked nothing like her. Well, truly it did look like her, except for that empty-headed expression on her face.

"I'm fine. Go back to your picture." Sally, slowly, experimenting with the pain and the balance, moved to the door. The crutch, tucked under her right arm, worked well to substitute for her broken right ankle. She'd have her hands full getting on and off a horse, but she could manage.

Somehow.

She might need to make a second crutch. Rig a strap to them to hang over the saddle horn. And she'd helped Beth once plaster a broken arm, so she knew how to do that, too. Two crutches and a plaster cast and she was on her way.

She wondered where in the world she was and how to get to Mandy's from here or find Luther from here. The thought of Mandy picked up the pace of Sally's heart. She felt a growing desperation to get to her sister. Or maybe to get away from Logan, she couldn't be sure, but the result gave her both: distance from the painter and her sharpshooting sister at her back.

She thought of Logan's warm kisses and her own odd expression in that painting and did her best to think about everything except here. She swung the door open just as Wise Sister came up to the cabin. "Did you see anyone?"

"I found tracks. Two groups. Four men. Much hunting." Her dark eyes gleamed. Sally felt like she knew this woman right down to the bone and she adored her. Smart, strong, quiet. A woman molded by the brutal West and thriving.

"Much hunting for you, Sally girl." Wise Sister didn't come inside. She headed for a stump near the house, stained rust brown from blood. With little noticeable exertion, she heaved the haunch onto the stump with a dull thud.

Sally didn't bother asking why Wise Sister thought they searched for her. She trusted Wise Sister's instincts. "Tell me about the men." She followed Wise Sister the few feet to her butchering block.

"I saw no one." Wise Sister produced a knife from a sheath on her waist.

Sally heard movement behind her and knew Logan had left his precious painting to listen to the talk. She did her best not to sniff at him—the pig who had kissed her and made her feel things then so politely told her he couldn't do her the enormous favor of keeping her as his queen in a fool's kingdom.

"Tell me." Sally watched Wise Sister sharpen

her knife with a little round stone that lay beside the stump.

With the scratch of metal on rock, Wise Sister spoke. "One group searches widely, the other wisely. The first, coyotes; the second, wolves." Wise Sister looked up with a smile as sharp as her knife. "I left sign for the wolves."

Sally smiled back.

"What's this talk of coyotes and wolves?" Logan asked, coming up beside her. Too close.

She was tempted to jam her elbow into his stomach. "Luther's close. Wise Sister left a trail for him to follow. It'll lead him here."

"Not a trail." Wise Sister shook her head firmly. "I feared the coyotes would find it. Even coyotes know the woods. But I let them know you lived. To keep searching. That *we* know they're hunting. Your wolves left markers, good, not easy to find. They weren't for me. So they must believe others come."

Nodding, Sally said, "Maybe. The people with me, the colonel and his wife, were important folks. Someone will come hunting. Luther is leaving a trail for those folks to follow." The smile was impossible to contain. Luther was close. She knew it. She fought off a horrifying urge to start leaking salt water. "How long until they're here?"

"Sally, Wise Sister said she didn't leave a trail." He patted her on the arm in sympathy.

The obvious had once again made its way out of Logan's mouth. Luther was going to find the man very annoying.

"Soon." Wise Sister ignored Logan. "They'll find their way."

"And the coyotes?" Sally knew Luther might be pressed to get here before the men who were searching for her.

Wise Sister frowned and told the straight, uncomfortable truth. She tapped her chest with her knife. "I was careful with the sign I left, but coyotes are wily. They may come, too. Even first."

A little shiver of fear ran up Sally's spine. "We'll need a lookout, day and night."

"I've hunted coyotes before." Wise Sister turned to her task and began skinning dinner.

"So have I," Sally said with grim determination. "I've got my Winchester."

"We can't shoot any coyotes or wolves this close to the cabin." Logan gave a firm nod of his head.

Sally pulled her own knife with relish. She raised it just enough to get his attention. Then, after his eyes had widened with alarm, she hobbled over to help Wise Sister.

"Maybe I'll thank that little cowpoke before I shoot him." Fergus stretched his legs out by their fire, enjoying the night and the campfire and the stars overhead.

"Don't know where he got to, but sure enough he hasn't gotten away." Tulsa poured a cup of coal black brew into his tin cup.

Fergus loved the wild land. Having someone to hunt up here was a pure pleasure. "We'll keep our eyes open and prowl around. Maybe I oughta build a cabin up here. Government threw me out of Yellowstone. Maybe they'll keep their paws offa me up here." The scalding coffee burned Fergus's tongue, but nothing could lessen his pleasure. A stick broke in the fire and sparks shot skyward, scenting the air with wood smoke. "I reckon I've been living in the high-up country for forty years now, Tulsa. Reckon I'll die here, rich on stupid travelers and fat elk. It's a good life."

Mountains loomed above them, the white caps dazzling in the summer sun. Quaking aspen shivered and twirled their leaves between the lodgepole pine and heavy underbrush. A man could get mighty lost up in this land. But time to time, Fergus had needed to get lost. So he'd come here, knowing well how to live until it was safe to get himself found.

"I ever tell you I had another brother, Tulsa?" Fergus was in a mood to spin a yarn, and thinking of these rough mountains made him think of Curly, and that led to wandering inside his head until he came to his boyhood.

"Cain't say you have. I've got me a coupl'a

sisters and a little brother myself. No idea if they're alive or dead. You know where your brother is?"

"Nope. Haven't seen my baby brother in the whole forty years I been up here. He was a lot younger." Fergus's memories soured as he thought of the drunken old man who'd married his ma the year before he and Curly had left. He'd had a heavy hand with Fergus's ma and wasn't against turning his fists on her boys. Fergus remembered well the day he'd finally gotten old enough and mean enough to make the old man back down.

"The man, Reynold was his name." Fergus shook his head. "He was kin to my real pa. He had the same white stripe in his hair that Curly and I have. Called it the family mark. Different last name though. He tended a saloon and helped himself to the whiskey. Moved around a lot because he'd get fired." Fergus had put himself between the old brute and Curly all the time and taken what beatings he could to protect his little brother. He'd done his best with his ma, too.

"Came a day when Reynold couldn't push me around anymore. He was giving my ma a thrashing and I stepped in, got in a lucky hit that put my ever-loving daddy onto his knees and ended up stomping the old man into the ground."

"Did your ma finally feel safe from him? Did

you throw him out?" Tulsa leaned forward and lazily refilled his cup.

"Nope, I got thrown out instead."

Tulsa froze with his coffee half poured, and the flowing liquid overflowed the cup, streaming onto Tulsa's leg. With a shout of pain, he dropped the pot and cup and jumped up to swat at his leg. The pot landed bottom side down. The coffee was spared, so Fergus made no mind of Tulsa's dancing.

Finally the man settled down and looked at Fergus. "Your ma tossed you out?" A cynical frown curved Tulsa's lips down.

Fergus knew Tulsa had a real good idea of how it'd been for Fergus and Curly. Fergus wondered what had happened to the baby Ma had just borne when Fergus had lit out. He'd always felt bad leaving the little one to his scared ma and brutal pa.

"Yep, Ma gave Curly 'n' me the egg money and told us Reynold would kill us if we were there when he woke up."

"Why didn't she go with you?"

"Scared he'd catch us, maybe." Fergus caught at the streak of white on his temple. "Ma used to talk about my real pa some. She said there was family, and if we could find them they'd take us in. Said there was family pride in sticking up for each other. Don't see how that's true. If my pa and Reynold were kin, then it seems like not beating on your children would be part of sticking with your family."

Shrugging, Fergus added, "Ma made my pa's family sound like good folks. Couldn't tell it by Reynold, though. I use his name as an alias. I like the idea of being an outlaw with that man's name. Hope I leave some dirt on it."

Tulsa grunted and reached for the coffeepot.

"So Reynold wasn't interested in whether we lived or died. Ma liked a man around and had her some trouble finding one. Ma wasn't a woman to be any better'n she oughta be, so decent men weren't interested."

"My ma neither." Tulsa poured more coffee and settled in again, ignoring the splash of wet on his thigh.

"I was sixteen. Curly was twelve but getting tall, and he could do the work of a man. We took out. I managed to steal a couple of horses and we rode west. We found a wagon train and signed on to work for a coupl'a families. Ended up in Denver and then headed into the mountains with an old trapper. Trapped when the trapping was good, stole a payroll and a horse when times were lean. When I found Yellowstone and saw all the people coming in, not wise in the ways of these mountains, I knew it was my own private gold mine."

That's when he and Curly had teamed up with Tulsa, younger than Fergus by a dozen years or so. Letting Tulsa join up with him and Curly was like having a little brother. Fergus ran his hand into his gray hair with the white stripe. The years were gone. His life more over than not. He sighed and wondered again about that baby.

"Always hoped that brute, Reynold, was nicer to his own child than he was to Curly and me. I've had an urge to go back, see if the baby needed saving. But it's a long way and that baby is a grown man now, and it's too late to change a thing." For all the sinning Fergus had done in his life, that was the sin that gnawed at his guts. Picturing that baby growing up with those heavy fists flailing at him. He'd protected Curly, but he'd left that baby behind to the wolves.

Fergus's yarn was spun and he felt the worse for having talked about it, so he turned his attention to what was in front of them. "I want that cowpoke dead. This is a good life. The livin' is easy. I don't want trouble on my back trail whether I stay here or go." And that long ago memory of his ma telling him the family stuck together, a family Fergus had never known, helped make him hungry for revenge against that cowpoke that had escaped while Curly had died.

Tulsa nodded and pulled his gun to check that it was fully loaded. "A good life for sure. We gotta make sure that cowpoke and whoever is takin' care of him are dead."

Fergus's family stuck together. Or so he'd been

told. So he'd stick with hunting the cowpoke for Curly's sake, and he'd stick with silencing a witness for his own.

When this was over, he'd still rule over this land—his own personal gold mine.

And that cowpoke would be dead.

Fourteen

Sally's alive." Luther straightened from the little pile of stones weighing down the leather. The leather had the McClellen ranch brand marked clear, newly cut. The stack of stones had obviously been deliberately left as a marker. "This is off her boot."

He looked up in time to catch a blurry wash over Buff's eyes, almost as if the man was ready to cry. Luther would have made fun of the old coot if he could speak past the lump in his throat. "This is Shoshone sign." Luther looked into an impassable pile of rocks at the base of a mountain. "Sally, or whoever left this, must know there are bad men searching for her because there's no effort to point us toward a trail."

"So where is she?" Buff asked.

Luther studied Clay McClellen's brand on a piece of leather. Only Sally would have known someone would come looking and understand what that meant. "Shoshone markings." Luther pointed to a few other cuts in the leather. "Makes sense that if someone carried her off, it'd be an Indian, a Shoshone. Them and the Nez Percé are almost the only ones left hereabouts."

"I heard they'd driven the tribes off Yellowstone. They might've come up here." Buff stared at the mountains around them. "I did a fair sight of trapping in Yellowstone in the early days, before we was saddle partners, Luth. Figures there might be some native folks in these hills."

"The rain wiped out the trail the same day we found it. But that first day we saw that someone rode away carryin' a load. Maybe Sally riding double with someone." Luther thought of the men they now followed and itched to face them. Two against two, even odds. He'd have done it, but he wasn't interested in arresting them and hauling them to jail a hundred miles away. And he didn't see any point in a shootout that would risk their lives and not bring them one step closer to Sally. So instead they'd dogged the other men. Luther hoped he'd find a sign of Sally first. And, if he didn't, Luther and Buff would be on hand to protect her.

"The marker was set up by a solid wall of rock with nothing to give us a direction. But it was left by a knowin' hand. Someone afraid the outlaws would see it first. So there's no clue to what direction to ride. We'll have us a time tracking our girl down. But maybe whoever was helping her will come again."

"And in the meantime, we'll hunt." Buff reached out and took the bit of leather from Luther's hand and stared at it a long time.

"See anything there that'll give us a direction to hunt?"

"Wise Sister." Buff closed his fist on the leather.

"What?"

Buff shook his head.

Waiting a minute, Luther decided his friend had no more to say. No surprise there. "Let's see if we can pick up a trail from whoever left it there." Luther looked at the wall of rock looming over that marker. "Could they be up in the highlands?"

"Don't see how." Buff's hand clutched at that leather as if he had to hold on to save his life. "There's no way up. Anyway, you'd be an idiot to climb up onto the top of a mountain."

"What kind of idiot builds his house at the top of a mountain?" Mandy was purely perturbed, and considering her earlier decision to stop restraining herself and let Sidney handle the real her as best he could, she would have asked her husband that to his face if she didn't have two sleeping babies on the ground beside her while she sighted her gun on a mule deer.

It was a long shot, but Mandy had to take it. This was the spot her girls had chosen to nap and she couldn't leave them to slip closer. And their cabin was right on the tree line. The new house would be well above it. So her idiot husband had chosen her hunting grounds for her. She couldn't quite bring herself to be grateful for his love of that mountaintop mansion.

The shot was five hundred yards. Worst part was she'd wake the babies up when she took the shot. No, worst part was she was doing her best to hide behind some rocks waiting for some game to wander close. Normally, she'd have stretched out on her stomach and gotten comfortable while she waited. She knew how to be patient when she stalked game. But these days, her round stomach was in the way.

The wee one inside of her gave her a kick and she smiled, looking forward to meeting the little tyke. A boy, she thought, just because it was time. Her ma was living proof that a woman could have long strings of one then the other, so she didn't put too much stock in any notion of it being time.

The deer moved a bit closer as it grazed. Then it lifted its head, maybe catching a scent of her, but she was downwind, though the wind up this high sometimes swirled around, defying a true direction. More likely there was something else in the woods bothering it. Even a bird taking flight or a raccoon too close at hand would startle a deer. Whatever the reason, the timid critter wasn't going to get any closer.

Mandy drew in a long, slow breath and steadied the gun on her shoulder, feeling her nerves cool. Her vision sharpened, her hands steadied, her blood chilled. Her finger tightened on the trigger. She released the breath halfway, then held it and took the shot.

Catherine and Angela jumped and woke up squalling.

The deer slumped to the ground.

She now had supper. And two crying babies.

With a sigh, she calmed her daughters, hung her rifle in place across her back, and then rigged Catherine on top of the rifle. She took Angela's hand and walked to the horse, tied back a ways.

Tom Linscott.

She caught herself thinking about him every time she got near a horse.

As she led the horse to the deer, she reminded herself that it was not *Tom* she thought of. She did her best not to think about him. It was that sturdy little foal and his massive, handsome stallion.

Tom?

No, nothing about him was proper to think about.

As she hung the deer and bled and gutted it, then slung it over the horse's shoulders, Mandy had plenty of time to wonder how Belle Tanner had fared with the foal she'd gotten out of Tom's stallion. But that wasn't thinking about Tom.

She slung the deer over the horse's shoulders. Next she settled Angela on the saddle, swung up behind the cantle with Catherine on her back, and made her way home. She wondered how Belle's mare had handled the long walk home over the rugged trail to the Harden ranch. Had Tom gone to visit the little foal? Had he approved of the care Mandy had taken of it that winter? It was the foal's health that was her real focus.

That had nothing to do with Tom.

Mandy prepared a huge stew that would feed even all of Sidney's workmen for a couple of days. And imagined the powerful muscles and sleek beauty of that magnificent stallion Tom had ridden.

But she didn't really wonder about *Tom*. Nothing there to wonder about.

With Catherine strapped on her back and Angela clinging to her skirts, Mandy finished preparing supper. When her stew was thick with venison and her garden vegetables, she set it to simmering, and the warm, savory smell of meat and onions began to fill the cabin. Then she went back to work finishing the deer.

It did cross her mind to try and figure when Tom would come. Would it be before or after the baby was delivered—a time fast approaching. Wondering about company wasn't the same as wondering about a man.

Returning to the butcher block outside, she lifted her razor-sharp cleaver just as Cooter, the younger of Sidney's bodyguards, came walking alone down the slope from the mansion site.

A chill ran up Mandy's spine. She took one quick glance then paid rapt attention to the work in front of her. Mandy had felt Cord Cooter's eyes on her many times. But both guards stayed close to Sidney. That was their job. So what was Cooter doing down here when Sidney might need his body guarded up by the big house?

Cooter was about Mandy's age, dark hair with a strange streak of white at one temple. He had reddish skin and lips that were too full. His eyes were a cold blue and they didn't miss much. The man had never spoken to her. He'd never come close to touching her. He'd never done a thing that could give Mandy an excuse to ask Sidney to fire him. But Mandy trusted her instincts, and she didn't like this man. He showed what kind of snake he was without saying a word.

Cooter went to the door of the bunkhouse. Then, as he grasped the handle, he turned and looked square at Mandy. Their eyes met and held. The chill in her spine turned to ice. A mean smile curved Cooter's lips. He caught the brim of his Stetson and tugged it, a greeting. But it felt more like a threat.

God protect me.

God protect me.

God protect me.

Cooter went inside.

Mandy turned back to her butchering and felt the ice flowing through her veins. So cold. And the cold went deep. It threatened to take over and rule her. Could a woman that cold love her children properly?

God protect me.

A squeal at her feet turned her attention. Mandy looked down at little Angela, clinging to her skirt, only a foot or so away from the lethal cleaver.

"Mama!" The little sweetie seemed to think she could help.

"You're a little young for meat cleavers, Angie." Mandy smiled and her heart warmed again. She had so much in her life. Yes, Sidney was a nuisance and a disappointment, but her children were wonderful. She noticed at that moment the wet spot on her neck. Catherine had dozed off. When that happened, she rested her baby-soft cheek on the back of Mandy's neck and often drooled in her sleep.

Carrying Catherine on her back, which she did a lot, had taught Mandy to sling her rifle differently, lower, so the hard length wasn't in

Catherine's way. The gun was slower to get into action with it that way, but Mandy hadn't needed to be fast in a while. She still needed to be accurate though.

Angela stood on tiptoes, reached, stretching her little body as much as possible, and screamed. "Mama. Mama hep. Andie hep Mama." Angie's voice rose as she tried to grab the knife, only missing by about two feet.

"Help . . ."

Smiling, Mandy knew she might not get much help from her husband, but before long her girls would be help. With a sigh at the high-pitched screaming, Mandy knew no one's life was perfect.

"Andie help, Mamamama!"

Mandy called her Angie and Angie called herself a slurred version of that. Today it sounded like "Andie."

With some ragged exceptions, her life was wonderful. She thought of how hard it had been hunting this deer, then carrying it home and the work of butchering. Luther usually did this. Mandy wondered where he'd gotten to and where Sally was.

God protect me.

God protect them.

"Mamamamamamama!" Angie bounced and screamed just as a hand landed hard on Mandy's shoulder.

She spun around with an indrawn breath so hard it became an inverted scream. One hand went to her rifle and jerked it forward. She clutched the cleaver in the other, which was a mistake if she needed to aim and fire. Her nerves iced over.

"Don't shoot, Mrs. Gray." Cooter put up both hands with a smile that didn't reach his eyes. He took a quick step back, but it was too small a step and well he knew it. He still stood too close.

Mandy didn't level the gun, but she had it in hand, the muzzle pointed toward the ground, her finger on the trigger. The cleaver she held high enough to keep it from Angie. If it seemed to Cooter like she was threatening him with it, well, that suited her just fine.

"Did you . . ." Mandy's voice shook with the cold, not fear. She cut off the words and drew in a long, slow, steadying breath as she got control of herself. "Did you need something?"

She had only to look in his eyes to know he'd deliberately put his hands on her. Angie had fallen silent as if she'd been frightened by this man. That was something Mandy took very seriously.

He'd touched her knowing she'd hate it. He'd scared her child. She felt a sudden, clawing desire to lift her rifle and pull the trigger. It shocked her so much that her nerves went even colder and she no longer felt anything but calm determination that this man would never come near her again.

"I was going to offer to butcher that deer for you, Mrs. Gray." The offer was a decent thing. But his eyes crawled over her like insects.

"I'm fine, Mr. Cooter. A person who lives in a wild land gets in the habit of pointing a gun fast. I will tell you clearly that I don't want your hands on me. I won't warn you again."

"Is that a threat, Mrs. Gray?" He licked his flaccid lips as if he liked the taste of something. His blue eyes had no lashes and seemed rimmed with pink. His brows were dark and heavy. Showing below his hat, she saw that streak of white in his hair that seemed to emphasize a coldness in the man so deep and wide it left frost on the outside. "You'll complain to your husband that I offered to help with some heavy work?"

That is exactly how it would sound to Sidney. Cooter offered to help, and Mandy caused trouble with her unladylike ways.

"I make no threats, Mr. Cooter. I tell you clearly to stay well away from me. How my husband feels about that doesn't come into it because I handle my troubles myself."

Their eyes held. Hers determined and clear and cold. His hungry and cruel.

After too many seconds of silence, Angie caught hold of Mandy's skirt. "Mama, Andie hep." Her daughter made a grab for the cleaver.

"If you'll head on now, Mr. Cooter, I need to get back to work and I'm sure you have work elsewhere, too."

Cooter stared a few seconds longer. Then a scornful smile quirked his lips. He tugged on his hat brim, pulling it low enough to cover the white, then turned to walk back up the hill.

Mandy never took her eyes off of him.

"I'd be glad to help you anytime you want, Mrs. Gray," he called over his shoulder. Then just as he stepped onto a trail that would twist upward and take him out of her sight, he turned back. "Day . . . or night . . ." He paused for too long. "You come to me if you ever need a *real man*." He stressed those words ever so slightly as his eyes crawled over her again, his insulting intent clear. "I'll be . . . watching . . . waiting for you."

The contempt was clear. Contempt for Sidney, as if he wasn't a real man. Contempt for her, as if she'd turn to another man for what his eyes insinuated.

The worst of it was Cooter had never acted like this before. She'd always known he was a dangerous man, but he'd acted loyal to Sidney from the first. He was showing this side of himself because Luther was gone. Was he the one who'd been prowling around the cabin at night, thinking he could find something in their cabin that would give him access to Sidney's gold, stashed in a vault in Denver?

A dishonest man might have many reasons for threatening a woman whose husband was defenseless. Sidney hiring bodyguards announced to the world he couldn't take care of himself and his family.

But what Cooter didn't know was that *Mandy* wasn't defenseless. She wasn't a woman to cower. Her hand reached down and clutched the muzzle of her trusty rifle.

She'd never shot a man. Never come close. Never drawn a bead on a human being and known she might have to make that choice. A bitter cold place in her heart knew she could do it. She took no pride in knowing it, but she did. She'd never be a helpless maiden in need of rescue by some big, strong man.

And then Mandy thought of Tom Linscott again. This time she didn't even pretend that she wasn't thinking of that strong, kindhearted man. Tom would use his fists on any man who treated a woman like Cooter had just treated her. He'd do worse if needed.

So would Pa.

So would Luther.

And Mandy stood here uncertain if Sidney would even *fire* Cooter. Unless Sidney thought Cooter was a threat to Sidney's gold.

The way to get rid of Cooter was to tell Sidney his money was in danger. That he'd take seriously. Something died inside her to know that—to get Cooter off this property—tonight she'd tell Sidney exactly that. And that might well force Cooter's hand and turn him from sly and threatening to a blatant danger.

Another interesting question: was he in league with Platte or not? If it came to shooting trouble, would Platte side with the Grays or with Cooter?

Mandy pictured Cord Cooter's dangerous, piggish eyes. Her skin crawled as she thought of his hard hand on her shoulder. She remembered his full lips moving as if they wanted to eat her up.

Not telling Sidney meant keeping a deadly dangerous man in their midst.

Telling Sidney might well tear this mountain-side wide open.

Fifteen

We need to cut strips of cloth." Sally tried to remember all Beth had done. "Then dip the cloths into the plaster until they're coated. Then wrap the strips around my leg."

The harsh rip of cloth pulled Sally's eyes around to see Wise Sister at work turning a pile of what looked to be old shirts into strips. Babineau's maybe?

Logan brought a bowl over. "I know how to mix it so it will set up solid. It should be the same as I'd use to mold my clay sculptures, right?"

"Makes sense, I reckon." Sally tried to be calm as she thought about unbinding her leg. It still hurt something fierce, although she could recall the first day she'd been hurt and knew it was much improved.

Logan kept his eyes respectfully on his work, carefully preparing the plaster and not looking at her leg. By the time he was done, Wise Sister had a small mountain of cloth. She gently removed the leather brace and unwound the cloth holding the splint in place.

"Much better." Wise Sister slipped off Sally's sock and ran a hand over a small swollen spot close to her ankle. "The break is right here."

Sally looked up to see Logan studying her leg, bare to the knee.

Wise Sister elbowed him in the stomach.

He jumped and quickly turned back to his plaster.

"I—I—uh—remember Beth wrapped the ankle in something before she put on the plaster, to protect the skin." Sally hadn't done much doctoring for her family. Beth had always stepped forward to do it, and Sally had been glad to avoid the chore. Being gentle wasn't really her way of handling things. She preferred a bullwhip.

Wise Sister got a clean sock and, with tender care, covered Sally's leg. It helped Sally feel less disturbed by Logan's touch. "You, soak the cloth." Wise Sister thrust the stack of fabric at Logan.

Sally was relieved that Logan wouldn't be allowed to touch her. Logan's touch had proved to be extremely unsettling.

When the first strip was soaked with the sticky white goo, Wise Sister took it and pressed it against Sally's stocking-covered leg. The damp cloth soaked through the sock and tickled. Then it downright itched. Reaching for her ankle, Sally's fingernails touched the cloth.

"Don't touch." Wise Sister slapped her hand with a scolding look that made Sally feel like a misbehaving five-year-old. "Don't move."

It was then that Sally remembered thinking disparaging thoughts of Logan when he'd sheepishly admitted he was scared of Wise Sister. Looking up, she caught his eye and he gave her a look that clearly said, "You see what I mean?"

It was all Sally could do not to laugh. But that would almost certainly qualify as moving, and she didn't want to be chastised again so she resisted the temptation. "Tell me more about Yellowstone, Logan. Or painting, or something before this soggy stuff makes me crazy." Sally looked at him, prepared to beg. But she instantly saw that she'd asked the perfect question.

His hands were busy pulling strips of cloth out of the plaster so he was trapped there just as surely as Sally and Wise Sister. "I first decided to come out here when I saw a painting by Thomas Moran. He came out with a group called the Hayden Expedition in 1871 and he made sketches and watercolors of all the beautiful, mysterious sights in what is now Yellowstone. I saw a lot of them as a boy, and it was just crystal clear instantly that I had to come."

Smiling, Sally said, "Like I wanted to be a cowboy right from the first."

"I suppose it's just like that." Logan handed over a strip without Wise Sister having to ask.

They were working like a team now. Wise Sister winding, Logan holding the strips, Sally being still. She suspected her job was the hardest of the three.

"I could hardly believe the stories I heard about the place, geysers and boiling mud. Ponds that changed colors and were hot right out of the ground."

"I have a little trouble believing in it now," Sally said quietly.

"My paintings of Yellowstone all got shipped back East already. I'd love for you to see them. I have some sketches I'll show you later."

"I'd like that."

"Moran's painting made the place so alive for me, and it made me almost crazy to see it and paint it myself."

"Almost crazy?" Sally made sure to smile when she said it.

Logan took her teasing with good grace. "It was more than just Yellowstone. It was the way Moran gave the whole world a look at something they could probably never hope to see. Until he came back from this expedition, there were reports of the wonders of the place, but a lot of people didn't even believe it, it was so outlandish."

"And you realized you could teach people with your painting. Open the world up for them."

Logan jerked his chin up and looked at her. His eyes blazed. "Yes, exactly. I could go, just me, and bring it back for everyone. It's more than just loving to paint. There are beautiful places back East. It's about sharing something rare and wonderful."

Logan handed over another strip then looked at her, and their eyes locked. The gaze shared something rare and wonderful. It changed Sally inside. Hardened and bound them together as surely as the plaster hardened around her leg. She knew this was wrong, wanting to learn more about Logan, wanting to feel more about Logan. But it couldn't be stopped. It could only be ignored. She had to get to Mandy, help her big sister. She had to and she would. But it wasn't going to be easy.

A grunt from Wise Sister broke the connection, and Logan quickly fumbled for a strip of plaster-soaked cloth and handed it over.

"Tell me more." Sally didn't want it to end, this tie that bound her to this man.

He talked but he didn't look, as if he knew that there was still time, that they weren't firmly encased in whatever wrapped around them. And he would do nothing to further that and maybe trap himself with her.

But Sally knew, at least for her, it was too late. She didn't know if she was in love with Logan, but she knew she loved him. Maybe at this point she could tell herself that she loved him as God called each to love others as themselves. It was more than a dutiful, Christian love though. It was laden with admiration and respect. And longing.

That wasn't romance and marriage and a home. But it was very, very close, and she pulled back from the brink before she tumbled headlong into love with a man who'd already told her he'd make a terrible husband.

The next morning she awakened alone.

Wise Sister planned on scouting the lowlands again today.

The plaster was dried rock solid and Sally felt an almost desperate need to escape. While she could still call her heart her own. She could get out of here now, but Wise Sister scolded and said the leg needed more time.

Sally hadn't been able to force her wishes on anyone while she lay there flat on her back with

227

her leg encased in stone and propped up high on a stack of folded blankets.

She began her second crutch that day and had it done by nightfall, including two handy straps of leather so the crutches would hang from her saddle horn.

The next day she practiced moving around on her crutches, with the heavy cast dangling, and knew she had to get better at this before she struck out on her hunt for Luther. But she found herself able to do the cooking chores, and she even found some vegetables ripe in the garden.

"I said I'd do that." Logan fumed from where he crouched beside her in the potato patch.

"You admitted you didn't know a potato leaf from a weed. I can do this faster if you just leave me alone." Sally knew she was being unfair. She'd chastised Logan for not helping, and now that he wanted to, she was shooing him away because he didn't know how. Sally knew better than that. She'd taught Laurie and her little brothers to tend the garden. She was a hand at teaching. "Fine," she forced herself to say, when she wanted him to go away. "Get down here."

Logan dropped easily to his knees and Sally envied him his two functioning legs.

They worked companionably together for about an hour before Logan looked up at a cloud that cast a shadow over them. "Look at that." He stood, staring upward.

Sally couldn't control following his gaze. Dark clouds boiled overhead off to the west, moving fast. Billowy layers and layers of clouds pushing lighter, thinner clouds ahead of them.

"We'd better hurry."

"You're right." Sally reached for a weed just as Logan caught her around her waist and lifted her to her feet. "Stop. I need to—"

"I'm getting them." Logan handed her the crutches and grabbed the cloth sack of vegetables they'd gathered.

"No, I mean I need to hurry and finish." Sally was talking to Logan's fast retreating back.

"You can get back to the cabin, right?" Logan didn't even look behind her. He was watching those approaching clouds. "You got out here alone. I'll miss it."

Get back? Sally opened her mouth to call after him, "Miss what?"

Logan dashed off and vanished into his cabin.

Sally shook her head to clear it of his strange behavior. Was he afraid of storms? Maybe he'd been scared by a thunderbolt as a child. The storm was coming but not that fast. Still, she might as well head in. She was halfway to the cabin when Logan reappeared with—of course—

Sally did her best not to groan out loud.

His paint.

"God, have mercy," Sally spoke to the building clouds. She'd never spent much time thinking clouds were beautiful, though they were of course, but clouds were God's way of warning people of an approaching storm. They weren't a call to start drawing. They were a call to close the windows and use common sense to come in before it rained.

She moved on to the cabin, practicing with her crutches, planning on starting a meal with those vegetables. She stopped. Her eyes were drawn to Logan as his arm slashed across the canvas—the intensity of his expression, the passion of his movements. The fixation on the boiling, advancing storm was like music.

Drawn closer, she knew he hadn't even noticed her. This is what he'd been talking about when he said he'd neglect a wife and children.

Dark gray splashed across white canvas. The violence and danger of the storm was there. Sally could feel it moving, threatening, as surely as the clouds did. She wondered if a man had this kind of gift and this powerful calling from God, could a woman maybe, just maybe, rejoice in that? Embrace all that was different about her life? If that man turned all that power and passion on a woman, could she live with the problems that came with a man obsessed with art?

It was like ripping away her skin to pull her gaze from Logan's work, but she did it. Forced herself to do it. Turning to the cabin, she thought of practical things like supper and learning how to walk on crutches.

With one tiny movement, she caressed the beads along the collar of the doeskin dress. Then she ran her hand over the seam where she'd hidden the tiny ribbon. She wouldn't have to hide that ribbon any longer if she stayed here. Logan wouldn't expect her to be boyish in her dress. Logan thought she was beautiful in anything she wore. The intensity of his art was there when he was drawing her, too.

Going soon was essential or she very much feared she'd never be able to go at all.

Wise Sister scolded her into staying home, and another week crawled by.

The only surprising fact was that Sally kept from strangling someone. "Let me ride out with you tomorrow." Sally and Wise Sister had retired to Wise Sister's cabin to sleep. Sally cared for the cabin while Wise Sister did her sneaking around.

Logan painted.

"Can't sneak. Broke leg." Wise Sister prepared for bed quickly and lay down on her pallet.

Sally hated putting Wise Sister out of her bed, but the plain truth was Sally still hurt. It was doubtful she'd have gotten any sleep on the hard floor. "My ribs are fine and my leg hardly hurts anymore since we put on the cast."

It might be more accurate to say Sally had gotten *used* to her leg and ribs hurting, which wasn't the same as *not* hurting, but she saw no reason to bury Wise Sister in details.

"Too many men. I go on foot. You need horse. Can't sneak on horse."

"Have you seen any of the men yet, even a glimpse?"

Wise Sister reached for the lantern she'd left burning until Sally was settled. "No, I see no one. Sleep now."

"Wise Sister, wait!"

To Sally's surprise, the Shoshone woman's hand paused. Usually Wise Sister did as she wished, and Sally had very little success changing the elderly woman's mind about anything.

She'd never get Wise Sister to agree to take her along, but she had a few other things she wanted to say. "The things in this cabin are beautiful."

Wise Sister sat up on her pallet with a small smile. "My home. I make it to please myself."

"Yourself and your husband, Pierre." Sally wondered at the lack of talk of Pierre. Though of course Wise Sister didn't talk much about anything.

"No, *my* home. *My* things."

Looking around at the handwork, the leather, the weaving, the soft animal pelts, the collection of feathers and stones and carved wood, Sally knew that was the truth. "Your husband wasn't here much, then?"

The smile on Wise Sister's face remained but was a sad sort. "Gone a lot. A wandering man, my Babineau. Didn't care after a while."

"You didn't like your husband?" Sally thought of Mandy. From the bits and pieces in her letters, Sally suspected Mandy didn't like her husband one bit.

"At first, yes. Very much. But he couldn't stay. Always itchy to move. At first I moved with him. Then the children came and I stayed in one place. I was a woman for home. He was a restless man drawn to the distant places."

"You have children?" Why hadn't Sally known this?

"Six children. Two girls, four boys. The boys took to the mountains like Pierre. The girls married to my tribe and left for the reservation. No one is near."

"That's sad." Sally knew how they all missed Mandy, hurt to know her babies were growing up as strangers.

"Just life. Not sad."

But Sally heard in Wise Sister's voice that it *was* sad.

"Those"—Wise Sister pointed to a woven mat on the wall, six sides, brightly dyed in six colors—"are my children. I find things of six. One for each child."

Suddenly Sally saw the sprays of feathers, spreading in six directions. The circle of stones, six stones, each a different color. A beaded wall hanging showed a six-sided sunburst. The number was in nearly everything. And in the midst of it hung that painting of Wise Sister and Babineau.

"Does Logan's painting of you and your husband please you, then? Or do you not like your husband's likeness on your wall?"

"Babineau was mine. I was his. We were together even when we were apart. I learned to be content in his absence and his presence. He was strong. He knew the land, and I respected that. I cared for him. A man who stayed with me would be good. But I chose him, not really knowing him, and I lived with my choice."

"I think—I think my sister is married to a man she doesn't like. I think that would be hard."

There was an extended silence as Wise Sister looked at the painting.

Quietly she said, more to the painting than to Sally, "Life is hard. There is right and wrong. We make our choices and live with them. Do what is right especially when it's hard."

There was wisdom in Wise Sister's eyes, and Logan had captured that perfectly in his painting. Patience. Suffering. Contentment. It truly was a beautifully done work. Sally looked closer at Babineau and saw strength and a look in Babineau's eyes of restlessness, wildness. But contentment was there, to match Wise Sister's. They'd found a way to exist together, even though they were very different.

In the end, Sally decided that's the way most marriages worked. Her ma and pa got on well and seemed happy. A painting of them would show little suffering. Beth loved Alex. Some of her sorrow for Mandy's life eased. Mandy would find her way somehow with no-account Sidney.

Sally almost spoke aloud of her confusion about marriage and adult feelings and Logan, but she turned from that, knowing the answer without asking the question. There could be nothing between them. And somehow that made it all the more important that she get out of here fast. "Let me go with you tomorrow, please. If we could ride straight to Luther, he'd protect us from the men who hunt me. We wouldn't have to sneak around."

"Too much hurt. You rest."

The light snuffed out. Sally barely controlled the urge to scream in frustration.

But whether because she was battered and healing took its toll or the high mountain air just agreed with her, Sally fell asleep.

Sally awoke to Wise Sister gone. It was the first night she'd slept through without a single nightmare, and Sally wondered if maybe, finally, she was getting well.

She dressed in her pretty doeskin and hobbled herself over to Logan's cabin. She came upon him standing near a ledge fifty feet in front of his cabin. From that ledge, the ground fell away, swooping to lower mountains, gentle swells, and jagged peaks.

They lived up where the eagle soared. Below the drop, the herd of elk stood in a circle watching a battle. The bull who led the group and the young upstart who challenged him. They'd played at this many times. Sally had seen it. But today seemed more serious. The two huge males snorted and charged, slammed their antlers together, fell back and charged again.

The steep drop reminded Sally of her fall. She hadn't had a nightmare last night. It might well be the first night she'd gotten through without one. But now, looking down, it was like she was plunging again. She had a moment of dizziness. She quickly backed away and sat on the chopping block. She saw his Stetson, pulling it on to block the view, and turned to watch Logan as a way of taking her mind off the memory of her haunting, plunging fall.

He stood, almost attacking his canvas with his knife. His strokes, wild, sweeping, almost violent, left trails of color behind that cried out with strength and vitality. The blue of the sky, the green of the grass, the gray of the rocks, all swirled into a blur around two bulls locked in mortal combat. Their massive antlers clashed, their heads down. Sally could hear the collisions, feel their anger and courage, smell their exertion.

It wasn't a proper painting, where the elk looked like real critters. It was a picture of motion and danger and power. Sally had seen a realistic sketch he'd made when the elk had battled another day. She didn't understand how he took that real world and turned it into feeling and motion and anger.

Sally thought he must be angry. But she watched him look from his canvas to the landscape sweeping away before him and the battling animals far below. Instead of anger she sensed power. Vitality. Strength. Passion.

It didn't sit well to think of him as strong. It wasn't a kind of strength she understood, and respecting something she didn't understand felt . . . dangerous. It was tied up with her sister Mandy marrying a man no one in the family respected. And Beth marrying a strange man that they all ended up loving, but who looked like a poor bet at first.

Thinking of the two times they'd kissed had awakened a feeling inside her that was as unfamiliar as it was alluring. Sally gritted her teeth. She wanted no part of a man who didn't feel like she did about the land and ranching. She wanted a man like her pa. Her second pa, Clay

McClellen. Her ma had married a poor excuse for a man first time out, too.

Sally was determined that, when the day came for her to marry, which she didn't intend to do for a long time yet, she'd pick a sensible man who fit in her life. A man would make a partner for her pa at the McClellen Ranch. Or a ranch very close at hand.

She wanted no part of the nonsense that had afflicted her sisters and ma the first time, when they did their choosing. Sally intended to use her God-given common sense to pick a sensible kind of man, and she'd be happy from the first day.

Logan took one more slash with his paint knife and left a trail of blue on the canvas that exactly matched the blue of the sky in front of him. How did he do that? He had a flat piece of wood in his hand that looked like a dinner plate, streaked with several colors. He'd mix them together with his knife and somehow come up a perfect shade. That in itself was a strange gift.

Sally had helped her ma dye fabric, and she knew how tricky it was to make colors do exactly as she wished. How did he, with sure, racing motions, mix his colors to capture a shade so rare and glorious?

He glanced over. He held another paint knife in his teeth, this one coated with a vivid shade of green. A knife in his teeth, another in his hand, the paint board he'd called a palette in his grip.

He had paint on his face and in his hair and on his shirt, and his eyes burned with fire that drew her like a moth.

It was to her shame that he drew her, a man who looked and acted like a complete lunatic.

He set the palette on a chair loaded with small pots of paint and removed the knife from his teeth, so he held one in each hand. He jabbed his blue knife at a second painting sitting beside the first. The one painted with his knives was wild, a confusing clash of color that almost vibrated with Logan's passion for art and the life and death battle of the elk. The other was of the area visible far below them. He'd painted, with complete realism, everything that swept away before them.

He had smeared green paint on his face from clutching the knife in his teeth. He didn't care one bit about being a mess. "I wish you could go down there with me and really be close to the land, hear it, smell it, touch it, taste it. I want all of that to come through in my painting."

"You want someone to be able to taste your painting?" Sally arched a brow.

A lighthearted laugh answered her skepticism. "No, I want someone to see my painting and *imagine* what it smells like and sounds like and tastes like." He wiped his hands on a paint-stained cloth.

"No one can do that. Painting is about seeing."

Even as she said it, she glanced at his odd, unrealistic painting and knew she hadn't spoken the pure truth. Sally had witnessed this fight, and Logan had brought it to the canvas in a way that was more than seeing. Logan's work called to all her senses.

"I planned to be out there in nature, ready to catch the sunrise or the racing wind." He stabbed at the landscape and the humor faded from his expression, his eyes snapping with impatience.

Sally saw in them the same passion that showed in his painting. She knew just how frustrated he was. "You're not the only one who's under lock and key, you know. I can't go down there either. Wise Sister scolds. Tells me I'll end up dead."

Logan looked at Sally's crutches.

With two she got around really well. She could do everything, except of course for the one thing she wanted to do most. Escape.

"Too many bad men." Logan frowned down at the view. "Her exact words. I'm going to have to paint this from a distance instead of from down there close. What's the point of being in the Rockies if I'm locked away on this hilltop?"

"I thought you built here because you loved the view." Sally came closer to see the detail of his painting. He hadn't used his knives and a blob of paint with the landscape painting. He'd used the same style she'd seen on her portrait.

"I do love it." Logan wielded his knife at the awe-inspiring panorama. "But Babineau built here for me because his cabin was already here. I wanted to see the whole area, and this was a good central location to all sorts of natural beauty."

"And why did Babineau live up here to begin with?"

"Because it's off the park."

"What?" Sally squinted her eyes to focus on his nonsense.

"Wise Sister's husband has done a fair amount of trapping in Yellowstone over his lifetime, but that's not allowed anymore. And they made it illegal to hunt, too. They'd been in these parts for years so they didn't go far."

Sally couldn't imagine a land where hunting wasn't allowed. What were animals for except to eat and ride?

"The first time Babineau took me up here, the view almost stopped my heart it was so beautiful. After that, I wanted to see more. I'd paint. Babineau hunted. Wise Sister cooked and sewed and tended a garden. I'd go off for a few days and camp. It gets so cold up here that it can snow even in August."

Sally thought of August in Texas and tried to imagine snow. It had snowed during that rainy spell, so she knew it was true. Wise Sister always kept a fire going at night in their fireplace.

"Wise Sister knows this area even better than Babineau, so they were content to stay here. It's close to where she grew up. Babineau built me my own cabin with the huge windows. It wasn't done when I left the first winter, but Babineau had it finished in the spring."

Sally moved closer to Logan's more outlandish elk painting, strangely drawn to it. She thought it was a waste of his life, but she couldn't deny it was skillfully done. She studied it and was only distantly aware that Logan was watching her.

He made a sudden movement of his head that drew her attention. He shook himself as if he wanted to shed water then smiled. "I'll bring a chair out." Logan set his knives aside and hurried into the cabin and back out with a chair.

"Thank you."

"We can sit together and watch the beauty we can't touch." He set the chair down. "How are you feeling?"

"I'm fine." Sally gratefully sank into it, careful to disguise her aches.

"You're still in pain. I can see it in your eyes." Logan leaned close and studied her in the strange way he did that seemed to be looking at the parts of her, to draw them. It made her feel bad, but she wasn't sure why.

Sally glared at him.

His eyes refocused, obviously seeing all of her. "What?"

"You're staring."

Logan flinched. "I do that. Always in my head I'm imagining the picture I want to draw. I've been told by plenty of people that it's a very irritating habit."

"Can't you stop?"

"I don't want to. That's part of why I live out here, mostly alone."

"You live in a wilderness in the West because you have the manners of a pig?"

A smile broke through Logan's discomfort. "No. Well, yes, but not *only* for that reason. I don't want to stop. I want to be who I am. Who God made me to be. I stare. People don't like it. So I stay away from them as much as possible."

Sally was a little tired of Logan blaming everything on God. "It's clear as day that God gave you an ability to draw. Most folks aren't born with such a talent, so it must be a special blessing. But don't tell me it's God's plan for you to be rude."

Logan's brow furrowed. "But it's all part of it. Part of the calling to art."

"No." Sally shook her head. "God sends each baby into the world with strengths—intelligence, a strong will, an easygoing nature, a sturdy back, quickness, or sharp eyes. You should see my sister Mandy shoot. It's a pure gift, no denying it. And Beth, her voice, the way she can whisper to a scared animal or comfort an injured child. I've tried to copy that when I needed to calm a horse. I do all right but it's nothing like what Beth can do. So I know God gives us gifts, but He just gives them to us. The raw material comes along with the baby. What a child grows into is all about his own choices in this world."

Sally thought of Wise Sister and what she'd said the night before about making a choice and living with it. Doing right. Doing one's best.

"Choices?" Logan shook his head.

"Yes, a child can follow the manners taught by her ma, or she can be rude. A little boy can take after his hard-workin' rancher pa, or he can chase after book learning, or he can be a no-account bum. And the choices can come from what their lives are like. How were they treated? Is a child the youngest of ten kids, pampered and babied and fussed over and never disciplined? Is she the oldest with heavy responsibilities resting on her shoulders that make her older than her years?"

Sally thought of Laurie. "My little sister, Laurie, is different from the rest of us. She's had from her earliest years a pa who loved her. Life hasn't been as hard for her as it was for the rest of us. She has no memory of life without a prosperous ranch and nice dresses. Mandy was fighting alongside Ma from the first day she was old enough to fetch and carry. Things got better, but Mandy's character had already been set. But no amount of training could explain my big sister's quickness with a Winchester. That was a gift she was born with, but Mandy had honed it, too, as we all have."

"My father pushed me hard to be a doctor, and I still became a painter." Logan looked down at the sweeping land. "Look, the elk herd has wandered away. Both bulls will live to fight another day."

"If he'd been really harsh with you, really *forced* you on threat of starvation or a beating, you'd have bent to his will, I reckon. But if he'd done that, he'd have broken you. A parent needs to figure out how to train a child without twisting him. How to understand the nature of the child and respect that." Sally shrugged and looked down at her clothes. "Ma's always pushed me to dress more proper, but she hasn't *forced* me, not out on the range. She thinks I'm an odd one, I suppose, but figures I'm not hurtin' nothin'. Your pa was probably the same. Guiding you, pushing you, but smart enough to let you make your own choices when it really mattered."

"You think what I do matters?" Logan gestured at his paintings.

She looked up at Logan's art and slowly hoisted herself to her feet to really study the elk painting. "I—I don't understand a man passing his days on such a thing. But what you do, whatever is inside of you that comes out onto that canvas—"

She turned from the painting to Logan and their

eyes met. "Yes." Somehow it was easy to say that. She held his gaze and felt something warm and beautiful, something already beginning to be born, come fully to life. "Yes, it matters."

"That means a lot to me." Logan's brown eyes flashed with gratitude and pleasure, but he didn't smile, almost as if his feeling went too deep for such a meager expression as a smile. "More than you could know." He reached out and rested one of his paint-stained hands on Sally's shoulder.

"I don't exactly understand what drives you, but I understand you have a gift and that it would be wrong to not use—"

Logan stopped the next word with his lips.

Sixteen

Sidney, we have a problem." Mandy had waited, choosing her time wisely. Or as wisely as possible when dealing with her notoriously difficult-to-deal-with husband.

Sidney was fussing with his stupid account book. Counting his gold—on paper—like some kind of half-crazed miser. Mandy often saw him swallow as he added and subtracted figures, as if he had to fight drooling over his precious gold. "Not now." Impatiently, he swept one hand at her, dismissing her, his gold ring on his fat fingers flashing in her eyes.

Mandy knew better than to interrupt him at his

book, but she also knew he went to bed directly after time spent savoring his wealth. And once on his way to sleep, he was useless. Odd how the man could sleep so well. She'd think he'd be a haunted man.

"Yes, now." She moved from her place at the sink, the evening meal all cleaned up. Facing him, only a few feet away, she plunked her fists on her hips. She'd gone over this a dozen times. How to approach him with this. She'd decided to, well, not lie. A Christian woman didn't tell lies. But to be wily. She couldn't remember a Bible verse specifically forbidding that.

"Behold, I send you forth as sheep in the midst of wolves: be ye therefore wise as serpents, and harmless as doves."

There were a whole lot of different animals in that verse. Mandy picked her favorite, squared her shoulders, and set out to be a sneaky little snake. "Something happened today that has me worried, Sidney. Your man Cooter, he said something to me that gave me the impression that he might be looking for a way to take your gold away from you."

Sidney jerked forward and rose to his feet, instantly on alert.

"I think he might have been who I heard outside the cabin the other night. I think he's prowling around." To Mandy's way of thinking, none of this was a lie. She just focused on something far less important—the gold—rather than discussing how Cooter had treated her.

"He came down the hill this afternoon." Sidney's eyes narrowed. Her husband didn't have much common sense, but Sidney could always be counted upon to be overly suspicious when it came to his money. "Is that when he spoke to you? What did he say exactly?"

Mandy needed to tread carefully now. If she spoke of Cooter's bold behavior, would Sidney decide that her complaint was about that and not about money?

Cooter clearly thought of being rid of Sidney. He'd never molest her otherwise. And the wretched man must suspect how bad things were between her and Sidney, or he'd have never treated her that way. Which meant Sidney was in danger from a man he paid for protection.

"It wasn't so much what he said. I felt like—well, he ducked out of my sight in a strange way. You know I'm good at hunting. A man doesn't sneak around without my knowing it. But Cooter did. I think, well, he went into the bunkhouse then came up behind me. He'd have had to slip away, down the back side of the bunkhouse, circle the house. I think he was inside."

"Did you lock the door?" Sidney rubbed his chin thoughtfully, his eyes narrowed and blazing, looking through her, considering all the possibilities.

"No, not just to step outside in the yard."

"You should always lock it."

This wasn't an argument she wanted to have. Sidney could always find a way to blame her for everything. "I will from now on. How brazen does a man have to be to sneak into the house when I'm just a few feet away? He must be planning something. Or maybe he's searching for the address of your Denver bank. Could he forge a paper sending for money?"

"Why now? He's been with me a long time."

Mandy knew why now but she'd never dare say it aloud. Luther and Buff were gone. As simple as that. They'd protected her. If only they'd come back.

"What are we going to do?" Mandy ignored Sidney's question and crossed her arms, thinking, knowing it might come down to shooting trouble, hating that danger could come close to her children. She felt a chill calming her as she considered all that could happen.

"I'll have to fire him."

Mandy doubted Cord Cooter would go quietly. "Easy to say. But if he's of a mind to act with violence, that might force his hand."

Sidney continued stroking his chin for long moments.

Mandy didn't offer to back Sidney if it came to shooting trouble. She'd do it when the time came, but it would upset him to speak of it now.

"I'll go to town."

"What?" Mandy felt as if the man spoke a foreign language suddenly. What did going to town have to do with—

"I'll go to town and take Cooter and Platte with me. Once I'm in town, I'll quietly seek out another assistant and hire him. Then, with a new man backing me, I'll fire Cooter. That will leave Cooter miles from the cabin. If I fired him here he might just ride away, only to circle back."

"He can ride out here from town just as well." And he'd have time to find friends and pick his moment and sneak up on their flank. What was needed was a strong man who could hold what was his, protect his home and family with his will and his fists and his gun if need be. Sidney had none of that, not even the will.

"No, *not* just as well. I'll make it clear that the money is untouchable."

But Mandy wasn't so untouchable. And while she thought Cooter's true aim was the money, he made his unholy interest in her terrifyingly clear. "I'm too close to birthing this baby, Sidney. I don't want to be left here alone. You are always gone most of a week when you go to town."

"I'll make a fast trip. I can do it in five days."

Luther and Buff made it in two all the time, three if things went wrong. It was a brutal ride to make in a day, early mornings, late nights, hunting up the storekeeper to open the store long after closing time so Luther could head out early the next day with loaded pack horses. Sidney liked the carriage and there was no way to make the trip fast with that. Even if he could, Sidney wasn't one to push himself.

"That might not be fast enough. I don't want to be alone here when the baby comes."

"I've never had much to do with birthing the babies, Mandy. I don't even need to be here." Sidney's hands clutched together as if the very thought upset him.

"But I had a midwife out from Helena the last two times. We lived close enough."

"But you didn't need them. It all went fine. No reason to believe it won't go the same this time. And anyway, I'll be back. And"—Sidney's eyes lit up—"while I'm in town I'll see about bringing a midwife back with me . . . or the doctor."

"A doctor can't ride all the way out here. Why are we living so far from town anyway?"

"No, you're right. A doctor probably can't be away from his office that long. But I'll ask around. I'll see if any woman is willing. Maybe someone will need work and be willing to come up here and help you until your sister shows up. You'd like to have a woman about when your time came, wouldn't you?"

Mandy would like that very, very much. And it really was probably still two weeks away or more, but babies had their own timing. It didn't matter anyway. She looked at Sidney's expression and knew he was going. At least he'd be taking Cooter away. "Yes, I'd like that. But I want you to make a fast trip of it, too. I don't like being here alone with the workmen."

Sidney nodded. "No, it's not proper for you to be here, though they seem like decent men mostly. And they'll stay to themselves and keep pressing forward with the house, so you'll hardly see them."

"Is there a man among them who can cook? I may not be able to keep up with feeding them all and caring for the girls." And then, though it pinched, she told him a truth that surprised her. "It's all harder when you're gone."

She wasn't even sure if it was true, because usually when Sidney was gone, Luther and Buff were here, and she'd honestly not noticed her husband's absence much. But now, with her old friends away and Sidney leaving, she felt more alone than she ever had in her life.

"I'll tell them they'll need to make their own meals. It will slow the work down, but it can't be helped."

Silence fell between them, Sidney plotting and planning to be rid of Cooter.

Mandy wanted that badly enough to let her husband go. If she wanted to send him on his way with a kick to his backside, that didn't change that it was worth his leaving to be rid of that dreadful bodyguard.

"You'll be safe here, honey. The men seem decent." Sidney came and rested his hand on her shoulder.

As if Sidney was any judge. He'd hired Cooter after all. "Yes, I'll be safe. But go right away, tomorrow, so you can get back soon."

He patted her like she was a well-behaved dog.

She was tempted to be less well-behaved and growl, then bite him on the arm.

"How long are we going to skulk around?" Buff tossed the dregs of his coffee on the fire.

"It's gnawing on me, too." Luther looked up from the campfire they'd built to boil up some coffee for their noon meal. The blaze was small so the men they followed wouldn't see it. "If we ride up on 'em, we need to be prepared for shooting trouble, or we'd need to haul them all the way to the nearest town. That's days away, and once we got there, they'd probably be released. We've got no proof they attacked Colonel McGarritt's party."

"It's them." Buff took a long drink of his blazing hot coffee. "As sure as if I'd seen it with my own eyes."

Luther stared at his coffee, tempted, mighty tempted, to find out what those men knew with his fists and his gun. Instead, here they sat drinking coffee while they kept a lookout on those outlaws, searching for any evidence of where Sally had gotten to.

They'd been slipping along in the wake of the men because they were sure these two hunted Sally. They'd fan out searching for markers from whoever was leaving them, hoping to find a trail that would lead to Sally. It was an itch under Luther's skin to worry about his girl and not do something more.

But they hadn't found a bit of evidence telling them where Sally might be hiding.

"I'm thinkin' it's a woman leavin' sign." Luther settled back against a rock wall that faced their fire.

It was a warm day so they didn't need the heat once the coffee had boiled and the beans warmed, but it gave comfort, and in this rocky area, surrounded by towering pines with their needles high overhead to diffuse the smoke, the fire posed no risk. They'd made note of where the two hombres they tailed had set up to cook a meal. Then when it was obvious the two were settling in for a long spell, they'd dropped back and built a fire.

"Yep." Buff poured himself more coffee and leaned back against the trunk of a tall, narrow lodgepole pine. "Woman sure as day. And she knows we're here now, and she knows those other coyotes are here, too. She's protecting

Sally, and she's let us know Sally's fine until we can get to her."

"Cautious woman," Luther added. "She knows she could lead trouble to Sally, and she'd rather lead us in circles than endanger our girl. A good woman. Knows the woods, too. Likely Shoshone."

"I knew a fine Shoshone woman once. Real fine." Buff stared into his cup.

Luther waited.

Buff didn't go on.

"Don't rightly know if I like the idea of a woman protecting Sally." Luther tossed his coffee away. "I'd feel a lot better knowing a man was close."

Seventeen

Logan pulled Sally close.

He tilted his head to kiss her better. His arms slid around her waist. He felt half mad with the pleasure of her saying she recognized his gift and knew he needed to use it.

As if he held the most precious thing in all God's creation in his arms, he deepened the kiss, cherishing the feel of her in his arms.

She jerked her head back, but that only made the angle better when he sealed her lips with his own. And she didn't pull back again. Instead her arms wound around his neck and he felt one of her crutches whack him in the shoulder as it fell.

It didn't distract him one whit.

A distant, barely functioning part of his brain whispered that he was better off alone. He was a self-centered man obsessed with his art. He ignored the whisper and pulled Sally closer.

"Trouble comes!" Wise Sister shouted from the woods. "We go!"

Sally jerked out of Logan's arms so fast he almost fell forward and knocked the poor broken-legged woman over. Sally was too quick for him, though. Dodging his clumsiness, she slung the rifle she always kept at hand over her neck, grabbed her crutches, whirled, and headed—Logan couldn't figure out where.

Away from Wise Sister. Was Sally planning to run? She couldn't last in the mountains, which were impassable to the west and north. Wise Sister was coming from the southeast.

While Logan tried to clear his head, Sally was already on the way to—he figured it out. The corral. Wise Sister said, "We go." So Sally was getting the horses.

She might be faster to react, but he could still outrun her, thanks to her broken leg. He caught up and passed her. He had the first horse caught and bridled before she got there. She whipped a saddle onto the horse, with her crutches firmly at hand.

Logan caught a second horse just as Wise Sister appeared from the woods running. He'd never seen her run before.

Sally glanced up, noticed, exchanged a look of alarm with Logan, and finished tightening the cinch then took over bridling the second horse.

Logan grabbed a third. "Just three or do we take all five? Will we need a pack animal?"

Sally shook her head. "I don't think we're gonna do much packing."

"What's going on?" Logan used every bit of skill hc'd learned in the West to cut down the time.

"I don't know, but if Wise Sister says we need to ride, I'm going to ride first and ask questions later." The rapid slap of leather as she tightened another saddle underlined the fear Logan knew he'd felt when Wise Sister, so soft spoken, so slow moving, yelled and ran.

Wise Sister ducked into her cabin as Sally and Logan finished with the horses. She emerged with a quiver full of arrows and a gun belt around her plump waist. It was Babineau's, but he'd never seen her with it. She moved so fast she didn't pause for even a moment to close her door.

Logan took one second to realize that while he led the third horse up to where Sally stood with the saddles, which lay hooked over the fence.

To leave a door open and ride away was to turn your home over. Bears would move in and eat what was there within hours. They'd tear the building apart from the inside out within days. Wise Sister was saying they were never coming back. Or there wasn't time to worry about whether they did. "Coyotes come." She rushed toward them carrying a heavily loaded cloth bag in one hand.

Logan grabbed the two prepared horses and led them from the corral. He went back to Sally. "Let me help you." Their eyes met. This young lady, who had more skill on a horse—or so Logan suspected—than most cowboys, didn't like needing help. But she had a broken leg and this moment was beyond pride. He grabbed her around the waist, hating the thought of her bruised ribs, and tossed her up with no ceremony. Then he rushed to the other horses and led one to Wise Sister's side. He went to boost Wise Sister, but she vaulted into the saddle with less trouble than a bird might have. Logan was mounted seconds later.

"That way." Wise Sister pointed to the most forbidding stretch of mountains Logan had ever seen.

A shiver went through his gut as he looked at those soaring, white-capped peaks and the dense woods on ground so broken he couldn't imaging walking through it, let alone riding a horse. He'd never even hiked that direction.

He jerked his head at Sally to go ahead.

Rebellion flickered across her face, and he knew she wanted to bring up the rear. He thought of her exposed back with gunfire possibly coming after her. "Go. Now!"

She tugged on her reins and followed Wise Sister. Logan followed, and before they'd left the grounds around the cabin, Wise Sister had them moving into that forbidding wilderness at a full gallop.

They passed into a thicket of trees with a trail Logan couldn't see even as he rode on it, and then Wise Sister pulled her horse to a stop and dismounted. Sally followed, so Logan did the same, not sure what their next move was.

Slipping silently up to the thicket, Wise Sister dropped to her knees. Logan knelt beside her on her right and Sally was on his right.

We're like wild game, hiding in the weeds from hunters.

He heard Sally whisper, "God, have mercy."

Logan leaned forward as two men emerged into the clearing around the cabins, riding hard. Wise Sister made a guttural noise of contempt. Sally shifted on her knees and swung her rifle off her back.

Logan had known her long enough to fight back the impulse to block the gun as she pointed it. Sally was tough, but she wouldn't shoot those men from cover, even if they were, as Logan suspected, the men who had killed her friends.

The men—one skinny with a potbelly and a twitchy manner that reminded Logan of a ferret, and the other a stocky man with massive shoulders and arms, wearing a coonskin cap, carrying a rifle on his saddle, and wearing two pistols and two ammunition belts slung bandolier style across his chest—pulled their horses to a stop in front of his painting.

Only then did Logan realize what an unexpected sight it must be for these two, who looked trail-wise and rugged and dangerous, to come upon two paintings, standing side-by-side on an easel, in the middle of nowhere. Logan had a sudden, world-tilting vision of just how odd he was with the life he led.

The broad-chested man swung to the ground and walked up to the painting Logan had just created this morning—the elk fighting, the swirl of color, his knife and his new love for the strange Impressionist style he'd learned over the winter. The man pulled his pistol and aimed it at the picture.

"No!" Logan lurched up.

They'd finally found what they were looking for and now no one was around.

Fergus itched to hurt someone. His eyes went to the freakish picture standing out here in the middle of nowhere. He was drawn to it just because he couldn't make out nothin' in it but two elk fighting. It was slopped on the paper like a baby had smeared paint on the wall. For some reason, he could feel the killing fury of the elk and it became his own.

Pulling his Colt six-shooter out, he emptied his gun into the stupid picture.

Gunfire brought Luther's head up. He sprang to his feet from where he crouched beside the tracks they'd found this morning. He was running for his horse before the first volley died away.

Buff swung up on horseback with an agility that defied his sixty hard years. They were galloping flat out before the gunfire died away.

"Straight that way." Buff guided his horse toward what looked like a jumble of rocks, spilled down from an endless, broken mountain. Trees grew out from what looked like impassable stone walls.

They'd ridden by this area before, but even with careful studying Luther had never seriously considered there was a way up the mountain here. This morning it was simple because the men they trailed had left sign easy enough to follow. Their horses picked their way and it was a treacherous ride, but the horses moved on, obviously following a clear route. About halfway up the steep, stony cut, Luther smelled smoke. They could go no faster. Panic rode Luther's shoulders as he thought of those bullets cutting into his sweet Sally.

"Luth!" Buff was coming behind Luther.

The hissed shout pulled Luther's attention from his fretting. He looked back at Buff, who pointed. One of those signs they'd been finding. A stack of stones whose main meaning was simply that they'd been stacked in a deliberate way. The Shoshone woman had left it for them, hoping they'd come up and see it but not directing them because she'd known that to direct Luther and Buff up this trail was to direct the men hunting Sally.

But those men had beaten them to the trail, and now Sally might be dead.

A hand slapped over Logan's mouth before the word had a chance to gain volume. Someone landed hard on him, carrying him backward onto the dank forest floor.

Gunfire rolled on up by the cabin. He was so desperate to stop the men from destroying his work, Logan wasn't fully aware of just what was going on for a few seconds.

"Shut up and lay still!" The words hissed at him like a Rocky Mountain rattler he'd sketched last August.

He focused and realized Sally was lying flat on top of him. Her hand was flat on his mouth, all her weight pinning him to the ground. Except her weight was negligible. That's when he realized Wise Sister was sitting on his legs and glaring at him around Sally's shoulder.

He quit fighting. The gunfire ended.

Sally leaned close. "Do I have to tie you up? Because I will."

"What was that?" Fergus turned to the far side of this little level spot, the only flat place for miles in a world that went up, down, and sidewise.

Tulsa looked at the place Fergus was staring at. They hadn't stayed alive in the wild all these years without trusting their eyes and ears and noses.

Nothing moved. No further sound.

"See if you can find anything in the small cabin, money or an idea who these people are." Fergus pointed to a small strip of leather lying on the ground in front of the bigger cabin. "Looks like Shoshone beadwork on that strap."

"Must be who took that cowpoke away from the cliff that first day." Tulsa strode toward the smaller cabin. "Brung him all the way back up in here. Makes no sense."

The whole thing made no sense and it grated on Fergus bad. They'd spent a long time in this country, which seemed bent on killin' anyone who passed through. And all over a witness to murder who should'a died that first day. Gut shot and the cowpoke rode away.

It made Fergus want to unload his gun into something else. "Get whatever's worth gettin' out of that cabin then burn it."

"Sorry." Logan's word was muted.

Sally got the idea, but she still didn't trust him, since he'd just proved himself to be a lunatic. She lifted her hand an inch.

When he remained silent, she caught a handful of hair and yanked it until his neck arched back. "Use your head." She did her best to burn him to death with her eyes. "You need to save yourself, so if they wreck your pictures you can paint more of them."

Logan nodded again.

It went against the grain to stop hurting the lunkhead, but Sally released his hair. Suddenly she became aware of the strength and weight and vitality of him and climbed off quickly, none too careful where she whacked him with the ten pounds of plaster on her leg.

Wise Sister eased to his other side with a glowering look of warning.

"We stay hidden." Sally reached down, grabbed Logan by the shirt front, and nearly lifted him back to his knees.

"Yes, I'm sorry." He acted contrite, but she still didn't trust him. The man didn't seem to have a lick of common sense.

"If you go running out there, I'm going to have

to open fire on those men. I've never killed anyone in my life. I don't want to start now." Though she spoke at a whisper, considering murderers were up the hill a few yards, she saw the impact. Good. It was almost as good as if she'd hit him with her fists.

Logan might cause her to kill and maybe die. For him. Because of him. To save him.

She saw him thinking it through and knew when he was done because shame washed over his face. Nodding, he leaned forward, hesitated, then looked.

The skinny man came out of the cabin with the painting of Sally in his hands. She felt tainted, as if the filthy man was touching her rather than a portrait.

Sally reached over and clamped one hand on Logan's arm. His muscled forearm clenched but he didn't shake her off.

The two men looked at the picture and laughed in a way that made Sally's stomach lurch. Skinny held the portrait, about two-by-two feet in size, in both hands, staring at it. Then he tromped on the elk painting, laying shot to pieces, flat on the ground, and heaved the portrait over the side of the cliff.

Logan's hand rested on top of Sally's but he didn't make a sound.

Skinny came back to the elks, talking as he moved. Sally heard the low rumble of their voices but couldn't make out any words. Skinny laughed, raised a boot, and kicked the bullet-riddled elk painting over the cliff, too.

The bigger man went into Logan's cabin. Sally thought of that huge painting in there, *Blazing Land*. He loved that picture so much Sally's grip on his arm tightened, just in case he lost control. Maybe they'd had their fun and they'd ride on.

She heard the first crackle of fire. A puff of smoke came out of Logan's cabin.

Wise Sister's hand slapped on Logan's mouth. Sally looked but saw he had control of himself now. He shook his head and gave Wise Sister an impatient look. She arched a brow doubtfully but lifted her hand.

"All I've got to do," Logan whispered, "is picture Sally and you bleeding to death. That's enough to keep me here."

Wise Sister nodded, her stoic expression showing a hint of approval. If Wise Sister was satisfied, that went a long way toward reassuring Sally.

Grimly squaring his shoulders, Logan turned back to face the destruction. All his work, all his paints, all his canvas and pencils and sketchbooks. The summer was over for him. He'd go home empty-handed.

A soft sound drew her attention to Wise Sister, watching the men do their damage. The skinny man walked into Wise Sister's cabin. Unlike

Logan, who had a home and family back East and money in the bank, that cabin contained Wise Sister's whole world. She had a lot more to lose than Logan did. Moments later Skinny emerged, carrying a cloth bag loaded down. Smoke began billowing out behind him.

All of Wise Sister's precious things. All her art made with six children in mind.

"Smoke signals," Sally whispered. "It'll bring Luther."

Logan turned to her. "So, I lose a summer's work. Wise Sister loses *everything*, but you get rescued. You're a lucky woman, Sally McClellen."

"I'm sorry. I wasn't thinking about my friends rescuing me. I was thinking of Luther and Buff fighting at our side. They're tough men. They'll help us. If these are the men who killed the colonel, then they're evil. We'll be a lot safer once Luther and Buff are here."

A shout from Skinny drew their attention. He pointed at the ground and his finger swept along a line that led straight to where they crouched in the undergrowth.

"He's found our trail." Sally grabbed for her rifle.

Eighteen

Luther didn't stop, nor even slow. The climb was steep and relentless. Their horses' hooves rang hollow on small stones that rolled and slipped.

Luther had lived in the mountains for years back when he'd been a trapper and a good friend of Clay McClellen's father. He'd watched Clay grow up and had a hand in teaching him how to live with the land. He'd felt like an uncle, and after Clay's pa had died, Luther had left the mountains to live in Texas near Clay and his family. He'd taken on the role of grandfather to his girls and now a great-grandpa to Mandy's young'uns. Though they were not blood relations, he was family and he'd fight for his family to the end.

The smell of smoke grew stronger as they neared the top of this precipitous climb. When they were within a few steps of the top, gunshots rang out again. It took every ounce of Luther's considerable self-control not to spur his mount. It would only abuse his horse because they were going as fast as they could.

They topped the cliff. Luther saw smoke and flames billowing up from two cabins. Nothing else moved. He slapped his horse hard on the rump and bent low over the saddle, mindful of that gunfire he'd heard. The ground was better here, a plateau that appeared to plunge down another mountain on the far side of the cabin. They were in front of the cabin in minutes. He threw himself off the horse, ground-hitching it as it shied back from the flames. An inferno ate at the log structure. Luther saw Buff rushing toward the smaller of the two cabins.

Could Sally be inside? Could she have been shot and left to burn? Could she, if she was in there, possibly be alive?

Bending low, Luther charged the door, ducking through the completely consumed frame.

Sally centered her rifle on her back then grabbed her crutches. She rushed toward her tethered horse. She felt strong hands on her waist as Logan hoisted her up on the horse before she could scramble up there herself. She'd've managed, but he sped things up some.

She jammed her crutches over the pommel of the saddle as Wise Sister took the lead. Sally kicked her horse into motion. Wise Sister headed down the wash of a dry spring.

Logan swung up on horseback just as a shot cracked the air. Wise Sister spurred her roan gelding and Sally moved fast behind her, glancing back to see Logan kick his horse. Over the thunder of their hoofbeats, Sally heard a bullet slam into the trunk of a tree only a few feet from them. Another bullet followed, then a third.

Sally leaned low on her horse until she almost hugged the back of her black mustang. She glanced back and saw Logan imitate her actions just as a bullet whined over his head. It passed over him and slammed into a tree, in such a perfect line it would have killed him if he'd been sitting upright.

The men must be able to see movement in the trees, though the forest was heavy. A few heart-pounding seconds followed as bullets rained on them. Sally's mustang moved deeper into the woods, the trail dropping sharply. The gunfire stopped, but galloping hooves sounded from behind.

Wise Sister raised her hand. At first Sally thought Wise Sister was stopping. Did she mean to stand and fight? Sally couldn't imagine pulling the trigger at another human being, killing a man. Then she imagined that bullet hitting Logan and thought maybe she could do it. She put her hand back to check, and of course her rifle was there, firmly in place across her shoulders as always.

Instead of turning to fight, Wise Sister slowed to a fast walk. Still, they continued at a reckless pace. This trail could trip a horse and break a rider's neck.

Sally stayed low, the trail nothing but the path of a dry waterway. Trees stretched their limbs out. Overhead were the branches of older lodgepole pines. Younger trees were thick all through the forest and they slapped at the horses. Sally looked behind her and saw Logan straighten for a second, take a swat from the needled branches, and then bend low again. He was trainable at least.

The horses seemed to understand what those bullets meant and kept rushing. Sally looked alongside her mare's neck to see where Wise Sister was going. She led them with the precision of a forest creature. The slope was downward, long and treacherous, and the dry spring bed was uneven and full of rocks.

They rode on, the silence broken by the harsh breathing of terrified horses and the racket of hooves on the rocky ground. Long minutes passed and they kept slowing. Sally could only follow Wise Sister and match her speed.

As they reached the bottom of the slope, Wise Sister veered off onto a patch of scattered rock. They now rode almost straight north along the side of the slope. They moved on until the rocks underfoot became bigger and impossible to traverse.

Wise Sister turned again, returning to a more westward path. They reached a solid stone ledge. A sheer cliff rose on their right, solid, impenetrable woodlands on their left. Sally knew this was no piece of luck. Wise Sister was very carefully choosing her way.

Her already huge respect for her Shoshone friend bloomed even bigger. Wise Sister had known exactly where they were going. She'd known this land long before anyone had had a thought of closing Yellowstone to private ownership or opening up Montana for settlement. Either that or she'd been practicing, preparing for trouble. Smart lady.

They approached a massive, sheer stone wall straight ahead, and Sally pulled up when Wise Sister did, waiting for the next move, loving the cunning old woman.

Logan had expected better of Wise Sister. She'd led them to a dead end, with murderers on their trail.

Wise Sister raised her hand again. Sally stopped and Logan followed suit. The Shoshone woman swung down off her horse with such agility, Logan's jaw went slack. She rarely sat a horse, or rather he'd never noticed.

It occurred to Logan that for a man obsessed with the world around him, he wasn't very observant, at least not when it came to people. He knew more about the habits of the bull elk that lived near his cabin than he did about his housekeeper.

Coming up beside Sally, Wise Sister spoke in a quiet voice. Logan had to lean forward in time to hear her say, "That trail." She pointed to what looked like an impassable wall of trees downhill of the rock. "I go." Wise Sister looked in the direction they'd come. "We lose them at the dry spring. Your people will come, Sally girl. They follow the coyotes, and the coyotes will go on downhill. I get your friends."

"If the coyotes don't find us first." Sally looked back the way they'd come, searching the trail as if, by staring hard enough, she could see all the way to those men and fight them.

"I'll go." Logan knew out of three people, one elderly, one wearing a cast, and one able-bodied man, he was least equipped for trouble. But it grated not to protect his women.

Sally and Wise Sister looked away from their back trail to him, as if they'd forgotten he was even along. They wore matching expressions that clearly suppressed smiles. It ripped at his pride.

"You stay, protect Sally girl." Wise Sister jerked a thumb at the wall of trees. She returned to her horse, caught its reins, and walked past both of them so swiftly Logan didn't get a chance to protest again.

Sally headed straight for that wall. Logan opened his mouth to ask how in the world they'd pass through that, when Sally turned her horse to the left and vanished.

Logan quickly nudged his horse forward, hoping the animal could do the same magic trick the other horse did. He glanced back at Wise

Sister. She'd vanished, too. For a few seconds, Logan had a wild wash of fear to be so completely alone in these woods and mountains. He'd haunted them for three years now, craved being alone in them. But he'd never faced danger.

He felt such contempt for himself at that moment it nearly choked him, to be protected by two women this way. Then his buckskin, far wiser then he on the trail—and why should his horse be different than everyone else?—turned onto an invisible trail between the rock and the closest tree. Because the tree was a bit closer to Logan than the massive stone, it looked like they butted up against each other, but there were in fact several feet between them and a faint trail that his horse moved along easily.

Logan heard Sally's horse snort ahead, but he couldn't see her in the dense undergrowth. To find Sally, he asked, "How did she find this?"

Sally's voice came from only feet away. "Scouting around you find these things."

Logan's horse turned at a corner that twisted the trail back on itself so sharply he realized he'd been side by side with Sally even though he couldn't see a sign of her.

"She was probably tracking a deer and saw it go down this way."

They were soon on the other side of that massive stone and once again moving along on a solid rock ledge.

"How far do we go?" Logan asked. He had a feeling he should know.

"Until we find a likely place."

"A likely place for what?"

"To hole up." Sally looked over her shoulder for too long.

Logan wanted to paint her smiling, daydreaming, working. He'd wanted to capture every one of the open expressions that passed so freely across her face. He'd actually felt hungry to explore every aspect of her beautiful face. But this expression . . .

"We need a good field of fire."

. . . made his stomach hurt.

"I'll hunt for shelter and—more important—cover."

It made him sick to think of putting this on canvas. He never wanted to see it again. "Cover from those men shooting at us?" He forced himself to say it aloud.

"That's right, Logan." She turned away from him. "We're looking for a likely place to kill." Nudging her horse forward, she added, "Or die."

Luther felt the flames cutting at him, his skin seared as he passed through the licking, consuming blaze. Once in, nearly blinded by the smoke, he took a desperate look around, rushing farther in to make sure no one lay unconscious in the corner, bleeding from bullet wounds.

No one. He headed out and saw a picture of Sally, drawn in pencil, lying on the floor near his feet. He grabbed at the drawings and felt a stack of things under it. He took them all as he staggered out of the choking blaze to drag fresh air into his lungs.

He looked around as he struggled to breathe and saw Buff abandoning the other cabin with something good-sized in his hand.

"No one in there." Buff had a picture, too. This one not a sketch but a painting.

"She was here." Luther lifted his picture as he and Buff moved away from the smothering fire. They saw the corral with two horses fidgeting and snorting because of the commotion.

"They either took her or she ran." Buff began studying the ground. It was the work of minutes to pick up the trail, grab their horses, and set off for the far side of this small flatland.

As they rode, Luther looked down at the picture of his Sally in his hand. She looked so much like Mandy, but she was completely herself. The toughest little wrangler in Texas, to Luther's way of thinking.

Buff held up what he'd brought.

Luther expected to see another picture of Sally. Instead he saw an old woman, dressed in a Shoshone doeskin dress, standing beside—"That's Pierre Babineau." Luther remembered the tough old codger well. He'd been haunting these mountains for years.

"And Wise Sister." Buff lifted the picture for just a second and looked at it. "She's gotten old. Reckon I have, too." He went back to his tracking.

"Never knew her." Luther saw where the trail dipped into the woods. Savvy spot to pick, with a dry spring eating a pathway, rough but passable, into that tangled forest.

"Babineau was a wandering man." Buff looked again at the picture. "Wise Sister stayed to home. I was in these parts before. Years ago. Did some trapping and mining on the Yellowstone River. I knew Wise Sister well, even before she married Babineau. If Babineau and Wise Sister have our Sally, then our girl's in good hands."

Luther's chest expanded with the most hope he'd felt since they'd found that first sign and knew Sally was alive. "Is she the one who drew these pictures?"

Buff shrugged. "Never heard of her doin' no drawing. S'pose it's possible. Shore cain't be Babineau. That man made a mark instead of signing his name. He drew me a map once to where he'd found good trapping, and I could barely make hide nor hair of it. He had no interest in anything that had him sitting around."

"Look at this trail. Three rode away first, then

two came after. The ones we've been trailing. Three. She's with Babineau and Wise Sister."

"Babineau was almighty savvy in the woods. But it was Wise Sister leaving markers for us. That don't make sense. Pierre wasn't a man to stay to home while his woman did the tracking."

"Maybe he's stoved up these days." Luther smoothed his heavy beard and thought about the harsh winters he'd lived through since following after Mandy. It suited him, these mountains did. He felt like he'd come home. But it was a rugged life, took its toll. "Hard, cold mountains might have gotten to his joints by now."

"Whatever's going on with Sally, those outlaws are dogging hard on her heels." Buff exchanged a grim look with Luther.

"We're close. We're almost there." Luther went down the trail as quickly as he dared, only to glance back and see Buff was off his horse. Luther pulled up. "What are you doing?"

Buff tucked the picture carefully into his saddle bag. It stuck out some, but he managed to fit it in. "I can't toss this away. If this is Wise Sister's, she can come fetch later."

Luther arched a brow as Buff took a long, close look at that painting. There was something in Buff's expression that Luther had never seen before. With a shrug, he said, "Stick these under that tree."

Buff saw them and mounted up. They moved

on down the trail, mindful of those men who had gone this way only moments ago. Men who had killed before.

That oughta be a lot more interesting to Buff than a painting of an old friend.

Nineteen

Sally pulled her horse to a stop so hard the animal fought the bit and reared. It backed away from the ledge while Sally's heart threatened to pound out of her chest. Her horse stumbled into the one behind it.

Then Logan was beside her. Not because he'd ridden up, but because she'd backed into him. Her horse had stumbled into Logan's then kept backing thanks to her iron-hard grip on the reins.

The trail wasn't wide enough for both of them. The mountain rose up steep on her right and rubbed hard against the cast on her leg. Then on the left the whole world slid away into a steep woodland. But somehow she managed to squeeze in beside Logan without shoving him off the trail on the downhill side.

Logan grabbed her horse's bridle as it came even with his hand. He stopped her or she might have backed all the way to Texas. "What is it?"

She realized what she was doing and eased up on her poor horse. Though her grip on the reins lessened, fear didn't lessen its grip on her. Her vision blurred and all she could see were trees rushing toward her as she fell and fell and fell. "We need to go back." She tore a hand from the reins to point back the way they'd come. "We must have . . . have . . . m–missed—"

"You said it was this way. You said Wise Sister gave you clear directions." Logan was watching her so intently she could hang on to that look, and some of the panic left her.

Then she looked at the trail ahead and saw rushing trees as she fell, then jerked her head around to look at Logan again. "We—we can't—the trail isn't—" Sally couldn't finish a sentence.

That searching look in Logan's eyes shifted from her to the trail. The awful trail Wise Sister intended them to take to reach safety. Logan tugged on the reins and pulled them free of her hand, as if he was afraid she'd turn and run if he let go of her horse. He began riding forward, leading her black mustang as if he meant to go straight over that cliff.

"No!" Sally's shout was more like a scream. Humiliating. Girly. Pa would be so ashamed. He might quit loving her. No man would love her if she acted like a weakling.

Logan stopped and twisted in his saddle. "I'm not going down the trail. I just want to see it."

But did he mean it? Or was he lying to make her face this stupid fear? She'd scrambled all over the steep, broken land back in Texas. There were no mountains like these, but it was plenty steep and plenty rugged. She'd never been afraid of a tough trail or a steep descent until—

"Is this because of the fall you took?" Logan turned his horse on the tight mountain path and rode up to her so he was only inches away.

Swallowing, nearly unable to force the words past her throat, she said, "I—I don't know. Maybe. I didn't know. I've never—I—I'm just being—a girl. I'm sorry." Sally tried to force her shoulders to square, but it was as if a thousand-pound weight of fear held them slumped. She swallowed again. "I—I can do it." She looked from the ledge to Logan and back to the ledge.

"Sally." His voice was hard. Commanding. Not at all the easygoing tone he usually took. She had so neatly concluded he was a weak, no-account kind of man. He didn't even mind a female crying. What kind of a man put up with that? But this wasn't the voice of a weak man.

"I'm not weak." Tearing her gaze from that drop, she faced him and knew she was lying.

"Of course you're not. You're the strongest woman I've ever known." Logan held on tight to her reins, belying his words.

"I can handle it." She could *not* go over that ledge. A scream built in her chest and began forcing its way out of her throat. Tears burned her eyes and twisted her stomach with the sickening admission of being a weakling, a female.

As if he knew she was on the ragged edge of control, Logan reached out and plucked her off her horse. He was so strong he lifted even the heavy cast so it easily cleared the saddle. He wasn't weak. Not at all. Not like her. Not about this.

He slid himself back on his horse, behind the cantle, and set Sally sideways on the saddle, still warm from his occupying it. This close, with one arm around her back against her pretty doeskin dress, holding his reins and hers, she felt some of his strength seep into her.

Shameful to need strength from another. She needed her own. Her pa loved her best when she was tough and didn't cry and did a man's work.

The need to scream fought to get free. Compulsively, her eyes went back to that awful, treacherous trail. "On—on a good mountain-raised horse we–we'll be fine." Her throat went bone-dry.

He caught her chin and tugged her face around so their eyes met. "You went through something no human being should ever face, Sally. Falling like that, somehow surviving. You're as strong and courageous as anyone I've ever known."

Sally couldn't pretend it was the truth. "I'm shaming myself. I've always pretended to be strong, but it was always a lie. I cry sometimes.

When I'm alone. And I love pretty, girly things—ribbons and lace and curls. I'm a coward." Panic had jarred loose her deepest secrets. Next she'd admit she got tired of riding the range and trying to outshoot the other cowpokes.

"No, you're not."

"I can do it." She couldn't imagine how. She'd faint or fall off her horse. She'd start screaming and crying and not be able to stop.

"We'll go back. We don't even know if those men found our trail. There's a very good chance they didn't. We'll be careful, go the way Wise Sister did, go past my cabin and ride out that way."

"Which might take us right into the teeth of those back-shooting coyotes. If they'd—if they'd face us, I could handle that." Sally realized then her fear went deeper than falling. Deeper than admitting to tears and softness. It turned her pure yellow to think of killing a man. She remembered firing, firing, unloading her gun, reloading, spinning it to cock it as her mother had taught her, as she'd fought with the colonel on that terrible mountain trail. She'd done it without thinking, but now it came rushing back. Had she killed a man?

Dear God, please have mercy if I took a man's life.

"Sally, it will be all right." Logan's eyes carried such strength, such calm. The calm helped. Not much, but some.

"What's wrong with me?" Her voice was barely above a whisper.

"It's normal, even reasonable to have a terrible experience leave behind fears, Sally." Logan's lips brushed hers and gave her something to think about besides sheer terror and wrenching guilt and her pa's love. Her pa had never asked her to be a tomboy. In fact, he'd often tried to shield her from the hardest work, and he'd assured her that he loved her for herself. The things she did. The way she acted didn't make a difference.

Beth had talked with her a few times, quiet talks, about their first pa and how much he'd wanted a son and how hard Sally had tried to be one for him. And how she'd kept that up when Ma had remarried. Beth had tried to encourage Sally to put on a dress and enjoy being a girl. But Sally hadn't trusted Pa to love her unless she helped him and never complained and never cried.

And now here she was, shaming herself in front of Logan. But Logan had never feared her tears. And yes, Pa might actually fear them, but he'd never withheld his love for any reason.

"There's nothing reasonable about what I'm feeling, Logan. Um, let's—let's get on with it." Her heart pounded faster. The trees, the falling, her vision blurred and she was somewhere else. Falling. Fighting it, she whispered, "Put me back on my horse. Give me a minute to steady my nerves, and we'll go."

"Are you sure?"

"Yes, yes, of course." Her voice barely worked.

"We can go back, Sally. There's no shame in not facing that trail. It's a bad one."

"Let's go. Help me back on the horse." She glanced down at her heavy cast, wrapped in Wise Sister's cleverly made moccasin.

Logan didn't obey her one bit about returning her to her saddle. Instead he backed his horse around and faced forward. Still holding her solidly, he made short work of detaching one of her horse's reins, tying it to the other to double its length, then lashed Sally's rein to his saddle horn.

The reins were long enough to leave her horse a couple of paces behind his. She wasn't sure what he intended by that. Did he intend to lead her down? That might be best. "Yes, put me down and I'll—" They neared the point where the trail fell off the edge of the world. Her vision blurred and trees rushed toward her and slapped her and clawed at her as she fell and fell. She wrapped her arms around Logan and buried her face against his chest.

"I'll just keep you right here, I think, pretty Sally."

"No, no, I'll be fine, I just need a little more time." Her voice rose until it was a squeak. Her eyes clamped shut. She felt the horse under her moving, heard its hooves clomping with dull, slow thuds on the rocky trail.

The ground suddenly sloped and Sally's eyes flew open. She looked along Logan's broad chest and past his left shoulder and saw . . . nothing. Air. The ground was gone for a hundred yards below. "Logan, no. I need time—"

"After I kissed you, you said you looked stupid in that picture. I thought you looked wonderful."

"What?" Sally's eyes were riveted on the vast expanse of nothingness as the horse picked its way down, sure-footed, slow and steady. Her heart hammered until she thought it would explode.

Logan caught her chin again, gently but unshakably. "What did you see in that painting that was stupid? I saw a woman who'd enjoyed a kiss. Who wanted another."

"Logan! Pay attention to the trail." Sally's hands clutched the back of his shirt frantically. She was going to scream. She was going to fall. Fall and fall forever, never stop. Never—

He kissed her. Pulled away quickly. "There you go. That's the kiss you wanted, right? That's what was in your eyes after I kissed you." Logan smiled at her.

"No." The man wasn't even watching the trail.
"Liar."

That insult got her attention. Calling a person a liar in the West was shooting trouble. "I *didn't* want another kiss."

"You took the second one I gave you without complaining."

"Watch the trail!" She felt her hands full of broadcloth on his back as if she could sink into him completely.

"A person has to trust his horse on a slope."

"But you should be watching."

"You want another kiss right now." It wasn't a question. He stated it as a fact.

And it wasn't true. What she wanted right now was to go back up to the top of this trail where it was safe. "That's the last thing on my mind, you big dumb—"

His hand slid from her chin and sank into her hair at the nape of her neck and he kissed her again. Deeply, gently. Sally thought of that picture he'd painted as she lost herself in the kiss. A woman whose mind had been emptied.

Of course her mind wasn't *empty* really. It was full, just full of only one thing. One huge thing that left no room for anything else. It was full of the notion that she'd arrived somewhere she'd been heading all her life. The notion that she'd come home to a man and a place. There'd been room for nothing else after that kiss, nor during this one.

Logan had captured that in his painting. Seeing

it had terrified her because he was nothing she wanted or respected.

Tilting her head back firmly, Logan slanted his lips hard across hers, which distracted her from thoughts of what she didn't want. In fact, he did a fine job of emptying her head of everything but him just as before. She shuddered to think what he'd paint if he had his brushes handy right now.

As he kissed her Sally knew, no matter what her plans were, they were all gone. All forgotten. She had to plot a new trail that ran alongside Logan's. Her hands let go of his shirt and slid until they wrapped tightly around his neck.

Rocks scattered and the horse shifted and slid a few inches, but all Sally could think of was Logan's strength, his wisdom, his talent for finding truth in his painting. For making a picture that a body could hear and smell and taste and feel. He'd made her beautiful with his art, and now he made her delight in being a woman with his kiss.

Logan raised his lips. "There, we're down."

"What?" Sally's eyes flickered open, her mind truly, once again, empty of all but one thing. "Down where?"

"Down at the bottom of the cliff of course." Logan smiled.

Focusing her blurred eyes, she looked up and up and up behind them. They'd come down a pencil-thin trail, and she'd never even noticed.

She realized she'd been nearly reclining against his arm with no mind to whether that might throw off her horse's balance on that death-defying trail.

Empty-headed indeed. Empty except for Logan.

Smiling, he tugged on his reins until he was side by side with her horse. "You ready to take charge of your life again, pretty Sally? Ride your own bronc?"

Her empty head filled again. He'd tricked her. He'd distracted her, this man who'd already broken the news to her that he couldn't do her the honor of marrying her. And because of her foolish fear, she'd let herself fall into a daydream of the future. One he'd already told her could never happen.

He reattached the reins then carefully lifted her with his unexpected strength onto her horse, mindful of her broken leg and her soft doeskin skirt. He had to put the reins in her hands and close her fingers around them.

She was too dazed to do it. Too ashamed.

She'd made a fool of herself for sure, because though he didn't need to know it, she'd just fallen completely in love with Logan McKenzie. And after all he'd said about never marrying.

He'd been dead serious when he'd said it. Which left her without a shred of hope that she could end up with him, even though—if he asked—she'd agree to stay forever and follow him wherever he went, to see whatever he wanted to paint next.

God, have mercy.

Because in the way of a wise Texas woman, Sally knew deep in her heart that he was the only man she'd ever love. And even if Luther came for her today and she rode away from Logan and never saw him again, she'd love him and only him for the rest of her life.

"Let's go." She turned to the trail, a game trail barely visible but not dangerous now. She'd need to take the lead. It was the only place she could put herself and be sure he wouldn't read what she was feeling with those sharp, all-seeing artist eyes.

God, please, please, please have mercy.

"Sally, wait." Logan reached for her. "We need to talk."

She kicked her horse into motion so he couldn't catch hold of her or see her or hear her. "No, let's go," she shouted over her shoulder.

They were the last words she spoke for a long time because the silent sobs choked her throat shut. And it was a good thing the horse was trail savvy because the tears made it so she couldn't see where she was going.

Twenty

Normally Mandy was relieved when Sidney went to town. Having Luther and Buff away had altered Mandy's thinking. She'd never realized quite how much she'd come to depend on her pa's old friends. For everything.

But with Luther and Buff hunting for Sally—
God, protect her. Protect my little sister.

Mandy had spent hours in prayer since Sally had gone missing. There was hardly the tiniest corner of her life that didn't, suddenly, seem to be a disaster.

Catherine cried from her crib in the bedroom, and Mandy felt that little voice center her. That's what her life was about—the children, protecting them, loving them, raising them to marry wisely . . . unlike their mama.

With the men here working on the house, and Cooter's frightening behavior, Mandy was on her own in a way she'd never been. She considered herself to be a tough woman. But maybe it was easy to respect your abilities when you never had to prove anything. She'd wanted to beg Sidney to stay. She'd wanted to shout at him, because he was no protection even if he was here. But if she'd said those words, they could never be taken back so she'd let him ride away.

The first hammer blow rang out on the house,

and Mandy glanced out the window to look up, up, up and see that ridiculous house really taking shape. It was stone. Gray stone. Everything in Sidney's world was gray. Mandy looked at her dress. A dull blue only because she'd gotten it before Sidney had become obsessed with his name and turning his whole world gray to match it.

But he'd bought Tom Linscott's blacks. Because no doubt they were so expensive Sidney couldn't resist.

Diverting herself from thoughts of Tom, she looked at her house again. To be surrounded by a mountain covered with logs yet build a house out of stone, at terrible expense, with an over-whelming amount of effort, was embarrassing. Most everything about her husband was an embarrassment.

The day, the third since Sidney had ridden away, caught her and dragged her into it. She'd hoped Sidney would be back by now. She'd told him to hurry. But she kept busy. There were the children to care for, the house to tend, the garden to weed.

Just after noon, with the girls fed and down for naps, she turned her attention to firewood. If she pushed hard she could get wood split before they woke.

She lifted a length of oak to the chopping block. Buff had cut a good supply before he left, but it was going fast thanks to the builders arriving and needing to keep the bunkhouse warm and cook their own meals.

Slamming the razor-sharp ax into the log with a single, smooth stroke, it split perfectly. She took pride in being able to turn her hand to anything, though it was a chore with her stomach so big. She should stick with this until she'd gotten four days' supply, but she already knew she'd be lucky to stay with the chore until she had wood enough for the evening meal and breakfast. And the evenings got cold so she needed more yet to keep a fire in the hearth.

Lifting another log into place, she raised her ax and swung. The impact shook her. She felt the muscles of her arms reach deep into her body, into her stomach, and pull painfully on something.

The sound of hooves spun her around, the ax in one hand, the other going for her rifle, strapped on her back as always.

That's when she admitted she'd been scared all morning, expecting trouble, expecting Cooter. Expecting to hear that Sidney had been shot and Cooter was back to do her harm. But it wasn't Cord Cooter who appeared on that trail.

Tom Linscott rode in leading two magnificent horses, a matching pair, shining black. Mandy barely noticed because her eyes were riveted on Tom.

She dropped the ax and felt his eyes on her, registering everything—that she was pregnant, that she was still doing Sidney's chores. That she was irrationally glad to see him.

The battle to keep herself from rushing toward him was almost more than she could win. And maybe she'd have lost the battle and shamefully thrown herself into Tom's arms.

If she hadn't felt a flood of warm liquid, as her water broke.

Twenty-One

Wise Sister!" Buff dropped from his horse and rushed toward the underbrush.

Luther heard Buff's words, saw his friend's actions, and pulled his horse to a halt in one short second. They'd found Wise Sister, and that meant they'd found Sally. He felt tears burn his eyes and covered them by blowing his nose and paying strict attention to urging his horse forward to the bushes.

In the seconds it took to reach Buff's side, an elderly woman emerged from the forest. "Here, get off the trail. Bad men come." Wise Sister caught Buff's hand and dragged him to his horse, caught the reins, and led both animal and man down a stony bit of ground eaten by water runoff. They would never have recognized this as a trail.

"Sally?" Luther followed after Buff's horse, aware that he was being completely ignored by both Wise Sister and Buff.

"Sally girl just ahead with Logan, the man whose cabin burned," Wise Sister answered.

"Logan? Is he the one who brought her here? Is he the one who drew those pictures?"

"Yes. No time now for talk." Wise Sister and Buff kept walking.

Luther couldn't help noticing that she was still leading both the horse and Buff, although from here it looked for all the world like two people holding hands.

Luther rode slowly. Wise Sister led Buff around a bend to her horse. She let go of his hand, they exchanged some words too quiet to hear, and then she swung up on her horse with the lithe agility of a young girl.

Buff mounted and followed her. Luther didn't expect Buff to say much to him, but had the man even asked if Sally was hurt?

It didn't strike Luther as a smart time to start hollering, so he fell in behind Buff and set out.

"They didn't come this far." Tulsa pulled his horse around with a savage jerk on the reins.

Fergus hadn't seen a sign of a trail for a long time, but on this rugged land, that didn't mean much. Right now they'd reached a flat land with some gathered silt that coated the entire narrow

295

trail. No one passed this way without leaving sign.

Tulsa turned and looked back up the trail. "I didn't seen no sign of 'em leaving the trail neither."

Staring at where they'd been, Fergus considered the time since they'd caught that glimpse of the riders, no more than an hour ago. "Then let's go look at places they could have left the trail *without* leaving a sign." He jerked hard on the reins as he wheeled his horse aside to let Tulsa go first. Fergus was good on a trail, but Tulsa was better, and only a stubborn fool didn't use the talents of the men around him.

Fergus wasn't sure about stubborn, but he was sure as certain nobody's fool.

Mandy's knees went limp as she realized what had just happened.

Tom was off his horse and at her side before she could hit the ground. He swept her up in his arms. "What's the matter? Where's the worthless bum?"

Sidney. Mandy hated to admit it. "He's gone to town."

"To Helena? When you're this far along with a baby? When is it due?"

A cramp made her grab for her belly. "Now."

"Now? You're having the baby right now?" Tom's light brown brows arched in pure fear right to his hairline. His hair had bleached to nearly white in the summer sun.

Mandy found her hand caressing the ridiculous length of it, hanging below his Stetson. It reminded her of her pa. "Never time for a haircut."

"What?" Tom turned toward the cabin, carrying her as if she weighed nothing.

At that moment Angela cried out, up from her nap.

"What's that?"

"My baby."

Tom's eyes went to her belly.

"No, my two-year-old."

Another thinner cry sounded with Angela. Catherine was up.

"And my one-year-old."

"I was here just over two years ago."

"Closer to three, actually." Mandy was sure.

"This is your third baby in that time?"

The pain in her stomach grew into a tight spasm, and Mandy didn't want to spend another second talking. "Tom, I'm going to have this baby." She couldn't mention her water breaking. It was too shameful. And there was no woman anywhere. Luther had stayed with her for the last two births while Buff had raced to town and brought back a midwife in plenty of time for there to be no need for a man dealing with something so personal.

"What do you need? What can I do to help?" His voice wasn't entirely steady and his darkly tanned skin turned a sickly shade of gray, but he said the words. A brave man.

The babies cried again and Angela yelled, "Mama!"

Mandy couldn't allow Tom's help. It was too outrageous to even think such a thing. No, this one Mandy was going to have to do on her own, but it would be all she could do to birth the baby, at least toward the end. She didn't have time for her little girls.

Which meant, "Have you ever done any babysitting?"

Logan goaded his horse forward and caught hold of Sally's reins, jerking her mustang to a stop. "You are not going to kiss me like that then ride away as if it meant nothing."

Sally was crying. He saw it the instant his words left his mouth.

"Sally, sweetheart." He leaned down, drawn to her so strongly it was beyond his power to resist the urge.

Sally was made of sterner stuff. She swiped the long sleeve of her dress across her eyes. "I'm not going to sit here talkin' while men hunt us."

Logan straightened. The flame that had drawn him had turned into a fire that threatened to burn him right to the ground. "We need to talk—"

"Wise Sister said to go to the top of this trail and I'd find a hidden cave." Sally stabbed a finger at the trail in front of her. "We can hole up there until she comes. Then we can talk."

The trail climbed again. Everything around here was at some kind of an angle. Up, down, and sideways—God had turned this place on its side rather than laying it flat. Logan was grateful for that because it was magnificent to paint. But it wasn't all that practical.

"No man with a lick of sense would want to jabber away when he's being hunted."

Logan handed her a handkerchief to save her pretty dress.

She took it and blew her nose.

Which gave him too much time to talk. "I'd say I had the sense to get us down that cliff side."

Sally's eyes went to the trail they'd just descended and some of the color leached from her tearstained face, leaving her eyes glowing red and her nose shining. And her lips still swollen from his kissing her all the way down that long, long trail.

Crazy thing to do. He hadn't even watched where his horse was going; though he'd have been little help to his horse so it might be just as well.

He could have kicked himself for reminding her of what she'd called weakness, as if a human being wasn't allowed to have serious doubts about a hairpin trail like that, especially when she'd recently gone sailing off a cliff.

Sally mopped her face off a bit then shoved the soggy kerchief into his hands.

"I wouldn't dishonor you by kissing you if my intentions weren't honorable, Sally." Logan knew his fate was sealed as far as finding a life with Sally now. He'd have to convince her to live in the mountains and spend the winters in New York. Or he'd have to change every plan he'd made. He wondered for a moment if the scenery in Texas was beautiful. It might be worth checking.

"I remember your honorable intentions well enough. You said your painting would always come first, and any woman in your life could plan on being ignored. No thank you, Logan."

"But that was before—"

"You're not going to say that's changed, are you? Because I won't believe you."

"I wouldn't lie." Logan was all stirred up. He was overreacting, but Sally calling him a liar made him furious.

"I don't think you would lie. I think any nice thing you said to me right now would be the absolute truth."

Mollified, Logan nodded. "Well then, good."

"But I think tomorrow you'd see an eagle flying over our heads, and you'd forget every pretty word you said to me." Sally's jaw firmed and the color was mostly back in her cheeks, thanks to her anger.

"I would not."

"And I'd expect you to, Logan. I'd respect you for that."

"What? You'd respect me for ignoring you?"

"No, I'd *hate* that you ignored me. I'd *respect* you for being yourself. For following your God-given dreams and using your God-given talents. And I'd understand that I had a weak moment, and you stepped in and saved me from that weakness, and because you're a hero right along with being an artist, it confused you for a bit about what you're feeling right now."

"You think I'm a hero?"

Sally pulled her Stetson off her head and whacked him with it. He lifted his forearm to protect his face. "Pay attention. Your words and feelings right now aren't the man I've been getting to know for the last few weeks. I've got to believe this is the exception, not the real you."

Logan wanted to argue with her, but he was momentarily distracted by the sight of a young buffalo emerging from a clump of trees far down the mountain. Its mother lumbered out behind it. His fingers itched for his sketchbook and pencil.

The Stetson swatted him again. "You've just made my point, Painter-Man."

Logan had forgotten she was there, but just for

a second. Well, a few seconds. No more than a minute.

"Now let's ride to that cave Wise Sister told me about and hole up until she finds Luther and brings him here. Then I can get out of here and go see my sister, and you can go draw another picture of an elk."

All his work was in ashes. All his paints and canvas were destroyed. He had to leave, go home. It was devastating thinking of all he'd lost. That's when Logan realized she was right. He felt so terrible about that loss that he'd gotten his priorities temporarily twisted. But this was only today, while he was saving her from her fear. Tomorrow he'd be right back to the self-centered clod he'd always been. And if he persuaded Sally to throw in with him, stay and marry him—the image he got of that drove every thought of painting from his head—he'd soon be back to his old selfish ways. He knew. She knew.

Logan looked at her. Their eyes caught, hers bright blue and red rimmed. He wanted to paint her when she'd been crying. But he had no paint. "You're right, Sally. But you're the only woman I've ever met who made me even want to think less about art. I doubt I could really be good to you, but I care enough that I'd feel awful when I wasn't, and that's no kind of life for either of us."

She nodded. With a tug on her reins, she turned

her horse to aim up the trail, searching for a place to hole up.

With a good field of fire. So, if called to fight, he might get a chance to kill a man.

Sick with dread, Logan fell in behind her and tried to force himself to think only about the scenery and what he'd do if he had a pencil and sketchbook and time. But instead he fixated on the beautiful woman riding away from him.

A woman he could try to capture on canvas for the rest of his life without ever exploring all the expressions that flitted across her amazingly lovely face.

A woman he'd just kissed mindless then thrown away with both hands.

Twenty-Two

Right there, Fergus." Tulsa raised his rifle in one smooth motion to his shoulder, sighted along the gun barrel, and took aim.

Fergus looked in the direction his saddle partner was looking and saw two riders. Far up the slope.

Tulsa jerked his gun down with a grunt of disgust. "Too far. All a shot would do is warn 'em."

"One of 'em looked like—a woman." Fergus couldn't take his eyes off what he'd seen. "An Indian woman with a gun strapped on her back."

"They're too far away to be sure of that."

"I know it. But I'm sure just the same. And the other one was too big to be the cowpoke you shot."

Fergus and Tulsa exchanged a long look.

"There could be other people out here. Maybe these aren't even the ones we've been hunting. That cabin might belong to someone with no stake in this game." Tulsa jabbed his gun muzzle at the place where the riders crossed just as they vanished into a cluster of trees.

"That gun, the one the woman had strapped on—that's the way the man I shot wore his gun. You don't see that much."

"You think the man you shot was a woman dressed in man's clothes?"

Slowly shaking his head back and forth, Fergus rubbed his hand over the bandolier crossing his chest. The belt of bullets reminded him of how the little Indian gal had worn that rifle. How the cowpoke wore his, too. He tried to sort it out. "He was little enough to be a she, I reckon."

"I regretted shooting that woman off her horse when we waylaid those folks. I haven't seen a woman in too long." Tulsa's smile was pure evil, and Fergus knew the man wasn't talking about *seeing*. "Maybe we can have another chance."

Fergus knew the man was now more determined than ever to catch up with that pair riding far above; and that suited Fergus just fine.

"They got off that trail somehow. We'll figure it out." Fergus gathered his reins.

"Not that way." Tulsa kept his eye on the spot they'd last seen the pair.

"How else?" Fergus looked at the land between him and the riders. It was a terrible thing to imagine, jagged, no broken trail, impenetrable forest broken in places by sheer rock.

"We go forward, find a way up from this end instead of going back. We'll cut miles off the trip."

"You think we're going to climb that mountain?" Fergus slung his reins around his pommel then lifted his hat with one hand and ran the other through his hair, agitated. Scared. Like that streak in his hair was a streak of cowardice.

"Yeah. It can be done. Even if we have to go on foot. We'll climb up there and get ahead of 'em, lie in wait, shoot 'em and strip 'em of their money and guns, and climb back down for our horses. Or we'll take theirs and spend all the time we want riding back to ours. Let's go." Tulsa kicked his horse into a trot without waiting for Fergus to say yes, no, or maybe.

Which made Fergus's fingers twitch to put a bullet in the man's back. When Curly had been alive, this'd been Fergus's gang. He made the decisions, and Curly backed him. Tulsa never did anything but go along. Now, without it being two

305

to one, Tulsa was giving orders, and Fergus didn't like it. He took one long moment to think of killing Tulsa, taking all the money in those stuffed saddlebags of his, forgetting that pair riding high above, and lighting a shuck for San Francisco. It would be easy. Tulsa wasn't even watching his back. But they'd been riding the outlaw trail together a long time. Right now, Tulsa Bob Wiley was the only friend Fergus had in the world.

On the other hand, Fergus knew how much money he had, and Tulsa had an even cut. If Tulsa died, Fergus was a much richer man. And he could stay rich if he kept away from poker and whiskey and women. A man got poor having that kind of fun. Though what was the point of being rich if you couldn't have some fun?

Fergus set aside the idea of blowing his cousin out of the saddle. He could always kill his only friend later, should the need arise. He kicked his horse into a fast walk to catch up. It was unwise to turn your back on a back-shooter. Family sticking together wasn't as tempting as cash in hand.

Tom carried Mandy into the house with such quick, determined steps she had the feeling he wasn't saving her so much as running to a place he could put her down so he could escape.

Both babies yowled now from their bedroom.

306

Tom looked at Mandy, his eyes so wide she could see white all the way around the pupils. His eyes darted from her, to her belly, to the door to the girls' room. Mandy suspected that if he'd been in a room with three sticks of dynamite, their fuses all lit, the man wouldn't have been any more upset.

He bent to set her down on a chair then straightened without letting go. "You should go to bed. No, you should sit out here. No, let me take you in with the babies. Two did you say? Two babies and one on the way? In under three years. Is your husband a complete idiot?"

Mandy could think of no response that should be uttered aloud.

"I left my horses standing there untied." He whirled around with her still in his arms as if he meant to go put up the horses, carrying her the whole time.

Mandy's belly relaxed and she could think again. And take charge. Someone needed to. Her husband wasn't the only idiot man around. "Put me down."

Why, oh why hadn't Sally gotten here in time?

"No!" He shouted the word and looked at her as if she'd asked him to hurl her over a cliff.

"I'm fine. The baby is coming but not this very instant. I'll go check on the girls while you tend to your horses."

"I'm not leaving you alone!" Tom practically

roared the words at her. "If your husband was here I'd snap him in two like a twig."

Mandy patted his arm. "Well, if he was here you wouldn't be all upset because he isn't here, now would you? So here or not, you don't end up getting to snap any twigs." She managed to catch his eyes, which were still darting around the room.

It reminded her of a little bluebird that had fallen into the house through the chimney one day. The brightly colored bird had crashed frantically into the walls and ceiling while Mandy rushed to open every door and window, hoping the poor little animal would get out before it hurt itself.

She hoped Tom's blue eyeballs didn't go flying out like that bird had once it'd found an escape hatch.

"Put me down." Small words. Spoken slowly, loudly. Direct orders.

He seemed to be responding. Setting her on her feet, he hovered as if he expected her to keep sinking right to the floor. When she stood, that went a long way toward calming him.

"Put the horses in the barn."

Shaking his head no frantically, he said, "Okay."

"Now, Tom. Hurry."

Those fluttering, flying eyeballs seemed to understand the word *hurry*. He turned and dashed out of the house so fast Mandy was

308

relieved the door was standing open or, right now, there'd be a Tom Linscott–shaped hole in it.

She focused on the crazy man who'd stopped by, to keep her from thinking of what lay ahead. Turning to the girls' bedroom, she went to it, forcing a serene expression on her face, hoping not to signal to the girls all her many fears.

The door swung inward as soon as she'd turned the knob. Angie, out of her crib, was working to escape.

"I'm sorry Mama was slow, honey." Smiling, Mandy scooped her up and gave her a hug. "I'm sorry I left you and baby Catherine to cry for so long."

"Mama sad?"

Mandy tried to decide if there was something in her expression that prompted Angela's question, or if she thought the word sorry meant sad. Giving the little imp another hug, she said, "No, Mama is very happy. We have company."

Angie's brow furrowed. And why not? How could this little one know what the word company meant? Since no one had ever stopped by to visit before.

Mandy carried Angie to Catherine's crib, did a quick diaper change for Catherine, and helped Angie with her own newly learned potty skills in the little commode they kept inside. Then she scooped both girls into her arms with a hard hug and went back into the main room of the house.

She settled them at the table and got two tin cups of milk ready and a slice of bread and jelly.

Thank heavens the cow finally bore her calf and we have milk again.

The girls finished their little snack while she had another contraction, this one so long and hard it scared her, but she didn't think the girls noticed. It passed, and she picked them both up and headed for the rocking chair just as Tom came sprinting through the door she'd still never closed.

"Put them down!" He rushed at her and scared the girls to death. When he reached for Angie, she shrieked and wrapped her arms around Mandy's neck so tightly it threatened to strangle her.

Mandy felt another contraction begin.

Tom started pacing back and forth across the room.

Oh yeah, you're going to be a lot of help.

Twenty-Three

Sally had an itch between her shoulder blades that told her to keep riding hard and fast.

"Stop!" Logan pointed.

Sure enough, there was a cave opening with rocks in the front that gave them nice protection and a good field of fire. Too bad all her instincts told her to keep moving.

"I wonder how far we are from Mandy's." What a dream come true it would be to reach Mandy's house. To have her fast shooting, deadeye sister at her side to face down these bad men. But Luther and Buff should be coming. Surely Wise Sister had found them. Surely they'd be here soon.

Logan shrugged. "You have no idea exactly where she lives?"

"There was a hand-drawn map from Helena to Mandy's house, but I never had it. Pa got it in the mail from Luther and gave it to the colonel, who died with it in the gunfight. One of the men in our party knew this area so we trusted to him when we left the train to take a shortcut. He did his figuring and we were following him. I saw the map from Mandy and I heard the man leading us talk about how he planned to go. But I don't know the area so it didn't make much sense to me. I just knew the general direction. Then after I was unconscious, you took me on a day-long ride in the *wrong* direction."

"Not the *exact* wrong direction." Logan shrugged.

"I can't even figure out if we rode toward Mandy's or away. I know you said we headed mostly west, some north. I think Mandy's cabin is mostly west, some south. We might be closer than we think."

And what if they were close? Sally thought of leading two back-shooters to Mandy and abandoned the idea of even trying to keep moving. "Up until now we've followed Wise Sister's orders; no reason to stop now."

Logan nodded and swung down from his horse in front of the tall cave opening. There was space between the pile of huge rocks in the cave mouth to lead the horses inside. Sally saw nowhere likely to tie them up out here.

Logan stepped in, leading his horse. "No, this isn't possible. It can't be." His voice echoed out of the black opening that swallowed up his mount. He sounded strange, almost scared.

Sally swung down and hobbled after him, not using her crutches. The cast supported her leg without pain. She was still a little edgy, as if even now someone was watching them, drawing a bead.

Entering the cave with her black mustang following placidly along, she stumbled over her feet to a halt at what she saw. Then she forced herself forward to get herself and her horse under cover.

There was a huge room that reached up at least twenty feet, but that wasn't the unbelievable part. Weird columns of stone stood reaching from floor to ceiling like a dozen support pillars. The columns seemed to glow in the dark of the cave. Sally leaned close to the nearest one. It was whitish gray and wet. She reached her hand out. "Don't touch it."

• • •

"Did you see that, Fergus?"

Snapping his head around, Fergus looked where Tulsa pointed. Straight up a sheet of rock that was mighty short on handholds. "See what?"

"A horse. We rounded this clump of trees just in time for me to see the back end of a black mustang going behind those rocks."

"Which pile of rocks? This whole place is nothing but a pile of rocks."

"That mound chest high, in that clear spot." Tulsa pointed as he urged his horse closer to Fergus. "There must be a cave behind that granite. I only saw one horse, but there's not room behind there for two."

Tulsa's eyes shone with a greedy, hungry gleam. "We've got 'em cornered if we can get up there fast enough."

Fergus looked all the way up that slope and gulped. It was a long, risky climb, several hundred yards. The last stretch looked purely impossible, but they'd decide if it was when they got up there. If they hurried, they could get within shooting distance in time to pin down this pair in the cave and take their time closing in on 'em.

Fergus ran a hand down the bandolier of bullets on his chest. They had enough ammunition to start a war. They could pin those riders down for a long, long time. One of 'em could cover the cave mouth while the other climbed and got into position. With two of them, they could take all the time they wanted climbing up there.

"Let's go." Tulsa rode his horse forward as far up the incline as possible. Then he swung down to use a scrub tree for a hitchin' post.

Riding along behind, it burned Fergus bad that Tulsa was giving orders again.

"Move faster," Tulsa said. "We finish this today, then ride for San Francisco for the winter. I've got a hankerin' for some whiskey and a hand or two of poker. I'm tired of living hard and cold."

Hard was the way Fergus wanted to hit Tulsa. Cold, well, that might well be how Fergus left his saddle partner. Cold and dead after they finished with those riders hiding in the cave. Fergus needed Tulsa to make sure there was no one left to tell the tale. They'd finish this then Fergus would double his money with one smashing bullet in Tulsa's back. It'd be the best day's work he'd ever done.

Tulsa yelled a few more orders as they clawed their way up that cliff.

Fergus almost enjoyed how much that irritated him because it would make killing his friend a whole lot easier.

Snatching back her fingers, Sally wondered if the columns held the roof up. "I've never seen anything like this before."

314

"They're stalactites. Dear Lord God in heaven, thank You." Logan's voice was so reverent Sally knew the man was truly praying.

And well he should be. She was glad these stone columns were here, too. "These are great. If those vermin catch up with us, we'll have a great shield. All we've got to do is get behind these. As far to the back of the cave as we can."

"Wise Sister had to know they were here. How could she not have told me?" Logan reached out and rested a hand on one a few feet ahead of the one he'd forbidden Sally to touch. He had no reaction to her mention of gunfire.

The man was a moron. A moron she was in love with.

And what did that make her?

"This is an artist thing, isn't it?" Sally's jaw clenched. She'd been being a good sport about his painting, hadn't she? But there were limits.

"I've got to get canvas. I've got to find a way to paint this."

He didn't seem to have heard a word she said. Well, his head would clear when lead started flying.

Of course maybe they were safe, far from trouble, and the itch she felt was just her being overly cautious. In which case, once she was sure they were safe, she might clear his head by slamming it into one of his *stag-tights*, or whatever he called them.

Ignoring him, she led her horse into the cave to find a place to protect the mustang. The cave was deep, too, as if it sank into the heart of the mountain. Water dripped everywhere, and those weird columns glowed like lanterns, yet cast no light, so she could only see with the bit of light from the cave door. The cave floor was wet enough she paused to take her crutches off the saddle to keep her cast dry. Then she wove carefully between the pillars on the rough floor until she found a small spring near the back corner. Her horse moved past her, its nose reaching for the water, its hooves echoing in the cave.

Though Sally worried about the water being safe to drink, a mountain horse like this little mustang was probably a better judge than she was, so she let the thirsty animal have its head.

Going back, she relieved Logan of his horse while he stared at the column as if he could use it to see into heaven. Logan's horse was soon beside Sally's drinking with soft, rushing contentment. Unable to resist, Sally lay down on her belly to drink. She wondered if she'd have to lead Logan to water, like she had his horse.

When she'd had her fill, Sally stood and wiped her mouth with her handkerchief. Then using one crutch only, she walked back to the front door.

As she passed him, since her broken leg wasn't

doing anything anyway, she used it to kick Logan in the shin.

"Ouch!" Scowling, he turned to her. "What did you do that for?"

Resisting the urge to give him one more sound kick, she asked, "Are you going to help me watch the front entrance, or do you want to start drawing pictures?"

"I don't have my sketchbook."

"You really don't have a brain in your head, do you?"

A deep furrow appeared between his brows. "I thought you said we were safe here. Why can't I look at these beautiful stalactite columns for a while?" He turned and pointed to one side of the room to where a column wasn't fully formed. It looked like a set of fangs, one upper and one lower tooth—each about five feet long. "Look at that one. It's dripping down from the top and building up from the bottom, but it hasn't met yet. Isn't it great?"

Sally spared the corner a look. "You shore 'nuff described it perfectly." She deliberately spoke her worst cowboy slang in her deepest Texas accent. Maybe it would remind him of why he shouldn't be kissing her. More importantly, maybe it would remind her of why she shouldn't be in love with him. They were from two different worlds. His was a world where you looked at a rock and wanted to draw it. Hers—where you looked at a rock and saw a place to duck behind when lead started flyin'. "When you're dodgin' bullets, I recommend you pick the fattest one."

She smirked at him. "And you know what? Choose one that's solid all the way through. That empty middle part on that one"—she pointed to the giant fangs—"won't stop a bullet worth nothin'. So solid's a real good idea. You can hide behind it while I protect us."

"Those men might shoot at us!" He wasn't asking a question. It was more like he had at last awakened to the danger. It took him long enough.

Well, good. Finally. He needed to be worrying about saving his worthless hide.

"We have to save these beautiful stalactites."

Sally's hands tightened on her Winchester. Oh, she wouldn't shoot him. That wasn't called for. But just one good whack with the butt of her gun. Just one to get rid of some tension and maybe knock some sense into his head. And if there was not a butt stroke hard enough to do that, at least he'd be flat on his back, out of the range of rifle fire. "You're in danger from more than just those coyotes on our trail."

She didn't identify herself as the threat. Instead, she whirled around and hobbled to the cave mouth. "Get a drink. There's water in the back. Just follow the horses. They're not so stupid they don't know to get some water in their bellies when they have a chance."

Sally was just resting the muzzle of her rifle against one of the rocks protecting the cave when Logan grabbed her arm, just below the elbow, and whirled her around.

"Don't treat me like I'm a fool." He leaned down until he nearly touched her nose with his, just like he didn't even see she was furious and heavily armed. "I know there's trouble. That doesn't mean I can't stop for a moment and appreciate something God created with pure beauty in mind. I think you're the one who's *stupid* to be able to see what's in that cave and go right back to water and bullets. You need to open your eyes and see the beauty around you. What's the point of living if you don't?"

Sally jerked against his grip, but he didn't let go so she rose on her tiptoes—well, one tiptoe; her broken foot wasn't of much use—to yell right in his face. "You need to open your eyes and see the ugliness around you. What're the chances of living if you don't?"

They glared at each other, mad enough to light a fire in the air. She yanked at her arm again and managed to drop her crutch and let her rifle swing down so it was out of the way between them. Logan tugged so her forearm pressed against the solid wall of his chest.

"Let me go," Sally spoke through clenched teeth.

"You're not going anywhere." Logan acted as if his height and weight and strong will were enough to force her to do his bidding.

The moment stretched. Sally's temper built. A red flush of fury darkened Logan's neck.

Then something snapped in Sally's anger and turned it upside down, to a different kind of fire. Sally caught the collar of his shirt with her free hand and dragged him down just as he wrapped an arm around her waist and lifted her off her feet—foot.

Logan's kiss wiped out every shred of common sense she possessed. He dragged her back into the cave, then turned and pressed her against the wall, turning his head to deepen the kiss. He raised his lips the least whisper of an inch. "Sally, tell me you'll stay here with me."

His words were nearly lost because Sally wouldn't let the kiss go long enough to let him speak a whole sentence. "I have to. I am so in love with you."

Logan shuddered.

Sally felt that all the way to her heart.

"Yes." His hands slid to her face, and he pulled away so she could see him. See he meant it when he said, "I love you, too. It's madness. You'll end up hating me."

"No, never." It was reasonable that she would get tired of a man who spent his time on nonsense, but she knew it would never stop her from loving him. "I can't hate you ever." She pulled him back to her and lost herself in his embrace.

Logan suddenly wrenched his head to the side, breaking the kiss. He rested his face against the side of hers and she kissed his cheek, his hair, his ear.

"Stop!" With a groan of almost pain, Logan pulled away from her and turned his back, running both hands deep into his hair.

Sally sagged against the stone, pressed a hand to her swollen lips, and tried to think of something, anything except this man and how strange he was . . . and how wonderful. She'd completely lost her mind.

She needed to be doing something else. What? What else? Watch the trail, find something to eat in the bag Wise Sister had brought along, study possible hideouts down the hill where someone could get a shot off at them?

"We're going to be together." Logan turned to her, his eyes blazing. "I'm not letting you go."

"Good." Now more common sense invaded Sally's muddled brain. Her dearly loved parents, the rest of her family back in Texas. Her big sister in need. Good reasons why she *should* go. She was staying anyway. "Because you're not getting rid of me no matter what you do." She launched herself into his arms again.

He caught her and laughed, his beautiful,

searching artist eyes seeking her every thought. Well, let him look. She wasn't hiding anything from him.

Then he dodged her kiss, grinned, and said, "You need to be a bit more practical, woman. This isn't the time and place for this."

Sally smiled, then even laughed. "Name the time and place, Logan."

"How about we live through this, find Wise Sister and your friends, then go hunt up a preacher in the nearest town and get married?"

"Go to town?" Sally widened her eyes in mock surprise. "Tell the truth, is that so we can get married or so you can buy a new sketchbook?"

Logan didn't even flinch. Instead he looked her square in the eye. "It is all about marrying you. If you promise to keep kissing me like that, I'll follow you anywhere."

"I had the same thought myself."

Logan leaned down and kissed her again, hard and quick. "Let's go stand watch to make sure no one sneaks up on us until Wise Sister shows up with your friends." Logan turned her so they were side by side. He slipped his arms around her waist, over her rifle. He helped her hobble along, and somehow they fit together just perfectly.

They reached the cave opening, more focused on each other than on the danger. They stepped out in the narrow space behind the rocks piled by the cave mouth.

A bullet whizzed between them, hit stone behind, ricocheted, and tore a hole through Logan's Stetson.

Sally grabbed at Logan, but he was already grabbing at her, and they dived to the rocky floor.

Gunfire whizzed overhead like murderous bees.

Logan threw himself on top of her to shelter her as the first bullet tore a chunk off one of the stalactites. With a shout of outrage, he said, "They're going to ruin this cave!"

"Those bullets are going to ricochet off the rock and kill us." Sally grabbed the front of his shirt in her fist and tried to decide whether to drag him to safety or strangle him.

Twenty-Four

Luther heard the gunfire and hit the ground before it made impact.

Silent as a ghost, he slipped into the undergrowth on the downhill side of the trail and advanced toward the shooters. He heard Buff and Wise Sister moving, separating whisper-quiet just ahead of him, using every ounce of caution and every shred of cover they could while still moving fast.

More shots rang out, but there was only the volley aiming up the mountain, no return fire. What if they were too late? What if they'd gotten this close to Sally only to have her shot dead minutes before they could protect her?

Luther moved faster, his jaw clenched to keep from roaring in fury. He was falling behind Buff, though Buff was going straight while Luther was on a downhill slant.

The bullets hit stone and caromed with a sharp whine. Two men. Rifles. Probably farther downhill from Luther. He eased on down the slope using the trees to hold him on that steep side of the mountain. It wasn't fit for a man to walk on, but Luther'd never met the mountain that could best him.

He saw a flicker of movement above and saw Buff waving to catch his eye. With a few quick hand gestures, he told Luther to keep moving down while Buff covered the higher end of the trail. It was more dangerous up there, but this was no time for Luther to jaw with Buff about a plan.

Luther faded down even lower, keeping silent, gripping sturdy trees that wouldn't give away his position by shaking their tops when he grabbed ahold.

He got below the shooters without their noticing, based on the fact that they were still unloading their guns on something up the hill. That made Luther feel a bit better. This was wild shooting, meant to get in a lucky hit. They didn't have a real target.

He hoped.

Grim determination twisted Luther's lips as he saw the first man just ahead, methodically unloading his gun up the hill to a cave opening about a hundred feet ahead and above them. Those hundred feet would be tough ones to climb, which probably explained why they were doing their dirty work from down here. This had to be one of the men who had waylaid Sally's party. For a back-shooter, he wasn't watching behind him a bit good.

The man's focus was fixed on that cave, firing, reloading, firing again. Luther knew what bullets could do inside a cave. A body could be riddled by the ricochet. A wild shot, bouncing off stone over and over, had more than its share of chances to kill.

Luther didn't aim his gun. No sense drawing that deadly fire when his first shot could only put down one of these rabid coyotes. Luther had no belly for killing either. He'd do it to save Sally, even to save himself. But he'd never killed a man and, if he could avoid it, he didn't intend to start now.

He moved fast while he studied the situation. Gunfire from a second outlaw told Luther that man was farther away and a bit higher on the trail.

A heap of stones covered most of the cave opening, but there was enough room to get a well-aimed bullet past them. Sally could already be cut to ribbons. Luther rushed recklessly now, hoping the shooting covered any sound he made, using cover for all he was worth but moving whether it was good enough or not.

He'd nearly reached the closest man when the outlaw whirled and fired into the brush, right where Luther figured Buff to be.

A muted cry of pain told Luther the man had hit what he'd aimed at.

Sally crawled on her belly toward the back of the cave with the front of Logan's shirt firmly in her grip.

She didn't have to drag him though. He was cooperating.

Bullets thundered and echoed in the cave. One caromed off the ceiling and struck within inches of her hand. She sped up. In the far back there was one big column, close to the water. There might be room there to hunker down and outwait this barrage of bullets.

Something smacked Logan and knocked him onto his side. Sally glanced at him as she resolutely hauled him back onto his stomach. Blood streaked the side of his face, dripped onto his arm and hers. His eyes were open but dazed. While she moved, Sally tried to see if he'd been shot in the head, but it looked like a graze to her. She hoped.

One of the horses screamed. Whether from fear or pain Sally couldn't say. They crowded the back of the cave, as many of those weird columns in front of them as they could get. Only the sound of the raging gunfire coming from the front of the cave kept them in place. They looked crazy with fear.

Sally was mindful of their stomping hooves as she headed for the corner they'd chosen.

A blow to her leg felt as if a bullet had found her. It was the broken leg. The pain wasn't enough to stop her, so she didn't bother to look back.

A loud crack in the midst of the nightmarish rolling thunder drew Sally's attention. She dropped flat on her face in time to duck a massive white stone hurtling toward her head. One of Logan's stalag-things. She was glad he wasn't thinking right, except that probably meant he'd been shot. But if he was only knocked for a loop, then she was glad. Because he'd have felt terrible about the destruction going on in this unusual and beautiful cave.

She felt terrible herself. But then she was being shot at. Feeling terrible made sense.

She dodged a horse's hoof, caught Logan by the front of his shirt, and lunged behind a thick white column. It was fat at the base, nearly three feet wide, and there was about two feet of space between it and the farthest back corner of this cave. There was nowhere safer for them to be.

She dragged Logan's feet behind the stone and sat him up, without much help from him. His eyes blinked owlishly. Blood coated the side of his face, black and ugly in the dim light. Awful to see.

Noticing her cast was busted up from where she'd been shot, she saw no blood pouring out, and the leg worked so she ignored it. Whipping out her kerchief from the pocket of her dirty, blood-stained doeskin dress, she pressed it to Logan's face.

His hand rose unsteadily to take over holding the kerchief. "Thanks, I'm okay. I think. It hit hard but it didn't go in. Just a scratch."

The gunfire stopped. Her ears still echoed with the deafening roar of it. The cave was thick with dust kicked up by the barrage.

Sally waited, gathering her strength. She needed to go to the cave door, see if she could spot their attackers, get her rifle into action. But just two more deep breaths first, if they didn't choke her.

Logan reached for her rifle. "I'll go."

"You can't go." She knocked his hand aside. No possible chance that she'd give up her gun. Not to anyone, least of all an artist who meant something all wrong when he talked about a fast draw.

. . .

The gunman raised his rifle to aim at Buff again. He rose so quickly his hat fell off and revealed a weird streak of white in his hair.

Luther recognized that and it twisted his gut, but he didn't have time to deal with it now.

The outlaw's finger tightened on the trigger, and Luther cracked a single butt stroke, hard enough to put down a bull buffalo, across the varmint's skull. The gun went off but the bullet went wild.

If this man had killed Buff, Luther wasn't sure he'd be able to keep himself from coming back and using the other end of his gun.

One more to go. As he thought that, Luther realized the shooting from the other outlaw had stopped.

That same instant a rod of cold steel jabbed hard against Luther's backbone. "Lower that rifle or I'll cut you in two." The voice was shaky and nervous, but that gun held as cold and steady as a Montana mountain peak.

One wrong move would end this for Luther and then, with Buff down, maybe dead, that left only Wise Sister to protect Sally and get her help if she was hurt.

Luther held his gun with both hands, because of the way he'd used it as a club. Now he lowered it. No chance to take a shot, not with the steady feel of that gun between his shoulders and the nervous edge to that voice.

"Drop it. Toss it away from you."

The voice did something to Luther, hit a chord, sent a chill down his spine that had nothing to do with the gun. He'd heard it before. But when and where?

With no choice to make, he tossed the gun well away from his body. He had a knife in his boot and another in a scabbard under his shirt. Getting to them would require that this hombre get careless. Wherever this man had crossed Luther's path, there was left only a whisper of feeling that he was dangerous. This was not a careless man.

"Get your hands up where I can see 'em." The gun jabbed so hard it would have cut Luther's back if not for his buckskin coat.

"Who are you, mister?" Luther's hands raised about level with his neck. He was closer to the knife in his shirt with his hands up. And Luther'd had plenty of experience getting it out fast. "What are you on the hunt for?"

"Shut up." The gun jabbed hard. "I'm not answerin' any questions. Fergus kilt your saddle partner in the woods. I saw him go down. Now we'll get your friends to come out and say howdy."

Down wasn't dead, and Luther knew it. He prayed this man was wrong about Buff.

"But why?" Luther hesitated, wanting to slow the man down, start him talking, give Buff a chance to wake up, Wise Sister a chance to get in

330

position with that deadly bow, Sally a chance to get away if she was still able. The cave had been as silent as the tomb from the first. "What'd they do to you?"

"One of 'em made the mistake of livin'. I ain't gonna leave no witnesses to talk about what we do out here."

Sally had gone over that cliff. Luther had read that sign. And this man hadn't been satisfied that she was dead. He'd hunted for her body. When he didn't find it, he'd stalked her like she was a rabbit and he a hungry coyote.

Luther's fingers itched to make a grab for his skinning knife. He wanted to take his chance, but that gun didn't waver. He'd die and leave Sally defenseless, though none of the McClellen girls could ever be described as really defenseless.

"You need to run. Forget this killing and get away. You killed a cavalry officer and his wife on that trail. People will come hunting you. I'm the first, but I won't be the last. Killing all of us won't stop what's on your trail now. You should quit this country, lose yourself in a city somewhere. That's your only chance."

"No one can find me in these woods."

"I did."

The gun jabbed again. "You call this you findin' me? I'd say I found you."

"Gettin' the drop on me just means I'm here. I found you. If you take out now, I won't come

331

after you. I'll mislead the posse that's gonna be on your trail, might be on it already. The only thing I want is for you to leave those folks alone in that cave."

"They won't be in there for long." Then the nervous voice rose. "Come out of that cave." The shout carried a long way in the mountains and echoed back, eerie and evil. "I've got your friend out here, and I'll kill him if you don't get out here *now*."

Luther would have shouted for Sally to stay inside if he didn't think this man would put a bullet through him on the first word.

The gun eased off Luther's spine as the man shouted again. "I'll give you the count of five, then your friend here dies!"

Luther swallowed, bracing himself for a bullet, easing his hands one fraction of an inch closer to his knife with each breath.

"One."

A rustle in the trees near that cave entrance drew Luther's attention. The scrub pines up there were mighty thin. Luther saw no way someone could find enough cover to slip out of that cave. And with Luther standing smack in front of this back-shooter, Sally couldn't get a shot off if she *did* get a chance.

"Two."

The voice was a few steps farther back and to Luther's left. Where had he heard that voice before? He eased his hand closer to his knife. There was a definite shake of a small scrub bush near the cave. Someone was alive up there. Sally. It had to be Sally. If only Luther could keep her alive . . .

"Three."

The man Luther had knocked cold stirred, and Luther knew if that man, Fergus, woke up and bought into this game, they were done. Right now the lone man had to split his attention, which gave Luther a fighting chance. The man couldn't kill all of them, so it stood to reason someone would survive this. Luther vowed it would be Sally before him.

But if Fergus came around and was up to covering his partner's back, both of *them* were a lot safer. And Sally's chances of surviving got a lot slimmer.

"Four."

"I'm coming out." A man's voice sounded steadily.

"No!" Luther shouted.

The outlaw smacked the back of Luther's head so hard stars burst in his vision and he sank to his knees.

Fighting to remain conscious, Luther didn't provoke the man again. Instead, with blurred vision, he watched the cave mouth, listened to the man behind him, waited, and inched his hand closer to his knife.

"Step out where I can see you. Hands up."

A tall, dark-haired man stepped out. This must be Logan, the man who drew the pictures. The man who had found Sally and saved her and hid her until help could come. Luther'd gotten that much and precious little else from Wise Sister. And now here Luther was, and no help at all.

The artist watched the outlaw with more sense than his chosen profession would have indicated he possessed. He carefully stepped away from the boulders protecting the cave, his hands in plain sight.

Seconds ticked by while Luther wished for a back way out of that cave, prayed Sally had found it and was running away right now.

But the man wouldn't have stepped out if there'd been one. And his Sally wasn't much of a one to run.

"There were two of you. A woman was ridin' with you. I want to see her now."

The outlaw's voice! If Luther could remember where he'd heard it, maybe he could use that to divert the varmint's attention.

Sally eased her head up from behind the biggest boulder. It covered her to the neck, but her head was right there, a perfect target, and this man had spent the last weeks of his life trying to kill her.

"It's you, isn't it?" The man sounded as if he didn't believe it. "You're the cowpoke Fergus gut shot who fell over the cliff. Bested by a woman. But your luck has run pure dry."

Luther heard the crack of the outlaw's hammer drawing back and grabbed for his knife, knowing he'd draw that bullet.

Somehow he'd stay alive long enough to save Sally.

Twenty-Five

Calm down. Let me sit." Mandy made her way to the chair as a new labor pain began tightening what felt like her whole body. She dropped quickly into the chair, trying to remain calm for the girls' sake.

Tom whirled from his pacing and followed her to the chair, his arms still outstretched, the panic on his face almost comical. Almost.

"Now girls, don't cry." Crooning to the girls while her belly tightened was about all she could do. Tom was going to have to wait if he wanted her to talk to him. She did look up, meet his eyes, and say, "Sit down, please. You're scaring the girls."

She did her best not to look at him again. The girls were both clinging. Angela had crawled up Mandy's body until she nearly wrapped around Mandy's head. Little Catherine had her face buried in Mandy's neck.

Tom stumbled backward without looking

335

where he was going and managed to more or less fall into a chair by the kitchen table.

Angela turned her head so her cheek was pressed to Mandy's. Tears soaked Mandy's neck while she patted her girls and murmured comfort. She hoped it comforted poor Tom, too.

She smiled at him. Almost more than she could do over the slowly receding wailing, the slowly growing tightening of her body, and the slowly building fear about what lay ahead of her, alone—yet not alone—miles and miles from help.

Mandy wanted her own mama so bad she almost started in crying and hollering "Mama" along with her girls.

God, protect me. Protect my girls. Protect this baby coming into the world. Protect Tom Linscott from panic.

That quirked a smile on her lips, which she would have guessed was beyond her at this point.

An afterthought shamed her. Because she hadn't prayed for her husband.

God, protect Sidney.

Cooter's cold eyes and that streak of icy white hair appeared in her mind, and she imagined Sidney telling the man he was fired.

Sidney's going to need protection more than all of us.

She rocked, quieting the girls, breathing slowly to conceal her discomfort until the labor pain ended. It had come hard and too fast. With the girls, her water hadn't broken until long after her pains had started. Things were much different already with this one.

Rising briskly, she said, "Now, Angie and Catherine, I want you to meet this nice man." Her tone carefully light, she eased Angela to the floor. Angela gave her only token resistance, which boded well if Tom could keep from yelling. Holding the toddler's hand and carrying the baby, she walked over to Tom, who seemed to have calmed a bit. "Tom, why don't you sit down on the floor so the girls can get to know you?"

"Why?" Tom blinked those clueless blue eyes at her. The man still hadn't figured out he was in for an afternoon, evening, and possibly night of child care. He might not have much time to get it in his head.

"Do it!" she snapped. She hadn't meant to yell, but that's the way it ended up.

Slipping quickly to the floor, Tom found himself at eye level with Mandy's two-year-old.

"Angie, this is Tom Linscott." For propriety's sake she should introduce him as Mr. Linscott, but Angie probably couldn't say Linscott anyway. Of course, maybe she couldn't say Tom either. But the odds were a little better.

"Hi." Angie grabbed the skirt of her little blue calico dress and bounced on her tiptoes, smiling shyly.

Mandy wondered how much longer it would be before the children were all dressed in gray.

Mandy was so proud of Angela. She loved her little girls, and she loved this baby on the way. They were the brightest part of her life.

"Hi, Angie."

With a sigh of relief she saw Tom playing along.

Thank You, dear Lord God in Heaven.

"Mr. Linscott is a friend of Pa's who is going to help us this afternoon. He brought us some new horses. Your papa bought them, and Mr. Linscott delivered them today.

"Sit down in front of Mr. Linscott, Angie. He'll tell you all about his horses." Mandy eased Catherine down, too, and the little tyke seemed almost jealous of her sister because she plopped down a bit closer to Tom than Angie.

Mandy walked around the little circle and pulled close the chair Tom had used. She very much doubted she'd be able to get up if she sat on the floor.

Catherine smiled at Tom then shoved a handful of her little dress into her mouth, flashing her diaper while she wiggled her bare toes.

Tom smiled at the two little girls. Then very slowly, using surprising wisdom for a man who didn't have children, Tom reached out his hands to Catherine, and when she didn't pull back, he lifted her onto his lap. "Hi, Catherine."

The baby giggled through her mouthful of calico.

It surprised Mandy. Then she had a thought that wasn't a bit comfortable. "Do you have children, Tom—uh—Mr. Linscott?" Why had it never occurred to Mandy that Tom was a married man? He was of an age to be such.

"No, I'm a bachelor, but my sister Abby has a baby between Catherine's and Angela's ages. A little boy, and he is almost as cute as these two." He spoke the words to the girls, not her.

Angela scrambled onto her hands and knees and crawled quickly to join her little sister on Tom's lap. Both girls seemed content there, which was good because Mandy felt another contraction coming on.

"So the horses?" she prompted, hoping Tom and the girls would sit and talk while she dealt with a labor pain far too strong to be happening so early. This baby was going to come fast. But it could never be fast enough that Tom wasn't going to have his hands *very* full with some *very* upset little girls.

Tom looked up and their eyes met. A furrow on his brow said he knew she was hurting.

So much compassion, so much worry, so much admiration that she was quietly suffering, so much gentle understanding that she was trying to keep things calm for the girls.

Mandy got more true respect and kindness

from one little wrinkle on Tom Linscott's forehead than she'd gotten from her husband during their entire marriage.

A devastating thing to admit while she was in the process of having her third child.

"Get back in there!" Logan spoke under his breath when he wanted to scream.

"No. I'm not letting you draw a bullet."

"So you'll get shot instead of me? No man would ever agree to that. And I won't live with knowing you died in my place."

"Not in your place, Logan."

Logan watched the man at the bottom of this nasty cliff. The skinny outlaw never took his eyes off of Sally. She was going to die.

Logan knew it. She had to know it, too.

With that watchful villain aiming straight at her head, there was no way to get her gun into action in time. Of course, Logan didn't have one. Like the idiot he was.

Sally inched her rifle higher behind the stone. Logan could see it but Skinny couldn't. If the gunman would look away for one split second . . . If anything, however small, would draw his attention . . .

Logan knew that had to be either Luther or Buff kneeling, bleeding from the back of his head. Unable to provide a distraction. From this vantage point, Logan could see the other one of

Sally's two friends lying sprawled on his back in the underbrush, out of everyone's sight, but in no position to help. Where was Wise Sister?

Searching the area, he couldn't see her anywhere, and he knew she was in this to the end.

Logan stood there, useless.

That rifle of Sally's inched higher. She was doing her best to look calm, not visibly move her shoulders, which the man could see. Logan had seen her handle that thing. One second of distraction and she'd have it leveled and fired. That skinny, twitchy man kept his eyes riveted on her like she was bread at the end of a forty-day fast.

So she was willing to die for him, was she?

Logan couldn't allow it. Couldn't live if it happened and he'd done nothing to save her.

When there was a crisis, Sally knew she reacted faster than almost anyone on earth.

Every movement was lightning-quick, but to her it felt like molasses. Her vision became almost painfully acute. Every sound was information she used without conscious thought.

She and Beth and Mandy had talked about this a lot. This calm in the middle of trouble. Mandy got cold, but Sally and Beth never did, and they'd decided long ago that it was the icy edge to Mandy's nerves that made the difference. So

Mandy could outshoot Sally, but precious few other people on earth could.

But this wasn't a quick draw. That outlaw had his gun aimed and cocked. No one could get a gun into action fast enough to beat the quick pull of a trigger. She needed one second, one split second of distraction. But the outlaw wasn't budging an inch.

Logan dove straight forward. Straight off the cliff. He flew off the ledge straight toward the nervous-looking man with his gun aimed straight between Sally's eyes.

He was a perfect target. His move meant sure death. If the fall didn't kill him, the gunman would.

And she knew why he did it, too. He'd known she needed the man to look away.

Logan was dying to save her. No greater love.

The outlaw's gun dropped away from Sally and aimed at Logan.

Her rifle came up, cool, smooth, unerring, despite wanting to scream and cry and give Logan a thrashing for what he was doing.

In one instant that didn't stop her aim or slow her speed, she saw the colonel's wife dying in a pool of blood. The colonel, shooting, fighting, honorable and good and courageous, battling this coward.

She felt herself falling, falling, falling. Trees slapping at her as she tried to grab hold. She saw

Luther bleeding and beaten to his knees. Buff was off to the side, visible from here. Down, maybe dead. Logan soared downward.

From out of nowhere, Luther had a knife in his hand and was spinning.

Sally's Winchester leveled and aimed straight at the outlaw's black heart. Her finger tightened on the trigger.

The gunman fired.

An arrow whistled through the air—and slashed deep into the outlaw's chest, slamming him backward.

Logan slammed onto the ground and skidded along flat on his belly.

Sally never fired a shot. She shoved her rifle behind her, mostly ignored her broken leg, and darted out from behind the rock.

Logan didn't move.

She saw blood. Too much blood.

The gunman was flat on his back, choking and thrashing and bleeding with an arrow surely pinning him to an afterlife of eternal torment and fire.

Wise Sister rushed out of the woods, tucking her bow over her head and one shoulder as she ran. Buff staggered to his feet and came limping behind her, bleeding through his right pant leg, his gun drawn. Luther stayed on his knees and reached for Logan, who lay still as death.

Sally looked frantically around for a way to get

to Logan. It wasn't going to be easy, but she'd do it. She dropped to sit on the ground, swung her feet over the lip of that trail, rolled over onto her belly, and slid over the edge.

Going over a cliff for the second time in her life. But this time by choice.

Sally clawed her way down that cliff, pain radiating out from her heart in waves a thousand times worse than when she'd gone over that cliff before.

Twenty-Six

Mandy fought against the scream.

This one, just control this one. Please, please, please.

"Please!" That last please slipped out long and loud. She couldn't control the cry for help. Her belly felt as if a grizzly had its teeth sunk into her, shaking, tearing her apart.

She clamped her jaw shut, listening for a cry. The girls had to be asleep by now. Poor Tom had a fight on his hands because Mandy had said good night and come to her room to have this baby in private and heard the racket. They'd made it through supper, though Mandy hadn't cooked it or eaten it. But she'd been there, doing her best to care for the girls as the contractions came closer and closer, harder and harder.

The sun had set, the evening had turned to

night, and finally she'd managed to get the girls into their night clothes and into bed. But she hadn't been able to sit there and sing and read stories. It was simply beyond her physical capabilities. So she'd put them in bed and left the girls to Tom. She'd come to her room and let their crying tear her apart along with her labor pains.

Now here she lay, close to an hour later, the pains coming one on top of the other. Nowhere to go for help, no one to turn to, not even for comfort.

"Mandy, I'm here."

Realizing she'd had her eyes slammed tight shut, she forced them open. Tom could not be in here.

"I'm right outside the window."

Frantic to find where this man was during this extremely personal time, she saw that her bedroom window was open but the curtains hung over them. Outside she saw a lantern, deliberately held so that Mandy would know someone was out there.

She could see his silhouette through the gingham curtains, his square jaw and straight nose, his Stetson pulled low on his forehead. She could see nothing more and, to her relief, he could see nothing at all of her in the darkened bedroom.

"You should step away. It's not right—"

"I'm not going anywhere unless—unless the girls need me." He sounded unsure and nervous, but so kind. "I understand why I can't come in, but I can be out here. I can't see a thing from here. But I'm close enough you don't have to go through this alone."

Mandy's contraction eased, but she knew another one would be coming soon. With the last she'd felt that terrible bearing down of her body that meant it was pushing the baby out. She was only too glad that had finally come, even though the contractions were agonizing.

"It will be soon, Tom. The baby's close to coming." Mandy would have blushed at the improper topic if she hadn't been exhausted and scared beyond embarrassment. She was in the mood to hurt any man she got her hands on, too.

"If you need me in there, I'll come."

"No, absolutely not. Never."

"We may have to forget what people say is right and wrong. I *will* come in there if I decide I need to. But for now, I just thought you ought to know the girls are fast asleep for the night, and I'm here. You may be in that room by yourself, but I am one second away. You're not alone."

Mandy only realized at that exact instant how terribly isolated she'd been feeling. Having Tom say those words was like someone had thrown her a rope as she dangled off the edge of a cliff.

"I'm glad you're here." Treacherously glad. Sinfully glad.

"Talk to me, Mandy. When your pains aren't bad, in between them, just talk. Anything you want. Just to know you're not alone."

"I—my life isn't a good one to talk about."

There was an extended silence, followed by a sigh. "You've got a lot of money. Two healthy daughters. A fine home. You just bought two of the prettiest horses west of the Mississippi." Even now she heard Tom's pride in his fancy horses. He added, "You don't have such a bad life."

Mandy laughed, or tried to. "You're right. I'm dwelling on the bad, and there's so much that's good."

"The bad." There was a long silence. "Like your husband."

And Mandy knew how improper it was to speak to another man about Sidney. But her mouth wouldn't obey her mind. "Sidney had a . . . a chance to be a good husband, I think. At the beginning."

Mandy didn't mention the part of the beginning where she'd found out Sidney was already married to someone else. True, that someone else had died before their wedding, but Sidney hadn't known that. No, he'd stood beside her, in front of her parents and family, and taken vows before God to be hers and only hers for life. All while he thought he was married. A vile, sinful falsehood.

Forgiving him for that hadn't come easy. With a slashing moment of honesty, Mandy realized she never had. She'd tried. She'd swallowed the shame and rage and betrayal and done her best, seeing as how the marriage was legal, to keep her vows to love, honor, and obey. But in her heart, in her soul, the soul that God had cleaned and forgiven, Mandy had not been able to do the same. It was a sin, and if she had been able to move, she'd have gotten to her knees and asked God to remove that sin from her heart.

She spoke of none of that to Tom. Instead she thought of Sidney after they'd had it out about his first marriage, after she'd pretended—even to herself—to forgive him.

And before the gold.

"The first winter together, Sidney seemed to respect the skills I brought to our marriage. He wanted to learn. He tried hard." Some days he'd tried hard. Others he'd been his usual pouty, sullen self. "He made some real progress taking on the chores of a pioneer. He tried."

"One winter?"

"We had part of the fall, then the whole long winter, and a short time in the spring where Sidney listened to me . . . and Luther."

"I've met Luther and Buff. Good men."

Where were Luther and Buff? Where was Sally? What had happened to them all? She didn't expect Sidney back, but she'd thought for sure Luther would move mountains to be here for her when her time came.

"Yes, Sidney let them teach him, and he treated me well." Once in a while. Even then he'd looked down on her. Mandy knew that now. "He showed promise."

"And then he discovered gold." Tom sounded so sure.

Mandy wondered what people said about her husband outside of his hearing. She suspected he was regarded to be a fool.

"Being rich hasn't been a good thing for Sidney. When there was no money, for a time he seemed to be trying to fill that hollow part of himself with working the land, caring for the cabin, learning to be a good husband. Then he found gold. Now, it's like he's hollow inside and desperate to fill that emptiness with the things money can buy. Worthless things for the most part."

"Hollow?" Tom just being out there, speaking, listening made this bearable.

"He was very poor growing up." Mandy couldn't relate the scandalous things Sidney had survived with a disreputable mother and no father. But poverty was enough of an explanation, though a poor one. Most poor people were honorable. "It's like he's trying to make up for a deprived childhood. He wants a bigger house, higher on the mountain, as if that makes him important, powerful. He wants a nicer buggy. A flashy ring, silk shirts, all of it just to brag. I hope you charged him a fortune for those two horses."

"I charged him a fair price." Tom sounded insulted.

Mandy's belly started tightening again, and she fought down a whimper, focused on Tom's arrogance. "Well, you should have doubled whatever you thought was a fair price because spending a lot on something seems to suit Sidney. And heaven knows he can afford it."

"He paid plenty." There was something smug in Tom's voice, and Mandy knew that Sidney hadn't bartered at all. Tom had made himself a pot of money on Mandy's foolish husband.

He'd more than earned every penny of the extra by being here today.

A cry of anguish slipped from Mandy's lips. Not loud—she fought that.

The baby pressed, ready to get out, more than ready. Mandy was ready, too.

"Are you all right?" Tom's worried voice drew her attention and she could see he was closer to the window, one hand on the sill. His silhouette looked poised as if he intended to leap through.

"Shut up," she shouted without meaning to and tried to sound more calm. "Just shut up for a second." Not so calm. "I mean, I mean, let me get—*ge-e-et*—" The pain turned the last word of what she'd hoped would be a rational little speech into a scream.

She was beyond listening for Tom, beyond telling him to stay out.

"Logan!" Sally fell most of the way down that cliff, but she got down fast and in one piece and it didn't matter if she had some bumps and bruises. She jumped up and stumbled to her knees because of her stupid cast, then crawled to reach her man's side.

He lay sprawled on his stomach.

Gently she leaned down and pressed her lips to his head. Then she reared back onto her knees, tears burning her eyes. "He's dead." He'd been shot! She turned to the man who had sent that bullet flying toward the man she loved. The only reason she didn't kill him was because he was already dead.

Luther knelt across from her, his skinning knife still in hand. Their eyes met. Sally felt the strength and relief in Luther's eyes that she was alive and well, and also the question. He'd witnessed her tenderness toward Logan. But this was no time for a talk.

Logan lay between them, flat on his belly, still as death. Luther's shirt was soaked with blood from his head wound.

Wise Sister joined them and dropped to

Logan's side, nearer his head on the same side as Sally. "Scoot. Let me see to him."

Pure tyrannical orders. Sally wouldn't have dreamed of disobeying them. She remembered Logan saying he was kind of afraid of Wise Sister. Sally knew exactly what Logan meant. She moved closer to Logan's feet.

Wise Sister looked up at Luther, fury in those black eyes. "See to Buff."

Luther might have been a little bit afraid, too, because he flinched and looked past Wise Sister to his decades-long friend. He jumped to his feet, staggered as if his head reeled, then steadied himself just as Buff limped up to them. "Where'd he hit you?" Luther spared one loathing glance at the still-unconscious outlaw, lying face down beside his arrow-shot friend.

"Leg. Not bad." Buff sank to the ground. "Just a burn. Slowed me down some."

Wise Sister pulled a good-sized leather pouch out of her belt and tossed it to Luther. "Bandages. Moss. Pack Buff's wound. See to your head. Hurry. Need it for Logan."

Sally got to her feet and rounded to Logan's other side. "Where was he shot? That man couldn't have possibly missed at such a close range."

"Tulsa Bob Wiley. That's the guy's name." Luther pulled his knife again. "Sit down and let me clean out that wound."

"No bullet hole I can see." Wise Sister ran expert hands down Logan's arms and legs. She ordered Sally, "Turn him over."

"Get away from me with that knife." Buff staggered to his feet and backed away as if Luther was aiming for Buff's heart.

"I'm just gonna cut open your pants leg. Bandage the wound." Luther advanced on Buff.

"No!" Buff's voice was a loud whisper, as if he only wanted Luther to hear, but every word was clear to Sally. "You're not cuttin' my pants offa me in front of Wise Sister."

Sally was distracted from her worry about Logan by Buff's strange behavior. She'd never seen him act nervous. Was he hurt more seriously than she'd thought?

His pants were slick with blood low on his left thigh, just above the knee. But it wasn't bleeding that fast, and why mention Wise Sister but not Sally? Buff wasn't a man to talk much, and Sally had never seen him worry for one moment about what anyone else thought.

"Help move Logan." Wise Sister glanced over her shoulder at Buff and sniffed. "We won't look. Just hurry."

Luther advanced toward Buff. Buff backed away quickly enough Sally had no chance to worry, because they reached a clump of aspen trees and vanished from sight.

Noticing the lengthening shadows, Sally

looked up to see the sun low in the sky, ready to set and leave them on this mountain in the dark.

From low muttered words, Sally could tell Buff was letting Luther tend his wound.

Sally and Wise Sister eased Logan onto his back. There was no blood, except for a single rivulet coming from his temple. A blood-stained stone under his head explained how that had happened.

"I can't believe he missed. I can't believe it." Sally dragged a kerchief out of her sleeve, folded it, and pressed it to the cut on Logan's forehead. Through her fear, she noticed Logan breathing steadily. His face was ashen under the blood, but if his only injury was being knocked senseless, it would take time and nothing else to fix him up.

Wise Sister gave one furious look over her shoulder at Luther, who had walked off with her bandages, then pulled the corner of Logan's shirt up, produced a lethal-looking knife, and slit the fabric. "Move your hands. Bigger bandage."

Leaving her kerchief in place, Sally let Wise Sister add her pad of cloth. Wise Sister pressed down hard to staunch the bleeding.

"Ouch! That hurts!" Logan's eyes flickered open.

Her husband-to-be was waking up. And wouldn't she just know the first words he said would be unmanly?

Sally was so relieved she felt another bite of tears just as Logan's eyes flickered open and locked on hers. With an unsteady hand, he reached for her and pressed his hand to her cheek, which jarred loose some of that blasted salt water.

"Logan." She leaned down and kissed him full on the lips. At least it hid her tears from Luther, who, if he could see through those trees, would be horrified and ashamed that she acted so girly. The kiss might horrify him almost as much. It didn't matter. Luther was ignoring her in favor of stopping Buff's bleeding.

When Sally pulled back, Logan was alert and—for a bleeding man who'd just jumped off a cliff into gunfire—he seemed pretty happy. She leaned down to kiss him again, and Wise Sister shoved at Sally's shoulder and shook her head. Probably not the time or place for kissing.

A sharp crack of a bullet being jacked into a gun barrel pulled Sally's eyes up straight into the muzzle of a rifle.

"Everyone just stay calm." A stocky man with a streak of white hair leveled his fire iron at them as he leaned against a sturdy tree.

Sally had seen him lying unconscious then forgotten all about him. One of the two coyotes Wise Sister said were hunting her.

The man's eyes darted toward his dead friend, but Sally didn't see a lot of grief. Then he scanned the area and must have known Luther and Buff were close by. He aimed his rifle straight at Sally's head.

"You men get out here or I'll kill her."

"Just back away, mister." Sally felt that odd, almost crazed calm that came over her in times of trouble.

"We stay right here." Luther's voice sounded as sure and solid as a mountain from where he was behind that tree. "We'll let you ride out like you rode in. But if your finger even twitches on that trigger, you'll die. You can't kill us all. Your only chance of survival is to walk away."

The outlaw's eyes stayed beaded on Sally for a long, long moment, and she felt as if she was staring straight into her own grave.

God, have mercy.

"Don't be stupid, mister." Buff added his voice. "There's only one way for you to live through this day."

Sally saw Luther move in the forest. He was making himself a target, she knew, trying to draw this man's deadly gun to himself. Sally's fingers twitched to reach for her own rifle. She saw Logan's hand slide to the sheath on his belt that held his knife, and she remembered that he'd tried to die for her once already today.

God, have mercy on us all.

"That streak of white hair," Luther said. "I've seen that before."

"Me, too," Buff added; and from the location of his voice, Sally knew Luther and Buff had spread out to make themselves even harder to hit.

Sally watched the outlaw and saw the instant he hesitated and shifted his eye. They had him. He'd figured out he had to run.

"You get out here." The man's voice rose with nerves. "I mean it. I'll kill the girl, and even if I die, you'll have lost your friend."

Sally heard the soft whisper of Logan's knife inching out.

No, please, stop this. Have mercy on us, God.

"You can't win this fight," Sally said. She had to save Logan. She couldn't let him die. She couldn't live without him. "You can kill one of us, and we don't want that, but then you'll die. One man alone can't take all of us."

"That thatch of white hair," Luther said, moving back and to the right as a snapping twig told Sally Buff continued to move forward and to the left. "It's just like—"

"How about two men?" A new voice entered their conversation.

Sally looked up high overhead, to the mouth of that cave, and saw another man.

"Two could do a lot of damage." A younger version of the man down here held two pistols aimed in the general direction of Luther and Buff. Sally wasn't sure what the man could see from up there.

"Cooter." Luther's voice sounded like he was spitting. "He has hair just like Cooter's."

"Your name is Cooter?" the man down on their level asked.

"Yep, that's my name. Least it was a long time ago. And my pa and my brother had that same streak of white."

The two men exchanged a long glance, but their guns aimed true.

"I think that makes you my big brother."

"Cordell, is that really you?"

"Yep, sure enough. I came west huntin' you. I heard tell of a man with this mark. I've kept my eyes open, but never run you to ground."

Cooter and Fergus held their whole conversation without shifting their eyes or lowering their guns.

"Cooter works for Sidney," Luther said.

Wishing Luther would shut up, Sally knew he was trying to draw the men's attention. Give her a fighting chance. She straightened slowly, gradually, to shift her gun so the muzzle wasn't pressed against the ground. Then Sally thought about what Luther had said. "He works for Sidney? Mandy's Sidney?" Which reminded Sally of her big sister and the fact that she was somewhere, very soon to have a baby—if she hadn't already. Sally needed to get to her.

"We're not gonna shoot it out with you folks." Cooter spoke like he was chitchatting over coffee and huckleberry pie. "I've got my eye on the mother lode, Fergus, if you want in."

"Why not? I'm shy a saddle partner." The older man jerked his head toward the dead outlaw.

"I think they're right that we won't be able to get out of here without taking some lead. But they'll take their share. Not a winning hand. We'll back off."

Sally straightened a bit more. No time for relief yet.

"I'll keep 'em covered while you get to your horse, Fergus."

Fergus shuffled back. A mighty careful man. "Head south and I'll catch up with you."

"Their only horses close to hand are up here in this cave so they'll be a long while climbing up here to get 'em. I'd steal 'em, but if I got in that cave, these folk'll scatter and I won't be able to get out. Their horses'd slow us down too much anyway, and the plan I've got, we can buy all the horses we want. I've already got a spare, and you'll have your partner's. With the climb ahead of these folks, we can be well away by the time they're on horseback."

Sally wasn't sure where Luther had left his horse, but it couldn't be anywhere close by. Luther, Buff, and Wise Sister had climbed down here on foot if they'd been on the trail she and Logan had taken. Cooter had it figured out about right.

No one moved as Fergus vanished from sight. The man above them kept his eyes and aim steady.

At long last, just as the sun slipped below the mountain, casting them into twilight, a whistle from far below caught their attention. The man above touched two fingers to his forehead and backed into the brush alongside the trail. He never once slipped up with his aim until he ducked out of sight.

Luther charged forward, still pale, his shirt soaked with blood from his head wound. "The mother lode is Sidney. We've got to get to Mandy's house fast."

"You stay with Logan and Buff," Sally ordered Wise Sister as she limped for the trail above and the cave where their horses were sheltered, hoping neither of the animals had been wounded.

"No!" Logan surged to his feet. "We're all going. You're not facing those two men alone with a broken leg."

Buff stumbled forward, too, pants blood-soaked but well in place, limping but moving. Wise Sister was the only one of them that was at full strength. Sally was second, but a poor second.

"We won't be alone. We'll have Mandy." Sally didn't think Logan understood, but she'd rather have Mandy fighting at her side than an army.

Sally kept moving toward the cliff and

scrambled up, using the meager handholds and sparing her battered cast as much as possible. It wasn't an easy climb, but she managed it, even in her doeskin skirt.

As she rolled over the lip of the cliff onto the trail, she looked back and saw Wise Sister right behind her. Logan, Buff, and Luther had vanished.

"They go for the other horses and come hard behind us. We tied the horses not far back that way. But there's no cliff. Logan and Buff get dizzy climbing this cliff, maybe Luther, too."

"Who decided that?" Sally would have preferred Luther at her side. She stood, testing her leg. Still no pain. She hoped that meant it was fully healed because the cast was a wreck. Her gaze went down to the dead man with Wise Sister's arrow in his throat. Sally centered her rifle across her back and decided having Wise Sister to back her was for the best.

"I lead." Wise Sister was issuing commands now. "I watch for coyotes. I know the woods."

"But do you know the way to Mandy's?" Sally hobbled into the cave, dingier now than ever with the sun gone. She snagged her crutch off the ground and hustled to the horses, which were back drinking at the pool. They looked no worse for being in a shooting gallery, though Sally saw a bullet lodged in her mustang's saddle.

"Buff and I talked as we came after you. He

told me where your sister's cabin is. I know enough to set out. He'll be with us before the trail branches out."

"Are you sure Logan and Buff are up to a long ride?" Sally caught her mustang's reins and led him out of the cave.

Wise Sister was right behind her. "Better they keep moving."

It ate at Sally, the worry over Logan, the strange, almost pulsating pressure she felt to get to Mandy. Almost as if God Himself was telling her to hurry. She got her horse outside, limped to the saddle, and, using her broken leg for support, got her good foot into the stirrup and climbed clumsily aboard.

"If those men head straight for Mandy's house, they may beat us there. And it's close to Mandy's time to have a baby."

"Then we hurry." Wise Sister pointed up the trail, the same direction Cooter had gone, and without asking, kicked her horse forward and passed Sally, taking the lead. Which also meant Wise Sister would draw the first bullet.

Swallowing hard, Sally let Wise Sister go. She knew the way, she knew the mountains, but Sally hated it.

As they rode fast up the ever-climbing, twisting mountain path in the ever-deepening darkness, another thought occurred to Sally. "You ever deliver a baby?"

Wise Sister shook her head. Then Sally heard a sound she'd never thought Wise Sister would make. Laughter. "All six of my own."

"Alone? You had all six of your own alone?"

"Oldest girl helped later. But the first four? Yes, alone. And I've helped with a few hundred others."

"Let's ride faster."

Twenty-Seven

Anyone else feel like a weakling?" Logan looked at Luther and his blood-soaked shirt, Buff and his bleeding leg, then touched the rough bandage tied around his own head. "You know Sally's got a broken leg."

It seemed necessary to point out that the women weren't completely unscratched. Wise Sister was, but that woman defied all attempts to stop her from anything she set out to do.

"Still carryin' that painting?" Luther rode alongside Logan. They set a fast pace, despite the pain they were all in.

"Painting?" Logan knew only one painter around here. He looked at Luther, who was looking back at Buff bringing up the rear.

Buff's saddlebag was tied shut funny, as if whatever was in there didn't fit, and the flap that closed over it was stretched.

"What painting?"

"One you did of Wise Sister. Babineau got mostly burned off, but Wise Sister is still there. Buff knew her back a long time ago."

"You knew Wise Sister when she was younger?" A branch slapped Logan in the face and he turned, bent lower, and kept moving. They weren't closing the distance with the women at all. Sally and Wise Sister were moving fast and had a good head start. Which meant if they got where they were going, they might run right into gunfire.

"Yep. And Pierre." Buff didn't add to that, and Logan got the impression Buff was a man of few words.

"How far to Sally's sister's house?"

"Not far. If we ride hard." Luther leaned down over his horse's neck to duck under a branch.

"Not far" was about the most useless bit of information Logan had ever heard. The trail could barely be called such. Tracks were clearly going this way.

"You're sure we're following Sally and Wise Sister, not those two outlaws?" Logan shouldn't have asked, but it goaded him that, yes, he could see two sets of hoof prints. *But what if the outlaws had met up? What if—*A particularly unfriendly aspen slapped Logan in the face and cut off his worries.

"Don't matter. This is the way to Mandy's and we need to get there. Sally and Wise Sister know that. Quit yapping and ride." Luther pulled ahead of Logan as the poor excuse for a trail got even more worthless. The three of them strung out in a fast-moving line.

Logan wanted to ask a lot more questions. But it stung to be accused of yapping so he fell silent and rode.

They reached a particularly treacherous stretch of the trail. The horses scrambled to find footholds. Faint tracks showed in the occasional bit of dirt blown onto what was mostly stone. They were on the right trail.

They crested the rise and found a trail clinging to the side of the mountain they were scaling. Luther kept climbing. Logan urged his horse forward. No small task because this easier trail let them move faster, and Luther was pushing his horse hard.

"Do they live clear on the top of this mountain?" Logan wondered if they had a pretty view and opened his mouth to ask.

"Yep. Mandy's husband is an idiot."

Logan closed his mouth. They reached a civilized stretch of the trail and the horses broke into a canter.

"So, what are your intentions toward my girl?"

Logan looked up to see Luther glaring over his shoulder. Cold eyes burned into Logan's hide.

"Your girl?" Logan considered dropping back. Luther hadn't shown much interest in talking, but this question he clearly thought was worth the effort.

"I have treated Sally with nothing but respect since she's come to stay with me." Logan thought if he got that out quick he might dodge Luther's fist.

Luther grunted and fell back by Logan's side. "Not what I asked."

Buff suddenly pulled up so Logan was between them. Logan felt trapped, with one mountain man on each side. He seriously suspected that was exactly what Buff and Luther wanted him to feel.

"I asked Sally to marry me. She's said yes. She has to get to Mandy first and make sure her sister is all right, but after that, we're riding to find a preacher."

"And live up here and paint pictures the rest of your life." Luther sounded like he was spitting when he said "paint pictures."

"Sally respects my work. Knowing she does is an honor. She said she'd be willing to stay with me, work beside me."

"You mean she's willing to break her back keeping your house and feeding you while you sit around and look at the scenery?"

"No, that's not what I mean," Logan retorted, embarrassed into anger because that sounded like what he expected Wise Sister to do.

"I'm used to people not understanding my work. I expect nothing else from most. But Sally understands." Logan hoped. And he hoped that the feelings Sally had for him right now, when their life and death struggle heightened everything, survived during the mundane years ahead when he neglected her to chase the elk or the spewing geyser or the crimson sunset.

He loved her and knew he always would. Right now, at this moment, she loved him. But how could that love survive disillusionment and hardship?

Giving her up would be the honorable thing to do. Send her away. Leave her while she still cared rather than binding her to him and watching her grow to hate him.

Logan looked at Luther. "I hate justifying myself to people. I live with contempt from almost everyone. But I can see you love Sally, and she loves you. It would mean a lot to me if you'd approve of us." But how could Luther approve when Logan didn't really approve?

"I might approve," Luther said, "if you followed her back to Texas, got to know her family, gave her parents a chance to know you."

And how could Logan go to Texas when he needed these soaring mountains to live? And all his time away from them was saved to see his own beloved family. And he needed New York City as a market for his paintings. The people who would open a museum or buy a sculpture were few and far between in the West.

"You'll drag Sally away from her family and ranch life, then hope she still loves you as the years pass." Luther urged his horse around a curve in the mountainside.

Logan saw that they had another hard climb in front of them. He silently thanked God that this conversation would have to end.

Just as Luther pulled ahead to the trail that narrowed until they couldn't ride abreast, he glanced over. "That's what Mandy did when she married Sidney. When you meet Sidney, you'll see why it's a bad idea to marry for love."

"Nothin' wrong with love," Buff interrupted.

Startled, Logan turned to the taciturn man. Could Buff possibly be on Logan's side in this?

"There is if your lives don't match." Luther scowled at Buff.

"Love's enough. Real love." Buff eased his horse back so he fell in behind Logan.

Looking back at his friend, Luther had an expression on his face Logan couldn't quite define. Annoyance, amusement, a bit of worry. Mainly surprise.

"Maybe love's enough." Luther glared at Logan. "Real love. But who's to say what's real?" Then Luther turned back to the trail and took the lead as they passed into a wooded stretch clinging to a steep mountainside.

From that point on they concentrated on not falling off the mountain.

· · ·

Mandy lost track of everything but the waves of pain and the man just outside, who seemed like an anchor holding her to this world while her body tried to hurl her into the next.

This contraction seemed endless and the next and the next. No break in between to relax and prepare to face another assault.

Then as if it was too much for the mind to deal with, Mandy felt an almost detached clarity. She realized in that moment something amazing about having a baby. God made her body to work. He created birth and women and babies out of His great love and endless wisdom. And He knew what He was doing.

This baby was going to come on out and join the world no matter if she had a doctor, a husband, a passing horse salesman, or two crying little girls. There was freedom in feeling that, even utterly alone, her baby would be fine. God created a beautiful world, and His world worked.

Her child, forcing its way into her life. There was no stopping it. No point in much planning ahead really, despite all her worrying. Her child would come in a way as natural as all newborn creatures. It would emerge to join the family on a wave of mother's tears. Mandy was only distantly conscious of crying out and giving an occasional shout she didn't plan and couldn't control.

As her time came closer, an almost audible snap in her mind erased her fear, leaving her with an almost insane serenity. A sense of power had her think fleetingly of Sidney's mountain and his mansion. That sense of independence and arrogance and victory and power. The power of it. Of surviving alone.

She'd decided to never twist herself around in Sidney's presence again to suit some notion he had of proper womanhood. She'd stood up to him a couple of times, but there hadn't been many chances. Now that confidence, pride maybe, though she knew that for a sin, exploded on a crest of pain.

She would never, never again back down from anyone. She had the strength to make her own life. And if Sidney or anyone got in her way, she'd trample him to the ground beneath a stampeding herd of longhorns.

Tom's voice intruded distantly on her heady fury. His words didn't make sense in the midst of her travail. She didn't need him. Didn't need anyone. And as soon as she was done having this baby, she'd prove that to the whole world.

Suddenly there was a massive surge of her body and another and another. It went on and on until Mandy knew she could survive it no longer.

Time stood still. It could have been moments or hours or days because to Mandy that moment was the stuff of eternity.

"This is taking an eternity!" Sally wondered why the menfolk didn't catch up. It wasn't like they were waiting for them, but still, they should have been here by now. Never a man around when you needed one.

Of course, Sally probably didn't need one, but it still would have been nice.

"God, have mercy, what is this?" Sally rode up closer to Wise Sister, who led the way. A trail blasted out of the heart of the mountain. Still narrow, so deep, but passable. Better than what they'd been following.

"We're close now. This is as Buff described. Sidney used blasting powder to widen the trail to his home." Wise Sister slowed her horse but continued forward on the steep uphill slope.

"Widen? This is widened? A wagon can barely pass." Sally entered the odd stretch of trail. The walls of the mountain rose over her head fifty feet. Someone above her on that trail could rain deadly fire down on anyone who passed. If Mandy's husband controlled the high ground, then his home was an impregnable fortress. But if someone else somehow gained that, no one could pass through this trail and expect to survive.

"Move faster." Sally thought of the two outlaws who had ridden off with their talk of the mother lode, Luther's certainty that they were talking about Mandy.

The really strange part was that no one seemed to be up there keeping a watch on this trail. That meant Sidney felt safe enough to neglect this single outpost. Sidney hired that vermin, proving he had poor judgment indeed.

Wise Sister didn't respond but she picked up the pace.

They rode on in silence until they'd passed through the gap.

Sally drew in a shaky breath as they found a mountain valley, still rugged but thick with grass and water. A small cabin stood at the far side of the clearing.

Mandy's house. They'd made it! In her excitement, her eyes followed the rising mountain and—"Good grief, look at that!"

A mansion. A huge structure was visible, half built, on up the mountain to the right near the peak.

Wise Sister grunted but didn't respond. She kicked her horse into a ground-eating gallop, and they drew near the house in time to hear a heart-tearing scream of agony.

Sally raced for the house and leapt off her horse as a stranger, a tall blond man, rounded the side of the cabin. They both froze for a second. Sally blinked. Who was this?

"Mandy's giving birth. She needs help." The man reached for the door, then froze and stepped back. "Uh . . . you go."

372

Sally didn't have time to consider who he was or how he knew something so personal about her sister. The only thing she was sure of was, though she hadn't seen Mandy's husband for years, this wasn't him.

Another scream spurred her into the house, Wise Sister on her heels. They ran inside in time to hear the high-pitched cry of a baby.

Twenty-Eight

New life. An eternal soul entering the world.

Mandy tried to force her body to respond. To reach for her wailing child, but she couldn't, not yet. But she'd manage it soon. Now she knew God had created her to be capable of doing what was needed, completely alone.

The door slammed open and Mandy clawed at the blankets she'd thrown off to shield her body.

"Mandy!"

"Sally?"

An elderly woman pushed past Sally, swinging the door closed. Mandy caught the smallest glimpse of Tom, just his form. He'd been coming in.

Thank You, God, that he didn't. It would have been a terrible sin to let him see her.

The Indian woman reached Mandy's side and smiled with a wisdom as solid as the mountain. She took a quick look to make sure the door was closed, then brushed the blanket aside and lifted the baby into her arms.

Sally came to Mandy's side and they looked at each other and both burst into tears. "Pa would have our hides for crying." Sally leaned down and pulled Mandy into her arms.

"It's a boy." The elderly woman looked down and a smile creased her wrinkled face.

"This is Wise Sister." Sally pulled away from Mandy, though Mandy didn't want to ever let go.

Mandy looked at the older woman holding her squalling, wriggling child. "A son." Mandy smiled through her tears.

Then new voices were added to the racket her little boy made. Two crying youngsters. No doubt disturbed by all the commotion.

Tom's heavy boots thudded as he went in to the girls. His deep voice began soothing them.

Mandy looked from Sally to her baby, too exhausted and confused to know what she should do next.

Wise Sister took the child and began bathing him in the water Mandy had prepared.

"Where have you been?" Mandy asked, suddenly furious.

Sally laughed and pulled Mandy into her arms again. There was considerable talking as Sally told of her adventure.

"You ran in here on a broken leg?"

"I'm a McClellen. Of course I did."

Wise Sister rested the baby in Mandy's arms. "Time for him to eat. I'll see to helping you clean up."

Mandy took the little boy.

Wise Sister tidied the room, changed the sheets with only a little help and a minor break in the talking, and made sure all was well.

"I'm no help at all." Sally sank down on the bed, her eyes fixed on the tiny baby. "I wonder what I expected to do if I'd gotten here alone?"

Mandy looked away from the baby and started to cry again. "I'm so glad you came."

"Too late to do any good."

"No, you're doing me a world of good right now, just by being here."

The door to the cabin opened again and they heard someone speak.

"Is that Luther?"

"Yep, he and Buff and Logan must have finally caught up."

"You've talked a lot about Logan?" Mandy made it a question.

"I'll explain later. Where's Sidney?"

Mandy's tears dried up, and she looked down at her son. With one trembling hand she reached out to touch the little hand that flailed near the baby's cheek. With a few gentle brushes, Mandy got the baby to open his hand and cling to her finger. "Sidney is in town."

"You're sure? We met a man named Cooter on

the trail, and Luther was afraid he meant you and Sidney ill."

"Cooter?" Mandy looked up. "Sidney was planning to fire him."

"He held a gun on us. He and the man chasing me lit out, and Luther thought they were heading here." Sally told Mandy briefly what had transpired.

"I wonder if he hurt Sidney." Mandy was exhausted and overwrought. That was surely the only reason that speaking of Sidney possibly being dead didn't give her a single twinge of sadness. She remembered her vow, as her child was born, to need no one, to stand on her own. Maybe that's why she wasn't overly worried about her absent husband.

Sally leaned close and whispered, "Who is that man out there?"

"What man?" Mandy knew exactly what man.

"A tall blond man who looked to be coming in at the same time I was."

"Tom Linscott. He brought a team by right when the baby started coming. He stayed around."

He did all her chores and took care of the girls when she couldn't. He saved her sanity. "I wouldn't let him in here, of course, but I reckon I did some hollering there toward the time the little one came. I must have scared him into ignoring my orders that he stay out."

Sally's brows arched nearly to her hairline. "He was coming in?"

Considering all she'd been through, Mandy was surprised to find out she had the strength to blush. "Must've been."

Wise Sister interrupted. "I take the baby. Show him to the menfolk. They will wish to know how you and the little one fare." She gently lifted the baby from Mandy's arms, adjusted the tiny blankets a bit, and said, "You need to sleep." Then she took the baby and left.

Mandy looked at her son as he disappeared. "Who did you say that is?"

Sally gave Mandy a huge hug. Mandy clung to her sister as if Sally was a floating log in a rushing river. A life saver.

"That's Wise Sister. She'll take good care of the baby, Mandy. When I was hurt and broke my leg, she took care of me. She's almost as good a doctor as Beth."

"How'd you say you broke your leg again?" Mandy's eyelids seemed to weigh about ten pounds each.

Sally lifted her battered cast and Mandy perked up, but soon her eyes grew heavy again. "I'm going to let you rest for a while." Sally squeezed Mandy's hands then rose from the bedside.

Mandy held on tight when Sally tried to let go. "You won't leave, will you?"

Sally hesitated for just a second. "Of course I won't leave."

For some reason Mandy was sure Sally was lying. "Please don't leave."

Tears burned her eyes again and she remembered how she'd decided to never need anyone again. But maybe she did need her sister. For just a little while.

"I'll be here when you wake up, Mandy. I'm here for a little while. Don't worry about a thing. You've got lots of help."

I don't need any help. Mandy thought it but couldn't quite manage to say it out loud for fear Sally would believe her and leave.

Sally's brow furrowed as she watched Mandy.

Mandy almost begged Sally to stay in the room with her. And that reminded Mandy again that she'd taken a vow to never depend on anyone again. She let loose of Sally's hands.

"You get some sleep now. I'll take care of your little ones."

Well, she'd start being independent just as soon as she woke up from her nap. "Thank you, Sally. I'm so glad you're here."

Mandy's eyes fell shut as she heard the door close, leaving her completely alone. Her last thought as she felt herself sinking into sleep was she'd have cried her head off if she hadn't been so tired.

Sally emerged from the room to find quite a party going on.

Luther held Catherine on his lap. The little girl was grinning and tugging on his beard. The tall, blond stranger held two-year-old Angela as if they were old friends. Wise Sister held the baby and stood next to Buff, who admired the little tyke, as proud as a grandpa rooster.

Sally limped over to Logan's side. Her foot didn't even hurt anymore. The cast was hanging by shreds of fabric. As soon as things settled down, she'd cut it the rest of the way off. As she stood by his side and looked at the people here, she could almost see him sketching the scene in his head.

Everyone was talking quietly, if they were talking at all, except Angela, who was jabbering away to the stranger. Sally caught the word "horsie."

"Yes, I have a big horsie." The stranger smiled at Angela, bounced her on his knee, and listened to her as if every word was etched in gold.

Who was he?

Logan smiled down at Sally. "Your sister's okay, then?"

"Yes, she is. She's fine. She was glad to see us, but she managed the whole thing herself. She's a tough woman." Sally looked at the three little ones. All three little more than babies. Her sister was tough indeed. "I've never even met my nieces before." Afraid her voice would break, Sally swallowed hard before she went on. "And a nephew. They shouldn't be so far away from family."

"Sidney is her family now."

Snorting, Sally looked sideways at Logan. Was she going to do this? End up somewhere so far from loved ones that her children never knew their aunts and uncles and grandparents? Was that a reasonable life? To give up everyone else for a man? It might be a good deal if it was the right man, but how could anyone know? Mandy had adored Sidney. Sally remembered Pa's unhappiness with Mandy's choice, but Mandy would not be turned aside from having him.

Luther turned Catherine so she straddled his knee and introduced the little girl to her new brother. Once Catherine's attention was caught there, Luther looked up. "We need to get ready for trouble."

"What trouble?" Tom Linscott responded immediately. Sally noticed he wore a revolver on his hip, and his weathered skin and sharp blue eyes spoke of living a hard life and conquering a hard land.

Luther explained about Cooter's threats, speaking calmly to keep from upsetting the children. "We need to put someone on lookout through that gap. If we own the high ground, no one can get in. Anyone who lives in here ought to have sense enough to post a guard."

"Where's Sidney?" Sally hadn't even though of him until Luther spoke of someone needing more sense.

"He went to town." Tom faced Angela outward and began bouncing her on his knee. Good thing, because the little girl might have been frightened by the fierce anger on Tom's face. He let none of it sound in his voice, and he kept jiggling Angela as if he didn't have a care.

Everyone in the room fell silent. The baby chose that moment to howl.

"See da baby." Angela reached up and slapped Tom in the face, then looked up and laughed. Tom smiled back—but there was no smile in his eyes.

"We need to post a guard." Sally looked at the wounded warriors around her—Luther still covered in blood, Buff needing his leg tended. Wise Sister needed to do the tending. Logan probably ought to be at least sitting down. Tom was healthy but this wasn't his problem.

That left her. "I'll go." Her cast was so battered she didn't think it was doing any good anymore. But her leg seemed to be holding up.

"I'll go." Logan stepped forward. He looked reasonably steady. But had the man ever even aimed a gun?

Sally couldn't help but *not* feel reassured.

Luther jabbed a finger at Sally. "You need to help with the young'uns. I'll go."

But Sally thought Luther looked unsteady under his gruff exterior.

"I'll go," Tom said. "I don't mind staying up all night. I just came way too close to helping deliver a baby. I probably won't sleep for a month. And I'll probably have nightmares for the rest of my life." Tom stood with Angela in the crook of his arm. "But if that no-account Gray comes riding through that gap, I can't promise not to fill his backside with buckshot."

All things considered, Sally wasn't sure she could make that promise herself.

"Then tomorrow I'm going to ride in to Helena." Tom handed Angela to Buff. "Find Sidney." Tom drew his Colt as soon as his hands were free. "Kick that worthless excuse for a man in the backside for going to *town* when his wife was ready to have a baby." He cracked open the revolver. "And send what's left of him home." Tom checked the load with quick, practiced motions then snapped the gun shut.

"Then I'll contact the U.S. marshal." Tom returned his gun to his holster with a soft *whoosh* of iron on leather. "And give him a description of the two varmints who drew their guns on you folks." Tom settled his Stetson more firmly on his head. "I've seen Cooter." With one tug, Tom drew his hat down nearly to his eyes. "If his big brother looks as much like Cooter as you say—"

"He does," Luther interjected.

"Good, then I can describe 'em both well enough that the authorities will know just who to look for." Striding to the door, Tom reached for the knob. "Then I'll make sure the sheriff rides out to find the body you left behind." He turned the knob hard as if crushing the doorknob was a substitute for crushing an outlaw—or Sidney. "And then I'll send a wire." Tom looked back, sliding his eyes over each of them.

Sally knew they were a battered-looking group. She suspected he was assessing their fitness to stay here and take care of Mandy. What was Mandy to him?

"And get ahold of someone who knew Colonel McGarritt." They must have measured up because Tom turned back to the door and jerked it open. "So they can get a bead on the men who killed the group you were riding with and wipe 'em out and put an end to the danger Mandy is in." Tom stormed out, slamming the door behind him.

Which set the baby to crying again.

"A man of action." Sally looked after him, impressed. That's the kind of man she should be marrying. She smiled up at Logan. Too bad for common sense, she was in love with the paint slinger instead of the gunslinger.

Wise Sister took control. "Sally, you get a bedroll and sleep on the floor in Mandy's room." She bounced the fussing infant. "I'll take the youngsters into the other bedroom and get them settled. Their eyes are heavy. They'll sleep soon."

Wise Sister turned to Buff. "Then I'll see to your leg. It needs tending. All of you men find a spot on the floor and get some sleep. We'll need you at full strength in the morning."

A woman of action. Sally was glad someone was taking charge.

Of course, Sally would have liked a bit of time alone with Logan to try and reassure herself that loving him was enough to overcome their differences. But who could stand up to Wise Sister?

They all obeyed like a herd of mindless sheep. Mindless, wounded sheep.

Twenty-Nine

Mandy woke to find an Indian in her bedroom.

She'd have screamed if she thought it was real. Probably a dream. Her eyes fell shut.

"No, come back. It's morning." The lady gently rocked Mandy's shoulder.

Mandy realized her shoulder being rocked was what woke her to begin with. She felt sleep ease away. It was the kindest wake-up she'd ever had. Mandy moaned and stretched, aching oddly, still mostly asleep.

"The baby needs to eat, little mama."

"Baby?" Mandy's eyes flew open and focused. She'd had the baby. "Where's Tom?"

Mandy clamped her mouth shut. That wasn't the first question she should have asked.

The baby let out a thin yowl, like a hungry kitten, and Mandy sat up, groaning at the battering her body had taken yesterday.

"Let me help, Mandy." Sally slid an arm under Mandy's shoulder.

"Sally!" Everything came back to Mandy in a rush. Mandy's eyes met her sister's, and they launched themselves into a hug.

While her little sister, who was taller than Mandy these days, held her in arms made tough by long hours doing a man's work, Mandy felt that stupid, weak urge to weep again.

That thin cry sounded again.

Sally eased Mandy back then smiled. "Hi. Yeah, I'm here." She propped a rolled-up blanket behind Mandy's shoulders.

Wise Sister carefully helped Mandy settle the baby in to a meal.

"What time is it?" That was a dumb question. What difference did it make what time it was? It was feeding time. That would be her only clock for a long time. Except it felt like she'd slept a long time. And she'd expected to be awake all night caring for a baby.

"The sun rises already in the east." Wise Sister, that was the Indian lady's name. Shoshone.

With a clear head and no baby being born, Mandy could recognize the dress and the beadwork as Shoshone. She looked at Sally and saw that Sally was wearing a doeskin dress similar to Wise Sister's. How had anyone gotten Sally into a dress?

"I can't believe I slept all night." Mandy's head cleared more with every word. That full night of sleep had been incredibly healing.

"We tended the little one," Wise Sister crooned, smoothing back Mandy's hair. "You needed rest."

Mandy took a few deep breaths and enjoyed the presence of women. So wonderful to have a woman around. Then her shoulders squared. She was the big sister, the pioneer wife, the tough Texas ranch girl, and the fastest gun and deadliest shot in the West . . . and she'd believe that until someone proved her wrong.

"Where have you been, Sally? What happened to you? Are you all right? Tell me everything even if you already went over it last night. Did you say you've got a broken leg?"

Sally lifted her leg up. It looked fine. "Wise Sister cut the rest of the cast off last night. I feel almost whole again after I got shot off a cliff."

"What?" Mandy felt her brows slam down over her eyes. "Start talking. I want to know everything that's happened."

Sally jerked her chin, sat down on the bed, and started at the beginning.

The baby was almost finished with his meal by the time Sally got to yesterday.

"Cooter! He held you at gunpoint?" Mandy's fingers itched to get her rifle. The nursing baby slowed her down.

"I think he'd have just shot us where we stood except Luther and Buff were a few steps behind some undergrowth. Buff was shot in the leg and Luther had to stop the bleeding. Wise Sister and I were tending Logan, who was knocked insensible after he dived off that cliff to save me." Sally kept taking fascinated peeks at the baby. "Even with two guns held on us it was too risky for the outlaws to start shooting. Cooter struck me as a cautious man and a thinking man. Which makes him mighty dangerous."

"The yellow-haired man stands lookout on the gap into your home," Wise Sister said.

"Tom." He was still here, still taking care of her. Mandy swallowed and turned her thoughts away from how much she admired him. Which made her think of her husband and how much she did *not* admire him. "What about Sidney? Did he come home? Do you think Cooter killed him?"

Sally's eyes widened.

Mandy realized how she'd sounded. Her voice had been too brisk, too indifferent.

"We don't know. Cooter talked about finding the mother lode then held the gun on us until his brother, Fergus, could get away. He didn't say anything about where Sidney was. Luther's sure Cooter was talking about you and Sidney and all your gold. The two of them rode off, and we headed here fast, afraid they were coming straight for you."

"No, there's no gold here." Mandy turned all the possibilities over in her mind. "I'm sure Cooter knows that. But I'm sure he's been working out a plan to get his hands on it. Somehow. He wasn't referring to a direct attack. Or at least I doubt it. Sidney put the gold in a bank in Denver and made sure people far and wide knew it so there'd be no point in attempting to steal it from here or there. He picked one that's got a safe that has never been robbed. Cooter must have some idea about the money, but I have no notion what it might be. I don't see how he'd think coming here would help him."

Sally nodded. "Good, then there's no immediate threat." Sally then told Mandy what Tom planned to do with his day.

Mandy relaxed. "That'll put the U.S. marshals on the trail of the right men. It'll make this area dangerous for them, and if they're not caught, it'll be because they quit the country, at least for now. But I very much suspect they'll be back."

"We'll be ready for 'em," Sally said with a mean look in her eyes that Mandy had missed very much.

"Yes, we will. Now, who's Logan?" Mandy watched fascinated as her mean, dangerous little sister turned all pink and shy.

A woman stepped out of the bedroom, dressed and a bit shaky, but not that much considering she'd had a baby all by herself last night.

Logan was stunned by how much she looked like Sally. They weren't identical. Sally was two full inches taller, her hair a shade darker. And while Mandy was a pretty woman, she didn't hold a candle to her beautiful little sister. But the resemblance was uncanny. "How many girls are there in the family?"

"Four." Sally walked out right behind Mandy, close, as if her big sister might collapse and Sally wanted to be handy to save the day. Sally held the baby in her arms, so Logan walked over, thinking he could do the big sister catching if it was called for.

"All as pretty as you two?" Logan was already dreaming about a painting. All four of them. Mandy the pretty little mother. Sally the rugged ranch hand. "You said one of your sisters is a doctor, right?" He could already see the doctor's bag and the no-nonsense intelligence. It would make a fantastic portrait, catching their similarities and their differences.

"Yes, and the fourth is almost a woman these days."

"She still as prissy as ever?" Mandy asked.

"Yep, and as pretty. Taller'n me these days. And she's got men coming around all the time courting. She has a parasol to keep her skin from getting burned. Can you imagine?"

Grimacing, Mandy said, "Pa must be as nervous as a long-tailed cat in a room full of rocking chairs."

Mandy and Sally shook their heads in mutual disgust. Logan wasn't sure if it was over their sister or their pa or both.

Luther came into the cabin carrying baby Catherine, with Angela dogging his heels and jabbering away. Luther had a free hand to lift his Stetson and scratch his head as if confused. "Strange doin's." Luther handed the one-year-old to Logan.

The tyke came to him easily. But the day was wearing on, and he'd spent considerable time with the little ones this morning. He'd never painted children before, but these were so pretty. He'd love to try, see if he could catch their innocence and softness, the love and trust in their eyes.

Logan wondered for the tenth time this morning where their pa was. Gone to town, leaving his pregnant wife alone with two toddlers. Then he thought of his own inclination for neglecting people when the sunrise called to him. Would he be any better of a father and husband than Sidney?

Catherine took that moment to grin at him.

He smiled back. A furious wolf awakened in him, and it was a struggle to keep that off his face. The thought of someone doing these babies wrong. He'd fight and die for his own child. By golly, he'd fight and die for *these* children. *Yes*, he would be a good father. A good husband, too.

He turned to look at Sally, standing there cradling a baby. Logan waited until she looked up, then he smiled. Her eyes slid to the precious child in her arms, and her brow furrowed. She came to his side, but too slowly to suit Logan.

What was going on in her female head? Logan leaned down to get a closer look at the little boy, and the baby's waving hands punched him in the face.

Catherine giggled.

Logan almost stole a kiss from pretty Sally, right there in front of everyone.

"Strange doin's about what?" Mandy moved to a rocking chair by the stove and sat down with a faint groan.

"About Buff." Luther went to her, frowning, with Angela clinging to the fringe on his buckskin coat. "Somethin' wrong with him."

"His leg?" Sally asked.

"Nope, that seems to be fine, sore but the wound is already closed. It's just that he was talking with Wise Sister for a while last night when she tended his gunshot. Quiet-like and I couldn't hear. But they were goin' on about something for a long time."

Logan realized that Wise Sister wasn't in the cabin. He'd seen her going in and out of the bedroom all morning. She'd fed them all breakfast with Sally's help. Her quiet efficiency was missing right now from the crowded house.

"Then Buff spelled Tom at lookout early this morning. Tom set straight out for town without even eating anything. I went to spell Buff and he said—he said—" Luther shook his head.

"Said what?" Mandy frowned.

Logan didn't think it was wise to worry a new mother overly.

"He said"—Luther swallowed with a gulp so hard it hurt Logan's throat to watch—"him and Wise Sister are getting . . . getting . . . m–married."

"Married?" Sally's voice rose. The baby jumped in her arms and started crying.

"Today." Luther looked dizzy. "He said he was sorry I couldn't go, stand up with him."

"Buff?" Mandy asked.

"W–We decided I'd better stay here and help out. He promised to be back in two days."

"Wise Sister is getting married?" Logan felt a sufficient flash of shame to stop himself from shouting that he needed her.

Bouncing the baby, Sally's brow lowered then it cleared. She exchanged a look with Mandy, and they both smiled. "That's wonderful."

"It is?" Logan was losing his biggest helper and a true friend who actually respected his work. Except now Sally was a mighty good friend. Still—

"I guess they knew each other way back. He trapped alongside Babineau in the early days. Babineau was always going off and leaving her for months on end. Sometimes he'd get snowed away from her for the whole winter. Buff got so he'd stop by her cabin, almost more often than Babineau, when she had little ones hanging onto her skirt. He'd stay awhile, do some hunting. Help with the chores for a time. He says he loved her even back then but never spoke of it, seeing as how she was married. She cared for him, too, I guess, because she said yes."

"Well . . ." Logan cleared his throat. He'd be happy for her if it killed him. "Buff's a lucky man." An impulsive need to stake his claim to Sally, before he lost another friend, made Logan turn to her. "We should have ridden along to town. Made it a double wedding."

Mandy gasped out loud. "I asked you about Logan. You never said anything about a wedding."

Sally gave Logan a surly look, and he considered that she might have wanted to make the announcement herself. Well, too late for that. "This is no time to discuss something like that."

Logan's stomach sank at the look in her eyes.

She was measuring him. He knew it. She compared him to Sidney and thought she saw a bleak future.

"I'm not leaving Mandy alone to run off with you." Sally made it sound definite and permanent.

"How 'bout if we get married, then come back here and stay with Mandy." Logan was willing to agree to almost anything Sally wanted, as long as they managed to include a wedding in there.

"I said we'd discuss it later." Sally's face was stiff with annoyance.

Logan wondered if by pushing her, he'd pushed her away.

Luther cleared his throat loudly. "I think you ought to wait awhile, Sally girl. You haven't known Logan all that long and—"

"Hey." Logan cut him off. "Don't try and talk her out of it. She already thinks I'm strange enough." He looked down at Sally uncertainly.

She softened a bit. "I'm a little strange myself."

"I'll let you wear cowboy clothes all you want." Logan leaned close and whispered, "And I'll let you wear ribbons and lace, too."

Her eyes warmed. Logan thought he saw agreement in her expression.

The door burst open, and Sidney barreled in. He had a black eye. "Mandy, do you know what Tom Linscott did to me? I've got half a mind—" Sidney fell silent at the sight of so many people.

No one spoke.

Logan wondered how long it would take the idiot to notice that his family had grown in his absence. He was tempted to blacken his other eye, but holding a toddler in his arms dissuaded him.

"So, Sid," Mandy's voice sounded distant, cold, hard, "I see Cooter didn't kill you." She didn't sound one bit relieved.

"Of course not." Sidney sniffed like an overconfident bull right before butchering time. "I fired him and that was that."

Logan looked from Mandy's chilly frown to the soft light in Sally's eyes. Could that coldness one day be aimed at him if he was a bad husband? He couldn't imagine the day he wouldn't notice, and Sidney didn't seem to.

Shaking her head, Sally said to her brother-in-law, "Hi, Sidney. I got here just a few minutes after Mandy had the baby all alone."

"Baby?" His eyes roamed the room and landed on the squirming infant in Sally's arms. His eyes widened in surprise. "Tom said something about me being gone from home when I was needed. I suppose he was referring to the baby. Is it a boy this time?" Sidney sounded petulant.

Logan clenched a fist.

"It *is* a son, Sidney," Mandy said from where she rocked. Logan noticed that a rifle had somehow ended up on the floor right beside her rocker.

Sidney came over to look down at the little mite. Unwise, considering Logan's uncertain control of his fists.

The child had a dusting of dark hair. Logan was afraid the little guy was going to be the image of his father. Hopefully only on the outside.

"I have a son." Sidney smiled and touched the baby's hand. The infant clutched Sidney's finger.

Catherine, in Logan's arms, said, "Papa!" and nearly threw herself out of Logan's grip.

Logan held on, and it was a good thing because Sidney only had eyes for his baby boy. He didn't even look at his reaching, smiling, yelling daughter.

He picked the baby up out of Sally's cradling arms. Logan saw Sally's scowl, but she didn't stage a tug-of-war, which showed some self-control.

The little boy's eyes opened. His arms jerked and he opened his mouth and wailed by way of saying hello.

"We'll call him Sidney Gray, Jr." Sidney didn't ask Mandy about it; he just pronounced it. Sidney took the child and went to the table to sit down and continue staring. Angela ran to his side and pulled on his pants leg. Sidney didn't seem to notice.

"Sidney *Jarrod* Gray," Mandy said. "My grandpa who lived in these mountains was named Jarrod."

"Fine." Sidney didn't even give his wife a single look. It would have forced him to quit staring at his son.

Sally gave Mandy a worried frown. "Are you all right, Mandy? How are you feeling this morning?" Logan knew Sally was hoping to jar black-eyed Sidney out of his fixation on the baby and remind him there were others in this family who needed attention.

"No, I have everything I need." Mandy's voice lowered, and it sounded as strong and unshakable as the mountains. "I've got my own strength, a charitable God, and my children are safe. I don't need a thing."

Logan thought he saw an almost irrational fervor strike Mandy. She really didn't need anything. She brought that baby into the world without a doctor or another woman or her ma or her husband. She didn't need anyone.

That expression held an almost crazed sense of power.

The baby thrashed its little fists, and Mandy looked at him as Angela gave up on her papa and ran to climb onto Mandy's lap. "Sidney Jarrod Gray for his father who couldn't be bothered to be home when his first son came into the world." She settled Angela on her lap.

"Huh?" Sidney looked up for a second then went right back to adoring his son.

Mandy didn't repeat herself. But when the

baby started crying, Logan noticed that Mandy, the independent, powerful warrior, hugged her daughter close and cried, too.

Sidney didn't notice.

Sally did, and when she looked between her big sister and her brother-in-law, her eyes went hard.

Logan felt her slipping away.

Thirty

Logan handed Catherine to Luther, then turned and grabbed Sally's hand.

"Hey, what are you doing?" Sally didn't have time to react before they were outside.

Logan strode along, dragging her and her only recently un-plastered foot.

She thought of using it as an excuse, but it didn't really hurt. "What are you doing?" Could this be one of his artistic quirks?

"I don't like what I saw in your eyes."

She must have been moving too slowly to suit him, because he turned and swept her into his arms, then continued walking.

"What you saw?" Sally's temper rose. She was going to *insist* that Logan quit reading her mind. She slid her arms around his neck, just for balance, not because she wanted to cuddle up to the big dope.

Logan stopped walking and turned to face her,

but he held on tight. "Yeah. I saw you comparing me to that worthless Sidney. Like you think I'd neglect you."

"You already told me you'd neglect me."

"Well, I take it back."

"You can't take something like that back."

Logan ignored her and kept talking. "I would *never* leave you when you were set to have a baby. I would *never* favor one of my children over the other. You know me better than that."

Sally let go of his neck and shoved against his chest. "Put me down."

"I'm not letting you go until we have this out."

She quit fighting and glared. Their eyes locked. Then her anger wavered. "How do I know?"

"What?"

"Mandy was completely in love with Sidney when they got married. He ended up being the wrong man for her in every way, but she didn't know that until after she'd married him and followed him halfway across the country. He lied about being married. He lied about being a lawyer. He lied about having a job waiting. Now here you are, wrong for me in every way. And asking me to follow you."

"But you just said it yourself."

"Said what?"

"Sidney lied. I haven't lied. You know exactly who I am."

"Yes, I do. I know you're all wrong."

"But you fell in love with me knowing who I am and what I do. Would Mandy have fallen in love with Sidney if she'd known the truth?" Logan's eyes widened, and he let her slide down to stand on her own two feet as if his arms couldn't hold her anymore. "He was already married?"

"Yes. Sidney's first wife died before the wedding, but Sidney didn't know that."

"Well then, would Mandy have fallen in love with a married man?"

Her jaw tightened, and for a second Sally thought she might slug him. "My sister is an honorable woman. Of course she wouldn't have fallen in love with him. He courted her, wooed her, flattered her, charmed her, showered her with presents and attention. She'd have *never* let any of that happen if she'd known. Plus Pa would have shot him right out of the saddle, so it wouldn't have mattered what Mandy thought."

"You're making my point, Sally. Sidney lied. I haven't. You may think we're not right for each other, but you love me." He leaned down and took a quick kiss.

Sally let him and knew she'd miss him terribly if she used her God-given common sense and sent him away.

"And I love you. Knowing exactly how different we are, I still fell in love. And you fell in love with me." Logan slid one strong, artistic hand along the side of her face and tilted her chin up. "Didn't you?"

He looked so vulnerable. So in love. And he was right. She knew almost too much about Logan—the good and the bad—because he'd warned her long and hard about what he wanted in life and how much he cared about his strange bend toward painting pictures.

She couldn't lie to him, which meant she couldn't lie to herself. "Yes, I did. I fell completely in love." She closed the inches between them and felt Logan's shoulders slump with relief, even as he slid both arms around her waist and lifted her to her tiptoes and kissed her. She clung to his shoulders then to his neck. His warm, thick hair was like silk beneath her fingers.

"No more doubts, Sally. We get married with our eyes wide open. Knowing how different we are, respecting those differences, and working hard to get along despite them. Whatever happens, we make this work because I never want to be without you."

"I never want to be without you either." Tears flooded Sally's eyes.

He leaned down and kissed them away.

"Do you mind much a woman crying?"

Logan pulled away to meet her gaze. "I love every emotion in you. I love that you're capable of love and rage, tears and tenderness. I love how you looked staring down at that new baby. I want every bit of how you feel to always show in your face. It's the most beautiful, expressive face I've ever seen. I don't even need Yellowstone or soaring eagles or snowcapped mountains. If you marry me, I'll have all the beauty I can bear, right in my arms."

His eyes studied her in that deep, detailed way, and she realized she'd gotten used to being stared at. She'd even learned to love it. "You mean you don't mind if I cry?"

"I never want to miss one second of what you're feeling."

It didn't sound true. No man *liked* a crying woman.

"I hate the idea of you being hurt by me or anyone, so if I caused any tears I wouldn't like that, and I promise to do my best to never make you cry." He snuck in a kiss.

Sally noticed she wasn't fighting him off, which must mean she liked the whole idea of being with Logan, no matter how outlandish it was.

"Besides, my mom raised four boys, and she cried at the drop of a hat. She cried when she was happy, when she was sad, when she was scared or tired or mad or . . . hungry. I swear that woman was always crying. I got real used to it and learned not to panic." Logan smiled then kissed her again.

It made a certain amount of sense. Her pa hadn't been around women as a child, out here in the Rockies. He might have grown up with no experience. Sally decided then and there to tell Mandy it might be fine to cry if she was of a mind. It might even be good and honest. And, unless Pa came to visit, there'd be no harm done.

Before today, Sally had never seen her big sister in tears, and she suspected Mandy had never seen Sally cry. Sidney didn't appear to notice. So maybe Mandy should save the salt water for someone who cared.

Then Logan broke off kissing her, and Sally realized she'd missed part of it for all her fretting about tears. She decided not to fret anymore. If she felt like crying, she'd cry and that was that.

Logan let her stand on her own two feet again. "We're getting married." It wasn't a question. It was an order.

Sally found she liked the idea of a man ordering her to marry him. As long as it was Logan. "But I need to stay here with Mandy for a while. I don't know how long."

"Then we'll stay. I'd like to ride to town and get married, then come back past my cabin and see if any of my paintings survived. Remember that one of you that outlaw threw over the cliff? We might be able to find it."

"But then we can come back here?" Sally hoped some bald eagle didn't distract Logan on the ride. Then she remembered he had no pencil or sketchbook and thought they'd probably be safe.

"Yes, for as long as you want. All summer . . . all winter, too." Logan looked up the mountain and grimaced at the mansion. "If they ever get that done, they ought to have plenty of room for us."

"Or maybe they could live up there and we could stay in this cabin." Sally looked at the really nice-sized cabin Mandy now lived in and wondered why anyone needed more.

"Unless Wise Sister and Buff want it."

Sally nodded. "We'll figure out something, because, yes, Logan. Yes, I will marry you." Her arms went around his neck again just as the cabin door slammed open and Sidney came flying out of the house to land belly down on the ground.

Sally saw Luther standing in the doorway and Mandy peeking out from behind Luther, holding the baby.

"You'll come back in when you can watch your mouth!" Luther raged.

Then he turned to Sally and Logan and said, "Get in here!"

Sally remembered thinking Wise Sister could give orders. She couldn't hold a candle to Luther in a rage. Maybe they'd just go on in. She reached down and took Logan's hand and they exchanged a look.

"Let's go tell 'em we're getting married," Logan said, not acting all that afraid of saying something as stupid as Sidney must have and incurring Luther's wrath.

Clinging to Logan's hand, Sally feared she'd have to drag him, but he came along willingly, walking past Sidney groveling in the dirt. They headed right into the teeth of Luther's rage.

Sally knew she'd finally found a man strong enough to let her be a cowboy, kind enough to let her have a few bits of lace and ribbon, and wise enough to keep his mouth shut about both. "Logan?"

"What, honey?"

"Luther's had a bad day with losing Buff and dealing with Sidney. Maybe you'd better let me do the talking."

"There's one more thing you'll find out as you get to know me better, Sally."

"What's that?" She smiled at Luther, who bared his teeth and glared at the hand she had entwined with Logan's.

"I'm not a foolish man." Logan shifted so Sally was standing directly between him and Luther. "I've taken so much abuse for my painting over the years that it's really hard to wound my manly pride."

"Which means?" Sally sort of felt like she was in a kill zone between the two men. Though in all fairness, no one would probably get killed. Exactly.

"I'd be glad to let you do the talking."

"Good, I'll start by inviting everyone to the wedding." Sally looked over her shoulder at Sidney, crawling to his hands and knees and spitting out dirt. "Except him."

Thirty-One

Buff and Wise Sister brought a preacher back.

Sally saw the man wearing the black suit and thought Buff had hired a new bodyguard for Sidney.

He might yet need one to protect him from Luther, and even more so from Mandy. Nils Platte was still hanging around, but whatever arrangement he'd had with Sidney for protection apparently didn't stretch to include protection from a wife.

When Buff dismounted, he had the most peaceful smile on his face Sally had ever seen on the taciturn old man. "We had our wedding." Buff nodded toward Logan, who was holding Wise Sister's horse. "Now it's time for yours."

A smile bloomed on Sally's face. "Luther isn't too wild about the idea of me marrying a painter. Looks like you're okay with it."

Buff jerked one shoulder. "Wise Sister likes him. Says he's a good man. I trust her."

Platte came out of the barn and took both horses. He didn't seem to be staying all that close to Sidney these days.

"How'd you manage to not get shot when Sidney ran Cord Cooter off?" Sally had been dying to know.

"Mr. Gray told me what he was planning. I convinced him to make a hard day's ride of it to Helena. He wouldn't do it for his wife, but he decided his own life was at risk so he was willing to get the firing done fast then run for home and set up a lookout over that gap. I've suggested guarding that gap before, but this time Mr. Gray seemed to believe he was in danger. I expected Cord to follow after us, thinking to get some lead into me and take Mr. Gray, maybe force the information about his gold out of him."

Wincing to think of how cruelly Cooter would accomplish that, Sally moved closer to Logan. They'd been under Cooter's gun. Either of them could have died so easily. Logan rested his arm across Sally's shoulders, and she couldn't believe the comfort of that single touch. She really did know him. It was all honest. Yes, they were different, but she knew that and she loved him anyway.

Wise Sister asked Platte, "Why didn't you get home earlier?"

Platte's jaw clenched. "Mr. Gray wasn't done with his town business. He insisted we leave the trail and let Cooter go past, then ride back into town."

"And leave his pregnant wife here unprotected, with Cord on the way?" Logan snarled.

Sally was happy to see Logan firmly on the side of those who despised Sidney. If he wanted to fit in the family, he really needed to do that.

"Mr. Gray didn't see it that way. He figured Cooter wanted him, not his wife. He didn't think she'd be in any danger."

"That man is mighty unconcerned about his wife and children." Logan pulled Sally closer.

"Seems right fond of his son." Platte spit on the ground with contempt. "Maybe he'll take better care of all of them now, with a boy in the mix."

Sally realized that if Cooter hadn't come after her, he'd have been back right during Mandy's birthing. Even her tough big sister would have had a time of it defending herself. "Why'd he go after us?"

"I talked with Luther some about the trail you took. You were close enough he probably heard the gunfire. Might've even thought it was Mr. Gray, gone off the trail."

"We were close to Mandy all this time, and I didn't even know it." Sally shook her head.

"There were a few things barring the way, Sally." Logan's grip loosened enough that she could breathe, but she didn't mind his holding on tight. "A cliff or two stood in the way. Miles of treacherous trail, a broken leg."

Nodding, Sally said, "It all slowed me down some."

"So why do you reckon Cord never came back? After he met up with his brother, I figured they were headed this way."

"Looked that way to me, too. Never cared for the way he looked at Mrs. Gray. I didn't agree with the boss that his wife wasn't in danger. But Cord's not in here, and I've posted a watch up there so he can't get in." Platte looked back in the direction of the gap then scratched at his bristly jaw. "Sometimes Cord would get to talking and he was crazy on the subject of his family. He asked everyone we ever saw if they'd seen a man with a streak of white in his hair. Said it was a family trait and he wanted to find two brothers he hadn't ever met. Or leastways not since he was too young to remember. He had a few folks say they'd seen such a mark, sometimes on one man, some would say on two. There were definite sightings around these parts, but no one could give him any solid information about just where the man lived."

"Fergus and the man Wise Sister shot had that white streak in their hair. Those must be his brothers."

"Cord talked about how his family always backed each other. Cooters stick together. He must've said it a hundred times. Figured it for big talk since I never saw a sign of any family. They sure weren't sticking by Cord."

"The dead man we saw where the outlaws shot Sally and killed the colonel and the others had that streak." Buff frowned. "He must be family, too."

"Then I say we need to be ready for trouble." Platte looked so serious it sent a chill down Sally's back. "Cord will be bent on hunting down anyone who harmed his family. Like I said, Cooters stick together. That's how he'll see it. He'll want revenge."

Sally watched Platte, Buff, and Wise Sister exchange a grim look. She felt pretty grim herself.

"So, is there gonna be a wedding or not?" Buff shook his head as if to throw off the tension.

Logan looked at Sally then turned to Wise Sister. "Where will you go? Will I ever see you again?"

Wise Sister moved to Buff's side so the two of them faced Sally and Logan. "Buff and I plan to build a cabin where mine was before. We'll build another one for you and Sally there, too, if you wish."

A smile bloomed on Logan's face.

Sally couldn't enjoy the moment, though she loved the thought of having Buff close by. "What about Mandy? She needs us here. She needs someone."

"I'm staying." Luther came up beside them,

with Angela sitting atop his shoulders. The little girl's hands were holding onto the long gray hair surrounding Luther's bald crown.

"And we'll be a day's ride away." Logan lifted her hand up and kissed it. "We can come several times during the summer to see your family. And as soon as things are settled down, I'd like to go spend about half the winter in Texas and get to know your family."

The thought of spending months with her family thrilled her.

"And then spend the second half of it in New York so you can get to know mine."

Sally's eyes went wide. The thrill was gone. "New York City?"

Logan lifted one shoulder sheepishly. "Only if you want to. We'll decide all of that together. After we're married."

"I'm kinda scared of New York City." Which made her a little mad because Sally didn't like being afraid of anything. "Maybe we'd better decide that before the wedding."

Shaking his head, Logan smiled. "Nope. We'll work out everything else, but there's nothing left to decide about a wedding. We're getting married. Today. Let's get your sister and get this wedding started."

Deciding that suited her right down to the ground, Sally said, "Don't move," ran to the house, and called Mandy's name.

411

Her big sister came out carrying a baby, with a toddler hanging from her skirts.

Sally plucked Catherine up so they could all move faster toward saying the vows.

They had their wedding guests gathered in two minutes—little more than the time it took the preacher to walk the kinks out after his long horse ride.

Sidney even waddled over and watched, though he'd been inspecting the house and no one had invited him. He just happened to be coming down to the house to gloat over his son at that moment. Both of his eyes were black now.

Sally stood Catherine on her own two feet, thinking it was a more proper way to conduct a wedding, but the little tyke hung from her doeskin skirt and babbled.

"Dearly beloved . . ."

Turning to Logan, Sally decided those words described him perfectly.

"We are gathered here . . ."

An absolute truth. They'd simply gathered everyone here and started in.

The ceremony, such as it was, lasted about five minutes, but Sally took those vows, to marry a man who painted pictures instead of herding cattle. Logan said his promises right back, and he'd seen her wearing chaps with his own two eyes.

When the parson finished, Logan leaned close and took both her hands in his. "There is truth between us, Sally. I know who you are, the tough wrangler, the pretty woman, the tears on occasion, the ribbon you always wear. I love you and know you and promise to respect you without trying to change you."

Sally heard some faint grunt from Sidney that sounded like he didn't agree with such a statement. A quick glance at Mandy told Sally her sister had heard that noise, too. The man was purely lucky he didn't have any eyes left to blacken.

But this was no time for her sister's problems or her brother-in-law's whipping. This was a sacred moment.

"We do know each other, Logan." She gripped his hands tighter. "We don't think alike about a lot of things, but about the big things, I think we're in wonderful agreement."

She looked deep in his eyes, those eyes that had a way of studying her, reading her every expression until he was almost reading her mind. Things that she'd come to depend on. "You can paint all you want and I'll still love you. In fact, I'll love you because you paint all you want."

"And you can wear anything you want and I'll still always love my little wrangler in petticoats." Logan leaned down and kissed her.

With that kiss, Sally sealed her vows, knowing as they began their future as two people, very different and very happy, they would always be true to themselves and to each other.

413

ABOUT THE AUTHOR

MARY CONNEALY is a Christy Award finalist. She is the author of the Lassoed in Texas Trilogy, releasing in the fall, which includes *Petticoat Ranch*, *Calico Canyon*, and *Gingham Mountain*. Her Montana Marriages series includes *Montana Rose*, *The Husband Tree*, and *Wildflower Bride*. She has also written a romantic cozy mystery trilogy, *Nosy in Nebraska*; and her novel *Golden Days* is part of the *Alaska Brides* anthology. You can find out more about Mary's upcoming books at www.maryconnealy.com and www.mconnealy. blogspot.com.

Mary lives on a Nebraska ranch with her husband, Ivan, and has four grown daughters: Joslyn (married to Matt), Wendy, Shelly (married to Aaron), and Katy. And she is the grandmother of one beautiful granddaughter, Elle.

Mary loves to hear from her readers. You may visit her at these sites: www.mconnealy.blog spot.com, www.seekerville.blogspot.com, and www.petticoatsandpistols.com. Write to her at mary@maryconnealy.com.

Center Point Publishing
600 Brooks Road ● PO Box 1
Thorndike ME 04986-0001 USA

(207) 568-3717

US & Canada:
1 800 929-9108
www.centerpointlargeprint.com